# Sand x250

James Soap Currie

**Sand x250**
First published in Australia by James Soap Currie 2022

Copyright © James Soap Currie 2022
All Rights Reserved

 A catalogue record for this
book is available from the
National Library of Australia

ISBN: 9780646854878 (pbk)

Cover photography by James Soap Currie © 2022

Typesetting and design by Publicious Book Publishing
Published in collaboration with Publicious Book Publishing
www.publicious.com.au

# Contents

# Sand x250

Have you ever looked at sand magnified x 250? Tiny different shapes and beautiful colours of crystals, minerals and shells, millions of years old. A sight that would have remained hidden, had we not gained the ability to look closer through a microscope.

We walk on the sand of beautiful beaches and appreciate the ocean and waves, the sea creatures and the stunning vista, but do we ever give a second thought to the sand underfoot?

We lie on it, play on it, build sandcastles with it, make glass out of it, but are we ever aware of the little things that make up the body of sand? Some of us will look closer and discover its secret beauty and some of us won't. Is it possible that some of the most beautiful things in this world are hidden for a reason? Are they designed to make us look closer?

Human beings are like that. Made up of lots of little things we cannot see with the naked eye. Lots of beautiful little things that go unnoticed and unappreciated. Little things that are hidden in plain sight, that we need to look at closely to discover.

Some of us will discover special people with a hidden beauty and cherish it, and some of us won't. It is the heart, not the eyes that recognises a beautiful soul.

# Chapter 1

# People

Every beach in Australia has its own vibe or character that is embodied in its locals or regulars. At Rainbows End Beach on the southern end of the Gold Coast, Queensland, it's business as usual at daybreak on a summer Saturday morning. A fit-looking, female surfer with a short surfboard tucked under her arm, walks across the sand and launches herself into the surf then paddles out through the break. Her name is Jessica. She has a hubby who also surfs regularly and seven beautiful children that surf every chance they get. Throughout the day Jessica designs and makes clothes on an old sewing machine at home, then sells them at the artisan markets wherever she can. She has been in the water for over an hour in the predawn dark, catching wave after wave after wave. In this part of the world she would be known as a local, and would be one of hundreds. Several more boardriders make their way up over the nearby headland to another surf entry point. The surf was going off.

The sound of an old red rusty tractor rattles through the air as a Rainbow's End clubby (surf club member) tows the inflatable rescue craft down the beach for the day's patrol. The lone clubby is the Surf Life Saving club's president, who is known as Starch. He is usually the first one on deck in the morning at around 5 a.m. and the last to lock up and leave in the evening. Starch is somewhere in his late forties and is an ex-professional Rugby League player who had a somewhat successful career at a Sydney club called St George. He was known as Starch because of his defensive tackling style which was very unforgiving. Unfortunately, he succumbed to a serious back injury whilst working and consumed large amounts of painkillers daily. He also drank a large quantity of beer which did not seem to affect his demeanour.

After unhooking the inflatable, Starch drove the tractor back up the beach to the clubhouse which was a two-storey building, being of a brick base and wooden upper level. The front of the clubhouse faced the beach with a huge verandah on the upper level that ran the full length of the structure. The top consists of a bar and restaurant plus the club management office. The ground level houses the male and female change rooms, showers, toilets, gym, kiosk, first aid room and storage areas for the lifesaving patrol equipment. The building was an Old Queenslander design, and retained all of its yesteryear charms.

The slapping of rubber thongs on the club pathway announced the arrival of another clubby.

'Morning Simmo, can you hose the grog off the front of the club, please? I'm running out of time. Don't know why these millennials bother! They spill more than they drink!' Fired off Starch.

Simmo, whose real name was Simpson, proceeded to hose down the front of the club. He was a local tradie with a wife and three young children who were nippers at the club. He was also coach of the ladies surfboat crew. Meanwhile Starch loaded up a trailer with signs, flags and other patrol equipment then hooked it up to the tractor and headed off back down the beach. The forecast was for a scorcher, so he knew he was in for a busy day.

The groan of a clubhouse roller door being opened signalled the arrival of Bean, the kiosk operator. He was also known as Mung, Green, Coffee, Has, Could've, Should've, Must-Have, Jelly and more. The kiosk fronted onto the beach at the base of the building, adjacent to the main entry. Bean was a likeable character, whose age was somewhere around the fifties. He had reportedly done it all, and by all accounts was still always up to something questionable.

'How are you going Bean?' Quipped Simmo, as he hosed down the club entrance.

'Normal,' replied Bean.

'The nocturnals have been at it again, mate,' said Simmo.

'Standard behaviour". Replied Bean. 'Who's on duty today?'

'Max, Geraldine, Shannon and Rooster', replied Simmo.

'Hope Rooster's sober! He was horizontal in the car park last night'.

'Probably looking at the stars,' said Simmo.

'As you do,' replied Bean.

The early morning surfers started to trickle into the kiosk for their bacon and egg rolls. Bean's bacon and egg rolls had become somewhat of an institution amongst the locals, so early morning trading hours were steady. About 8 a.m. Max, Geraldine and Shannon, the volunteer lifesavers for the day, made their way down the beach toward Starch. They were young, bronze, and fit, and loved what they did. Rooster, however, had still not surfaced and Starch was becoming impatient.

'You lot heard from Rooster? He'll bloody wanna turn up! I haven't got anyone to fill in and it's going to be a big day. Half this mob wouldn't float on a log, let alone swim', said Starch.

'Yeah Nah, Yeah Nah,' replied Shannon.

The trio staked out the safest area of the beach, then planted the red and yellow boundary flags. Starch made his way back up to the clubhouse, on the hunt for Rooster.

'Hey Simmo, have you seen Rooster?' yelled Starch.

'Nah mate, he might have gone M.I.A.' Replied Simmo.

'That'd be right! I hope he's not a no-show', said Starch.

'You know he sleeps in the first aid room when he's got a skin full and can't drive home' said Simmo.

'What! How long has that been going on?'

'Awww about 12 months. Thought you knew', replied Simmo.

'Bloody hell', exclaimed Starch, as he headed to the first aid room.

Standing at the entrance to the room going through his bundle of keys, looking for one that would open the door, Starch heard a deep rumble, then another, then another.

'What the!' he muttered.

Finally opening the door he was greeted by the sight of a very asleep Rooster who was on his back with mouth wide open, legs straight, and arms crossed on his chest. The room reeked of the smell of beer, and Rooster exhaled more and more with every breath.

'Rooster! Fair dinkum mate! what's going on?' Roared a very annoyed Starch.

'Is that you Starch? I think someone mugged me and dragged me in here. Where am I? I can't remember a thing. I don't know what happened'. Said Rooster.

'OH, CRAP! And that stinking smell in here, is?' Roared Starch.

'Dunno, I must have fallen over in a puddle of beer mate, when they mugged me'.

'Fair dinkum Rooster this is bad mate! I need you out there today and look at what you're giving me. Stuff me, it's your first roster in 6 weeks and look at you', he blasted.

'Nah mate, no! I'm good to go. Bloody champion!'

'Well, we'll see. Mate don't come in here when you're gone. It's a first aid room, not a halfway house. There is something seriously wrong with you'. Fired back Starch as he turned and walked off.

'No mate, no never!' yelled Rooster.

Simmo rolled up the hose and finished tidying up the entrance to the club as Rooster wandered out of the changerooms, and made his way to the kiosk.

'Morning Bean, can I have a bacon and egg roll please'. He quietly requested.

'Give it a nudge last night. Did we mate?' Asked Bean.

'Nah, think I might have got some food poisoning from upstairs but I don't want to say anything', Rooster quietly replied.

'Food poisoning mate? Really! Maybe you were bitten by a beach snake, or maybe it could have been an ex-wife. They're harder to see at the bar, you know,' said Bean understandingly.

'Don't know mate, can't remember. It's given me amnesia'.

Bean rolled his eyes skyward and gave a slight head shake, as he cooked the troubled Rooster his bacon and egg roll.

'Well, I hope it gets better for you. Take it easy. Can't be too careful you know. All those bugs and all that amnesia floating around out there. Scary!' Said Bean with a wry smile, as he handed the troubled man his roll.

'Good to go mate! Champion!' Said Rooster, as he jumped to attention.

Heading down the beach to join the patrol, Rooster was a striking figure. He did not in any way, shape or form resemble the archetype of a lifesaver. He was a tall man with a huge stomach that folded over his nylon swimmers. His legs were thin and his physique showed little if anything of his younger years spent swimming training. He had tanned arms up to his short-sleeve line where his torso was lily-white. His legs were brown up to a line where his work shorts were worn, then they were white. He had white feet and ankles up to where his socks ended. All this was highlighted by his nylon maroon club swimmers, commonly called Dick Togs or Budgie Smugglers. Emblazoned across the backside of the swimmers were the bright yellow letters RESLSC, which was an abbreviation for *Rainbow's End Surf Lifesaving Club*. Rooster was a larrikin and generously enjoyed his beer. He loved being a clubby and relished his time on duty as it gave him a sense of purpose. Although he rarely volunteered for other duties around the clubhouse, he would be there in some sort of condition if asked.

Rooster's reputation preceded him as he arrived at the patrol tent to subtle eyeball rolling.

'Morning you blokes', he said to Max. Geraldine and Shannon. 'Take it easy and don't panic if we get the call. Always be vigilant. I am by your side', he assured them.

'Thanks Rooster, we'll do our best,' replied Shannon.

Rooster then sat down in the patrol chair, ate his bacon and egg roll and fell asleep. The others were happy with that.

Back at the club kiosk, two old timers called Danny and Grizz, had arrived for their morning coffee and breakfast. They arrived at the same time, sat at the same table and ate the same meal each Saturday and Sunday morning. Unfortunately there was a love triangle, as both of them had designs for the same lady. A wealthy widow named Liz. Liz was well aware of the boys' intentions and played their affections brilliantly.

Danny was a short fat sociable man, who routinely walked around five hundred meters on the soft beach sand once a week and called this walk his training. He was also a perennial dieter. Although this was hard to understand due to his frequent consumption of sweets, especially cakes.

Grizz or Grizzly was tall and thin, well-tanned and very fit. He walked with a lean to one side and any conversation with him was usually bruff or short. Grizz rode his carbon fibre racing bicycle from one end of the coast to the other every chance he got, and could be described as a fitness fanatic. Grizz was also a rehabilitated alcoholic.

The pair approached the kiosk servery counter to order.

'Morning Bean, can we have the usual, please?' Said Danny.

'How are you going, men? Is Liz coming this morning?' Enquired Bean. Both men replied at once with different answers.

'Oh! So maybe we'll just see what happens'. Said Bean and left them to answer each other's questions.

Grizz and Danny sat at their usual table and busily quizzed each other about their respective answers to Bean. The kiosk continued to trade with the regulars and tourists or day-trippers from Brisbane.

It had been an uneventful day so far for the lifesavers, with Rooster still asleep in the chair and the other lifey's answering questions and directing swimmers. The sun had crept higher and its sting could already be felt, signalling a very hot day unfolding. A few longboarders surfed the beach break on either side of the flags whilst the swimmers continued to build in numbers. Up on the beach, the club Nippers started to arrive with their parents. The Nippers are children aged between 5 and 14 years old who join the life-saving clubs to learn water-based skills and safety. The club had a modest but keen number of the youngsters who were starting to prepare for training. Their coach Jodie, a very fit, muscular, bronzed young lady had begun preparing a section of the beach for some of the activities. Jodie was also a regular Ironwoman competitor and the Nippers idolised her. It wasn't long before the beach came alive with the barking of orders and lots of chatter.

Adrian, the club restaurant chef, arrived for work and started his prep for the day. It was a requirement of Rainbow's End Surf Life Saving Club that all employees have a bronze lifesaving medal or current lifesaving certificate which was to be renewed every year. This included the restaurant and bar staff.

'Morning Starch', said Adrian, 'Haven't seen Rooster around, have ya?'

'Sort of, is everything alright?' Asked Starch.

'Should be. He owes me fifty dollars and his memory gets foggy after a couple of days', replied Adrian.

'Oh well he's on duty, so he's around the place'. Said Starch, full of sympathy for Adrians unrecoverable fifty dollars.

Downstairs at the kiosk, the conversation had turned to a controversial dredging operation in the area known as the Tweed River bar. The topic was very inflammatory so Bean tip-toed into the conversation between Danny and Grizz.

'You blokes going to the meeting about the bar'. Asked Bean, as he served the pair their usual bacon and eggs.

'Yeah for sure', replied Danny.

'Bloody ridiculous! It's all about bloody money, that's what it is. If the bar bothers you, don't go near the bloody thing'. Growled Grizz.

'They'll end up stuffing all the surf breaks. That's what will happen', added Danny.

'If brains were dynamite they wouldn't have enough to blow their bloody noses. Fair dinkum'. Snarled Grizz.

As the boy's were getting fired up, Liz made a timely entrance.

'Good morning gentlemen', she said. Her arrival had caught both of them by surprise.

'Very good morning Liz', said Grizz as he jumped to his feet. 'I'll just get you a coffee and maybe something to eat if you like'.

Danny was quick to react. 'Oh, it's ok Grizz. I've already organised a very special smooth latte. It's new you know, and very special'.

'Grizz's hair stood up on the back of his neck as he tried to contain his anger. 'Little piece of crap', he muttered under his breath.

'Well good on ya mate', replied Grizz. 'I'll have one too. How's your day going Liz? Is anything special planned? Thanks for that Danny'. He added as he pointed towards the kiosk counter.

Grizz made the most of his time alone with Liz and she was flattered by his advances. Although both of them were unlikely suitors, she did enjoy their company and attention. Danny arrived back with the special coffee.

'There you go Liz. It's the smoothest coffee ever produced in this country. I had to be in the know, to get some. We are so lucky', said Danny. 'Oh gosh, Grizz. I've had to leave your coffee on the counter. I was hauling a full load. Could you help me please?' He added.

Danny obviously sought to undo Grizz's smooth-talking with Liz by sending him off to fetch his coffee from the counter. Leaving Liz at the mercy of his charms. Danny was delusional.

Grizz was seething as he approached the counter. 'Hey Bean is this coffee mine? Danny's going on about how special it is. He reckons it's the smoothest coffee ever produced in this country, and how lucky we are to have some'. Muttered Grizz.

'Nothing special about that mate. Sounds like coffee embellishment to me. The last time I looked, this was Rainbow's End, not bloody Monte Carlo'. Snorted Bean.

'You little wanker', mumbled Grizz as he made his way back to the table.

'Ahhh, there you are, young Grizz. I was just about to send out a search party. Is Bean OK?' Asked Danny.

'Yeah, seems alright to me. Didn't have a chance to talk to him', said Grizz. 'You OK, Liz?' He added

'Living the dream, Grizz, living the dream', she replied, relishing the jousting male competition.

Every club has at least one member that everybody likes. There are always individuals in clubs that don't appreciate each other fully, and occasionally personalities clash. But there is always at least one person that everybody likes. In Rainbows End SLSC his name was Jackson, affectionately known as 'The Big Fella', 'The Little Fella', 'Jac' or 'Jacko'. Jack was a chubby boy of around 14 years of age and most people regarded him as a living legend. Although it wasn't because of his athleticism, but because of his undying will and determination to come back from defeat again, again and again. Jack had failed to pass his surf rescue certificate 8 times but was still diligently training for his next attempt. Although he had the willingness and dedication, Jack suffered from severe exercise-induced asthma which was a major obstacle for him. He had lost his father when he was 9 years old, when a drunken motorist veered onto the footpath where his dad was jogging and hit him in the back. He died at the scene.

Jackson was an only child and his mum was doing her best to care for him. They existed on a very modest income. Starch became a father figure for him as the two were usually inseparable on Club days. Jack was learning the ins and outs of Surf Lifesaving very well and Starch had secretly taught him how to drive the inflatable surf rescue craft and jetski. It was his dream to be a professional lifeguard. Jack had so many positive traits to like, he was just one big bundle of little things. One did not have to look closely to find the specialness about him, every time people saw him coming they smiled. He was chock-a-block full of likeability.

Weaving around the traffic and dodging pedestrians on the footpath. Jac steered his rusty old bicycle into the club car park, then round the base of the club and parked it in the storage shed.

'Morning, big fella', said Simmo. 'Starch was looking for you a moment ago and Jodie wants a hand with the Nippers'.

'Yeah, no worries. If Mum comes in can you tell her where I am, please', replied Jack.

'Yeah, mate. I'll keep an eye out for her', said Simmo.

'Thank you', replied Jack.

As he was making his way down the beach the first surf rescue of the day unfolded. A very overweight man had gone out too far and panicked when he couldn't get back to the beach. Shannon had recognised the man was in trouble and alerted Geraldine and Max. He grabbed the rescue board and sprinted into the surf. The break wasn't messy so they reached him quite quickly.

'Help, help, I need help', the man shouted at Shannon.

'You'll be alright, just listen to what I say'. Yelled Shannon as he grabbed the man under the arm, and dragged him onto the board.

'You're safe, I'll get you back in', Shannon reassured him.

The man vomited up some water then nodded his head, he was exhausted. Shannon skillfully negotiated the break and caught a wave back into the beach. Geraldine and Max ran into the water to assist them. The three of them carried the large man on to the beach and laid him on his side, he was conscious and continued to vomit up small amounts of seawater. After about 5 minutes he was able to sit up, although he was too tired to move.

'You alright mate? That was close', said Geraldine.

The exhausted man looked up at Geraldine and in between breaths quietly said, 'Thank you. Thanks to all of you. I was stuffed. I thought I was going to die'.

'That's OK. How are you now?' said Geraldine.

'Oh, I'll live. I think I've swallowed the Pacific Ocean and threw it back up again, but I'm ok, thanks to you. I will never do that again,' he replied.

The Trio stayed with the man for another 20 minutes and by then he was able to walk about and appeared to be fully recovered. The three then made their way back to the patrol tent and sat back in their chairs. Rooster, who had not moved the whole time and whom they thought was still asleep muttered: 'Not bad. Not bad for kids'. He didn't open his eyes and re-commenced snoring immediately. Shannon, Geraldine and Max looked at each other with disbelief and never gave a reply.

Jackson continued his way along the beach to join Jodie training the nippers. Most of the parents had left or were having a surf or swim. Starch was on his way to the patrol and stopped to check on them both

'Everything okay, Jode?' asked Starch.

'It's all good Starch, we're having a great time', replied Jodie.

'Hey, Jack, can you give me a hand after nippers if your mother doesn't need you. We've got to check some of the equipment', said Starch.

'OK, I'll ask Mum. It'll be OK', Jack answered.

Starch continued his way down the beach to the patrol.

'Well done ladies and gents, that was very well handled. I noticed you were all over it like a rash Rooster'. Said Starch as Rooster continued to snore. 'Fair dinkum', he added. 'This bloke's a non-event'.

# Chapter 2

# The Place

Rainbows End Surf Life Saving Club was in a dire financial position. Whilst the neighbouring Surf Lifesaving clubs resembled large nightclubs on the beach with rivers of gold provided by their Poker machines. Rainbows End club policy was, no Pokies. The members were unanimous in support of this policy. They maintained they were a family Surf Life Saving club and not a nightclub. This position however, left them with very little revenue coming in. The only income was from the bar, restaurant, chook raffles, meat trays, memberships (when paid) and coin collections from local shopping centres and markets.

Starch was well aware of the club's predicament and it was a constant burden for him. A meeting with the local council had been arranged and an application for a state government grant was being finalised. The clubhouse needed a lot of repairs, which in the past had always been carried out by club volunteers, however, the current problems were structural and major. Which was beyond the volunteers.

The paradox facing Starch was although Rainbows End was foremost a Surf Life Saving club that put the community first by way of the volunteer lifeguards, nippers programs, etc. The club membership was small in comparison to the large nightclub-style clubs that neighboured them. This steered the behaviour of the local councillors and politicians, who gravitated toward the more members means more votes logic. So although Rainbows End was a community-centred club and was applying for a community-based service grant. The smaller community-based membership was a handicap for them when being considered for government assistance. Especially with dodgy politicians.

Between the surf club and the beach, was a concrete path that attracted a lot of regular walkers, joggers and sightseers. The kiosk looked out onto the path. One particular lady who walked by most days had unwittingly stolen Bean's heart. Although Bean had never spoken to the lady, and she probably didn't even know he existed. He was hopelessly and secretly madly in love with the woman. She had short black hair and a very pretty face, with a very trim figure that resembled a fit teenager. Although she looked around 50ish or late 40s. Bean had tried on a couple of occasions to initiate a conversation with her, but his confidence had let him down at the last second. This caused him to become breathless. So he continued to live with his affliction. One of the restaurant staff named Mel, a shortish well-fed woman, had picked up on Bean's situation. So, from time to time, Mel would offer him advice on how to approach his problem. This was well-received from Bean, and Mel had now become his confidante.

'Good morning dear Bean', said Mel. 'Seen anyone interesting today? Maybe, someone, you would like to know better'.

'No', answered a despondent Bean.

'Look, I know we've talked about this before but... maybe…. Why don't you try handing out something like free coffee vouchers. Only to her of course. Then when she comes into the kiosk for the free coffee, you could talk to her'. Suggested Mel.

'She would probably bring her boyfriend, or husband, or whatever'. Replied Bean.

'Well, at least you will know! Won't you!' Mel fired straight back.

'I've tried to talk to her but the words just won't come out'. Exclaimed Bean. 'It's in the too hard basket anyway'.

'So what, you're just going to mope around for the rest of your life wondering?' Said Mel.

'She doesn't even know I'm alive,' answered Bean.

'Well, you've never done anything to let her know you are alive or did I miss something?' Said Mel.

'Oh, she is just so beautiful,' romanticised Bean.

'Oh, for heaven's sake! This is sad, this is so sad,' roared Mel as she left and made her way upstairs to the kitchen.

After he had finished talking to the patrol, Starch made his way up from the beach to a meeting with Robyn the club accountant. They were to meet at the kiosk so Starch took a seat and waited. Robyn was a very neat, attractive lady whose appearance was always impeccable. Starch liked her a lot because she was so very efficient. Along with being a qualified practising accountant, Robyn also held a law degree and had a mountain of experience dealing with legal matters. He didn't have to wait long, for Robyn was also prompt.

'Hi Starch, I have the financials and the application for the government grant. The committee can check it over, then I'll make any corrections if need be'. Said Robyn.

'Thanks, Robyn, we appreciate your input on this. There's a meeting next week so I'll get them to go over it, then I'll let you know the next day what the outcome is. At the moment it seems everybody's waiting to see what's going to happen to the bar and this dredging fiasco'. Said Starch.

'When are they having the meeting for that?', asked Robyn.

'Next week, and I'd say there will be some fireworks'. Replied Starch.

'Interesting', said Robyn.

At that moment, Starch received a call on his radio from the lifeguard patrol.

'Hey Starch. Ya there?. Come in. Over'. Said Shannon's crackly voice over the radio.

'Yeah mate, what's up 'Shan. Over'. Replied Starch.

'Yeah. There's a couple of White Pointers on the beach. We're just not sure how to handle them. Over'. Said Shannon. (White Pointers was slang for untanned topless female sunbathers. The name was drawn from a species of shark).

'Are they around the families? Over.' Asked Starch.

'No, not really. Over', said Shannon on a very crackly radio.

'Oh well just leave them, but if it becomes a problem or there is a complaint, handle them the best you can. Over.' Said Starch.

Then a different voice interjected over the radio.

'Do you want us to handle them for you boys? hahahahah.' Said the voice, which belonged to the Greenmount lifeguards next door who eavesdropped on the radio conversation. 'We'll come around and handle them for you all day long, hahaha'. The raucous laughter bellowed out of the two-way radio like a loudspeaker.

'Thanks for your concern, but that won't be necessary,' Starch answered politely.

Then another different voice dropped into the transmission.

'Awwww, sounds like a job for specialist White Pointer handlers to me. We'll put our hands up, hahahahhahaha'. Blurted one of the Cooly Beach lifeguards, over the two-way. Cooly was another neighbouring club.

'Thank you, gentlemen, but your help is neither sought nor required'. Replied a gentlemanly sounding Starch. His reply was met with more raucous laughter, and another quip from Cooly lifeguards.

'Gotta love those pointers'.

Robyn sat through the conversation, observing the male behaviour and rolling her eyeballs like they were in a pinball machine.

'Ok Starch, I'll leave that with you and I'll talk to you next week. Any questions, just phone. Bye.' She said, then left, shaking her head.

The Gold Coast is pretty much a tale of two cities, with a cultural divide between North and South. During the '50s the coast was renamed the Gold Coast, drawing reference to the money being made by developers. Over inflated real estate prices and goods and services were common. In the '60s the coast elected a retired bicycle manufacturer from Melbourne with the name Bruce Small, as the new mayor. Mayor Smalls' advertising slogan was "Think big, vote Small" and featured a picture of a very big breasted, petite, cartoon lady. The committed Calvinist toured Australia and Asia with charming scantily-clad bikini girls called Meter Maids. He promoted the Gold Coast as a family holiday destination, with the advertising mantra, "Sun Surf Party". Which in time, produced its share of melanomas and drunks. The mayor was inspired by property development in the United States and became a major developer on the coast - when there were no conflict of interest laws. It was open slather, and the money rolled in as his dream of Americanising the place took shape.

The popular mayor had a good run up until the 70s when the Gold Coast City Council was deemed too dysfunctional under his leadership, to continue. So it was dismissed by a state government that was itself later dismissed for corruption. But the greed is good mentality was now normal on the northern end of the coast, and the developer/councillor mates game prospered. Higher and higher towers sprouted all along the Surfers Paradise beachfront consequently casting afternoon shadows all along the beach. The lesson in how to kill an environmentally blessed patch of coastline, was learnt well.

The strange, knock everything down and build something else attitude is like a disease among councillors. Some continue on their quest to put Australian beach culture and heritage to the sword. The little things that make up the coast are walked on every day by politicians in all levels of government, who don't seem to know or want to know the value of conservation. Sadly, Surfers Paradise resembles a beautiful woman, who has been used and abused by greedy men until she has nothing further left to take. Nevertheless, the northerners made a bronze life-size statue of their favourite developer pollie, and placed it in a position for all to admire and reflect upon. Some would say it's the northern Gold Coast's answer to the redeemer statue in Rio de Janeiro.

The south or southern part of the city has a completely different mindset. The over development has so far been tempered and the beach is hallowed turf for locals. In contrast to the north, the south originally identified the name Gold Coast, as being derogatory. However, eventually it came to represent the colour of sand on the beaches. The southern Gold Coast is blessed with some of the world's best beaches. Surf culture is inherently linked with environmentalism and in the south, surf culture is dominant. The dark shadows of boardriders can be seen in the water off the points before the sun comes up, most, if not all mornings of the year. Kids before school will get a surf in, workers before work will get a surf in. Then as the sun goes down the shadows will still be there in the water. All of them waiting for that perfect wave to go home on.

The people who looked after the beachgoers, including the tourists, were the Surf Life Saving clubs. The surf lifesavers were the volunteers and Lifeguards were the council paid professionals. To the people they help, they are like angels and the things they do, save lives.

Rainbows End was the last Queensland Beach before the border with New South Wales. There wasn't any physical border between the states, just a row of Norfolk pine trees on a grass median strip that divided the road up to Point Danger. There was a cement obelisk type of structure at a roundabout intersection in Coolangatta. The obelisk had a line engraved into the centre of it with the words Queensland on one side and New South Wales on the other. That was the only state marker in that part of the world. During the summer months states ran on different time zones. Queensland ran on AEST (Australian Eastern Standard Time), while New South Wales utilised Daylight Saving Time, which pushed their clocks ahead one hour. This meant that on one side of the Norfolk pine trees it would be 6 a.m. while stepping around to the other side of the tree in New South Wales it would be 7 a.m. This could at times be confusing for tourists and an inconvenience for locals. It was, however, a favourite spot for New Year's Eve revellers. The celebrations for the new year in New South Wales would happen, then in another hour Queensland would do it all again. This was fine with the locals.

The coastal geography in that part of the world was a series of headlands, beaches and the Tweed River, with the unpredictable Tweed River bar at the mouth. Next to that was a beach called Deebah, then up past Lovers Rock to a tiny beach called Froggies. Then came Point Danger and the classic surf break of Snapper Rocks. Rounding Point Danger heading north was Rainbows End beach. Next to that was Greenmount Beach then Coolangatta Beach, then around another Headland to Kirra Beach. The environment was pristine and vibrant.

# Chapter 3

# The Problem

There had been much conjecture about the Tweed River bar and the problems associated with crossing it. Sand would build in the mouth of the river making it a challenge, and at times dangerous to negotiate. The local trawler boat fisherman and tour operators had lobbied the government for years to find a solution to the problem. There had been no improvement so far, although there had been a considerable amount of taxpayer money spent on failed fixes. The latest proposal for the problem was to dredge the mouth of the river periodically as part of a permanent maintenance operation. The sand from dredging would then be pumped through different pipelines to a kilometre offshore where tidal movement would take the sand away. The proposal became a hot topic and spirited debate was constantly taking place amongst the locals. They had seen enough mistakes or stuff-ups.

The stakeholders in this proposal were the Surf Life Saving clubs who control the beaches, the boardriders, the recreational and professional fisherman, the boaties, the dive tour operators, the whale watching boats, and the three levels of government, plus the residents. The most influential of the groups were the boardrider clubs, because of their numbers. They could also be the most affected by the shifting of sand. A European company had begun to lobby government officials for a contract to dredge the bar. But this was not being disclosed by the government officials, at this time.

The day came for the discussion and information evening regarding the dredging and public input was being sought - or so it was thought.

As was expected the atmosphere inside the council hall was very tense and apprehensive. The pro dredging camp was the trawler fisherman, recreational boaties and recreational fisherman. The 'find another solution' camp were the surf club members, environmentalists, boardriders, dive operators and beachgoers. The tour boats and whale watching boats sat on the fence. The politicians present were divided into 'for' and 'against' camps.

The evening started with an address by the local state member of parliament who was leaning towards the dredging solution. His obstacle was the local surfing fraternity, represented by club spokesperson Mick Underwood. Although Mick was an excellent surfer and nice bloke, he was very light on critical thinking. Another spokesman for the board riders was Tim Llittlebottom, who was the proprietor of a large surf shop in the area. Littlebottom had a reputation as a shifty businessman, and many thought he milked the surfing fraternity for all it was worth.

As the meeting progressed the complexities of the problem became clearer, mainly because of the proximity of the state border. The dredging of the river mouth would be carried out in the state of New South Wales. However, if there was a problem with tidal flow, the enormous amount of sand being dredged would impact the beaches, reefs and diving wrecks in the state of Queensland. This would be a political nightmare as both states were governed by opposing political parties. The balance of power was held by the boardriders who enjoyed some of the world's best surf breaks that were scattered along the points and beaches of the lower Gold Coast. The surf industry was worth hundreds of millions of dollars to the coast, and any damage to the surf breaks would be a financial as well as an environmental catastrophe.

The meeting saw several heated exchanges between the opposing parties. The last speaker was to be an expert from a European dredging company, who had been touted as a world-renowned environmental problem solver. The expert was a very confident speaker, although his message seemingly lacked a solution. This was until he gave an unconditional promise. According to his calculations and using his company's methods to extract sand from the bar. Not only would they fix the problems with the bar. They would create a whole new surf break. The new break would allow surfers to ride from Snapper Rocks to Kirra, around 2klm. It would be called the 'Super Bank'. The meeting ended with all parties still arguing and the problem remained unresolved.

The following morning at the club, emotions were still running high. Starch was organising the patrol for the day while Simmo was once again cleaning the club's surroundings. The boardriders were making their way down the beach, and Bean was in the kiosk. The thing on everybody's mind was the dredging.

'Morning 'Simmo', said Bean. 'What did you think of that fiasco last night?'.

'I'd say they don't have a clue what they're doing! It seems to me all they're doing is talking,' said Simmo.

'Yeah, I just don't know mate. It's a problem but I haven't heard anyone that has a solution. That is beside the expert, who sounds to me like an educated bullshit artist', said Bean.

'So what do you think the Surf Clubs will do, Bean?', Asked Simmo.

'Not much they can do, mate. The problem is in New South Wales so we don't have much of a say. The Boardriders are the ones with the numbers on both sides of the border, but their two representatives aren't exactly environmental scientists'. Said Bean.

'Good morning Romeo', quipped Mel, as she passed by on her way to work.

There was no reply from Bean, but it prompted an inquisitive look from Simmo.

As Mel made her way upstairs, Starch appeared at the kiosk counter.

'What's going on you blokes?' said Starch. 'Can I have a bacon and egg roll with tomato sauce and the bacon crispy, please?'

'Ok, it'll be 5 minutes. Hey Starch, I had to ring Bull about the hot water playing up. He said it's probably a thermostat and he'll get here as soon as he can'. Said Bean.

'BULL!!!' Said Starch alarmingly. 'Oh mate, don't ring Bull'.

'Why?' questioned Bean. 'He's a club member'.

'Oh mate, but he charges like a wounded bull!! That's how he got his name. He thinks we call him Bull, because he speaks no bull. Never ring Bull', said Starch emphatically. 'I'll get someone to fix it, that's reasonable. In the meantime spin Bull a yarn, and tell him it's fixed itself or something'.

'Yeah ok,' said Bean.

'So what's the verdict on the dredging, Starch?' Asked Simmo.

'Mate, at the end of the day, money will make the decision. The rest is just a sideshow. The lot of them are as bent as mountain roads. Believe nothing of what they say and half of what you see them do', replied Starch.

'Yeah, I'd agree with that,' said Simmo. 'Who's on patrol today?'.

'Not sure mate. Haven't checked the roster yet, but I'll do it in a minute. No one's phoned in for a no-show, so no dramas so far,' said Starch.

Jackson came wandering up from the beach looking for some work. 'Morning everybody'.

'Good morning Jack', said Simmo.

'Morning Jack', said Bean.

'Morning Jack. We've got a bit of time up our sleeve, so we'd better test that inflatable and jetski'. Said Starch. Bean and Simmo smiled approvingly.

'That sounds great', said Jack trying to contain his excitement.

'I'll deal with this bacon and egg roll, and check the roster on the way down'. Said Starch as they started to head off down to the beach.

The surf was reasonably calm, but the waves were dumping close to the shoreline which made things a bit testy for Jack. Starch decided to supervise from the middle of the inflatable, where he could shift his weight around.

'Take us around the point, Jack,' he prompted.

Jackson's modesty shrouded his ability to handle watercraft. Starch was very proud of him, and greatly enjoyed their time together. After rounding the headland, Jack flirted with the Tweed River Bar for a while testing his ability then headed back to the beach. Starch had a huge grin on his face as he let the young fellow give the inflatable a workout. At times it felt like he was riding a bucking horse, with a firehose of seawater spraying in his face. The two were having a great time as the boat thumped, thump, thumped it's way across the waves. The outboard motor was screaming like an angry swarm of bees, when a crackly voice blasted out of Starch's radio.

'Hey clubby, keep your toys out of the bar or you might bruise your soft little arse', shouted the obnoxious voice.

'Radio working is it Walton? 'That's a first. Thought I could smell rotten fish', barked back Starch.

The obnoxious voice was Fins Walton, a fisherman who was notorious for alleged illegal shark fin fishing, and multiple safety breaches on his trawler fishing boat. Fins didn't believe in radios or safety equipment, arguing the radio was a people nuisance and his experience was his safety equipment. He had been fined for numerous infringements including trying to surf the break between the beach flags in one of his boats whilst heavily intoxicated - then assaulting lifeguards and police.

Fins had a dog of sorts called Sharkbait. A small type of terrier that wandered onto the boat one day and stayed. Unfortunately, the Fins-Sharkbait, man to dog relationship was anything but harmonious. Fins would constantly threaten to use the dog as shark bait while the dog would threaten Fins by showing his front teeth and growling in an extremely hostile manner. He also slept on Fins' bunk pillow, making it stink. There was no middle ground between them. Sharkbait received his name from the two Japanese deckhands or 'deckies' on the trawler, whose names were Sushi and Ben. The pair of deckies and Sharkbait, plus a one-legged seagull that always sat on the mast, were the trawler crew. The little terrier was always busy running from one end of the boat to the other.

'Who ya got with ya. Another yellow shirt-wearing Cinderella?' Blasted Fins back across the radio.

'Jackson is doing a little open-water training in the inflatable', replied Starch.

'Jackoooo', bellowed 'Fins' in exuberance. And the mood suddenly changed.

'Hey, little buddy, I have some beautiful reef fish here for you and your mum. Caught them last night so I'll drop them off at the club for ya'. Said Fins.

'That's so appreciated, Mr Walton. Thank you so much. Your fish are always beautiful and fresh. If you need help cleaning your boat please call me. It's a great boat'. Said Jack.

'That's OK, little buddy. Just let me know if you need anything,' said Fins.

'Thanks, Mr Walton', said Jack and the radio fell silent.

Starch rolled his eyeballs and said. 'I suppose I'd better warn the club in case he decides to stay for a drink.'

The clubhouse was reasonably quiet as the staff and members were going about their business.

'Who's been sleeping in my bed?' said Rooster as he unlocked the first aid room. He was checking the first aid supplies and loading the freezer with ice that was used to treat bluebottle or marine stinger venom.

'Hey Bean, chuck me on one of your best, will ya mate.' yelled Rooster.

'Yes Rooster. You alright? You sound reasonably healthy'. Said Bean.

'Yeah mate, I went to the meeting last night. It was a very dry affair,' replied Rooster.

'And?' asked Bean.

'And what?' asked Rooster.

'What do you reckon?' asked Bean.

'No comment, except there's a hell of a lot that can go wrong if they stuff this up,' replied Rooster.

'Yep. That's the problem', said Bean.

# Chapter 4

# The Neighbourhood

Matthew was Bean's casual helper and most trusted friend. A teenager that possessed a manner and social understanding way beyond his years. He was an indigenous Australian, extremely intelligent, and a naturally gifted sportsman. A good looking young man with an athletic muscular physique. He stood around 180cm and excelled in everything he involved himself with.

Having finished his high school years with a mark that placed him in the top 1% of the state, Matt was waiting to start university study. There were several scholarships on the table including a double degree in law and medicine. There were also offers of sponsorship for a professional career in surfing, rugby league, rugby union, AFL, cricket and a US college basketball offer, which complicated things. At this point, Matthew did not have a clue what he wanted to do.

Matthew's family were very close and very supportive, but never interfered with his choices. They were a family of non-drinkers and hard workers. His mother was a nurse and his father a health inspector for the local council, and weekend park ranger.

Bean needed some free time from the kiosk to do some errands, so he gave Matt a phone call.

'Hey, Matty. How ya going? Are you free for a couple of hours today?' He asked.

'Yeah Bean, what time?' replied Matthew.

'Whenever you're free mate, we're on Matty time', said Bean.

'Ok Bean. Appreciate it. Let's schedule it for around 2 p.m.. Unless you need help for the lunch period'. Said Matt.

'Done, sounds good,' replied Bean.

Having an insider knowledge of Bean's personality. Matthew decided to set off for work early before lunch, knowing that Bean would need help for the busy time but wouldn't impose.

'Hey Matt, how are you going?' Said Bean as Matty walked in. As expected, he was relieved to have some extra help onboard for the busy period.

'Great, thanks Bean. I decided to come in early,' said Matt.

'Yeah, that's real good mate. Now I can try and get away a bit earlier after lunch'. Said Bean, wondering how Matty always seems to get things right.

Danny, Grizz and Liz were just finishing their morning get together and exited past the servery counter.

'See you blokes later', said Danny.

'Thank you gentlemen', said Liz, with a wry smile, which prompted Bean to roll his eyes.

'Have a good one', said Grizz. His eyes were firmly fixed on the back of Liz's anatomy, which prompted Bean to roll his eyes even more. Matt looked down and slowly shook his head from side to side in disapproval of the Grizz behaviour.

'Thank you', said Bean to the departing trio.

The lunchtime kiosk trade was not that busy considering the number of people on the beach. Although there were new up market coffee franchises, and American fast food takeaways further up the street. The kiosk did not enjoy as much trade as it should. One of the reasons for this was the people preferred to stay on the beach swimming and sunbaking for most of the day. Matthew knew Bean was struggling financially and had decided to intervene and stimulate the kiosk economy.

'I might duck off now Matt if that's ok with you', said Bean.

'Yes Bean that'll be ok. Do you mind if I get something out of the car before you go?' answered Matt.

'Yeah mate', no worries', he replied.

Mathew darted out to his car then returned with some rolls of wetsuit material and PVC piping.

'Errr, what's going on Matt?' Asked Bean as he noticed all the stuff he was carrying.

'Nothing much Bean. Just testing material consistency and stuff,' replied Matt.

'Oh!' said Bean, and he left to go on his errands. Matty was always up to something scientific so this was nothing unusual.

There had been quite a lot of bad blood between the Boardriders and Clubbies not so long ago, but things had been quite calm for a few years. However, there was the occasional flare-up.

Around midday the beach was busy and the points were ideal for weekend Surfers. The Boardriders were packed in like a can of sardines. As usual, there were heated exchanges relating to who had right of way on the waves (surf etiquette). Adding to this the animosity between the locals and the out-of-towners was at fever pitch.

To avoid the aggression a couple of the out-of-towners had let themselves drift into the area flagged for beach swimmers, and started to surf there. The flagged area is a strict No-Go zone for surfers. Two of the younger lifeguards asked the pair to leave the restricted area and received a zero response. Another more experienced lifey ventured out to warn them. The boardriders still ignored the request and suggested the lifey compartmentalise and insert the request in a certain part of his anatomy.

Patiently watching the exchanges from the beach, Starch had just about had enough.

'I'll be back in a minute'. He advised Jackson and Jodie who were nearby training Nippers.

Starch launched the inflatable and made his way out to the back of the breaking waves. It didn't take long before one of the boardriders drifted into the flagged area. Starch reacted immediately.

Leave the flagged area, please boardriders. This is a restricted area'. Said Starch through a megaphone.

'Get stuffed', yelled one of the Surfers.

'Who do you think you are? You don't own the beach! Stick ya megaphone up ya arse'! Shouted the other surfer.

Putting the megaphone down, Starch moved closer to the pair, and replied.

'I've got a better idea. How about I stick your board up your arse, then you can begin life as a popsicle'.

There was something about Starch's voice and manner that left the pair of surfers with no doubt about his intentions. He was a formidable character when challenged, which prompted them to paddle off and not return. Starch then made his way back to the beach to a waiting Jodie.

'Are you ok?' Asked Jodie.

'Yeah Jode, no problem. Just a couple of young blokes from somewhere else that didn't speak English. All good. We communicated very well', replied Starch. And with that problem solved, everybody went back to their duties.

Back at the kiosk, Matthew was busy with his material and PVC piping when an unexpected customer appeared at the counter.

'Hey, Matty! Shove these couple of reefies in the fridge for young Jackson, will you mate'. Said the gravelly voice of Fins Walton. 'What the hell are you making there?' He added, noticing the cut-up wetsuit material and PVC piping Matt was working with.

'Oh, nothing really. Just doing a bit of study into the different temperature variables of different coloured wetsuit materials'. Replied Matt.

'Why black and blue?' Asked Fins.

'Oh, no reason. Just the light spectrum and the way UV radiation works'. Replied Matty, hoping that would be the end of the conversation.

'Why do I get the feeling you're spinning me a yarny, young Matty? Why do I get the feeling? Enquired Fins. 'Make sure young Jacko gets that fish, and I'll look after you next time... Ok?'

'Yep! No problem. I'll let him know straight away. He's on the beach with Starch and Jodie. I'll call him on Starch's radio', said Matthew.

'Thanks, mate', said Fins. Then, as he was leaving he took another quick look at the wetsuit material and added: 'You're spinning me a yarny, Matty. You're spinning me a yarny'.

As Fins made his way through the car park to his truck, he noticed two out-of-towners loading their surfboards onto the roof of a car. It was the same two who had wandered into the flagged areas and refused to leave. They had just come out of the water and both had freshly acquired black-eyes.

'Bit rough out there, boys?' Smirked Fin's. They didn't answer.

'Gets a bit like that'. He added as he drove off.

The next few days passed without incident. Starch was flat out on the phone tying up loose ends, and chasing much-needed sponsorship dollars for the club.

'Hi Robyn, Starch here'. Sounded the husky voice through the phone.

'Hi Starch, what's happening?' Quizzed Robyn.

'The committee had a meeting and were unanimous in accepting the application for the assistance you prepared', Said Starch.

'That's great', replied Robyn.

'We don't know how to thank you, you've done so much for the club', said Starch.

'That's ok Starch, my pleasure. I'll get the original in the mail with the relevant documents straight away. Oh by the way, have you heard the news?' Asked Robyn.

'Thanks for that... What news?' asked Starch.

'The New South Wales government has accepted the European company proposal for dredging the bar', answered Robyn.

'You're joking!' said a surprised Starch.

'No. I have a friend in the New South Wales Premier's Department', replied Robyn.

'You are joking!' said Starch in a state of somewhat disbelief.

'No Starch, I'm not joking. I believe there was a meeting between the dredging company and the representative from the Boardriders Association, and Tim Littlebottom. Michael Flower, the local MP for Queensland was also present. The dredging company sold the boardriders and Littlebottom the promise of a super bank that would always have a wave and what not. This would add to tourism dollars and provide jobs, jobs, jobs.' Recounted Robyn.

'This is unbelievable', said a bewildered Starch.

'Yes. I tend to agree with you. Something is amiss here', said Robyn.

'I'm stuffed for words', said Starch.

'Would you like me to dig a little deeper?' Asked Robyn.

'Well, that'd be, yes please,' answered Starch.

'OK. I'll make a few calls and see if we can find out the details in the contract, and the terms of the arrangement etc.' Said Robyn.

'Do you think they're operating in the best interests of the community?' asked Starch.

'Based on what I already know. Definitely not.' She answered.

'That'll do me! Can you contact me as soon as you've got anything?' Asked Starch.

'Will do', said Robyn.

'OK. Bye,' said Starch.

'Bye, Starch', Robyn replied.

The news of the dredging was met with mixed emotion amongst the parties involved. No one knew what the benefit or consequences would be. The only certain thing was the complete lack of trust in the decision-makers because of the controversy surrounding the decision. Realising this, the government directed the dredging company to begin work immediately, hoping this would negate any protest or opposition to the project.

# Chapter 5

# Fishful Thinking

A small 60's retro type motorcycle glided into the car park. The female rider skillfully maneuvered the small bike into a tight parking space beside the kiosk then dismounted and removed her helmet. She was a very pretty young lady with long thick dark brown hair and eyes to match. The sound of the bike prompted Matthew to look outside.

'Momo... Legend,' he said loudly.

'Hey, Matty, where's Dad? Said the young lady.

'He's out the front on the path. He's handing out free coffee vouchers,' said Matthew.

'Moey', 'Mo', 'Momo' or 'Motank' was Bean's daughter. The nicknames were short for Monique Sian. She was a couple of years older than Matty and the two were great friends. Whenever he needed quick help with an academic problem Matt would consult Moey, who would always have the answer or know where to find it.

Mo was currently at university studying to become a medical doctor. She had previously spent time studying law, medical science, dentistry, midwifery and dabbled in economics. It seemed she had at last found her passion. Before leaving school and starting university Moey had completed aircraft solo training and attained her pilot's licence. She was 16 at the time and a full year before she could qualify for a car licence. Bean often questioned her about being a bit more stable but she always gave him the same answer: 'A girl's gotta do, what a girl's gotta do'.

He doesn't ask too much anymore because he's reconciled with himself that, 'A girl's gotta do what a girl has gotta do' - and no matter what advice he gives, she'll probably do it anyway.

'Dad, what are you doing?' Asked Mo as she approached him on the pathway.

'Handing out some free coffee vouchers', replied Bean.

'Why?' Asked Mo.

'To generate more business', replied Bean.

'Well you don't seem to be handing many out', said Mo.

'It's called Target Marketing. So I'm targeting my market'. Said Bean trying to sound logical.

'Dad, are you waiting for someone?' Asked Mo.

'No. Everyone knows where to find me', replied Bean.

'Well okay, I'm going up to have breakfast. Are you nearly finished? Asked Mo.

'Of course, let's go', said Bean.

Back at the kiosk, Mo, Bean and Matthew took advantage of a quiet break and settled down to have some breakfast.

'Moey, do you mind if I access the Uni site for some data?' Asked Matty.

'No problem, I'll log in for you. What data are you after?' Replied Mo.

'Just the migratory pattern of sharks', said Matt.

'What are you doing with sharks?' Asked Mo.

'Oh nothing much, just researching a bit about them. Nothing important', answered Matt.

'Hmmm, you two are acting a bit strange. Dad with his coffee vouchers and you with your shark research. Sounds a bit suspicious to me'. Said Moey in a drawn-out tone.

'Dad, I know it's none of my business. But I was chatting with some of the lecturers at Uni, and they have never heard of the environmental problem-solver that's involved with the dredging company'. Said Mo.

'Surprise, surprise', quipped Matthew.

'That doesn't surprise me at all Momo', replied Bean.

'Did you object?' Asked Mo.

'Well there wasn't any opportunity, apart from the meeting', replied Bean.

'Then, we have the border problem!' Said Matt.

Bean paused for a moment, then said: 'It's now a wait and see'.

The three of them sat there enjoying the quiet time until the kiosk phone rang.

'Hello, Rainbow's End kiosk.' Said Bean into the phone.

'Gidday Bean, Grizz here. Is Danny there?' Said the non-eloquent voice of Grizz.

'No mate, haven't seen him today,' replied Bean.

'Is Liz there?' Asked Grizz.

"No mate, haven't seen her either", replied Bean.

'What? Are you sure?' Blurted Grizz.

'Yes mate, I'm very sure', replied Bean.

"Ok thanks, mate. See you later". Said Grizz abruptly, and hung up.

'No problem'. Said Bean into the disconnected phone then rolled his eyes and went back to the quiet time.

Along with the volunteers, there were the professional lifeguards who were paid by the city council. The professional lifeguards were a good crew and were usually top tier athletes of different sports and being a full-time lifeguard suited them, as they were all very fit and handled the job requirements easily. Another section was the helicopter rescue teams. The helicopters were sponsored by private corporations in return for naming rights, but the crew were all highly skilled volunteers. The pilots and paramedics manning the local chopper were familiar with the different volunteer surf rescue patrols on the beach, and would socialise at the surf club.

Two of the regulars at the Club were a pilot called Rotors, and a paramedic called Stitches. The paramedics were also known as Drop Bears because of the way they are winched down or dropped into a rescue situation. As Starch was going through the paperwork in the office, the crackling sound of the club's two-way radio rattled into life.

'Helicopter rescue to Rainbow's End Surf. Come in. Over', said a voice over the radio.

'Rainbows End Surf. Copy. Over', replied Starch.

'A Tiger shark is moving north along the coastline, just behind the break. Its present position is Casuarina. Will keep you advised if it moves closer. Do you copy? Over.' Said the chopper voice.

'Yeah, I copy. Over', replied Starch.

'How ya goin, Starch?' Said the chopper voice.

'Not bad, Rotors. All I needed was a Tiger shark in my backyard', answered Starch.

'It's a decent-sized fish, so if it gets much closer I'll let you know straight away. Over', said Rotors.

'Thanks for that, boys. I'll brief the patrol. Over and out', said Starch.

Deciding to tell the patrol in person, rather than over the radio. Starch headed off downstairs past the kiosk window, on his way to the beach. Bean was in the kiosk and noticed the look on his face.

'You alright, Starch?' He asked.

'Yeah mate. Just got a bloody shark moving up the coast', answered Starch.

'What kind of shark?' Asked an inquisitive Matty.

'Bloody Tiger shark', answered Starch.

As he kept walking he crossed paths with a muscular Jodie who was running along the beach on the soft sand.

'Hey Jode', said Starch. 'A Tiger shark is hanging around Casuarina and heading our way. Probably pay you to rethink your ocean swim'.

'Oh OK. I'll go to the pool. I'll see if Jack wants to come. Is it true they're going to be dredging the bar?' Asked Jodie.

'Yes it is. Let's hope they know what they're doing', answered Starch.

When he reached the patrol he let them know about the shark situation then decided to stay with them for a while in case anything else happened. They also wanted to talk about the Tweed Bar dredging.

Back at the kiosk, the phone was unusually active as Matthew tried to get some work done. He threw his head back and looked skyward when it rang again.

'Hello kiosk', said Matt, into the phone.

'Yeah Matty, it's Bull here. Do you know if that problem with the hot water has come back?' Asked 'Bull'.

'Ahhhh no, not that I know of.' Answered Matty cautiously.

'Awww righto. Call me if it comes back, will you mate?' Replied Bull.

'Ahhh okay. Hey, Bull I was just wondering what happened to those scuba tanks you made? The body contour ones', asked Matt.

'Still got them, mate. I just don't get the time to use them. Why?' asked Bull.

'I have to do some scuba diving for a volunteer environmental study program. Would you consider selling them?' Asked Matt.

'Well no. But if it helps with environmental protection and you're a volunteer, I have a spare tank you can have. Complete with gauges'. Replied Bull.

'Whattttt! Are you serious? Wow! Bull, that's fantastic! What the heck, man! That is a seriously cool thing to do. Bull what the heck, man! I don't think the things they say about you are true. No way', blurted Matt.

'What do they say about me, and who's they?' Bull immediately fired back.

Matty realised he had put his foot in it, and had to think fast. This was a 'situation'.

'Oh, nothing bad Bull. You just don't seem to be around the club much anymore, and I think people miss your company. I guess they might have thought you gave them the flick'. Said Matty, scrambling for an explanation.

'What bullshit, I've been working 7 days a week. I'll make it a point to get down there more often. Bloody sooks! I leave them alone for a while, and they fall in a heap'. Bull blurted over the phone.

'Yeahhh', said Matt cautiously.

'OK. I'll drop the tank off for you tomorrow'. Said Bull and hung up.

As the phone went dead, Matty hung up the receiver and muttered to himself in a mournful tone: 'What have I done?'. He then went back to work with the wetsuit material and piping he had laid out all over the floor.

As the days passed, the locals were amazed at how swiftly the dredging company had started work. Pipes were delivered, surveyors were busy, heavy digging machinery was parked on-site. It was almost as if they had everything waiting, and the locals' weren't feeling comfortable about it.

The surf club crew were carrying on as usual, including Simmo who religiously did his outside cleaning chores. About mid-morning young Jackson turned up to lend a hand.

'Morning, Jackson', said Simmo.

'Morning, Mr Simpson', said Jackson.

'Jack, it's ok to call me 'Simmo'. I don't mind', said Simmo.

'Oh sorry, Mr Simpson. I'll remember to do that from now on. Thanks a lot, Mr Simpson. I appreciate it', replied Jack.

'Is everything alright, Jack? You've been a bit quiet. How did the surf rescue certificate go?' Asked 'Simmo'.

'Oh pretty good. I just got a bit tight, so the instructors thought it would be best if I sat this one out', answered Jack.

'Oh, that's too bad. Sorry to hear that. Personally, if I got into trouble in the surf I'd be looking for your help. Trust is the greatest acceptance Jack, and I'd trust your help, any day'. Said Simmo.

'Really, Mr Simpson. That means so much to me. I don't know what to say', replied Jack.

'Well, you could start by calling me Simmo, instead of Mr Simpson. It makes me feel more like your friend when you call me Simmo'.

'Sorry sir, errr Mr Simmo. I mean Simmo', replied Jack.

'That's OK mate. Let's look for something to do', suggested Simmo.

As the pair walked around the clubhouse, they came across some raw meat on the walkway.

'What's that'? Quizzed Simmo.

'Looks like a big steak', Jack suggested.

'Wonder how it got here?' Quizzed Simmo.

'Maybe it fell out of the garbage', suggested Jack.

'Nah, the garbage is on the other side', answered Simmo.

'It stinks!' muttered Jack.

'You're not wrong! We'll get rid of it then have a yarn to Adrian. Let's find out what's going on', said Simmo.

After disposing of the rotten meat, the pair headed upstairs to the club restaurant. Adrian, and his new part-time kitchen hand named Brian, were prepping for the day's work.

'Adrian, how 'ya' going'? Said Simmo, as they walked into the restaurant kitchen.

'Not bad mate. I haven't got anything to eat yet, you'll have to see Bean downstairs', replied Adrian.

'Nah, it's alright mate. We just found a couple of raw steaks on the footpath downstairs, and they were pretty rank. Just thought you oughta know', said Simmo.

'Freaking Brian! Freaking Brian! Stuff that kid!' Said a frustrated Adrian, trying to control himself. 'Hey Brian, did you clean the cold room out?' Yelled Adrian.

'Yeah, you told me too'. Replied a composed Brian.

'Did you throw out any food?' Asked Adrian.

'Yeah, you told me too', answered Brian.

'What do you mean, I told you too?' Asked Adrian.

'You said, clean out the cold room and throw out anything suspect', said Brian.

'Well what was suspect?' Asked Brian.

'Only a bit of meat', answered Brian.

'Well, what was suspicious about it? All the meat in the cold room was fresh', said Adrian.

'It just looked suspect', said Brian.

'Well I'm glad you're not a copper, or we'd all be in the jug,' blurted Adrian. 'And what do you mean it looked suspect? Please explain'.

'It had blood', said Brian.

'Fair dinkum! Fancy that! So did you smell it?' Said Adrian.

'Why?' Said Brian.

'Fair dinkum, Brian. You get me! Seriously mate! What's going on upstairs, mate? Lights are on but nobody's at home'. Said a strained sounding Adrian.

'Please explain', replied Brian impertinently.

'If food is off, it smells off. Is that not hard to understand? Hello', said Adrian.

'Well, you said if it's suspect, throw it out. So it was suspect and I threw it out', said Brian.

'Well, where did you throw it out'? Inquired Adrian.

'Well, just out', replied Brian.

'What is out? Where is out? Out in the garbage? Out the window? What? Where'? Said Adrian, getting increasingly impatient.

'Out the window', stated Brian.

Whatttt!!! Are you serious? What freaking window?' Replied a horrified Adrian.

'The office window' answered Brian.

'What the hell are you talking about? Why on earth did you throw two perfectly good, prime beef, Aussie export quality steaks, out of the office window? You lunatic!' Screamed Adrian.

'Time mate. I'm busy', said Brian. 'It's called task time expenditure'.

'Gee Wizz mate! I'm about to lose the freaking plot here'. Blasted Adrian, who was now glowing red with flared nostrils, and a death stare.

'Just deal with your emotions, and breathe, it'll pass'. Said a calm Brian, with a parental type tone.

'BRIAN! If you ever throw any more food out the office window, you will pass to the next life'. Snarled Adrian, beginning to explode.

Simmo and Jac were starting to feel very uncomfortable and looked for a way out.

'Yeah, well ok, we'd better be going'. Interjected Simmo, in an effort to calm the situation.

'I think they've got a communication problem'. Jack surmised, as they headed downstairs to the sanctuary of the kiosk.

'I think they've got a Brian problem', replied Simmo.

The kiosk was reasonably quiet and Bean noticed the look on their faces as they approached the servery counter.

'You two alright? You're looking a bit dusty', quizzed bean.

'Yeah, we're ok. There's just a bit of fireworks in the restaurant between Adrian and Brian'. Replied Simmo, giving an eyeball roll.

'Not again. What's it about this time?' Enquired Bean.

'We found a couple of raw steaks on the club walkway that had been there overnight and they were a bit rank. Brian had thrown them out of the office window because they were suspicious', answered Simmo.

'What was suspicious about them?' asked Bean.

'They had blood on them', answered Simmo.

'Struth! Lucky he's not a copper. We'd all be out the window', blurted Bean.

'Yeah, I think Adrian's about to blow a gasket with him', said Simmo.

'Well, he's a pretty hardy kid because he did an hour on the Grommets

Pole yesterday. The boys reckon he was still giving it to them when they let him go'. Said Bean.

'OH NO!!' Blurted Jack.

The Grommet Pole was a steel pole embedded in the concrete footpath of the Kirra Beach Esplanade. Being tied to the pole was a form of punishment for grommets (a term for young surfers) who mouth off or abuse older Boardriders. Learning respect and surf etiquette could be a painful process for young surfers who couldn't tame their tongue, or curb their obnoxious behaviour. Once tied to the pole, the senior surfers would urinate on the testy grommet as they walked past. This would usually last an hour depending on how remorseful or resilient the grommet was.

# Chapter 6

# Not Having
# a Bar Of It

'Hello', said Starch into his phone.

'Hi, Starch, it's Robyn. How are you?'

'Good thanks, Robyn. What's going on?' Asked Starch.

'I have some interesting bits and pieces of information about the dredging contract', answered Robyn.

'Hmmm, This will be interesting. Fire away', said Starch.

'Well, according to a very reliable source. The most astounding thing is, the actual amount of dredging does not have any limit'. Said Robyn.

'What do you mean?' Asked Starch.

'Well the company can dredge as much, or as little as they like', answered Robyn.

'What!! That's ridiculous! That's totally without guidelines. That's like a game of footy without rules. Not that a game of footy without rules, wouldn't be fun', said Starch.

'Well, at the very least, it would seem highly inappropriate for a government to sign a financially open-ended agreement with a private foreign company. They are giving the foreign contractor a blank taxpayer cheque', said Robyn.

'Stuff! Well, when you put it like that, it almost seems criminal'. Said Starch.

'Criminal? Starch, this deal has dirt all over it. No one is that stupid.

Not even a politician. Well maybe some politicians. But it is fairly obvious from the lack of transparency, someone is profiting greatly from this'. Explained Robyn.

'Wooooo. What are we going to do?' asked Starch.

'Keep digging. Keep tugging at the string till we have enough to form a conclusion'. Said Robyn.

'Should we get a lawyer or something?' Said Starch.

'I am a lawyer, Starch. Please forgive my language, but these people are the scum of the earth. There is no excuse for wasting or rorting taxpayer dollars. We'll hunt them down like the scum they are'.

Starch was a bit taken aback with Robyn's seething determination. He had never heard her speak like this before.

'Well, I'm certainly glad I never faced you in the front row of a scrum. I'll try raising some money to pay you for your time'. Starch said quietly.

'That won't be necessary. Everything for the club is pro bono. I spend my day preparing tax returns and when you see the amount of money that people are being penalised for working hard being squandered and stolen by some unethical grub in government. It makes your blood boil. It is so unfair, unjust and in a word disgusting. I'll keep you up to date with what I find. It would be prudent not to discuss this with anyone else at the moment. Talk to you later'. Starch waited until he thought it was safe to speak.

'Okay, thanks, Robyn. We all appreciate what you're doing. Please call me if you need anything. Bye', said Starch. After hanging up the phone, he paused for a moment to think about what had just gone down. He then muttered 'Strewth', and wondered what would happen next.

The epicentre of breaking news around the club was the kiosk, and Bean the perennial listener was always prepared to give away pearls of wisdom as free advice to troubled locals. Bull the plumber was seeking temporary refuge from the world, and wandered up to the servery counter for some "coffee counselling".

'Hello, you blokes'. Announced Bull in his typical "I'm about to say more tone".

'G'day Bull. What are you doing here? Shouldn't you be working or something?' Asked Bean.

'Awww, they're giving me the proverbials mate'. Said Bull, drawing Bean into the conversation.

'That doesn't sound right. Don't know what the world's coming too', replied Bean.

'Whinging, they're always whinging. They want the work done. You climb up their sewer and fix their problem. Then they whine about the cost', said Bull frustratingly.

'That's terrible', said Bean.

'Yes, bloody unthankful mate, that's all I can say. I mean. They're getting a plumbing demigod for a song and they whinge and whine about the cost! I mean, the last bloke is taking me to court! How ungrateful is that? A little bit of cost overrun and they go stupid. I mean, what's a fair dinkum bloke got to do these days. The world's stuffed!' Proclaimed the serious-sounding Bull.

'I don't know what to say, mate. I just don't know what to say'. Said Bean compassionately.

'That's alright mate. Can I have a coffee please, and I might have a bacon and egg roll too please, mate'. Said Bull.

'Yeah, okay mate', replied Bean.

'I'll just grab a seat. Yell out when it's ready. Oh, did that hot water problem come back?' Asked Bull.

'No. Must have been spiritual. Probably a poltergeist or something'. Answered Bean, guardedly.

Just as 'Bull' settled down at a table, Mel (Beans confidante) walked past on her way to work upstairs. 'Hello Bean. Free coffee vouchers were a nice touch. Keep me posted on any developments', she quipped.

Straight behind Mel was Liz. Who approached the servery counter.

'Excuse me Bean, have you seen the boys?' Asked Liz, who sounded like a cop.

'Ahhh, no Liz. Not today', answered Bean.

'Thank you, Bean'. She replied, then abruptly left, leaving Bean feeling puzzled until the phone gave an impatient ring.

'Hello Kiosk'.

'Hey Dad. Is Matthew there?' Asked Moey.

'No, Momo. He's working on his shark study thing'. Said Bean, who was now feeling a lot happier after hearing Mo's voice.

'Oh okay. He wanted my login details for Uni. Can you ask him to call me? He just doesn't answer his phone', said Mo.

'I think it's broken', replied Bean.

'Oh okay. Thanks Dad. Bye. Love you', said Mo.

'Love you too Mo. Bye'. Said Bean as they hung up the phone. There was so much going on at the moment he started to wonder when things would go back to normal... If ever.

Matthew's project was taking shape. There was a type of frame made out of PVC pipe, covered by a two-colour wetsuit skin. The skin would change between ocean blue and grey by rotating the frame. Attached to a part of the frame were the contoured scuba tanks that had been donated by Bull. On one side of the frame was a telescopic rod that would lengthen and contract with a lever attached. Similar to an old car aerial. He had decided to extend himself and integrate a mobile phone into the design. The problem of course, was his project was submersible. This did not deter him as he was very confident in his ability to solve problems. But if he did find himself in a jam there was always Moey as a backup. Even if she didn't know what he was up to.

The woes of the club had begun to mount up for Starch. The condition of the building. The uncertainty of the community grant from the government. The Tweed River Bar dredging fiasco, which could have catastrophic consequences for the tourist trade if something were to go wrong. Were all taking their toll. On top of that was all the little day to day things that add up to problems. In an effort to cheer him up, Starch's children had decided to personalise the ringtone on his phone as a surprise present for him. The ring tone was a dodgy rendition of his favourite football club theme song, 'When The Saints Go Marching In'. Although he appeared very excited in front of his daughters, the ring tone was sending him over the edge and he was desperate to get rid of it.

Starch was not technically minded and despite his best efforts, he could not figure out how to get his old standard ringtone back. So, until he could find someone to help with his problem, he had to grin and suffer another rendition of "O when the saints, O when the saints come marching in" - every time his phone rang. Some days the phone rang constantly and life was challenging for the tough ex-footballer.

As he did his rounds he fumbled through the settings menu on his phone looking for a solution, the song blurted out once again announcing an incoming call. 'Oh When the Saints, Oh When the Saints, Oh When the Saints Come Marching In'. Gritting his teeth, he punched the answer button with his finger, and muttered 'Hello'.

'Hi Starch. It's Andrew Coleman from Kirra Dive Tours'. Said the friendly voice on the phone.

'Hey Colmy. How ya going?' Replied Starch.

'Not bad, mate. Just wondering if you have any information on the bar dredging?' Asked Colmy.

'Only that it's a very suspicious operation', answered Starch.

'Yeah, I had the same feeling. They've started work already. I hope they don't stuff the reefs', said Colmy.

'Well, like I said. The only mail I've had is all bad, so it's a wait and see thing.' Replied Starch.

'That's about all we can do. I've gone over their proposal and it states the sand will be pumped between 500 to 1000 metres offshore. I've had a look at the pipes delivered, and it's not five hundred or one thousand meters of pipe'. Said Colmy.

'Yeah, we can't do too much at the moment. But between you and me, it's looking very dirty'. Said Starch.

Colmy groaned and let out a heavy breath. 'We'd better keep an eye on them. They're gunna stuff this right up', he urged.

'Agreed. But I think they think we haven't got a clue. From the information I'm receiving it's as if the government has given them a licence to be stupid'. Said Starch.

'Scary, very scary! If anyone has the qualifications to hand out licenses for being stupid, it's this government. I'll catch you later on Starch. Thanks mate. See you'. Said Colmy and hung up.

Starch paused for a moment then pressed the 'off' button on his phone. He took a deep breath and decided to go for a walk and clear his head. Sometimes, you have just got to go for a walk.

Back at the kiosk Matty had just arrived to give Bean a hand.

'Hey Matty. How's that project going?' Asked Bean, as he walked in.

'Good, there's so much to learn'. Replied Matt, acting kind of coy.

The buzz of a motorcycle pulling up next to the kiosk signalled the arrival of Moey. So Matt went outside to check.

'Hey Moey, how's it going dude?'

'Normal. What's happening?' said Mo.

'Oh, nothing much. Hey Mo, I was just wondering if you ever see sharks when you're doing your loops around Cooly airport?' Asked Matt.

'Not really, but I'm not looking for them. I do see the occasional whale', said Mo.

'Wow, sounds fun. What days do you go up?' Asked Matt.

'Usually when I can get an aircraft, but Tuesday and Friday seem to be the days. Why? Asked Moey, getting a little suspicious about the sudden interest in her flying.

'Oh, I was just wondering if you could keep an eye out for sharks. If you see one, could you take a video of it with your phone and show it to me?'. Asked Matt, innocently.

'Sure, I can do that, but you still haven't told me why... Where's Dad?' Said Mo.

'He's inside. Let's go', said Matt. The two of them headed into the kiosk, as Jodie came through the front door.

'Jodie, my girl', welcomed Bean.

'Is Jules coming in, anytime?' asked Jodie.

'Yes, he's coming for a surf tomorrow. Or so he reckons', answered Bean.

'Oh great, can you ask him to have a look at my shoulder? I think I've torn a rotator cuff muscle', said Jodie.

'Oh I'm sure Jules will be only too glad to have a look at your rotator cuff muscle, Jode'. Replied Bean with a wry smile.

'Jules or Julian was Bean's son and a high profile Exercise Physiologist that Jodie liked to take full advantage of when she sustained any injuries. He was a tall, handsome young man with an athletic build and very amiable personality. Just like his father, Julian had a touch of Aussie larrikin in him and tended to look on the humorous side of life. He was gifted with a natural ability to adapt to different types of problems rapidly and remained calm in challenging situations. Which his sister Moey, greatly appreciated. Her little brother was her rock.

Although he was athletically gifted and another all-round whizz kid, Julian's passion was music. He was a guitarist in several bands on the coast playing different styles of music and occasionally would go on tour around Australia or overseas. Jodie had a mini crush on him and whenever the pair met there was an abundance of smiles and sparks flew. This was a source of entertainment for Bean who likened the pair to a couple of prizefighters feeling each other out in a never-ending first round. Jodie's injuries were an opportunity for the pair of them to get together. Physiology is very hands-on.

# Chapter 7

# Club Life

Some of the lifeguards were training and had paddled around the headland to the bar. Starch had taken a jetski and decided to head out to keep an eye on them for a while. He reached them as they were turning around and starting to head back, as the bar was very choppy and extremely treacherous. Just as he was turning around to follow them, he noticed a fishing trawler approaching from the ocean side and recognised it immediately.

'Hey clubby. Don't get too close to the big, bad bar, or you might break a fingernail'. The familiar and unmistakable voice of Fins Walton, bellowed out of the radio speaker.

'Walton!' Muttered Starch as he looked in disbelief at Fins Walton, steaming toward a seemingly certain catastrophe.

Fins ploughed his trawler head-on into the bar. Starch and the lifeguards held their breath as the trawler was tossed about like a cork. Unfazed, Fins went full steam ahead with the waves crashing over the trawler. Starch was on the verge of calling the rescue chopper as he felt sure the Trawler was about to roll over. Fins kept the throttle on full and his experience as a skipper shone. He had seen and sailed much bigger waves than this.

'Is that all you've got?' Yelled Fins as his deckies, Ben and Sushi hung on for dear life. Starch and the lifeguards held their collective breath as Fins made it out of the bar and into the relative calmness of the Tweed River.

'That guy's a freakin lunatic', yelled one of the lifeys.

'That's an understatement! Psycho freakin mad seadog that's a danger to the bar, is more like it'. Said another.

Starch smiled. He had seen a lot worse from Fins Walton.

High up, on the side of the headland, Jackson and his mother were having a picnic and had watched Fins negotiate the bar. Fins looked up from his boat and instantly recognised Jackson waving.

'Jackoooooo'. Came the bellowing voice from the boat loudspeaker.

'Loved the fish, Mr Walton'. Yelled Jack, from the headland.

'Jackoooooo'. Came the bellowing voice out of the loudspeaker, again.

Jackson's Mum gave a rare chuckle and remarked: 'If ever a man was born to roam the sea, it surely was Mr Walton'.


Matthew had continued working on his project and the prototype was ready for testing. He decided to phone Moey and see if her plans for the day involved flying.

'Hello Mo. It's Matt. Are you going up to do loops at Coolangatta today?' He asked.

'Yes Matty, why? What's up?' Replied Mo.

'Oh, nothing much. Just wondering. If you see any sharks around the headland today, could you let me know, please? It's to do with my research', said Matt.

'Yeah, I can do that. But you do know the rescue chopper will report all shark sightings anyway. You are in a surf life-saving club Matt, you do know that don't you?' Drawled Mo.

'Yeah, yeah sorry. I just like your feedback, that's all. What time are you going up?' He asked.

'The plane is booked from 10 till 11 a.m.' Answered Mo.

'Ok, thanks. Bye'. Said Matt.

'No problem'. Replied Mo, feeling a bit suspicious about what Matty was up to - knowing he was up to something.

Matthew's indigenous heritage coupled with his father's weekend job as a Park Ranger provided him with an intimate knowledge of the local coastal environment - especially around the headlands and beaches. During his childhood, Matty spent most of his time exploring the area and had discovered several secret caves that were only accessible during low tide. The local folklore told of secret caves that the convicts hid in when they escaped the early penal colonies. Matty had kept his discovery a secret between himself and his father.

At around 9 a.m. Matt grabbed his surfboard and walked up to the headland. Crossing over to the southern side he climbed down the rocks and waited till there was a lull in the breaking waves. At a calm moment, he jumped in with his board and wasted no time paddling round to the front of the headland. He tried to stay reasonably close to the rocks where he was hard to see from the top. When he was safely out of sight, he dived just beneath the crashing waves and dragged his board under with him. He let the current drag him about 10 meters then came up in a beautifully formed cave about the size of a household single garage. There was a naturally formed rock shelf on the wall where he had been hiding his project - the shelf was high enough above the high tide mark to safely store things. A crevasse in the roof let enough light in for him to see during daylight hours. The floor of the cave was sandy and flat.

Rummaging through a waterproof bag he had bought with him, he found his mobile phone and sent a text message off to Moey, that read: 'Hi Moey. Just wondered if you were in the air yet?'

Mo was at Coolangatta airport doing her pre-flight check when she heard the message come through and replied: 'Errr, just about to taxi out now. Over and out'. She then turned her phone off and muttered: 'Far out'.

Matt waited 15 minutes then slipped into the wetsuit material and revolving PVC frame rig that he had built. The contoured oxygen tanks were full and fitted snugly around him. The oxygen was delivered via a full-face bubble mask with a safety feature built-in, so that if he had an accident and was knocked unconscious - the system would automatically keep functioning for hours. Alternatively, if he was within a metre of the surface, the system would switch to fresh air that was supplied via a snorkelling device.

Slipping into the water and diving under the surface, he paddled out through the mouth of the cave. The current was strong and indicated some strengthening of the frame was needed. He managed to stay in the deep water and made his way out to about 50m offshore. The sea was calm so he moved up to about a metre from the surface, then used a lever to rotate the wetsuit covered frame around him.

The dark coloured material was now facing the surface and the blue-green was underneath. Matt spent the next hour moving about and testing the rig just below the surface. When satisfied with his test run he made his way back through the current to the cave. After he packed his rig on the shelf he took advantage of the sunlight shining through the top and did a mental calculation of where the cave was positioned - reasoning that there might be a dry entrance. Although he had never discovered one, it didn't mean it wasn't there. After giving this some thought he took hold of his board, dived into the water and made his way out through the entrance, taking careful note of its proximity. He then headed back to the kiosk.

Ben and Sushi were two Japanese surfers that were deckhands or deckies on Fins Walton's boat. Both were highly paid professionals in Japan, before deciding they wanted to surf around the world. Australia was their first stop, and that's where they had stayed for the last 12 months. Fins needed a couple of deckies, so he wandered into the Cooly Pub one night and picked them off the bar - promising them a highly paid life of adventure on a luxury boat. The Japanese names were too hard for Fins to remember, so he called one of them Sushi but before he came up with a name for the other, the man declared: 'Just call me Ben'. Sushi and Ben were excellent deckies and worked hard for Fins, although at times they had serious doubts about his sanity. Fins, in turn, hailed the boys as good fishermen and often stated: 'It'd be a pleasure to drown with them'. All in all, they were part of the community and quite popular around the clubhouse. The boys lived to surf and surfed to live.

Matty arrived back at the clubhouse just as the boys were washing off their surfboards.

'G'day, Matt-san', yelled Sushi.

'How you going, Mat-san?' Yelled Ben.

'Hey bros, how was your surf?' Answered Matt.

'Full sick', answered Sushi.

'Very busy, Matt-san', answered Ben.

The conversation was interrupted by the distinct sound of Starch's new phone ringtone. "Oh when the saints, oh when the saints go marching in". The Trio turned to see Starch coming up from the beach and trying frantically to press his phone answer button.

'Hello', said Starch into the receiver.

'Is that Rod?' Answered a male voice.

'Yeah, that's me', said Starch.

'Rod, my name is Michael Flowers. I'm the local state MP. I'm just looking at the club's request for a state government grant', said the man.

'Oh yes', said Starch.

'I'm not saying anything at this stage but congratulations on the request. It has been very well prepared and so far it looks very good. However, Rod what I need to make you aware of is, there is going to be some dredging of the Tweed River bar - and the New South Wales government department and dredging company would like your support'. Said Flowers.

'Well, why would they want that? We're in Queensland and so are you'. Said Starch.

'Oh, I guess it's just good inter-state relations. I think the dredging company and relevant New South Wales government departments would appreciate a show of support from the Life Savers, in the local media'. Continued Flowers.

'Well, I can't do that, mate. We're in Queensland, and we don't have a clue what they're doing. No one consulted us', said Starch.

'Rod, let me put it this way. I would hate to see this very well prepared and deserving request for assistance, stalled or rejected because of some silly politically-minded reason. Think about it. What is best for the club? Thank you, Rod, Goodbye'. Said Flowers and hung up.

The hairs on the back of Starch's neck stood up as he tried to mentally digest what was just said. He struggled to believe someone had just threatened him, so he decided to head up to the kiosk and settle down and not say anything about the call to anybody - except, maybe Robyn. For the next few moments, all he could think was: 'This is blackmail, this is bloody extortion, this is bloody wrong'!

Down on the beach, the ladies surf lifeboat crew had assembled and Simmo was preparing the boat for the day's training. One of the girls had called in sick so the call went out for a replacement. Rooster, who was sitting at the clubhouse bar, had gotten wind of the situation and decided the girls needed him. Dragging himself away from the bar, he headed down the beach to help out. Simmo saw him coming and muttered: "No, no, no, no, no".

Rooster had filled in once before and his flatulence had been a huge, monster problem. The rowing team turned around to see what Simmo was saying 'no' about, then froze in fear and foreboding at the sight of Rooster striding towards them. Annika, the boat Sweep, stood next to Simmo and declared: 'Oh my grandmother. This isn't happening Simmo. The team is still recovering from the last Rooster fart fest. He is not an option!'

Steph, who was another of the boat crew, had scorn on her face and drawled: 'And what about the poetry!

Where ever you be.

Let your wind go free.

For do not seek.

From where the wind blows.

For the wind blows.

From me.

Have you ever heard worse? We are not going through that again, Simmo! It's not happening!' Blasted Steph - sounding very not negotiable.

'Talk about gone with the wind'. Said another rower named Charlie, who had a disgusted look on her face.

'What about at the bloody end when he stood up to give us a pep talk and the Family Jewels escaped out the leg of his DT's. Talk about gross!' Said another of the crew called Sam, bringing a collective moan of abhorrence.

'Bloody disgusting! Ugliest balls I've ever seen! Give me Ball Trauma'. Moaned Annika.

'Yeah. I couldn't sleep, it was that disturbing', said Steph.

The level of disapproval was huge and hostile, so the girls started to look for alternatives.

'Where's Jodie?' Asked Annika.

'Jodie and Jackson, are busy with the nippers and everyone else is on roster', replied Simmo.

'Anyone got a phone? Quick!' Said Annika.

'I have the radio. Why?' Quizzed Simmo.

'Just give it here', said Annika. So Simmo handed it over.

'Hello kiosk, are you there? Over'. Said Annika, urgently.

'Yeah I'm here, who's this? Over', replied Bean.

'Annika from the boat crew here, Bean. We're one short in the boat for the day and need a volunteer straight away. Is there anyone at the kiosk that might be prepared to help some nice ladies?' Appealed Annika.

'Yeah well there's Ben and Sushi, but they've been surfing all day and I think they've got to start work soon. Matthew's here, but he's helping me. Hang on. Jules has just turned up. He might do it', said Bean.

'Who's Jules?' Asked Annika.

'My son', answered Bean.

'Ok. Is he fit enough to do it?' Asked Annika.

'I'd say so, and he's house-trained', answered Bean.

'Sorry Bean', but I've never met your son,' said Annika.

'Give me a minute and I'll ask him', replied Bean.

Jules had parked his car and was taking his surfboard off the roof when Bean yelled out from the back door of the kiosk.

'Hey Jules, can you fill in for the ladies boat crew? They're one down and haven't got anybody. They sound desperate', yelled Bean.

'I'm going for a surf, Dad', yelled Jules from the car park.

'So do you want me to tell them, no?' Yelled back, Bean.

'The surf, Dad! The surf! Listen to it! The sets are calling me', shouted Jules.

'So, do you want me to tell them, no!' Yelled Bean again.

'Dad, I'm not a female. I've never been in a surf boat', Jules shouted back.

'Well, it's not rocket science. You just pull your pants up your arse and row! What will I tell them? They can't get anybody', yelled Bean.

'Alright, alright, I'll do it, just this once, if they can't get anybody else. But forget about the pants thing'. Jules shouted a little quieter, having resigned himself to the fact he would have to do without his surfing fix.

'Boat crew, boat crew, are you there? Over', said Bean into the radio.

'Yes Bean, what's happening? Over', replied Annika.

'Yeah, he'll do it. He's coming straight down', said Bean.

'That's one we owe you Bean. We'll look after him', said a much relieved Annika.

Rooster had arrived on the scene and announced he was up for a bit of rowing, and directed the girls to get the show on the road. Annika hastily intervened.

'Sorry Rooster, but we promised Bean's son Jules that he could help today. He's very excited and we'd hate to hurt his feelings'. Tactfully explained Annika.

'Yeah, Nah, Nah. You need someone with experience. I'll talk to him and explain the situation', replied Rooster.

Simmo started rolling his eyeballs. With the team ready to quit and sensing a disaster he decided to use the diplomatic approach.

'Yeah, everybody knows you're the real deal when it comes to surf boats, Rooster. But the young bloke's been asking me for ages, so we gotta give him a go. Anyway they need you up at the clubhouse', pleaded Simmo.

'What do they need me at the clubhouse for?' Asked Rooster - baffled at Simmo's statement.

'Well, mate, everyone else at the bar speaks rubbish. They need you up there mate, to talk some sense mate'. Said Simmo, really laying it on.

'Nah, yeah, yeah alright then. I suppose you're right, the young bloke can have a go as long as it's alright with the girls. I don't want to let anybody down', said Rooster.

'No, no, all good', said the girls hurriedly.

'Alright, I'll see you later', said Rooster, and headed back to the clubhouse.

Annika looked around then asked: 'So where's this kid?'

'Here he comes now', replied Simmo.

'Where?' Asked Annika.

'There!' Said Simmo, motioning the girls to look in the direction of the clubhouse where Jules was running across the soft sand toward them. He was wearing a pair of board shorts and no shirt, his skin was a bronze colour and he looked very fit.

'You're joking', gasped Annika with her mouth staying open.

'We've gone from the outhouse to the penthouse', quipped Charlie.

'You didn't tell us he looked like that!' Said Steph.

'Hi everybody, I'm Julian. Dad told me you need a fill-in for an hour.' Said Jules as he approached the crew.

'Looks like he gets the gold medal for all fill-ins', said Annika quietly.

'Oh yeah', answered Steph.

'Definitely', added Charlie.

'OK, let's get the boat in the water, seeing we're all smiles'. Simmo suggested, with a smirk on his face.

'Julian, could you be Stroke for today, please? That'll push us all along'. Asked Annika as the rest of the girls added their support to the idea. Simmo thought it was a bit suspicious until he figured out the Stroke is at the back of the boat in front of the Sweep, and in a position that allowed the other three crew to look at his back the whole time.

'Oh dear,' Simmo said quietly to himself. 'So much for training'.

Rooster arrived back at the kiosk as the sound of Moey's scooter could be heard arriving in the carpark.

'G'day Bean. I let your young bloke have a go at rowing, seeing as he was so excited and I didn't want to upset him by saying anything wrong'. Said Rooster.

'Oh really! Well, thanks for that Rooster I appreciate it', said a somewhat puzzled Bean.

Just as Rooster was leaving, Moey came through the back door of the kiosk. 'Hey Dad, can you make me something to eat?' Came the request without any hesitation.

'Yes ok, grab a seat, and by the way. Hello Dad, and great to see you Dad, and yeah, great to see you too Mo', replied Bean.

Moey whisked through the kiosk and sat herself down at one of the tables, then dragged a laptop out of her backpack which she fired up and started busily tapping away on. Matty wandered over to see what she was up to. 'Hello Mo, what's going on?' He asked.

'Hi Matty, I'm so under the pump with this assignment. I've got to have it in today', replied Mo.

'Oh no! Do you want a hand with anything?' Matt asked.

'It'll be okay, but thanks for offering. I've just got to check and cite my references. Everything else is done', said Mo.

'What's it about?' Asked Matt.

'The history of Western Medicine on South Pacific Indigenous Peoples', answered Mo.

'Wow! That sounds so interesting. Can I read it when you're finished?' Asked Matt.

'Yeah sure'. Answered Mo, trying to concentrate.

'Ok, I'll leave you to it. Ahhh, I was just wondering if you saw any sharks today when you were whizzing around up there?' Asked Matt tentatively.

'Errrr, no', replied Mo.

'What, none?' Asked Matt, with a surprised tone to his voice.

'Yes Matt, none'. Replied Mo, who was now tired of the conversation.

'What none? As in nothing? Nothing at all?' Blurted Matt.

'Matty, do you still speak English? None, nothing, zero, zip, zilch. None! Alright? The only thing I did see in the water was a log floating around the headland', replied Mo sternly.

'A log? A log?' Questioned Matt, starting to sound frantic.

'Yes, a log! Look, dude, I've got to get this done, so why all the questions? Is this something to do with your research? I get the feeling you're not telling me everything', said Mo, feeling irritated.

'Oh, no, no. I mean, yes, yes. It's my research. I thought there would have been more sharks around, that's all'. Explained Matty - backpedalling.

'Well, there are these things called shark nets out there, that the sharks are probably not interested in getting caught in. Helloooo', said Mo.

'Oh yeah, I forgot about that. Anyhow, I've got to get going. Cheers mate', said Matt as he retreated to the kiosk counter. Bean had prepared Moey something to eat when he noticed the glum look on Matt's face as he walked through the kiosk door.

'You alright? You look a bit off', asked Bean'.

'Who me? No, I'm fine', replied matt.

'Oh okay, I'll be back in a minute', said Bean. He was still wondering what Matty was up to as he placed the food and coffee on Moey's table, being careful not to disturb her.

'Thanks, Dad,' She said, with a big smile.'Hey Dad, I've been watching the tidal flow and the way the sand moves during the tides. I know I'm not a maritime or environmental expert but I think they have got this bar solution wrong. Even if they pump the sand 1000m out to sea the tide will still bring it back onto the Southern Gold Coast beaches'.

'I hear you sweetheart and I trust your judgement, but there is nothing we can do, it's a closed shop', said Bean.

'Do you think I should mention it to Starch?' Asked Mo.

'You could but Starch is doing all he can, so it'd probably just stress him out more'. Replied Bean.

'Yeah, that's a good point. Where's Julian? I saw his car in the car park and his board is in the kiosk', asked Mo.

'Filling in for the girl's boat crew. Last-minute emergency', replied Bean.

'Ohhh, that'll be interesting', said Mo.

Bean walked back to the kiosk and sat down for a rest, but just as he began to relax, Danny suddenly appeared at the counter.

'G'day Bean have you seen Liz here today?' He asked as he scoured the landscape.

'No mate, she comes and goes but I haven't seen her here today. Is everything alright?' Asked Bean, raising an eyebrow.

'Awww, it's all smoke and mirrors mate. She's playing games with me. Have you seen Grizz?' Asked Danny, sounding a little more intense.

'No mate, haven't seen Grizz either. Can't help you', answered Bean.

'Yeah, see what I mean!!! She's playing games with me', Danny blurted out, clearly agitated. 'I'd better get one of those chocolate bars, I'm going to do some training and I better get my energy levels up'.

'Oh okay. Got to have those energy levels'. Bean said, wary of carrying on the conversation any longer.

Danny scoffed down his chocolate bar, also called his energy bar and headed down the beach to do his training. Bean had noticed Matt wasn't saying too much which was a little unusual, so he asked: 'You seem a bit quiet Matt. Everything alright?"

'Yeah Bean, all good, no probs', answered Matt quietly.

It was clear Moey's log observation comments had seriously dented Matt's confidence. His project needed some significant improvements and this had him in deep thought. He decided to change materials and be a lot more creative. The costs involved would blow his budget out of the water but having his imitation shark mistaken for a log had badly bruised his ego, and stung him into action. Matty's Shark Phase 2, would be terrifyingly realistic and certain to cause chaos.

# Chapter 8

# Lives Around the Club

The lifesavers were having a very quiet day on the beach, or so it seemed. Shannon had noticed a surfer lying flat on his board trying to paddle into the shallow water near the beach. As he reached the sand he tried to stand up but stumbled to his knees, his back was covered in blood and was still bleeding badly. The young surfer had come off his board on a crowded wave and another surfer had gone over the top of him, accidentally slashing his back with the surfboard fins. This was one of the perils associated with surfing crowded breaks, as surfboard fin slashes could be a very serious injury.

Geraldine, who was another of the lifesavers on duty also spotted the surfer and sprinted across the sand to reach him. Untying his leg rope whilst assessing the cuts across his back she turned to Shannon, and without panicking said: 'This is bad!' She then applied a towel in an attempt to stop the bleeding, as Shannon called Starch on the radio.

'Patrol to Starch, come in. Over'.

'Yeah, I'm here, what's up? Over', replied Starch.

'We're bringing up a young male surfer with a deep fin cut across the width of his back. He's lost a lot of blood and we require an ambulance urgently, over', said Shannon.

'On its way.' Said Starch as he contacted emergency services who dispatched an ambulance immediately. The lifeys then arrived carrying the young surfer who looked very pale and exhausted. Geraldine held the towel firmly on his back as Starch started to clean around the wound. The sound of a siren coming from the distance was a welcome sound. Paramedics arrived, quickly disembarked and very professionally attended to the young fellow's wounds. They then placed him face down on a stretcher and loaded him into the ambulance.

'Thanks, Starch, see you next time. Good job lifeys'. Said the paramedics as they blasted off, siren blasting on their way to the hospital.

Starch, Shannon and Geraldine breathed a sigh of relief as they watched the ambulance pull out of the car park. The situation could have been much, much worse and it was a timely reminder of how quick things can change. No matter how peaceful and serene the beach appears anything can happen at any time. The environment can change in the blink of an eye, so it is best to be prepared as much as possible and expect the unexpected. For volunteer lifesavers this wasn't easy, Starch was aware of this and was always around to settle the nerves after the more serious rescues.

'Do you two want to go back down the beach and I'll bring you some food from the kitchen', said Starch.

'Thanks, Starch', said Shannon, who welcomed the change of atmosphere.

'Sounds good to me', added Geraldine, still holding the blood-soaked towel.

After the lifeys had left, Fins Walton and Sharkbait the ragged terrier dog, arrived at the entrance to the club. Fins turned to Sharkbait and muttered: 'No dogs allowed'. In response Sharkbait showed his front teeth and gave a rattly growl. 'Idiot!' Said Fins as he walked in the door and upstairs to the bar. Sharkbait followed as usual.

Starch had made his way back down to the patrol and gave them their food from the kitchen. A bit of drama tends to sap the emotional energy out of people and Starch was no different, so he decided to take a few minutes of quietness to rest. That was until his phone rang.

'Hey Starch, it's Tommy Green from the bar up at the club', said the caller.

'Yeah mate, what's up?' Replied Starch.

'Just letting you know, Fins Walton is at the bar drinking. I wasn't sure what to do, seeing he's supposed to be barred and suspended'. Said Tom.

Starch gave a long breath out and muttered to himself: 'It's just one thing after another'.

'What'd you say?' Asked Tommy.

'Errr nothing', replied Starch. 'Is there anyone with him?' he added, aware that Fins didn't have any mates.

'No, only Sharkbait', said Tommy.

'His dog? Where's the dog and what's it doing?' Asked Starch.

'He's at the bar having a pie with Brian from the kitchen', answered Tom.

'Whaaaaaat?? Are you serious? Fair dinkum the place is turning into a bloody zoo! Get that bloody dog out of there and tell Adrian and Wendy there is a zero-tolerance level on Brian!! How much has Walton had to drink?' Gasped Starch.

'He's on his second pint and rum chaser'. Answered Tommy, bracing for the reply.

'How long's he been there?' Blurted Starch.

'About 5 minutes', replied Tom.

'5 minutes!!! Stuff a duck, and he's on his second pint and rum', said Starch.

'Yeah, he sort of just swallows it... Hang on, I think he's leaving', said Tommy.

'We can only hope', muttered Starch.

'Yep, he's heading for the door and Sharkbait' is right behind him. Okay all good'. Said Tommy as Fins walked out the door.

'Good. Make sure you give Adrian and Wendy my message. Everyone's got a right to be stupid but that kids abusing the privilege. Thanks, we'll catch up later', said a relieved Starch. He then put his phone down, shook his head and muttered, 'unbelievable'. Elsewhere on the beach, Jackson had finished helping Jodie with the nippers and decided to look for something to do around the clubhouse. Andrew Coleman from Water-Town Dive had just arrived looking for Starch, and met Jackson at the club entrance.

'Hi Jack, is Starch around? Asked Andrew.

'Yeah Mr Coleman, he's just down with the patrol. He should be back shortly'. Jack replied.

'OK, I'll just grab a coffee and wait at the kiosk. Jack, it's ok to call me Colmie', said Andrew.

'Ok, thanks, Mr Coleman. I'll do that from now on', replied Jackson.

'How's the surf rescue certificate coming along?' Asked Colmie.

'Still getting there', Jack replied.

'Have you ever thought about maybe having a look at what's underwater as well as what floats on top?' Colmie asked.

'Oh yeah, for sure, but we don't have a lot of money and diving costs money. Mum works long hours and I'm looking for a job after school, so maybe one day it'll happen'. Replied Jack.

'Well, I'd like to offer you a job. We need a well-mannered junior to answer the phone when we're out on dives and also a few hours tidying up the shop and dive boat through the week. The phone is a mobile that is redirected from the landline and shop number so we have no objection to you carrying the phone around with you. The job would pay around $200 plus a week, plus unlimited free diving tuition and free equipment hire and free time on the boat for you and your mum. We will teach you to control your breathing and relax in the water, and I'm sure this will help you with your rescue certificate', said Andrew.

Jackson stared in disbelief, his jaw had dropped and his mouth was gaping open.

'Well what do you think?', Asked Andrew.

'I don't know what to think, Mr Coleman, sorry, I mean Colmie. I think you could get someone better than me. I'm happy to clean your shop but you don't have to pay me'. Jackson replied.

'Jack we need someone well mannered, polite, honest, trustworthy, reliable, someone we feel comfortable with and is local. We have been watching the way you work around the club and we're very impressed. If you want this job it's yours', said Colmie.

'Oh yeah, I'd love to have the job but I just don't want to disappoint you', Jack explained.

'You're a hard man Jack! Is it the money? Do you want more money?' Colmie asked with a smile.

'No, that's heaps of money and I'm so wanting to learn about diving', replied Jack.

'Well, how about you talk to Mum, and she can call me and I'll explain it to her.' Colmie suggested.

'Ok, it's a big yes from me but I'll get Mum to call you. I'll just race down and find Starch for you', said Jack.

'Thanks, Jack. There's no hurry, I'll be at the kiosk so take your time', said Colmie.

Jackson's head was spinning with excitement as he ran down the beach. 'Starch, are you busy? Andrew Coleman is up at the kiosk and wants to have a yarn to you about something'. He blurted out between breaths.

'Yeah OK, thanks. I'll go up and see what he wants. You alright Jack? You look a bit giddy', said Starch.

'Yeah, yeah, all good', said Jack excitedly. 'Colmie offered me a job'.

Starch made his way up to the kiosk and found Colmie sitting at a table by himself. 'G'day Colmie, how are you doing?'

'Pretty good Starch, how about you?' He replied.

'What's going on?' Asked Starch.

'Just a query, Starch. The local state member, Flowers, has just phoned me. He told me you're excited about the bar dredging operation and you've labelled it as a brilliant piece of maritime engineering. Also, you're going to endorse it in the media and you're encouraging everybody to support it. I just wanted to ask you, if that is true?' Rattled off Colmie.

'Pigs arse!!!' Barked Starch. 'I said nothing of the sort! The idiot phoned and tried to pressure me into making a positive statement about it in the local paper. He's using an application for a Community Grant the club needs, to leverage his position'.

Colmie looked relieved and replied: 'I thought it sounded a bit suspect'.

'A bit suss!!! Mate, it's a whole lot more than a bit suss, it's beginning to look like a sideshow. I'm starting to think this dredging business has nothing to do with the bar and everything to do with money'. Declared Starch.

Colmie pushed a breath out and replied: 'Yeah, I'm getting the same feeling'.

Then with a sober tone to his voice and poker face, Starch added:

'That Flowers! The so-called state member is as bent as a mountain road. And I'll tell you what. He's sailing very close to the wind'. Colmie could sense the conservation getting wound up so he tried to settle things.

'Yeah, very definitely. He just laid a whole pile of crap on me. What do you think we ought to do?'

Starch thought for a couple of seconds then answered firmly but reassuringly.

'Well we know something is wrong but we don't know exactly what is wrong. These blokes are professional snakes and they cover their tracks very well. Just play it by ear, for the time being. Maybe we'll get lucky and one of these low-lifes will upset Walton, then that'll be the end of them. He's mad enough to do anything!'

'OK, good idea, I'll keep in touch. Oh, by the way, I've offered Jack a bit of paid part-time work. I think he'll be great'. Replied Colmie, still smiling at the thought of Starch's Walton solution.

'Yeah', replied Starch with a chuckle. 'He just blurted it out to me on the beach! I've never seen him so excited'.

'That's great, I'll let you know if anything happens. See you later', said Colmie.

'Yeah okay, thanks for keeping me in the know', Starch replied, as the pair shook hands. Then, just as they went to leave they noticed Fins Walton and Sharkbait standing at the entrance to the club talking to a couple of fishermen. Colmie turned to Starch and gave a knowledgeable wink, declaring, 'There's our man'... 'And dog!' Starch answered, as he walked off shaking his head.

After he finished the discussion, Fins dropped into the kiosk to pick up something to eat for Sushi and Ben, who were preparing the boat for work. Fins and the boys had a concoction of goat's milk, avocado and orange, that they consumed regularly. Matthew saw him coming so he had the food ready and waiting for him.

'There you go, 3 GMAO's, special edition', Matthew spruiked.

'Yeah, righto Einstein', replied Fins as he grabbed his food. But just as he was walking away, Matt had a question.

'Errrr, excuse me Fins. You wouldn't happen to know where I could get some large shark fins, would you?' Asked Matty, cautiously.

'What kind of shark fins and why are you asking me?' Replied Fins.

'Oh I just thought because you're a fisherman, you might know', said Matt nervously.

'What do you want large shark fins for? It's not bloody Asian soup so scratch that one'. Growled Fins.

'No no no, it's just to do with my shark migration study', explained Matthew.

'SHARK MIGRATION!!!' Shouted Fins. 'Are you having a go at me? You told me you were investigating temperature variables and light spectrum effects on different colours of wetsuit materials. Now it's shark migration. So, are the sharks wearing wetsuits when they migrate these days, are they? Getting their little shark arses burnt from the light spectrum are they?' Finn's red hair and beard highlighted his red face and the slight smell of rum on his breath indicated to Matty that he was in dangerous territory.

'No, no... it's the... same study'. His voice became quieter. Matt felt depleted and was more hesitant. Fins stared him down with a set of eyes that would have bored a hole through concrete.

'Now listen here young fella. You come from a good family and I know your folks well. They're decent people so whatever you're up to it better be legal or you better not get caught, cause, if you do you'll be going swimming with Sharkbait out the back of the boat'. (Fins was interrupted by a very aggressive snarling Sharkbait who was also showing a set of very sharp front teeth). 'So don't play me for a mug and stop bullcrappin your head off. You could try asking the boys who check the drum lines and nets out the front, but if you want to go big - the taxidermist has a few someone donated. Tell him I sent you'.

There was a moment of sober silence when Fins finished speaking until Matty assented and replied in a subdued manner. 'Thank you. Sorry about that'. Fins walked off with Sharkbait following closely behind him as usual. Matty gave a huge sigh of relief as he looked skyward. Any conversation with Fins was good when it was over!

# Chapter 9

# Experts?

Weeks passed and the work on the Tweed River Bar continued with the installation of a pumping station, and the announcement of several outlet sites for the dredging. There was no announcement for the main outlet, which was to pump sand more than 500 meters offshore. Previous attempts to solve the bar problem included extending the groin on the southern side of the entrance to interrupt the tidal flow - however, this solution had made the bar more treacherous. Then, after consultation with another expert, the solution was to extend the groin even further. Which made the bar even more treacherous. Thus the dilemma continued with more solutions, proposals, studies, working models, experts, consultants, non-binding opinions, observation trials, controlled studies, etc, etc. Thus, the locals were subjecting any work on the bar to closer scrutiny, with a high degree of mistrust and scepticism. The for and against camps were becoming more and more polarised with each day, as the sand pumping system was being built at an extraordinary pace. Everything was set up and just about ready to start.

Unbeknown to the locals, the dredging company finished an environmental impacts study a year in advance of its proposal to the government. The whole process only had to be rubber-stamped. After community consultation and objections were screened, the government decision-makers were satisfied the community consultation process had been fulfilled. In their opinion, there were no scientifically valid objections to reject the dredging company proposal. However, the dredging company had amended the design, citing new scientific data. Instead of laying the outlet pipes 500 meters out from the shoreline, the amendment allowed them to pump it just 50 meters out, at its main outlet. They had reasoned this adjustment from a working model and the adjustment had resulted in quicker build time for the project. The pumping would begin in a matter of days, when the local member of parliament would be opening the operation with invited media only - which was not publicised.

Jackson was still giddy with excitement about Colmies job offer. However, his mother had insisted he finish his school assignments, before she would be speaking to anyone about a possible part-time job. He would never argue with his mother, so he buried himself in his schoolbooks and completed all his study obligations. Suzanne knew how hard he had worked and had some news for him.

'Jackie, I spoke to Mr Coleman today about your job offer, and he would like you to start ASAP'. Related Suzanne.

Jac's jaw dropped, his eyes lit up and he stared at his mum in disbelief before blurting.

'REALLY!!! REALLY!! I'll start tomorrow, if that's okay with you, Mum... Can I?'

With a mother's knowing smile, Suzanne answered. 'Yes Jackie... Of course'.

'Thanks, Mum. Love you mum'. Gushed Jac, in enthusiasm overload..

'I love you too, Jackie', she replied.

'I won't let you down', said Jac trying to contain his excitement. Suzanne could sense that he might be a bit too excited, and didn't want him to place his expectations too high - so she reminded him of bigger responsibilities.

'Jackie, just remember, you have to keep up your schoolwork. If the job gets too much we may have to cut the hours back', she explained. And with that sobering thought, he grounded himself.

In the following week and a bit, Jackson handled the responsibility of the new job with ease. His maturity and polite, friendly manners were an instant hit with the customers. Jac progressed rapidly through the diver beginner's course and was feeling good about himself. However, Colmie could sense some apprehensiveness in him and decided to address it.

'Jack', said Colmie. 'Can you help me load up the van, we're going to the pool for an inauguration class. I also want to do some work with you while we're up there'.

'OK, I'll start loading.' Answered Jack, as willing as ever.

Once at the pool, Colmie and Tanks, the diving instructor, were very busy with the class whilst Jack tendered the gear and assisted the learners. After an hour and a half in the water, the class took a break and Colmie asked Jack to put on a weight belt. He then pulled out a snorkel mask that was covered with black tape to prevent any visibility for the wearer.

'What's that for?' Asked Jack, referring to the mask.

'It's a stress inoculator', replied Colmie.

'What's a stress inoculator?" Continued a curious Jack, puzzled by the appearance of the mask.

'Let's jump in the pool and I'll show you', suggested Colmie.

A somewhat pensive Jack lowered himself into the pool, and Colmie fitted the mask but didn't pull it over his face. He explained to Jac the purpose of the mask.

'Sometimes when we're diving, loss of visibility can be a big problem. It can happen if the bottom gets stirred up or we're in a cave and we lose light. So, we try to prepare ourselves for it to avoid panic or overreacting'.

'Oh, okay', replied Jack. Taking it all in.

'Now this is what we're going to do. I want you to pull the mask over your face then we'll get out from the edge of the pool. I'll have a hold of you, then when I say - take a breath and go under. The weight belt should have just enough to help you sink. When we're under the water I'm going to spin you round a couple of times then let you go. You have five seconds to find your equilibrium and head to the surface. If you haven't started towards the surface after 5 seconds I will grab your hand and take you up. Don't remove the mask until we get to the surface. Is that clear?' Questioned Colmie.

Jack immediately replied: 'Yep'.

'Ok, let's do it'. Colmie declared. The two of them then let go of the poolside and paddled out a couple of meters. The weight belt felt heavier for Jack the longer he had to tread water.

'Okay Jack, put the mask on, take a deep breath, and down we go'.

Following directions, Jack pulled the mask over his face. Without any vision, he immediately felt more vulnerable and the feeling of sinking in darkness was awful. In a matter of seconds, he was feeling apprehensive, then without warning Colmie grabbed him by the ankles and dragged him down further. This caught Jack totally by surprise. Colmie then spun him in a somersault. Following that he spun him around horizontally. This left Jack totally disoriented, and not panicking wasn't an option. Precious seconds ticked by and a feeling of helplessness swept over him. The weight belt made buoyancy difficult so he started to paddle his way to what he thought was the surface - but he felt Colmie grab his hand and pull him in another direction. Colmie was strong in the water and to Jack, he felt like a large tugboat. They burst through the surface water and Jack gasped for air as the face mask was pulled off.

'How was that?' Beamed a smiling Colmie.

'Far out', blurted Jack. 'That was so bad, it scared the crap out of me'.

Colmie gave a hearty laugh and replied: 'Get your breath back and we'll do it again.'

Jack rolled his eyeballs, then the pair spent the next 30 minutes going over and over the same drill until Colmie called time. 'Ok Jack, that'll do for today. How do you feel?'

'Exhausted, totally stuffed'. Declared Jack, sounding every bit like he was exhausted and totally stuffed.

'Hah, I mean mentally,' asked Colmie.

'Exhausted, totally stuffed'. Replied Jack, still trying to get his breath back.

'That's exactly what we want. You did very well Jack. Next time we'll do it in open water with a current', proposed Colmie. He was very impressed with how Jack had handled himself. Jack just rolled his eyeballs again, wondering what he had got himself into.

After the lesson finished the team packed up and headed back to the shop. Today was a special day for another reason. It was Jackson Gave's first payday. Two hundred and ten dollars of hard-earned cash. This was a very special moment for him. For the first time in his life, he realised his time and talents were of value. He was exhausted but inside he was different. He had grown and acquired a confidence that wasn't there before. He wished his dad was there to share it with him and to talk about things, but he knew this could never be. The loss of his father had always been a burden for him but he kept it hidden, he knew his mother was also suffering. He tried to be as strong as he could, that is why he kept going back and trying again, and again, and again for his Surf Rescue Certificate. He wanted his mum to feel proud of him for achieving something. But this was different, not only was he doing something that lifted his mother's spirits, but there was also the very big advantage that this achievement came with a payday. So, on his way home, Jack called into the local florist and bought the biggest, most beautiful bunch of flowers in the shop. The shop owner knew about Jack and the loss of his father so she went the extra mile and secretly cut the bill to cost.

Jackson arrived home on his pushbike struggling with the very large bunch of flowers. As he came through the front door of their modest home his mother gave a look of bewilderment.

'Hi, Mum, these are for you. It's ok, I got paid. Here's the money for groceries and stuff', exclaimed Jack. His mum was more than a bit surprised.

'Oh Jackie, it's your money, you earned it and it's yours to do with whatever you want'. She answered.

'No, Mum, the money is for us. We can share it and buy stuff that we need. Please Mum, this is important to me', insisted Jack.

Suzanne could sense the need in his voice and compromised.

'Well if it's important to you, that is the way it will be. But, only if we can give you an allowance'.

'Ok, but I don't need anything at the moment, so let's save up for something', Jac assented.

Suzanne looked at him reassuringly.

'Jackie, I am very proud of you. You are such a thoughtful young man. You are the best son a mother could ever hope for, and those are the most beautiful flowers I've ever seen in my life. You have made me feel very, very, special. Why don't you go down to the club and see what's happening with your friends. I'll come down later and we'll have a meal to celebrate'.

'That's a cool idea, mum'. Jac replied, and headed off to the club with a happy heart.

Unfortunately, not all hearts were happy at the club where the social jousting and one-upmanship between Danny and Grizz continued with great fervour. The undivided attention of Liz being the ultimate prize, and both had committed total passion to their quest. Nothing was considered off-limits or too low in this battle of deep affection. It was a man against man in a quagmire of desire, with no quarter asked and none given.

In the kiosk, Bean continued with his quest. Wandering down the long and lonely road of unrequited love. Although he had begun to think of it as the impossible dream he was still constantly handing out free coffee vouchers. But, the target of his affection continued to elude him. Mel from upstairs was growing tired of his long face and far away looks, so she decided to intervene with some practical female know-how.

'So Romeo, how's the love vouchers going? Made contact yet?' Asked Mel in a slightly satirical manner.

'Nope, it's impossible. If I go out and wait, she doesn't show. If I don't go out on the path she walks past. It's impossible'. Bean anguished.

'So what's the plan if she does walk past and you give her a voucher? What next?' Quizzed Mel.

'I don't know. I haven't got that far yet', he lamented.

Mel was starting to feel his pain so she looked for a plan. 'Bean, Bean, Bean. If this woman walked in here right now, what would you do?'

'Probably die', he muttered.

Sensing a possible approaching tragedy Mel realised this was a trainwreck romance, so she consoled him.

'Well that's positive! I suppose we'll just try and make it to first base then see what happens'.

Bean paused for a minute looking at the floor then sighed:

'Well to tell you the truth I've been thinking of putting her in the too hard basket. I just wish I could stop thinking about her'.

In a last-ditch effort to save the situation, Mel suggested:

'Well, how about if I hand out some vouchers, as a favour of course. Then if she shows up, I'll quiz her and find out if she is available. I'll be your wingman'.

'Yeah, why not', replied Bean immediately.

'Ok, I'll let you know if anything happens. I'm going upstairs so I'll see you later', Mel replied.

With the situation seemingly under control and a plan in place, she headed up to the kitchen where the sound of Adrian's voice was once again raging at Brian.

'YOU DID WHATTT?' The ballistic screech came.

Mel couldn't hear the muffled response from Brian.

'Brian! An Ibis is not and never will be a chicken in this restaurant', yelled Adrian.

There was another muffled response from Brian which sent Adrian into another screeching meltdown.

'An Ibis is not a freaking chicken. They are paying for chicken. Get that freaking bird out of here or I'll call the animal ambulance and have you arrested for attempted bird murder. You are incredibly freaking stupid'.

Mel was struggling to believe what she was hearing. But the mindless rage Adrian had whipped himself into prompted her to intervene and try and calm the situation.

'Is everything alright, Adrian?' She asked tentatively.

'Yes, thank you, Mel. Brian and I are just discussing a culinary technical issue'. He replied, trying to remain calm.

'Well you had better sort it out before Starch gets wind of it. Why is there an Ibis in the kitchen?' She queried.

'It flew in through the window. Brian was just taking it out. Everything's sorted now. Thanks for dropping in'. Adrian replied, hoping to brush her off.

Mel walked off to the bar area as the sound of muffled rumblings continued in the kitchen.

# Chapter 10

# Sharks, Stingers, Drunks & Danny

Starch had enlisted Jack to help him with some routine work around the clubhouse and as usual, Jack was relishing the social interaction and banter with the other clubbies.

'How's the new job going, Jack?' Asked Starch.

'Oh great, I love it. They're teaching me how to slow down my breathing and how to control myself when I'm under stress. I feel a lot better, I hope they're happy with me. They're nice people,' replied Jack.

'They're very happy with you Jack. I spoke to Colmie this morning and he asked if you were happy', explained Starch. 'Just be yourself, that's all we can be. On the club front, we'd better start spending more time in the power craft. You'll be old enough to get a license soon so when you get that you can do a patrol in the inflatable - you can handle the blow-up better than anybody".

Jack was relieved, encouraged and excited by Starch's remarks.

'Wow! That's awesome. I'm all over this Starch, can I ask Simmo or Jodie to take me out if you're busy?' He urged, seizing the moment.

'Yeah, that's OK. Just let me know when you're going.' Replied Starch, who was smiling inside. To see Jackson happy was a very satisfying feeling. The pair finished doing the clubhouse rounds then headed down the beach to check in on the Lifesavers.

'How's it going? Looks pretty quiet', quizzed Starch.

'It is quiet except there's a pile of clothes over there that have been there since we arrived this morning, which means they could have been there last night'. Explained Jesse, who was one of the lifeys.

Starch looked toward the pile of clothes with the dreaded, here we go look on his face. 'Oh that doesn't sound good,' he slowly remarked.

'No, we thought we'd give it another hour than say something', explained Jesse.

'Well if they've been there that long we'd better have a look now'. Said Starch, feeling uneasy because of previous experience.

'Well for a start they don't look like clothes you'd wear to the beach, so let's have a bo peep'.

Jodie was on patrol so she started looking through the pile.

'It's not beachwear'. She murmured holding up a pair of black business trousers. There was also an expensive shirt and a pair of black Italian shoes.

'This is starting to look bad. What's in the pockets, Jode?' Asked Starch.

Going through the pockets she found a wallet with money, credit cards and personal items. There was a strong smell of alcohol emanating from the clothes, which prompted Starch to think about the dire consequences of combining alcohol and a nighttime dip in the surf.

'I'm starting to get the dreaded awfuls about this', he groaned. 'I hope this bloke hasn't gone out last night, got tanked and decided to come down here for a dip in the dark'.

The patrol had the same uncomfortable thought. 'We were wondering the same thing', sighed Jodie.

Starch was faced with an unenviable decision of what to do. Does he call on a search for a missing swimmer and alert the police and possibly waste everybody's time? Or does he do nothing and wait a bit longer? If he does nothing and waits it may cost this person his life - so he decided to call the police and give them the man's details found in the wallet. After calling the police he directed the lifesavers to start looking out the back of the surf break and around the headland. Meanwhile, he and Jack would look around the rocks at the base of the headland to see if anything had washed up. As they started to search, Starch alerted the rescue chopper to the situation. They were doing a sweep along the coastline when Rotors, the chopper pilot, answered the call.

'Do you have any idea what time he went into the water, Starch?' He quizzed.

'No, not exactly. We know the clothes have been left on the beach for at least 4 hours but that doesn't include last night. Over', replied Starch.

Rotors pondered the situation for a moment then responded:

'Ok, gotcha. We'll do a sweep and follow the current to see if that turns up anything. In a worst-case scenario, he probably would have washed up on the beach by now. Over'.

A lifeless body on the beach wasn't what Starch was hoping to find but he lamented.

'Yeah well, let's hope it's neither that or he's cuddled up to a Noah's Ark. Over.' ( Noah's Ark was slang for shark). Although rarely seen, they were always a factor to be considered in the search for a missing swimmer.

After looking around the rocks at the base of the headland Starch and Jack walked back to the kiosk. The radio was silent and all that could be done was being done. Bean was working in the kiosk and unaware of what had happened but noticed the look on Starch's face. 'Struth, what happened to you?' He asked. 'Looks like you've got the weight of the world on your shoulders.'

After giving a big breath out, Starch patiently explained.

'It looks like some blokes got tanked last night, gone for a swim and didn't come back'.

It was something everyone in the club dreaded hearing and Bean was no exception. So he tried to be helpful.

'Has everyone been notified? Can I do anything?' He offered.

'Yes and no. There's nothing much else we can do other than look. It might be a false alarm but it feels bad'. Starch answered.

Bean handed him a bottle of water and gave another to Jack, then dialled his phone.

'Moey, are you up in the air?' He asked.

'Yes, Dad, I'm down at Byron. Why what's wrong?' Came the reply from Mo.

'There's a missing swimmer up this end. Could you keep an eye out on your way back, please?' He replied.

Moey was quiet for a moment then answered.

'OK, I'm on my way back now. Bye'.

Just as Bean finished the call, Fins Walton and Sharkbait walked past on their way up to the club bar. 'Couldn't help but overhear. I'll let you know if I drag anything up', said Fins.

Starch looked up when he heard Finn's voice as they were heading upstairs to the bar. He just shook his head and didn't bother to challenge them. He already had enough to deal with, and took a moment to ponder the lunacy that sometimes happens around the club. Just as he thought there was a logical explanation for all the bizarre behaviour, Danny appeared at the servery window. He sensed that all those logical behaviour assumptions were about to be blown out the window.

'How are you going, men?' Barked the quirky voice of Danny. 'Can I have a couple of energy bars and a banana smoothie, please?'

'Thought you were on a diet?' Quizzed Bean.

'Yeah, I am. I'm toning up, I can't believe how fit I am, I'm in the best shape of my life'. Blurted Danny as Starch, who was trying not to listen, rolled his eyes. Bean gave a very sober look and approached his next question to Danny with much trepidation - knowing this could be another one of those, here we go moments.

'Well, what do you need energy bars and smoothies for?' He asked, dreading the answer. Danny looked at him with his mouth open and wondered why he'd ask such a question.

'Oh, mate! It's my metabolism. I'm just burning fuel at ridiculous amounts. I can't afford to lose my shape, I've worked so hard for it'. He explained, which caused Starch to look at the floor and shake his head from side to side. Bean couldn't resist another question.

'How much of this training are you doing?' He asked.

'Ahhh, just the stuff out the front mate... It's called high impact, multi-angle, soft sand power training'. Answered Danny, as Starch groaned whilst still looking down.

Bean served him his smoothie and chocolate bars and commented:

'Danny, all you are doing is walking across the sand and back'.

Danny was still a bit bewildered at Bean's ignorance of advanced training methodology and calmly explained:

'Nah, it just looks like that to the untrained eye, mate. You have to know about serious fitness techniques before you can understand what I'm doing'.

For a second, Bean started to doubt his sanity, but snapped out of it and asked:

'Well, why don't you get Jodie to join you? She's always up for that sort of thing'.

'Oh no!' Beamed Danny. 'Liz mightn't like that. We're getting on very well, you know'.

Starch gave a mournful groan and muttered. 'I can't take any more of this'. Then stood up and walked off.

'Well, I've got to get into it', declared Danny sucking on his smoothie. 'Did you give me those energy bars?'

Looking at him in disbelief, Bean politely answered:

'Yes, they're called chocolates. You ate them!' And with that, Danny turned around and marched off down the beach to do his training. Bean paused for a moment and watched him walk off chewing on another chocolate bar and sucking on his smoothie. He wondered what was going on inside his head but then concluded, whatever it was might be catching - so it was best not to give it too much thought. Just as he went to clean up, the phone rang with Moey on the line.

'Hey Dad, I've just spotted a shark off the headland. I'm doing a loop to get another look, but it was a shark. And a big one'. Said Mo.

'What the!!! I'll tell Starch, straight away'. Bean replied alarmingly, trying not to overthink the situation.

'Kiosk to Starch. Urgent. Come in. Over'. He blurted over the radio.

'Yeah, what's up? Over'. Replied Starch, hesitantly.

'Moey just spotted a large shark off the headland. She's doing a loop to keep an eye on it. There is no mistake, this is a big shark. Over'. Exclaimed Bean.

'Stuff a duck! What next? OK, I can see her, I'll sound the alarm'. Replied Starch, trying not to jump to conclusions about the missing swimmer and the shark sighting. The Clear The Water siren sounded as the patrol tried to get everybody up on the beach without starting a panic. Starch's radio barked into life again:

'Come in Rainbows End this is Greenmount, over'. Rattled the incoming voice.

'Yes Greenmount, this is Rainbow's End. What's up? Over'. Answered Starch.

'Heard the transmission. We're heading up in the dinghy to take a look, Starch. Are you all good? Over'. Quizzed the comforting voice of the Greenmount Lifey.

'Yeah, thanks for the help. The choppers up the other end. Over,' he replied. The call from Greenmount gave Starch a little bit of a lift. They were a good crew and very professional at what they did.

'Ok, we'll be there in a minute, we've told everybody to clear the water until further notice. Out'. Finished off the lifey.

After a long few minutes waiting in the kiosk, Bean's phone finally rang and Moey's voice barked out of the handpiece:

'Dad, I'm over the area where it was but I can't see it anywhere. It couldn't have swum off that quick but I can't see it. I'll go round one more time'.

Bean listened and replied: 'Ok, I'll tell Starch'.

As he put down the phone he reflected on the worsening situation. The only thing worse than a large shark around the swimmers - was a large shark that couldn't be seen around the swimmers. The patrol had managed to get everyone out of the water and onto the beach. But there were still a considerable number of surfers who stayed in the surf. Starch was sweating on the feedback from Moey, so he pumped his radio again.

'Patrol to kiosk. What's going on with the visitor, Bean?' He asked.

'Can't locate it mate. She's going round again. Over'. Bean replied.

'OK. Out'. Answered Starch, just as his mobile phone rang: 'Hello', he barked into the phone.

'Hello', came the reply. 'Could I speak to Mr Lawless, please. My name is Senior Constable Kelly Follent from Coolangatta Police'.

'Yeah, Kelly, it's me'. Replied Starch.

'Sorry, Starch, I didn't recognise your voice. I'm just keeping you up to date with the missing swimmer. We went to his address but there wasn't anyone we could find there. We have made enquiries with the neighbours and they have not seen him for at least 24 hours. So we will notify you immediately if he is located. How is everything on your end?'

Starch thought about her question and the only word he could think of in reply was, mayhem. But he tried to sound professional.

'Well, we just had a shark sighted off the headland to add to our missing swimmer, so it's all hands on deck at the moment. The rescue chopper is sweeping the coastline and the three clubs have watercraft out searching. So we're giving it everything we've got'.

'Well the last thing you needed was a shark to join the search so let's hope we can find this bloke. We'll keep looking on our end so just keep us in the loop. I'll be in touch straight away if we find anything. Thank's Starch', she replied. There was something very no-nonsense like but compassionate in Kelly's manner, that Starch liked. She was a good cop and he was glad he was on the right side of her. To be on the wrong side could be worse than swimming with the shark. His thoughts were suddenly interrupted by the crackling radio.

'Kiosk to Starch, come in. Over'. Bean's voice resonated.

'Yes Bean. What have you got? Over'. Replied Starch, expecting to hear the worst.

'Moey has done another loop but cannot sight the shark. She is adamant it was a large shark but cannot sight it now. Over'. It wasn't what Starch needed to hear as a missing shark just added to his problems. But he accepted the situation and replied:

'That's OK. Better to err on the side of caution. I trust her judgement so we'll give it thirty minutes or so and see if the chopper is down this end. They can do a final sweep. Over and out. Thanks Bean'.

The patrol gave an announcement over the loudspeaker letting everybody know the water would be off-limits for about another half an hour. So the crowd slowly made their way up to the kiosk where Bean was starting to get swamped with orders. Mel had just turned up for work and saw the people starting to line up outside the kiosk server - so she ventured inside to find out what the rush was all about.

'Hello, lover boy. What's going on?' She inquired.

'Shark alarm! Everybody's wandered up here. I've got the orders backed up on the grill and more people waiting at the counter. Can you give me a hand? If you do the counter, I'll work the grill'. Pleaded Bean.

Mel raised an eyebrow and replied:

'I've got 30 mins before I start upstairs, so where are you up to and where's Matty?'

'I don't know. I've phoned him four times and sent three texts. He never does this, he always answers his phone. This has never happened before. I hope he's OK'. Mel could sense the concern in Bean's voice and felt the same.

'Hmmm, me too', she replied.

Starch was on his way back to the headland to look for any sign of the missing swimmer and decided to check in with the rescue chopper.

'Rainbows End to Air Surf Rescue. Come in. Over'.

'Air Surf Rescue. Copy. Over', came the reply.

'Any news? There's nothing to report down here', asked Starch.

'Nothing so far Starch, but there is something else we've noticed that is very unusual. There seems to be some sort of shift in the current, which is altering the sand flow. Over'. Remarked Rotors, the chopper pilot.

'A shift? That's interesting. In what way?' Quizzed Starch.

'Well, it's not tidal. The build-up of sand on the beach is getting worse and it seems to be creating a lot more gutters. It sounds odd but I've never seen a change like this. Over', he explained.

'Hmmm', pondered Starch. 'It doesn't look any different down here. At the moment there's no one in the water, but we'll check the flag positioning before we give the all-clear. Over'.

'Okay, good idea. We'll do a double check on the shark sighting and keep looking for the missing swimmer. Over.' Replied Rotors.

'OK. Thank you. Out'.

Starch wondered for a moment about the change in sea current Rotors was talking about. Then decided to go up to the top of the headland where he could get a good view of the rocks below. When he got to the top and climbed under the safety barrier, the first thing he spotted was Matthew paddling his board close to the rocks. The roar of the waves crashing made it near impossible to get his attention by yelling. So he waved his arms until Matthew spotted him, then pointed to the beach to have a chat.

'You didn't see anything floating around on point, did ya?' Asked Starch, as Matty pulled his board out of the water.

'No, why? What's happening?' He replied in between breaths.

'We found some clothes on the beach but no human to go with them. Looks like they've been there since last night and reek of alcohol. On top of that, Moey spotted a large shark in the water off the point. Which meant, we had to start a search for the missing human and sound the alarm to clear the water because of the shark.' Starch slowly explained as Matty's mouth dropped open further and further.

'You're joking!!! When did all this happen?' Matty gasped in reply.

'30-45 minutes ago, maybe'. Answered Starch.

'Oh no! Bean's on his own. I've got to get to the kiosk, pronto.

Are there many people on the beach?' Tucking his board under his arm, he was desperate to get moving as Starch answered.

'Well there were a lot of people on the beach but most have gone up to the kiosk. Matty, doesn't the idea of swimming with a large shark bother you at all?'

Matty started to run off and replied:

'Yeah, yeah, definitely', which caused Starch to raise an eyebrow at the oddity of the man-eating, predator shark-related response behaviour.

Continuing on his search from the top of the headland, he paused and took note of the sand starting to build-up on the beach. It could have been seasonal but the build-up was too sudden and something that he had never seen before. Thinking about the earlier conversation with Rotors, he wondered if this could be due to the shift in current the pilot had observed. But he had enough to deal with at the moment so he shrugged it off and continued looking for the missing swimmer, and any sign of the shark.

Matty arrived back at the kiosk and burst through the backdoor to find Bean and Mel trying to cope with the torrent of customers. Bean felt the pressure ease, as he saw Matt come in and fired off a barrage of, please explain questions.

'What happened to you? Where have you been? What's wrong with your phone? What's going on?'

'Long story. What do you want me to do?' Before Bean could reply Mel interrupted:

'Just take over the counter for a minute while I run upstairs and tell them I'm going to be late. While I'm up there I'll have a look at what stock we can borrow and I'll get the boys to bring it down. We're running out of everything. Alright?'

Before the boys could answer she was out the door and racing up the stairs. Bean and Matty looked at each other and nodded in agreement, as they both threw themselves into the customer apocalypse. It was only a few minutes when Mel burst through the door with an armful of buns and vegetables.

'The boys are coming down with more stuff. We should be alright'. She announced confidently then rolled up her sleeves and murmured: 'OK, let's do this'.

The customer onslaught lasted for another thirty minutes before Starch sounded the all clear siren and reopened the beach. The crowd slowly finished their food and dispersed, leaving the three of them exhausted. The kiosk looked like a hurricane had gone through the place and demolished everything.

'Strewth! Nothing like a nice friendly people-eater to get the place rolling'. Babbled Bean.

Mel was exhausted and on information overload, so she just nodded her head then announced: 'I'm outta here, boys'. Then gathered her things and headed upstairs. The restaurant door was open and the screaming voice of Adrian was once again raging. She wasn't in the mood for any more drama but stopped to listen as to what the fuss was about.

'You are not freakin gender-neutral you idiot, so don't go in the women's showers'. Yelled Adrian, and as usual Brian replied in an aloof and irritating manner.

'But the club has turned off the men's hot water and I identify as gender-neutral'.

A look of astonishment swept over Adrian's face as he struggled to contain himself.

'Listen. Wood duck. You'll identify as unemployed if I tell Starch. Which I will do if you go in there again'.

Thinking that was the end of the conversation Adrian walked off but brian followed him with more to say.

'You do realise you're being discriminatory! I'm being progressive and you are stifling my growth in self-discovery'.

Sensing a looming homicide Mel intervened.

'Sorry Adrian, but I couldn't help but overhear... Again... May I say something?'

The tone and coldness of Mel's voice put the boys on notice that something bad was about to happen. Adrian was still boiling mad at Brian's attitude and replied respectfully:

'Yes, of course, Mel. Sorry about the yelling'.

Mel turned her gaze to Brian and it was the look of cold, far away, don't care eyes. Brian suddenly felt very queasy and kept quiet as she spoke.

'Brian. The Grommet pole will look like a luxury holiday in comparison to what will happen to you - if you keep insisting on being the smart arse you insist on being. If you ever go into the female showers or change-rooms again. The female boat crew will relieve you of your so-called gender identifiers, and hoist them up the flagpole out the front. Don't test me on this. I know what they're like'.

After speaking, Mel turned and walked out of the kitchen leaving the boys with an angry woman hangover. There was very little said for the rest of the day, which was turning out to be an all-round disaster.

The anxiety was starting to creep up on Starch. A drowning and a shark were two of the biggest revenue killers a beachside economy could experience, and something the club couldn't afford. After searching for the body he hoped he wouldn't find, he went and reassured the patrol that they were doing everything that could be done - and not to jump to unnecessary conclusions. After all, it might just be a pile of clothes and money from a forgetful drunk. After sorting that out he decided to head up to the clubhouse and check on things up there. Walking across the sand he found himself on a collision course with another looming disaster. Danny was trudging across the beach toward him. Starch kept his head down and hoped for the best but Danny was always up for a bit of self-promotion. 'If I get any fitter I'll be dangerous', he confidently blurted as he walked past. 'Unbelievable', groaned Starch without making eye contact.

At the kiosk, Matt and Bean were still cleaning up and trying to get organised when Matty noticed something unusual. The cash register had a decent amount of money in it.

'Hey Bean, have you seen how much money is in the till? I think you better empty this. There's a lot of money in here'. He slowly advised.

'What are you talking about? Mel was on the till, it should be right'. Bean replied.

'Have a look! There is a heap of money in there, then lift the tray and look underneath! Just empty it! That's way too much money to have sitting in there', repeated Matt.

'Hang on, give me a look', muttered Bean as he opened the till. 'Holey dooley!! What happened here? Stuff a duck!! I'd better empty this and count it up'. He blurted as Matty smiled to himself. A till this full had never happened in the kiosk and there was something else that caught his attention. 'Bean, do you realise we have no stock left? Zero, naught, nothing'.

Then, as he reconciled the EFTPOS machine his jaw dropped and he gasped:

'Woooo, how long were you two getting smashed before I got here?'

Bean looked up at him after counting the cash with a concerned look on his face, and mumbled.

'There must be a mistake. There's over two grand in cash here. That's impossible!' He said quietly as if there was something wrong with earning that much money.

'Well, you better look at the EFTPOS receipts'. Replied Matt, still smiling and feeling excited at the takings.

Bean looked at the print-out and struggled to digest the figures.

'That's a misprint! It's gotta be! Two thousand two hundred dollars just isn't possible'.

Matty gave him a reassuring smile and explained the windfall:

'Bean, it's no misprint. Look at the number of transactions. You had fifteen dozen bread rolls that are gone. Wendy even borrowed more from upstairs along with the drinks and other stuff that are all gone'.

Bean listened and accepted his explanation with a smile saying:

'Wow! We have never made that much money before. Never!'

'You've never had that many customers before'. Matty fired straight back as Danny appeared at the counter window and promptly made his presence felt.

'Men, can I have a bacon and egg roll, please. I need to get a bit of post-workout protein into me', he blurted.

'Sorry, mate. I haven't got an egg or any bacon in the place'. Bean apologised.

'Yeah right. Can I have extra tomato sauce too, please', replied a disbelieving Danny.

'Would do it if I could, but haven't got any of that either'. Explained Bean.

Danny took a step back from the counter and stood there with his hands on his hips not accepting what he was hearing. He turned to see Starch and Jackson approaching and deduced that the concerned look on Starch's face was due to the sudden lack of food in the kiosk. So he voiced his displeasure.

'Hey Starch, what's going on? There's no food in the kiosk! I'm a member in training and there's no support. What's going on?' He declared with his hands still on his hips.

A very strained Starch rallied his patience and responded with a look of nausea on his face.

'Danny, you could not call anything you do training. Get over yourself. Go on a diet and stop wearing out the beach. And by the way, I just saw Liz and Grizz sitting privately up on the headland sipping champagne'.

Danny took a step back without saying a word then retreated to the carpark, hopped in his car and headed straight up to the point. Starch appreciated this as a small victory until he saw Bull the plumber pull into the carpark. Bull hopped out of his truck and headed straight toward the bar, Starch cringed and stayed out of view. The 'unbearables' were coming at him in waves and now wasn't the time to engage with them.

As he walked past the kiosk server heading upstairs, Bull fired off a question: 'Hey Bean, what's going on with that thermostat?'

'All good mate, no problems. Why aren't you at work?' Bean immediately replied.

Bull paused, looked down and took on a wise demeanour before replying. 'I have to go to court. Some blokes disputing my bill. Unbelievable!' He then moved on.

As he walked upstairs past the kitchen, Adrian's voice could be heard screeching through the doorway again, so he paused to listen.

'I know she doesn't identify as the boss, but if you don't pull your head in you'll identify with a tag on your big toe. Those rowers don't take prisoners. Understand!' Adrian shrieked. Wondering what it was all about but deciding not to intervene, Bull continued on to the bar.

'Give us something wet, please Tom'. He asked the barman in his wise sounding self.

'Errr, not water?' replied Tom.

'Did I say I wanted a bath? Where's Starch? I need to have a chat about the hot water system in the kiosk'. Bull snapped, without sounding wise anymore.

'He's got his hands full at the moment, but I'll let him know'. Replied Tom and walked off before the conversation could go any further.

'Good. Well done', Bull muttered and settled in at the bar.

Starch was still downstairs doing his best to avoid the time-wasters when his phone rang once again. He recognised the incoming police number as he pressed the answer button:

'Hello', rumbled his gravelly voice.

'Hi Starch. It's Senior Constable Kelly Follent from Coolangatta Police. We spoke this morning about the missing swimmer', said the police lady.

'Yes, Kelly. How ya going? Have you found someone?' Asked Starch, hoping for some good news.

'No, not yet unfortunately. But his mother is on her way down from Brisbane so we can have a look inside his unit'. Answered Kelly.

'Oh okay, but haven't you done that already?' Quizzed Starch.

'No, we didn't go inside. Just knocked and made inquiries with the neighbours', replied Kelly. Starch went silent for a moment, wondering why they needed to go inside until Kelly enlightened him:

Things similar to this happen occasionally, Starch. I'm hoping we don't find it but we're looking for a letter or note that might help explain things'.

'Ohhh, I see', he replied. 'I never thought of that'.

'That's okay, we'll keep you informed. Thanks Starch. Talk later. Bye.' And the phone fell silent.

Standing there quiet for a second he pondered what Kelly had said and what a difficult job the police have. Jackson was standing beside him and had not heard the conversation but sensed by the look on his face, things were looking grim.

'What do you want me to do, Starch?', he asked.

'Nothin mate, just hang around in case I need you. We'll play it by ear', he replied.

Having successfully dodged Bull, the pair decided to have something to eat from the kiosk where Bean and Matty were still busy cleaning and getting organised.

'Back on your feet yet, Bean?' Quipped Starch as they approached the servery.

Bean looked up from his cash register and replied:

'Getting there. What a day!'

'What were you up to hanging around the point, Matty? There's no surf there', asked Starch.

'Ahhh. Just got caught in a sweep and I was making my way back'. Answered Matt, as all eyes gave him a suspicious look.

'A SWEEP!!! You've never been caught in a sweep in your life', blurted Starch.

'Ahhh, I was feeling a bit exhausted and couldn't be bothered fighting it, so I just decided to go with it'. Matt sheepishly explained as the suspicious looks intensified.

'What crap! What was there a White Pointer or someone sunbathing on the rocks or what?' Pushed Starch as he began to get curious.

'No, no. Just like I said. I just decided to go with the flow'. Came Matt's unconvincing reply.

Bean decided to change the subject and get Matty off the hook.

'What's going on with the missing bloke down the front, Starch?'

The question brought Starch back to the reality of his current problems.

'Still looking!' He moaned. 'He could be sitting on the bottom for all we know'.

'Strewth! Don't say that. Imagine if Fins drags him up! He'll end up at the taxidermist'. Blurted Bean, which bought a big smirk from Matty who added: 'Yep'.

The mention of Fins made Starch roll his eyes and change the conversation again.

'Do you have anything left to eat or are we going upstairs?' He asked.

'Yeah, Nah.' Bean replied. 'I made a couple of rolls for you blokes and the patrol before I opened this morning. Made a super big one for Jacko, with all that scuba diving and work around the club you've been doing, you've earned it'.

'Yeah, bloody champion'. Added Starch as Matty winked at Jacko.

The pair took the lunch rolls and sat down at a table, appreciating a respite from the morning's events. As Starch took his first bite he looked up to see Danny walking through the carpark and heading straight toward them. 'Here we go again', he murmured to Jacko.

'Hey Starch, where did you say you saw Grizz and Liz up at the point?' Bellowed Danny.

'Just on the Southern side on the grass. Looked like they were having a picnic or something'. Answered Starch politely.

'Well, I was just up there doing stair work, and I didn't notice anyone'. Danny replied.

The thought of Danny doing stair work had Starch rolling his eyeballs and looking for a way out of the conversation. He turned his head away and quietly said: 'Maybe they left'.

Danny gave a sinister look then turned and walked off without saying another word. Starch took a second bite of his roll, then the rattle of his radio interrupted him. 'Patrol to Starch. Come in, over'. Said the crackly voice.

'Yeah patrol, over', answered Starch.

'We have a 12-year-old boy that has multiple Blue Bottle stings. We're bringing him up to the Med room. We need an ambulance urgently. Over', said the crackling voice.

'OK, I'm on it. Out'. Replied Starch as he pressed the emergency quick dial on his phone and summoned the ambulance.

The patrol came running up the beach carrying the young boy who was in a great deal of pain from the venom that was injected by the Blue Bottle Stingers. There were large red, angry-looking welts across his chest, stomach and legs. Jackson grabbed some ice from the medical room freezer and the patrol lifeguards started to apply it around the welts. Starch poured water over other areas trying to reduce the swelling. The young fellow started to have trouble breathing as his airways began to contract and his face started to swell badly. The boy's family were distraught as his mother did her best to comfort him. They were a farming family from regional New South Wales and this was the lad's long-awaited holiday trip to the beach.

'Come on Ambos'. Starch quietly beseeched as the sound of an approaching siren brought a sense of relief to all of them. It was a diabolical situation with the boy now struggling to breathe and the ambulance battling its way through traffic to reach him. The team knew it was coming down to a matter of critical minutes.

The ambulance drove up the beach access ramp and stopped beside the kiosk. Two paramedics jumped out, one unloaded the stretcher and the other quietly assessed the boy's condition. The lifies gave them as much information as they could, then within a matter of minutes they had loaded him into the van. With one medic in the back treating him and calmly giving updates and instructions over the radio - the other drove, with sirens screaming and lights flashing, dividing the traffic in front of them. The group watched the ambulance drive out of sight and felt full of hope that the boy would recover. Nevertheless, once again it had come down to precious minutes between saving someone and losing them. Starch mumbled: 'What next', and gave a sigh.

'Any news on the missing swimmer?' asked Charlie, who had come in to help with the beach patrol.

'Not yet', replied Starch with the weight of the day starting to show in his voice.

'Okay. We'll head back to the beach and keep looking', Charlie responded as the rest of the lifey's started to walk off. There was no time to rest, they had to keep looking. The hours passed and the club was reasonably quiet giving no indication of the tribulation going on behind the scenes. The search for the swimmer was fruitless and the likelihood of the outgoing tide sweeping him further away was now more plausible. The hum of Starch's mobile phone bought a feeling of apprehension as the police number came up on the call identifier.

'Hello', mumbled Starch into the phone.

'Hello Starch, it's Kelly Follent from Coolangatta Police', said the friendly voice.

'Gidday Kell, what's happening?' Asked Starch.

'Well, we've located your missing swimmer. He's high and reasonably dry although he looks as though he has had a very big night', Kelly answered.

'Starch couldn't help himself and gasped: 'Well thank the powers that be for that! What's his story?'

'We located his mother who let us into his unit where we found him very asleep in his bed. His story is that his fiance dumped him so he attempted to drown his sorrows with generous amounts of cheap wine. He then wandered or staggered off to the beach where he decided to throw his $70,000 dollar engagement ring into the sea. However, he had a panic attack when he realised the cost of what he had done. So he stripped off and dived into the surf in his drunken state searching for the discarded ring. After some time searching and getting dumped by the waves, he gave up, got out of the surf and staggered back home naked. He states he never gave his clothes a thought and doesn't care about anything anymore. He seems to be still intoxicated, although he did apologise for any alarm he might have caused'. Related Kelly.

Starch frowned heavily and struggled to process what he had just been told. On one hand he was relieved there was no missing swimmer, but on the other hand he was angry at the waste of resources. 'Unbelievable!'

He gasped. 'Fair dinkum, unbelievable! I wish these people would stay away from the beach when they're drunk. Complete morons. Hopeless drunks!' He rambled on, lost for words.

'My sentiments exactly, Starch. It's been a very expensive night for him, let's hope he's learned something. What happened to the shark you mentioned?' Quizzed Kelly.

'Lost sight of it and has not been seen since, thankfully. I'll call off the search for this lunatic straight away, and let everyone know what's happened. Thanks, Kell, I appreciate your help. I'll see you later on if you need to write a report', answered Starch.

'Well, what a day you've had. If there's anything else we can help you with, just call. I'll catch you later', said Kelly. And the call ended.

Starch turned to see Jackson with a concerned look on his face, so he briefly told him the news about the drunk, broken-hearted swimmer. Jackson quickly deduced that broken relationships and alcohol are not a good mix. The rescue teams and chopper were all notified and the search called off with mixed emotions of anger and frustration. The only upbeat people were the beach patrol who immediately started looking around the beach for a very large diamond engagement ring.

Starch and Jac then made their way back to the clubhouse where Starch phoned the hospital to check on the young boy with Blue Bottle stings. The lad was in a stable condition although the situation would have been much worse if it wasn't for the rapid response of all involved. Seeing as there wasn't anything else they could do, the pair made another attempt at eating their rolls at the kiosk.

'What a day', recounted Jac.

'Unreal! Sharks, stingers and drunks!' Added Starch.

'And Danny!' Blurted Jac, as they both burst into laughter.

'Sharks, stingers, drunks and Danny", bellowed Starch. 'Shocker!' He added as they both roared with laughter.

Back in the kiosk, Matty was getting ready to finish work. 'You all good now Bean?' He asked.

'Yeah mate, unreal. I've paid all my bills in one day. What a rip-snorter of a day'. Bean replied happily.

'That's great news. I've got to do some work at home so I'll get going if that's alright?' said Matt, acting pretty coy.

'Yeah, thanks mate. Strewth, that was a good day. If I could meet that shark I'd give him a great big kiss on the lips. I might even throw a bit of mullet off the point on the way home, just in case he's still around'. Chuckled Bean.

'Oh I'd say he's long gone now and I think he'd pass you up on the kiss thing. Why don't you take yourself out to dinner for a change?' suggested Matt.

'You know what? I might just do that. You're a top young bloke, Matty. They don't come any better. I reckon you'll be famous one day. Thanks, mate, I'll see you tomorrow'. Bean assented honestly.

Matty was humbled by what Bean had said and struggled to keep his poker face as he walked through the car park. As he reached for the door of his VW Kombi van and out of sight of the club, a huge smile broke out on his face. He clenched his fist in jubilation and shouted "YES".

He had managed to fool everybody, even Moey. His shark dummy had been an unequivocal success. He had stimulated the kiosk economy and helped Bean's financial dilemma enormously. There were still improvements he needed to make to his shark including some safety issues that needed addressing, but what a day it was. What a day.

# Chapter 11

# Who's Who?

Some of Rainbows End Beach's most prominent regulars or locals, were the Penguins, also known as The Mad Old Blokes or the M.O.B. The Penguins were a group of around a dozen elderly men who swam up and down beyond the break at sunrise every morning, rain, hail or shine, year-round. The only time they were absent was when the conditions were deemed unsafe and the beaches closed. To watch the early morning ritual was intriguing. Occasionally they came down to the water in a group with a few stragglers. Other times they came down in a signal file line.

All of them had similar physical characteristics and were clad in skimpy nylon swimmers known as Budgie Smugglers. To watch them entering the water was like a natural phenomena such as the migration of Wildebeest or the March of the Penguins. Slowly and resolutely without speaking, they came with all the mystique of Stonehenge. Into the waves like large seals they plunged, then out to the calmer water, where their arms flopped lazily along for 100m or more. Up and down parallel to the shore, behind the break. To watch them from the beach with the sun's rays appearing over the horizon, was a beautiful, inspiring sight. Here were these elderly men who, in the twilight of their years, had found contentment, fellowship, and an appreciation of life - when most had surrendered physical activity to the years.

The exit out of the water was a much more disjointed affair, with most exiting when they had done their time and distance. All of them gradually made their way up to the beach showers positioned along the cement walkway, where they exhibited a complete absence of self-consciousness. Elderly men with large bellies in skimpy nylon swimmers taking a shower, could be a challenging site to some people walking by.

Once showered, the migration continued back to the change rooms where the conversation topic centred around the, 'It was a lot better country in those days' topic. The conversation took off in full uncensored flight when the old days were compared to the modern mess called Political Correctness - and the way the hopeless, braindead, bloody ratbag politicians were ruining Australia. After this fiery conversation, the morning ritual came to an end unless there was a special occasion such as a birthday or new grandchild to celebrate. The celebration involved the birthday boy or new grandfather buying discounted bacon and egg rolls and coffee for all other penguins. Bean at the kiosk was generous in his support of the Penguins, although the fact that Danny wasn't one of the group may have had something to do with his generosity.

There had been some conjecture as of late, directed at the penguins from some of the mature female club members. The ladies had labelled them chauvinistic, sexist, machiavellian, misogynistic, among other things. However, this view was not shared by all the women, in particular, the wives of the Penguins. They thought it was a good thing to get rid of them out of the house for a while each day. Then there were other women who admired the stoic discipline to a hardy, active lifestyle that the Penguins engaged in - these were real men. By and large the penguins were like heritage-listed buildings, and the longer they stayed the same, the more people appreciated them.

Starch had arranged a garden setting of tables and chairs next to the lifeguard storage shed, where the Old Boys could meet, have a few drinks and chinwag throughout the day. This was their turf.

The little group had formed themselves into a money-raising charity for disadvantaged children and homeless or abused people. Their mode of operation for raising money was anything but normal and somewhat questionable. A few of the men were retired owners of international companies they had built themselves and were very familiar with import laws and restrictions, including patents. All of them were familiar with the rise in popularity of surf brands and leisurewear, so they focused on that for a revenue stream - copying popular upmarket brands and reproducing them cheaply in Southeast

Asia. The clothing was imported by piggybacking in containers of stock belonging to their former companies - with the result being, pirated clothing brands at a fraction of the cost of the original. They then sold the fake brand clothing dirt cheap in the local pubs and clubs and gave the money to the charities. The locals were aware of the pirated clothing but everyone turned a blind eye, whilst the tourists thought they were getting a bargain.

Whilst there were the beach regulars and locals and beach traffic was somewhat predictable at different times of the year, on the other side of the border things were changing. The sand dredging continued around the clock with huge volumes of sand being shifted. Most of it was being pumped about 50 meters offshore, and it wasn't going unnoticed. Starch was doing the rounds of the club when his phone rang:

'Hello, may I speak to Mr Lawless, please?' Asked the female voice on the phone.

'Yeah, speaking', replied Starch.

'Mr Lawless my name is Molly Baxter. I'm a journalist with East Coast Media and I was wondering if I could get your views on the Tweed River Bar sand dredging?' Enquired the journalist.

'What do you mean, views?' Questioned Starch.

'I'd like to ask you some questions relating to changes in the environment, possibly caused by the sand dredging. I have a report in front of me from Queensland University who have been monitoring the shoreline along the Gold Coast. There is a rapid build-up of sand happening around the southern end of the coast that is being caused by the dredging operation on the Tweed Bar'. Related Molly.

'Well if that's the case, shouldn't you be showing that to the powers that be'. Replied Starch.

'The government is paying for the impact assessment but they're ignoring the findings'. Explained Molly.

Starch was puzzled by the young journalist's interest in his opinion, and answered: 'Well there's not much I can tell you'.

'If you could find time for a coffee and a chat, that'd be enough, and you would be helping the environment'.

The tone of Molly's voice was an indication of her determination to get Starch's opinion, so he relented.

'Yeah okay. Let me know when you're coming and I'll make myself available'.

'Fantastic!' gushed Molly. 'I'll phone you in a couple of days. Thanks'.

Starch had been trying to ignore the dredging operation but thought it best to bring Robyn up to date on the issue, so he gave her a call which she answered with her usual no-nonsense, straight to the point manner:

'Hi Starch, any news?'

'Yeah, I've just had a journalist from East Coast Media called Molly Baxter, phone me wanting to know how I felt about the dredging. I didn't give an opinion but I agreed to have a chat over a cup of coffee. It's about some study she has from Queensland Uni, showing a rapid build-up of sand on the southern part of the coast being caused by the dredging. Have you heard anything about this?' Asked Starch.

Robyn was silent on the phone for a few seconds then replied:

'Hmmm. I haven't heard anything about that but Molly Baxter is an excellent freelance, investigative journalist. Her father is Russell Baxter, who is a very respected QC, so I'd say she is onto something and is looking around for information. Molly's a big hitter, Starch, so there's obviously something going on. I'd love to get a look at that study'.

'I'll ask her to bring a copy', replied Starch.

'Great. There isn't any news on the club grant yet, and information is very hard to get. Has anyone spoken to you about it?' Robyn asked.

'No, only the local boofhead called, asking me to give some favourable comments about the dredging to the local paper. I took that with a grain of salt', answered Starch.

'What local boofhead?' Asked Robyn.

'Boofhead Flower! He told me if I didn't get positive about the dredging, things like the club grant could get bogged down in red tape'. Blurted Starch.

Robyn was flabbergasted at Starch's story and struggled to believe what was being said.

'Why didn't you tell me this? When an elected servant of the people threatens a community group with withdrawing government assistance. That is a very serious thing.'

Starch knew straight away he had just inadvertently lit the wick of a very big firecracker called Robyn.

'Yeah, but who's gunna believe me? They're all tarred with the one brush and I just thought he was full of crap'. He reasoned, trying to calm the conversation.

'Well that might be true most of the time, but we need to help Molly Baxter as much as we can. In the meantime I'll try and find out where the application is, then we'll walk it through. Flower is obviously trying to use it as leverage for community backing of the dredging, which doesn't make sense because he is on the wrong side of the border. You'll have to keep me up to date with any developments or conversations that are relevant, straight away, please. I have to go now, so we'll talk later. Bye Starch'. Replied Robyn, and ended the call.

Starch stood there for a moment listening to the dial tone on his phone, then let out a relaxing breath and continued his walk around the club. The phone call to Robyn had made him realise that although he was trying to ignore the dredging fiasco - it had become a major stumbling block to the club grant. The repairs to the club building needed to be done as soon as possible, so he began to ponder his options. Thinking about Flower and his demands, he wondered why he was pushing so hard. He decided to give Robyn more time and hoped there wasn't a bad storm or weather that could wreck the building. He also hoped he was doing the right thing. Diplomacy, politics and business were not his strong points.

As he made his way to the equipment shed, he spotted Jackson pedalling through the carpark on his bike.

'Hey Jac, what are you doing here today?' He asked as the young fellow rode toward him.

'The reef is too covered in sand, so we're not doing as many open dive charters. How are you doing? Do you want a hand with anything?' He asked in between breaths.

Starch gave a smile and replied: 'Yeah alright. I've got to go through the Nippers stuff for Jodie. If you want to give me a hand we'll get it done quicker then I've got some stuff to do at home'.

'Yeah okay' replied Jac. As the pair turned to go to the storeroom they were confronted with Fins Walton walking straight toward them.

'Hey, Clubbie!' came the unmistakable growl of Fins. 'What's that little worm Flower in your ear about? And how are you, Jacko?' He added.

'Gidday Mr Walton. Good thanks, how are you going?' Answered Jac, as he bent down to pat Shark Bait. Jac's manner temporarily diffused the tension between the two men, so Starch answered: 'Not much. Why do you ask?'

'He's been pumping the skippers, trying to get them to talk to the media about how the bar has improved, which it hasn't. He's also saying how wrapped you are in the improvement and maintenance program'. Explained Fins.

'Nah. I haven't and don't have anything to say about the bar'. Replied Starch, very cautiously.

Fins raised an eyebrow and took the answer with a grain of salt, but pressed the matter further.

'What about the sand drift? Ya lagoon is just about gone and it's a three-day walk from the club to the water'. He continued.

Starch was starting to feel boxed in but reasoned. 'We don't know if that's from the dredging or just natural drift of the tide'.

Fins was having none of it and blurted back.

'Come on, cut the bullshit! We both know what's happening. They've got two pumps going round the clock and they're shifting heaps. They're not pumping it out far enough so it's drifting straight around the headland onto the beaches. They've already stuffed the reef!'

Starch interrupted. 'As far as I know there's only one pump'.

But Fins was adamant and continued.

'They've also put in a pumping barge because the original idea left a doughnut-shaped hole wherever they pump from - so the barge has to dredge the mess the other pump leaves behind. They're both running through the same system and the sand is loading onto the beaches. They've been trying to get it to bank up, but the swell's not cooperating'.

'How do you know all this?' quizzed Starch.

'Never mind, just be aware of what's happening. Someone is going to get dragged under because of the way they're stuffing the beach around... On another matter, Jac, I've left some reefies in the kiosk fridge for ya'. Replied Fins.

This brought a smile to Jack's face as he greatly appreciated Fin's kindness. 'Okay, thanks, Mr Walton. Do you need help with anything?' He offered.

The big fisherman was as tough as they come but Jac's politeness and manners melted his tough exterior every time they spoke. He gave a grin and replied:

'Nah, allgood little buddy but thanks for the offer. I've gotta get going. I've got an appointment with my gastrointestinal tract'.

He let out a huge burst of laughter and walked off which prompted Sharkbait to let out a growl and trot along behind him. As they walked off Starch yelled:

'No dogs in the clubhouse'.

Without turning or stopping Fins replied: 'Don't own a dog', and Sharkbait snarled again as if to add approval.

'What do you think, Starch?' Asked Jac.

'Starch was still digesting what could best be described as Fin's forced reasoning, and answered:

'Well he's right mate. I don't know how he gets his information but he gets it. What's the Dive Centre saying about the reef?'

'Andrew said we had to cancel the reef dives because of visibility and the reef is 70% covered in sand. He's pretty concerned about how quick the sand built up and they seem to think the beaches are going to go the same way'. Answered Jack.

Starch gave a surprised look and replied: 'Whattt!!! He hasn't spoken to me about it'.

'I think the politician called Flowers has been ringing him quite a bit and telling him you are very much in favour of the dredging. So, he's not sure what to think'. Explained Jac.

'You're joking! This is getting out of control. I'll give him a ring. Thanks, Jac', blurted Starch as the conversation was interrupted by a crackly voice from the 2-way radio.

'Patrol to Starch, are you there over?'

'Yeah, Starch here', he answered, still feeling a bit flustered by the dredging revelations.

'Ahhhh, we've got a complaint from a couple of white pointers regarding a man hovering above them on the rocks at the headland while they were sunbathing. Over'. Rattled the crackly voice.

'Well, tell them to put some clothes on. Over', barked Starch.

'Well they're also saying that he exposed himself to them, and he was wearing a pair of club swimmers. Over', came the reply.

'Well, who was stupid enough to give this fruit loop a pair of club swimmers?' Questioned a bewildered Starch as Jac tentatively listened to the conversation.

There was a few seconds of silence before the patrol replied: 'Ahhh, we spoke to the man. Over'.

'And what did he say?' Starch fired straight back.

'Ahhh, it was Rooster. Over', came the reply which was enough to send Starch over the edge of reasoning.

'WHAT!!! Why did bloody Rooster give this bloke a pair of club swimmers?' He blasted.

'Errr. No. Rooster was the alleged "Exposer". Over.' The lifeguard tried to be as diplomatic as possible as he sensed Starch becoming increasingly frustrated.

Starch's face went blank as he tried to fathom what the lifey was telling him. Jackson was dumbfounded by what he was hearing. He tried to act normal, but found himself walking around in a little circle, thinking, 'Oh no!' This was unfathomable, even by Roosters standards.

'You have got to be joking! What's his story? Over'. Sighed Starch, almost dreading the answer.

'Well… He said, and verbatim I will quote it. "He was taking a leak and the pair of white pointers were ogling him. He couldn't break-stream and they wouldn't give him any privacy". He believes. "They were awestruck at the measure of the man and in wonderment of his dimensions". Errr, they were his words not mine. Over', patiently explained the lifey.

Starch paused to think. Rooster was a larrikin but this was a whole new level. Even for him.

'Fair dinkum!!! This bloke is so far over the line. I'm on my way down. Out', he told the lifey. Just as he started to walk off, the radio crackled again with another voice: 'Greenmount Surf Rescue to Starch. Come in. Over'

'Yeah Starch here. Over', he answered.

'Ahhh, we are just seeking clarification on that last transmission. Was that a couple of white pointers? Left and right white pointers or two individual white pointers? Which would mean there were four white pointers (the voice paused for muffled giggling) and did he say they were browned off?'. This was followed by raucous laughter before saying, 'Out'.

Before he could reply, the radio crackled again with loud laughter and sounded like someone trying to say something about Coolangatta.

'Coo, Cool, Coolangatta Surf Rescue to Starch. Over', said the voice.

Reluctantly, Starch answered: 'Copy. Starch here. Over'.

The radio crackled back: 'White Pointer handling crew here Starch, if you need our support. We heard your patrol has got their hands full up on the headland. Over'. The Coolangatta lifesaver's voice burst into full-bellied laughter, which tested the speakers on the small 2-way radio.

Starch promptly replied: 'Thank you, Cooly. Out'. Then headed down the beach to confront Rooster. Jack tagged along to watch the fireworks. By the time he reached the scene the White Pointers had returned to sunbathing and Rooster had taken the long way back to the clubhouse. The patrol was keeping an eye on the swimmers, so he briefly quizzed them on the whereabouts of Rooster.

'Oh, he wandered off', said Max, who was one of the lifesavers. 'He said he wasn't seeking an apology, even if he was visually interfered with'.

Starch never replied, but both of them just looked down at the sand for what seemed like a long period of time without saying anything.

'I'll have a yarn with him later on. I can only take Rooster in small doses'. Starch eventually drawled.

'Yeah he's a bit of a boy, that's for sure'. Max the lifey, replied.

# Chapter 12

# A Girl's Gotta Do, What a Girl's Gotta Do.

The ladies surf boat crew had decided to hold a birthday party in the club for one of their rowers called Charlotte. They had invited female rowers and lifesavers from the other clubs on the coast, ruling it an all-female affair. Charlie, as she was affectionately known, was Asian in appearance but spoke with a strong Australian accent. She was a school teacher, but was planning to switch professions at the end of the year with one of her friends. Their plan was to work as high rise window cleaners. Neither of them had any abseiling experience but the thought of it didn't seem to bother them.

As the day unwound the ladies enjoyed free reign of the bar area making it a temporary male no-go zone.

Downstairs at the kiosk everything was quiet, so Matty finished early to do some safety improvements on his project or pet fish. Grizz and Lizz sat enjoying each other's company at a table while waiting for Danny to finish his training. Jodie went upstairs to join the girls and Jackson had gone to work at Kirra Dive Centre. Bean was working the kiosk alone when Rooster sheepishly appeared at the servery.

'Hey Bean, can I have a bacon and egg roll with avo and tomato, and can I have that put on my TAB, please mate? Thanks, mate,' appealed Rooster.

'NO!' Bean swiftly replied.

'What, are you out of stock? That's OK, just make whatever you like mate. I'm easy'. Reasoned Rooster.

But Bean wasn't having a bar of it, and once again replied: 'NO!'

Rooster was very thick-skinned and wasn't the best at listening or taking a hint so he pressed the matter further.

'No? What is everything gone? Is the power off? I'll have a sandwich. No problem. Thanks mate'.

Bean gave him a stern look and explained patiently: 'No. You can't have that on your TAB because you don't have a TAB. But, there is fifty dollars that has been owing for four months on the TAB you don't have. Would you like to pay for that?'

'Rooster gave an unconvincing, shocked look on his face and stuttered back: "Fifty dollars? What? No one told me. What did you say? I had no idea mate.' He then pulled out a $100 dollar note and gave it to Bean.

'Thank you. Take a seat and I'll bring it over'. Said Bean as he rolled his eyes and shook his head.

As 'Rooster' walked off, Ben and Sushi rolled up to the counter carrying their surfboards.

'Hello Bean San, may we have two specials, please? Thank you'. Ben requested as Sushi washed down the boards.

'Yeah boys. How's the surf?' Replied Bean.

'Surf bit flat for short-board and Point very crowded. Much argument. Much angry.' Replied Ben.

Bean gave an understanding look and consoled him; 'Yeah, bloomin board riders. They whine and complain and get crappy when there is no surf. Then when there is surf, they whine and complain and get crappy about each other in the surf. Then, if there is a really good break and the sets are rolling in and they have to work, they are intolerable. I'm sick of 'em.' He reasoned.

'Oh, many apologies to Bean San. Some nice board riders are everywhere'. Ben quickly replied.

'Nah, you've had too much Sake, Ben, my man. You're hallucinating. They're all mad'. Bean countered as he took Rooster his roll and change from the $100 note - which he checked with a painful grimace. Feeling diplomatic after paying his bill, Rooster rose out of his chair like a statesman. He then glanced over at the avocado, orange juice and goats milk smoothies (or specials) Ben and Sushi were enthusiastically devouring.

The sight of the specials was enough to turn Rooster's, bacon and egg loving stomach. Which prompted him to comment:

'Don't know what's going on with you blokes. Don't know at all'.

And with that, he headed upstairs. As he got to the top, the unmistakable angry sound of Adrian and Brian turmoil, came blasting out of the kitchen. Still feeling a bit diplomatic and statesman-like, Rooster ventured inside to give them the benefit of his presence. He was confronted with the bizarre sight of Brian standing there in his underclothes, while Adrian was yelling his head off at him.

'Are you not sick of people yelling at you? Are you not tired of the Grommets Pole? Some people are beginning to think you've got a mortgage on that thing. Are you not learning anything about yourself? Has it not dawned on you to just shut up?' Shouted Adrian.

Feeling empowered by his current diplomatic mindset, Rooster intervened: 'Do you blokes ever let up? What's going on now?' He enquired in an authoritative tone.

'The girl's boat crew and their mates are in the bar celebrating Charlie's birthday. So, Einstein here, a club employee, walks in and tells them he identifies as gender-neutral. Then he insists on being part of the boat crew, and having a seat on the boat. If they refuse it's discrimination, so he'll be forced to pursue and accept compensation.' Adrian frustratingly explained.

'Whattt!!!' Bellowed 'Rooster'. 'Well first off I'm letting you know. No bloke gets in that boat except me, and that's the way the girls want it. I'm the only bloke they want for a fill-in. Mate, they would have been furious if you tried to replace me. And what happened to your pants?'

Brian didn't answer so Adrian spoke up: 'Well they didn't give him a verbal reply, they "dacked" him! They turned him upside down and ripped his "dacks" off. They're now up the flagpole out the front. Blowing in the wind'.

'Strewth!!! Have you got another pair?' Sympathised Rooster.

'No', Brian, quietly answered.

Still enjoying the air of a man in charge, Rooster once again took control of the situation. 'Just go downstairs to the change room and there's a spare pair of shorts in my locker'. He counselled Brian with an understanding tone.

'Thank you', murmured Brian as he headed off downstairs.

'Righto', declared Rooster. 'I'll go and sort these girls out'.

Adrian felt a chill go up his spine and was compelled to offer Rooster a last-minute caution.

'Well mate, I can tell you right now. You could be next up the flagpole. They've been in there knockin 'em back for a couple of hours. It'll be a game man or a fool that walks in there and tells 'em what to do, because he will come off second best. I can promise you that'.

But a confident Rooster was having none of it and boastfully replied: 'Nah Mate! Allgood. They love me'.

Adrian could only look down in silence slowly shaking his head. As Rooster walked off to the bar he sadly muttered to himself: 'There goes the folly of men'.

The girls were pretty much stacked into the bar with great camaraderie between them. Together they had seen the highs and lows of competition, the satisfaction, pride and relief of saving someone in the surf. The heartbreak, sorrow and lingering aftermath of losing someone in the surf. They were rarely granted the respect they deserved as athletes. Theirs was a gruelling and sometimes very dangerous sport where things could go very wrong, very quick. Not only did they have to compete against each other, they also had to compete against an unpredictable and sometimes hostile environment. A surf boat competition in treacherous surf conditions could be a very dangerous place to be.

Rooster took one step into the bar area and was met with an avalanche of wolf whistles and woo-hoos. The verbal onslaught took him by surprise.

'Hey girls, it's the atomic XY chromosome', yelled someone.

'The apex male has arrived'. Yelled someone else, and the hits kept coming.

'Hey Rooster, how they hanging?' 'Hey organ arse, play us a tune'. 'Hey Rooster, is that your guts or did you swallow a rotten watermelon?' 'Hey Rooster, give up farting and save the planet'.

The raucous laughter was deafening and Rooster was rattled. Feeling a sense of enormous inferiority, he feigned a concerned look on his face. He patted his pockets as if he had forgotten something. Then, seizing the moment, he backpedalled out the door and headed downstairs.

As he got to the bottom of the stairs he had a thought bubble, then did a u-turn and headed back upstairs.

Adrian was still standing in the doorway as Rooster confidently sprouted:

'Thought I'd better check on young Brian, see that he got the right locker and everything. That must have been an awful experience he had. Poor kid'.

Adrian never said anything but looked down and curled his bottom lip then nodded his head up and down. He was under enormous pressure not to burst out laughing and stood very still. Although his self-control was enormous, he was still visibly shaking and strained to keep his jaw clenched until Rooster turned and made it back to the bottom of the stairs. Adrian then buckled over and broke into hysterical laughter.

As the girls continued to party in the bar, Jodie, who was helping run the show received a text message on her phone. She gave a wry smile and remarked to Laurel:

"Charlie's surprise is here. He's in the car park and will be up in five minutes".

Laurel giggled and replied: "This'll be good".

About five minutes passed before a very obese, long-haired man walked into the Bar. Jodie waved to him and pointed towards Charlie. The man was big enough to block out the sun, with rolls of fat that wobbled as he walked over to Charlie.

The girls quietened down and were not sure what to make of the situation. Charlie had no idea what was happening. 'Charlie'? The large man eloquently asked as he approached her.

'Yes.' Charlie nodded nervously in reply.

'My name is Jay'. Said the big bloke introducing himself. He was carrying a large portable sound speaker system which he placed on the floor. The room was silent as he raised one arm in the air and spoke with a voice of authority.

'Your attention please. When I raise my arm in the air, loudly shout, Charlie'.

He then reached down and switched on the speaker system. The system was connected to an ear-piece type of monitor and a very thin clear microphone attachment - mostly hidden by his long hair. He reached up, touched his ear-piece and the speaker boomed into life. The ladies were transfixed. Their mouths dropped open as the sound of his beautiful, classically trained voice filled the room.

The girls were as still as monuments and just as quiet, as the big bloke sang a sensual love song to Charlie. Her eyes started to well up. Towards the end of the song, the large man knelt down on one knee in front of her. Charlie now had tears running down her face. When he finished the song and while he was still on one knee, the man gently declared: 'For Charlie'.

This was a special moment and one that would stay with Charlie forever. As the applause settled down, the big man started to sing: 'Happy birthday to' then raised his hand as the girls yelled 'Charlie', and the song continued wholeheartedly. Adrian and Brian had come out of the kitchen when they heard the singing, and were enthusiastically applauding. Brian who was still wearing Rooster's pants remarked: 'I feel touched'.

Adrian looked down, then turned and walked back inside without saying a word...

Starch was on the beach with a little time to spare so he decided to have a chat with Rooster about his behaviour. He gave the club a call on his radio: 'Patrol to base. Come in, over'.

'Yeah Starch, Tommy here. What's up? Over'. Replied Tommy Green, the bar manager.

'Is Rooster up there? Over', asked Starch.

'Yeah. Nah. He stuck his head in the door and the girls gave him a touch-up, so he took the bolt. They're having a birthday bash for Charlie. It's her lifey and boat crewmates from all over the coast. Over", answered Tom.

Starch was unaware of Charlie's birthday bash and what was happening in the club bar: 'What girls? Are they still there?'

'Yeah mate, very much so. Over'. Answered Tom.

'Well, as long as they're not out of control. Other people want to use the place. They haven't bothered anyone, have they? Over', asked Starch.

'Well they dacked Brian earlier, but he asked for it, and they gave it to Rooster, but it was in good spirits. Now, some fat bloke has just come in and sang Charlie a love song and happy birthday. At the moment they're all weeping. Over', explained Tom.

'You're joking. Fair dinkum! Are you serious? Is Brian alright? Over'. Starch muttered, as the What Next feelings were slowly creeping up on him.

'Yeah mate, he's fine. He's wearing a pair of Roosters pants. His are up the flagpole out the front. Over', said Tom reassuringly.

Starch groaned and massaged his forehead wondering, whatever happened to normality?

'Mate, if you see Rooster can you tell him I need to have a chat with him. Ask him to hang around, please, and I'll come straight up. Over'.

'Yeah, okay mate. Out'. Replied Tommy as he pulled beers with his right hand, and held the radio with his left.

Starch gave a deep sigh then started to slowly walk toward the clubhouse. Before he got too far he was halted by two small voices in a panic.

'Starch, Starch, Mr Lawless', Came the cry from two little nippers, who were running flat out across the sand toward him. 'We just saw a shark! It was huge! It'd eat you', cried out nipper #1. Who was a red-haired, freckled-faced boy with copious amounts of zinc cream on his face and shoulders.

'It was monstrous!!! It'd eat you in one go', shouted nipper #2, a bronzed skin lad with curly sun-bleached hair.

'Okay, okay, where did you see this shark?' Asked Starch, calmly trying to quell the situation.

'Up the headland. It was humongous. Then it disappeared', blurted nipper #1.

'What do you mean it disappeared? How do you know it was a shark?' Asked Starch.

'Its fin was out of the water. It wasn't a dolphin. It was right on the surface, then it just sort of disappeared. It was so big'. Babbled nipper #2.

Starch was having trouble believing the nipper's sighting and started to suggest they might have made a mistake.

'Sharks just don't disappear'. He started to say, but was cut off by the nippers who were adamant.

'IT DID!!! It must have dived or something! Mr Lawless, it was huge!' Yelled nipper #2.

'Ok, calm down and tell me where this was again', said Starch.

'On the point of the headland, when we were collecting driftwood for school. Then we saw it. You better warn everybody before it eats someone.' The boys were not letting go of their sighting and were desperate for Starch to believe them.

'Ok', he relented and reached for his radio. 'Patrol, patrol. Come in. Over'.

'Yeah, Shannon here, Starch. Over', came the crackly reply.

'Shannon, can you get on the ski and go around the point and check on a possible shark sighting? Over'. He asked, much to the relief of the nippers.

'Yeah ok. On my way. Out'. Shannon replied.

Starch looked at the two nippers who were still puffing from their sprint down the headland, and across the sand to raise the alarm.

'If you two want to go back up to the headland, you'll see Shannon in the water looking for the shark.'

'Thanks, Mr Lawless'. The nippers then turned and bolted off across the soft beach sand at breakneck speed. Starch continued on towards the clubhouse wondering about the two recent shark sightings and how the shark mysteriously disappeared. Maybe it was a coincidence, maybe not. It was very unusual, that's for sure.

Tommy Green, the bar manager, was still working flat out when he spotted Rooster at the top of the stairs and heading for the kitchen. 'Hey Rooster, I need to see you for a minute', yelled Tom.

Rooster turned sheepishly and replied with a somewhat confident tone: 'Of course Tom. How can I help?'

'Starch needs to talk to you about something. Can you hang around? He's on his way up', explained Tom.

'Gee whizz, talk about bad luck. I've just been called out on an emergency. Tell him I'll call him straight away. As soon as I charge my battery'. And with that, he did a U-turn and headed straight back down the stairs.

Tom stood there with a stunned look on his face. He had just been sold a dummy, and he didn't like it.

It wasn't long before the girls called it a day and started to make their way home. Shannon couldn't locate the shark but the nippers were very adamant it was there, and it was very big. A female lifey rescued Brian's pants from the flagpole. Whilst Adrian continued to wonder if the young cook was learning anything at all from his self-discovery ordeals.

Tommy Green shouted the big fat bloke a big fat beer and found out he was studying for a Doctorate of Musical Arts at the Conservatorium of Music - and did Sumo wrestling as a hobby. The big fellow had sung and played multiple instruments in concert tours of Japan and Europe. During one of those tours of Japan, he had found a passion for Sumo wrestling. He did the singing for Charlie's birthday as a favour to the girls.

As the sun began to go down, Shannon and the patrol packed up the equipment and pulled the flags for another day. The conversation mainly centred around the second disappearing shark and the mounting beach sand. Fins Walton, Ben, and Sushi headed out through the Tweed River bar to the open sea for another couple of nights' work. Sharkbait stood on the bow with his nose in the wind and the one-legged seagull sat perched on the mast. It was business as usual for the boat crew.

The sand dredging continued every day, seven days a week with the sand continuing to mount up on the beach. The only plus side to the dredging was that a sandbank was beginning to form a wave out from the point. But, everyone remained sceptical except for Flowers the politician, the non-local board riders, and of course the dredging company.

# Chapter 13

# Mums

Despite the extra help from Mel, Bean's love quest had not improved. He decided to implement what he called a time management approach. Instead of standing out front on the footpath for one hour a day, handing out vouchers waiting for his desire to come along, he made an A frame sign. The sign had a list of menu items and a box full of the free coffee vouchers. He called this strategy, his Shotgun Approach. The approach meant giving away a few, or possibly, a lot of free coffees, but it was only a matter of time before his desire took a voucher. This was his master plan.

Mel listened to his plan with a less than impressed look on her face. 'Is that so?' Was her dry reply. 'Is that so?' She repeated. 'Well fancy that! Who would have thought? This is sad, Bean. This is very, very sad', she retorted.

'Whaddaya mean, sad? Wait and see, I'm telling ya, it'll work!' Countered Bean.

'Oh fair dinkum, is that right? Bean's love guide to the universe. Just give them a coffee and away you go. Unbelievable! What is it with you men that you think you can buy your way into a woman's heart? Can I buy you a coffee? Can I buy you a drink? Can I take you out and buy you dinner? Do you think we are animals that react to positive reinforcement? Is that it? Are you training us to be good companions? No wonder things don't last, you're all control freaks'. Blasted Mel.

But Bean wasn't copping a spray from the fairer sex without some retaliation.

'Hang on! Hang on! Those things are just nice gestures, I'm a thoughtful bloke. And, what about you females and your obsession with diamonds? And how about shopping? Strewth! Going shopping in a store sale with a female is life-threatening. You whip yourselves into a frenzy. You don't shop, you hunt for bargains! It's predatory! Then if you get a bargain, it's like satisfying a bloodlust. That is till the next day when you take it back to the store and exchange it for the "other one"'. Bean's female information speech was interrupted by Bull, who perched himself on the servery counter.

'Mornin all. What's goin on?' He said.

'Morning Bull. We're normal. What's goin on with you today?' Bean replied.

'Workin mate. Just on my way to another job and need a coffee from you.' Said Bull.

'Okay, is that the lot?' Asked Bean.

'Yes, mate. How's that hot water system going?' Asked Bull.

'All good mate. How did your court case go?' Replied Bean, cautiously.

'Ahh, that one is over. I have another one on the go at the moment. I installed some gold plated taps for a bloke and he reckons I scratched them. No way, I say'. Bull retorted.

As he wandered off with his coffee a young lady dressed in business attire approached the counter.

'Excuse me. Could you tell me where I could find Starch, please?' The young lady asked.

'Yeah, he's around here somewhere. If it's important I can call him on his radio', replied Bean.

'No, no, that's okay. I'll just have a look around and see if I can find him.' Said the lady, and walked off.

The lady aroused Bean's curiosity. 'Wonder what that's about?' He said aloud.

Starch had just walked up the beach and was heading toward the clubhouse when the young lady approached him. 'Starch?' She asked politely.

'Yep', answered Starch.

'Hi Starch. My name is Molly Baxter. I spoke to you on the phone a little while ago about the beach conditions', said Molly.

'Oh yeah, weren't we going to have a chat when we weren't busy or something', replied Starch.

'My apologies, you are absolutely correct. I was just going past and thought I would touch bases. But I won't keep you from your work. It was nice to meet you Starch'. Molly then turned to walk off.

'Hang on, hang on', relented Starch. 'Sorry about that. I've just had enough of the sand dredging fiasco. If you want to have a chat, I'm on my way to the kiosk for a break. You're welcome to come along'.

'That'd be great, thanks. But, only if I get to shout', said Molly.

'No it's okay I'll take care of it', replied Starch.

'Too late. I offered first'. Molly fired back straight away.

Starch liked the young journalist and sensed she had a fighting spirit - so he decided to go with the flow and see what she had to say. After the pair had ordered their food and Molly paid the bill, they sat down at a table together.

'Okay, so what do you want to know, Molly?' Asked Starch.

'Well, I'll be open with you, Starch. I've been talking to Michael Flowers, the local member, and he tells me, and verbatim I will quote it: "Starch is one of the staunchest supporters of the Tweed River bar dredging operation". So my only interest is - what are your reasons for supporting this operation?' Asked Molly.

Starch sat there for a minute with a bewildered look on his face, then replied: 'Well, I haven't got a reason because I didn't say I support it'.

They looked at each other for a moment, seemingly confused.

'Well, could I ask why you think Flowers would say that? And why would he involve you?' Queried Molly.

Starch hesitated again, then tried to answer her question with as much diplomacy as possible:

'Molly, the club has applied for a state government grant, which it is entitled to do. The club needs that grant to survive because, as you might have noticed, we're not exactly the Opera House. It takes a hell of a lot of raffles to keep this place afloat. I don't know what the connection is between Mr Flowers and the dredging company that is doing the work on the bar. But, he has made it quite clear our grant could be jeopardized if we were to give unfavourable comments to the media. I haven't given an opinion to anybody, including flowers. I don't know why he keeps telling people I'm in favour of it'. Explained Starch.

Molly looked at Starch and acknowledged the strain on his face.

'Thanks, Starch, I really appreciate your honesty. I think it's obvious that he is leveraging his position with the grant, to get what he wants. But why? What's the payoff?'

'I wouldn't have a clue, Molly. I wouldn't have a clue. Sorry, I can't help you more', replied Starch.

'Oh no, I appreciate your time. There is something going on, but they've hidden it very well. Just off the record, what do you think of the dredging?... Honestly', Molly asked.

'Look at the beach! The reef is stuffed. Our lagoon has gone. The only people talking it up are a couple of wannabe developer boardriders called Underwood and Littlebottom. One is dumb and the other is greedy. There is a lot of vacant space between the ears of those two. They're both singing the praises of the yet to appear Superbank. Although the sand is starting to bank, so you never know, they might be right'.

The frustration in Starch's voice was a good indicator of his honest answer. Molly felt satisfied that Starch wasn't hiding anything and decided to call time on their chat.

'Yes, I see what you mean. If you don't mind, I'll keep you informed of what I find. And next time, coffee is on you'.

Starch gave a big approval smile. He had found lots of things about Molly to respect. She was a straight shooter, and he was glad he had her in his corner.

Walking back to her car, the young journalist pondered the paradox Starch had found himself in. As an investigative journalist, she could smell the corruption all over the dealings between the foreign dredging company and the individuals in the government decision making process. The lack of transparency and veiled threats by both state government MPs created anger inside her, but time will tell. It will all come out in the wash'. She thought to herself.

Matthew's Kombi rattled into the car park and pulled up beside the kiosk. Out jumped Matty and headed inside with a large bag full of stuff.

'Hey Bean, sorry I'm late', he announced.

'That's okay, it's quiet anyway', replied Bean.

'See ya later, Shakesphere. See ya Matthew', said Mel on her way out.

Matt started emptying the contents of his bag. There was something that looked like pieces of wetsuit material. There was also a buoyancy vest, glucose tablets, bits of hose, gloves and bits and pieces of electronic equipment.

'What's all that for?' Asked Bean.

'Ahhh... It's just a project thing. Nothing exciting', answered Matt.

'Looks complicated', said Bean.

'Yeah, but it's not exactly', replied Matt.

'Ok. I'll leave you with it'. Said Bean, as he walked off to do some errands. Two minutes after he left, Starch came around the corner.

'Gidday Matty, is Bean in?' He asked.

'No mate, he's just gone out for a bit. Is everything okay?' Matt asked.

'Just the usual dramas. Not too bad. Nothing we can't fix. Except for the bloody disappearing sharks', said Starch.

'Disappearing Sharks? Never heard of them. Maybe it's something to do with quantum physics'. Suggested Matt with a grin.

'Probably. Whatever that is. Mate, if you spot Rooster, can you let me know please. Before the quantum thing gets him', replied Bean.

'Yeah, sure thing. I'll let you know straight away. I didn't hear about another shark sighting. When was that?'

'The other day a couple of nippers repeatedly insisted they had seen a very large shark, but I'm stuffed if I know. They were up on the headland and very adamant about seeing it just off the point, pretty close in'. Replied Starch.

'Ahhh well you never know. Better to err on the safe side and protect the people in the water'. Said Matty, sounding very understanding.

'Thanks for that advice. If you see Rooster let me know please', Starch replied and walked off.

Matty paused for a minute thinking he might have sounded a bit too understanding but shrugged it off and set to work on his project. He wasn't aware someone had seen his last swim so he started to think of a possible way to give him an awareness of what was happening above the water. His project was evolving and he was enjoying it more and more.

Liz, who was the much-wanted catch of the Danny and Grizz desire trap, had decided to cast her man net further afield. Liz had joined an online dating site and had made contact with several mature men, so she decided to meet one of them at the kiosk. They were having a quiet chat and a cup of tea at one of the tables when Grizz wandered around the corner and stopped at the kiosk servery.

'How ya going, Matty? Can I get a ham and salad roll in a takeaway, please mate'.

Matty looked up from his project and replied: 'Yeah, sure'.

Grizz turned around for a stickybeak and spotted Liz and her date seated at one of the tables. 'Who's that with Liz?'

'Well you didn't hear it from me, but I think it's an internet hook up', said Matt.

'Stupid woman', mumbled Grizz and walked over to the table;

'Hi, Liz. I've never met your father. How ya goin, mate'. He said, extending his hand to the stranger.

'Grizz, this is Roger and he is not my father! Roger is my friend', Liz let fly.

'Sorry about that mate, you look just like her old man. Nice to meet ya Rogahhh', drawled Grizz. 'Great to see you again Liz, always a pleasure to meet your family. Errr friends'.

Not wanting a reply and happy with his little disruption, Grizz picked up his roll from the servery counter and headed to the car park - but before he drove off he thought he'd better give Danny a call, on a "need to know" basis. Blokes being blokes of course.

'Yeahhh', Danny's voice leaked through the phone.

'Yeahhh, it's Grizz here, mate. Just thought I'd let you know, seeing you're my mate and everything. Liz is down at the kiosk living it up with some lover-boy she trolled off the internet'.

'Whattt? Are you serious? Came the shocked reply.

'Yeahhh, mate. I had a bit of a yarn to him, trying to be polite and everything but they were just too aggressive, mate. Mate, I think they're on drugs'. Testified Grizz.

'Whattt? Are you serious?' Came another, shocked reply.

'Yeahhh, mate. Mate, I really don't care, but they were running you down, mate. Mate, they were saying all sorts of nasty things about you. Very upsetting for me, mate. Like I said to them, don't say things like that because Danny's my mate. Mate ya know'.

'Awww, mate. This isn't happening, mate. Is it? What'd they say?' Danny's mind was on tilt.

'Awww, mate. Very low shots. Character assassins at their worst, mate. Made me ill, mate...I deplore all kinds of physical violence, but this pair had me upset, mate, ya know. Like, you're a nice bloke, mate'.

'Yeah, thanks for that, mate. You're a good bloke. But what'd they say?' Danny pressed while starting to get wound up.

'Awww, just silly stuff, mate. Like, she said you're an "impotent bean bag" and an "unimpressive male" and stuff. He said you're a "refugee from a retirement home" and "watered down beer", and "all hat no cowboy" and a "stationary object", and "all tail no bull". He told her, "if that lout ever bothers her in the future, to let him know and he'll straighten your paths out". Mate, just stuff like that. I think we should let it go, and don't let it bother ya, mate'. Came the watery advice from Gizz, but Danny's wick was lit.

'THAT'S IT!!! I'm on my way down there, and I'll sort this bloke right out. Bloody Liz, she's at it again. Playing me for a mug. Trying to get attention. She's all bullcrap, mate. Can't trust her, that's for sure. There's gunna be trouble. This bloke's gone! See you later, Grizz. Really good of you to ring me, mate. You're a top bloke. That took guts, mate'.

Grizz gave a wry smile, started his car, then drove off along the esplanade with a very smug look on his face. Danny arrived at the club, disembarked from his car and made his way to the kiosk, with a posture that resembled a frill neck lizard.

'Hey Matty, have you seen Liz?'

'Ahhh no. She was here before but I didn't notice her leave', answered Matt.

'Was she with anybody?'

'Yeah, some bloke. They might have gone upstairs. I don't know, Danny', said Matt, hoping that would be the end of the conversation.

Danny made his way upstairs to the bar and restaurant, then as he passed the kitchen doorway he heard people shouting. Cautiously, he walked inside to see a red-faced Adrian yelling at Brian.

'If you ever tamper with the menu boards again, I'll do ya! I'm not freakin joking Brian, I'll do ya!' He screamed.

'Are you blokes alright?' Interrupted Danny, hesitatingly.

'Yes mate, what can I do for you?' replied Adrian in a more civil tone.

'Have you seen Liz around?' Danny asked.

'Nah, mate, not today. Have you seen Rooster?' Asked Adrian.

'No, I haven't, sorry. Thanks for that. I'll let you get back to it'. Danny retreated out the door as Adrian resumed shouting at Brian.

'Like I was saying, Brian. It is not up to you to redefine the culinary dictionary. This is yet another train wreck you've bought on yourself. If Starch would have seen that menu board, we'd both be on the rack, so WAKE UP!'

'Well, yelling won't get us anywhere. This is an issue that is clearly divisive', replied Brian, in his usual aloof manner.

'Freakin hell Brian! I'm gunna lose it again! If it bothers you, LEAVE THE COUNTRY!' Screamed back Adrian, clearly on the verge of an apocalyptic breakdown.

'Well I think you need an anger management course. You're the people who are de-genderising the birds, which isn't right. I will talk to Starch about it'.

'Brian, listen to me. You've gone past stupid and need to get over it. We do not serve "Curried Bird", it is chicken. We are not concerned with what the chicken identifies as. IT IS A FREAKIN CHICKEN!!! Not negotiable! What are you trying to do, ask the chicken what it identifies as before you turn it into food? End of story'. And with that, Brian wisely turned and wandered off muttering to himself, while Brian gave the usual, look down head shake and tried to calm himself down.

Danny couldn't find Liz or her date upstairs, so he headed back down to the kiosk.

'Thanks, Matty, see ya next time'.

'Thanks, Danny. No luck finding Liz?' Asked Matt.

'No, lucky for them. I would've knocked his block off'.

'Whose block? What block?' Quizzed Matt.

'That big-noter she's hanging around with', sniped Danny.

'Oh yeah, okay. Dunno', said a puzzled Matt.

'Just as Danny left, a lady came to the counter with a free coffee voucher. 'Hi, just wondering if the free coffee is available in takeaway?'

'Absolutely. What would you like?' Answered Matt.

'Just a flat white please, no sugar'.

'Coming right up', said Matt as he got to work.

'It's quite a nice little kiosk you have. I haven't been here before, although I walk past the front occasionally', remarked the lady.

'Oh right, yeah that path gets busy. The kiosk is not mine, I just work here. It's great meeting all the people and my boss is tops'.

The lady smiled and looked around as Matt made her coffee and placed it on the counter.

'Well, thank you very much for the voucher, it is very much appreciated', said the lady.

'Aww thanks, that is so nice. I'm just filling in for my boss who's out at the moment, but I'll make sure he gets your message', said Matt as the lady waved and walked off. Unbeknown to Matty, the lady was number one on Bean's "desperate to talk to list" and Bean had just missed his golden opportunity.

It was business as usual for Starch as he did his rounds chatting and solving little day to day problems around the club. He was on the beach with the patrol when he decided to head up to the kiosk and see if Jack had arrived.

'Hey Matty, what's going on?' He quizzed.

'It's pretty quiet here, although Danny just came and went', said Matt, rolling his eyes.

'Here we go. What's happening now?'

'Well, he was looking for someone and apparently that person is lucky Danny didn't find him, because Danny was going to knock his block off', recounted Matt.

Starch paused for a moment and scratched his head wondering if Danny had finally lost his marbles.

'Whose block is Danny gunna knock off? Danny couldn't land a blow on fresh air at the best of times, let alone another human being. I mean, anyone with a pulse rate would be a physical challenge to Danny. He's as formidable as a feather duster and about as threatening as a doona cover'.

Matty tried to keep a straight face and not laugh before explaining. 'I believe he's a friend Liz found on an internet dating site'.

Starch gave a chuckle of disbelief and astonishment. 'Awww mate, this could be epic. Does Grizz know he has more competition? Mate, this could blow up to be huge. The love triangle becomes the passion square. Major dramas coming up here'.

'I did see Grizz have a brief chat with Liz and her new man, earlier this morning', added Matt, diplomatically.

'What? Strewth, that would have been as amiable as a dog fight. Was that before Danny got here?'

'Yeah, maybe about an hour before', replied Matt.

'Ahhh, set up. I'll bet you anything, old Grizz has baited him and he's bitten like a marlin. Bloody Grizz would have wound him up like a cuckoo clock, and Danny is bloody cuckoo at the best of times. I'd better have a yarn to dangerous Danny and tell him, we don't want any trouble here and don't go beating up on people. You know, because he trains and could seriously hurt someone'. Starch was smirking and relishing the Danny dumping.

'Do you think that's necessary?' Asked Matt.

'No, but I can't resist, mate. Can't resist. Have you seen Rooster yet?'

'No, I haven't seen Rooster for a while. I'd say he's around, but I haven't run into him', answered Matt.

'Disappearing Rooster, disappearing sharks. Strewth! This place is starting to look like the Bermuda Triangle'.

As if on cue, Jackson came whisking through the car park on his pushbike, and rode up to the kiosk.

'Jac! Where have you been? That inflatable needs a workout'. The greeting from Starch was well received by the young man.

'I've been out on the reef since sun up this morning. Andrew got me to go on the dive and help with the clients'.

'You must be getting good at this diving caper. What's the reef look like?' Asked Starch.

'Pretty sad at the moment, it's just being choked by sand. Andrew thinks it'll be buried in about a month so he might have to relocate his business'. Replied Jac.

'Really! That's bad. That's not good news. Did he say where he would go?'

'No. Not yet. We've been doing night dives at the rock wall on the Tweed River, which is going well and he heard a rumour the navy might be going to scuttle an old ship for a diving site out the front. He said he'd wait and see', recounted Jac.

'Ok, here's hoping. That's not good news about the reef, but the elephant in the room has raised its ugly head again. Anyhow, the outboard on the inflatable has just been serviced so can you give me a hand to put it back on and test it, please. I've heard you're a pretty good open water test pilot', said Starch.

Jackson seemed a bit embarrassed by the praise and modestly replied 'Maybe'.

116

The pair then set about fixing the outboard to the inflatable and launching it off the beach. Jac steered the craft through the break and motored out about 200 meters.

'Ok, give it a run around the headland', said Starch.

The young fellow steered the craft back toward the beach then skillfully turned before the break and headed toward the headland. Rounding the point everything looked normal so they kept going to the river mouth. It was reasonably calm conditions so he cruised around the edge of the bar for a couple of minutes commenting: 'It doesn't look much different'

'I think it's more about what's happening beneath the surface, Jack. Let's head back round the headland', replied Starch.

Jack turned the inflatable toward the headland and gave it full throttle. The craft skipped across the open water like a stone thrown across a calm river with Starch grinning the whole way back. He was very proud of Jack and was impressed with the maturity he was showing as he continued to develop into an outstanding young man. As the pair arrived back at the patrol flags, Jack asked: 'Do you think there's a sandbank starting to form off the headland?'

'Yes, definitely. But, we don't know how stable the sand build-up is. It's slowly smothering everything else', replied Starch.

'Oh well, at least the boardriders will be happy', reasoned Jack.

'That'll be the day', replied Starch and the both of them burst into laughter.

'I've got to head off. Andrew gave me a bonus so I'm taking Mum out to dinner. It's a surprise and for the first time ever, we'll be going out to a proper, sit down restaurant. This is going to be so good', explained Jack.

'Whattt? Are you not going to shout the bar? We could party for days with that bonus', smirked Starch.

Jac gave a hearty laugh and quipped: 'Maybe next time'.

The pair shook hands with Starch full of praise for the young man. 'That's a very good thing to do, Big Fella. Have a great time and we'll see you when we see you.'

Jackson headed off on his bike with the feeling life was starting to get better. He knew that his mother and himself would never recover from his father's death, but moments like shaking hands with Starch were very special to him. His ability to contribute to the household expenses had given him new hope for the future. He briskly cycled home and asked his mother if they could go to a certain restaurant, as he had been saving up and always wanted to go there. He knew if he suggested it was for her she would argue against him because she liked him to save for something that was for himself. So, he tactfully persuaded his mum by suggesting he always wanted to go to the special restaurant, but he needed her company.

The pair went out to eat and had a wonderful time. They laughed and shared stories about the diving, the club, the characters on the beach, whilst his mum told him stories about her childhood. These were stories he had never heard before and he greatly appreciated them. He had always thought of his mother as 'mum', as if her life had begun when he was born. But, the stories of her childhood and growing up, let him realise his mother was so much more than just Mum. There were stories of her school teacher, her friends, the day she got her car license and went "cruisin" with her friends with the music turned up loud. Stories about the holidays, the sports competitions, the trips to the dentist, the groundings, the world of no internet, no mobile phones, no Instagram, no Facebook, no Twitter.

There was the story of the last day of year 12 school when the girls piled into her dad's car and she did doughnuts on the school oval, which landed her in all sorts of trouble. There were stories of the unfinished university years and the little surprise called Jack that came along and blessed her life. The tales of her role model Mum and the happy years with her best friend, Dad. The adventures of her childhood where her dad was her hero and her mum was her guiding light with whom she had many secret "girl" talks.

Jack could recall little things about his grandparents but he had never heard his mum talk about them so openly, and that night before he went to sleep, he thought about his mum in a completely different manner. He had never imagined the person that is his mum. He thought about her as a child and a toddler and how she would have grown up in a far different world than his, where she would have been so vulnerable. He thought about the relationship with her parents and the love in her voice when she spoke about them. He thought about the overwhelming tragedy in her life, her enormous strength of character and resilience to life's adversity. The more he thought about the person that is his mum, the bigger that person became. Her life was one big sacrifice and although he loved her more than anything, it seemed so little compared to her neverending giving.

He couldn't help but think about other mums. Were they all like that or was he just super lucky? He thought about "Mother's Day" and groaned, thinking 'what a hopelessly inadequate so-called day of appreciation'. 'Should be a bloody decade', he murmured to himself. He immediately followed the murmuring with a thought of: 'Did I just say bloody?' Gosh! I'm starting to sound like Starch. Could be worse. Imagine sounding like Rooster or Brian, or Danny. 'Nightmare!' He thought and smiled to himself. Life was getting better, he had the lovingest mum ever, heaps of friends, a roof over his head, a belly full of food, a job and a purpose in life. But, he was determined to do more and make something of himself. He would not let his mother's sacrifice go unrewarded. One day he would build her the biggest house, buy her the bestest car, and would have an income that would enable him to give her whatever she needed. This was his mission.

# Chapter 14
# Making Plans

The following weeks passed without incident at the club. Apart from the colourful personalities, it was business as usual. The girl's boat crew had found another level and with the help of Simmo, were training very hard. The club gym was fast becoming their domain and physically, they were looking very much like a top tier rowing team. The Australian Surf Boat Titles were being held on the coast in the coming months, and if they kept improving, Simmo was going to suggest they have a go. Starch had been watching their improvement and quizzed Simmo on their muscular transformation.

'The girls are looking good, Simmo. What's going on?'

'They're just really committed, I don't know what happened. They just fired up!' Replied Simmo.

'They're not roided up, are they?' Quizzed Starch.

Simmo gave a laugh. 'Nah, not, as far as I know. They've just been working fair dinkum hard. They love getting in that gym, then getting in the water and ripping on those oars. The bigger the surf the harder they go. It's just good old fashioned grunt, but I will say this, they have got heart. Every single one of them has got a huge, huge ticker. They fear no wave and as a team, they behave as one. They'd surf a tsunami, this mob. It's an honour to train them'.

Starch could feel the pride in his voice. He had felt the same pride years ago in the voice of his football coach. He knew that when someone believes in you that much, anything can happen.

'So what's the plan?'

'What do you mean?' Replied Simmo.

'Well they're obviously very fit and they know what they're doing in the rough stuff, and they've got that little streak of mongrel in them. What are you going to do with them? Nothing is not an option'. Said Starch.

'Well, to be honest. I was going to suggest having a crack at the Aussie titles on the coast in a couple of months, but I didn't want to interrupt their improvement. At the moment training is fun and they're loving it so I thought I'd leave it. Maybe in a month or so I'll ask and see how they feel about it'.

'Okay, sounds good, you're the boss. Do you want us to start putting on a few raffles to raise some money?' Asked Starch.

'Nah, Nah. I don't want to put any pressure on 'em. I'm happy to pay for everything myself. The kids love watching them, and the Old Boys will weigh in with some cash anyway - whether we ask them or not. Although, I'd shudder to think where it came from'.

Starch laughed and replied: 'Yeah, they definitely do their own thing, and you're right they'd have something old school up their sleeve'.

Simmo gave a chuckle then replied: 'In the past, it was more about the money than the ability. All the travel and accommodation adds up and when it comes to a female crew, sponsors are thin on the ground. But this time it's in our own backyard, so it's do-able if we can self-fund. The girls are just everyday working mums and daughters, and we've even got a grannie! They're not a pro athlete bunch, so let's not throw them in the deep end - but keep this to ourselves until I ask them'.

Starch was impressed with the humble and modest nature of Simmo. He was a good bloke with three daughters of his own, so the girls identified with that side of him. He was also easy for them to push around. The more Starch thought about it the more he understood the chemistry behind his coaching philosophy, and he wanted to help. So he agreed to Simmo's suggestion.

'Yeah okay, for sure. We'll keep it between us. It'd be a big thing for the club if we had a team in the titles, especially the girls. I don't think the club has ever had one. Oh, just one other thing, you haven't seen Rooster around have you? I haven't spotted him in weeks'.

'Yeah, he pops up now and again. Are you still chasing him about the flasher episode?' Questioned Simmo.

'Nah, I've filed that one. At the moment he's due for patrol again and he doesn't answer his phone'. Answered Starch.

Simmo cast his eyes downward and explained: 'Ahh, you didn't hear this from me, but I think he had a bit too much to drink and told someone's wife he was attracted to her. He actually wrote a love letter to her on the bar upstairs. Apparently, it's full of poetry and stuff. Five pages of it'.

'You're joking!!! Whose wife was it?' Asked Starch.

'Donga's'. Replied Simmo.

'Donga's!!! Stuff a duck. No wonder I can't find him. He's probably dead', blurted Starch.

'Yeah… Donga's walking around with a piece of rope. Reckons he's gunna tie him to the shark drum lines out the front'. Explained Simmo, rolling his eyes.

'We'll leave that alone! Let's hope they meet somewhere else. I'll see ya later', said Starch. As he walked off he wondered if the worst came to the worst, should he rescue Rooster if he's tied to the shark drums? Or just leave him there? His thinking was interrupted by his phone ringing. It was Robyn.

'Hey Robyn, Starch here'.

'Hi Starch, I'm just touching bases about the grant. Do you have any news?' Asked Robyn.

'Nope, but the dredging is drawing its fair share of interest'. Replied Starch.

'Yes, I'm not surprised. The only people who do not want to talk about it are the government. I notice they're appointed their own environmental scientists to do an impact assessment, and they don't want to talk about that either. All I'm told about the grant is, "it's going through the process", but I'm sure Flowers is sitting on it.' Said Robyn.

Starch sighed and replied: 'Well maybe I'll have to talk to the dickhead'.

'Not yet. Talk but don't commit. We don't know what we're aligning ourselves with. Let's just give it a bit more time.' Said Robyn.

'Yeah, you're right. I'll let the board know what's going on, and I'll let you know straight away if anything happens'. Relented Starch.

'Thanks, Starch. Here's hoping. I'll catch you later. Bye'.

Up on the headland, Matthew was trying to find a safer way into his cave. He had survived a couple of close calls while trying to enter through the ocean entrance. Both times unexpected waves had resulted in his head hitting the top of the opening, so his fish had undergone a safety overhaul. The full face mask now incorporated a surf helmet in case he had a bad head knock and lost consciousness, whilst the mask now had an automatic valve that would regulate the snorkel and oxygen tanks. The whole system was running through a small computer about the size of a mobile phone - and had a back up that would provide air supply even if he fell asleep. The only thing he wasn't sure of was, how long the system could operate before it lost power.

With the addition of a small electric motor from a foil board, the project was starting to look like a one-man submersible craft. He started to wonder about the viability of making something similar for recreational use. But at the moment, deception and rescuing the kiosk economy were his goals.

Back at the kiosk things were relatively quiet, aside from the regular boardriders who kept the bacon and egg rolls ticking over. Liz sat alone at one of the tables flicking through a travel brochure, whilst Bean perused the local newspaper between customers. Danny and Grizz walked past the kiosk within minutes of each other but didn't stop or say anything which was strange. After a couple of minutes, Bean got up from his newspaper and curiously looked outside to see what was going on. Grizz was standing next to the servery window checking messages on his mobile phone, so he decided to test the waters and maybe get some answers;

'Good morning Grizz, how ya going mate? What's going on?'

Without looking up, Grizz grumbled: 'Dunno why people say that I mean, why say good morning when it might be a bad morning? Why say, good morning when no one knows what kind of morning it is? It's bloody stupid!'

Bean stood there quiet for a moment and admonished himself for opening a conversation with Grizz. His personality was no secret but in a moment of weakness, Bean had let his guard down. He dared to be pleasant to the Club Bear, and he was mauled... So he headed back inside.

'Can I have a coffee, please?' Said Grizz as he stood at the kiosk counter, head down counting his money.

'Yeah, how about Danny, is he joining you?' Asked Bean.

'Dunno. He invited me here, but he wandered off. Probably gone to adjust his activewear or something'. Grizz snorted.

'Oh, okay. Do you wanna grab a seat or something and I'll give you a yell when it's ready'. Replied Bean.

When he started to make the coffee and Grizz had wandered off, Danny suddenly knocked on the counter and announced his arrival.

'Top of the morning to you my good man. I trust all is well. Can I have a coffee please and I'd better get one for my fine friend Grizzly. Oh, can you put some of that caramel stuff in mine please. I burn a helluva lot of energy and I've got to keep my lean tissue replenished'.

Bean paused for a moment wondering whether to reply or not, but decided not to go there and kept all conversation strictly business.

'Good morning Danny. Grizz has already ordered. He just went for a wander, he'll be back in a minute'.

'Whattt!!! Fair dinkum! Fancy that! Oh well, better just make that one coffee. Better throw me on some raisin toast with banana and honey and a whisper of whipped cream too please mate.' Danny said humbly.

'Okay, do you want to find yourself a seat and I'll bring it over to you. Liz is over there', replied Bean.

'Yeah, Nah. She's playing games with me. But I'll be polite and say hello to her, because I'm a gentleman'. Just as Danny finished speaking Grizz wandered around the corner.

"How ya going, Danny. I didn't order anything for you because I thought you'd want some high protein training thing", said Grizz.

Danny gave an understanding look and replied: 'Yeah, no worries mate, let's grab a seat. Suppose we oughta go over and bow to the dragon'. So the two of them went over and pulled a chair at Liz's table.

'Gentlemen, what a shame. I'm just leaving for my appointment with my overseas travel agent. Goodbye', said Liz. Standing up before either of them managed to get a word out.

'Well, how rude is that? That internet thing has got in her brain. Can't communicate, silly woman. No manners whatsoever. That'll do me. She's reached a new low'. Spat a gobsmacked Danny.

'Standard behaviour', snorted Grizz as Liz walked off.

Back on the headland, Matty had found a new way into his cave. It was situated halfway down on the point and well hidden from view, with the entrance safely above the high tide mark. So he started to plan another test swim. Although happy with the authentic look of his pet fish, he was concerned about the flip side of the wet suit material - and his ability to disappear in near-surface water. He decided to get creative and use a couple of dyes to break up the mono colour. The new design was ready for a trial so he gave Moey a phone call to see when she was going past.

'Hi, Mo. It's Matthew. How are you?'

'Allgood dude, what's up?' Replied Mo.

'Oh nothing really, I was just wondering when you were flying past the front again'.

'Why? Came her reply.

'Oh nothing important. There is a major shift in the ocean terrain due to the sand dredging and I'm investigating the effect on the migratory pathways of the larger fishes'. Explained Matt.

'What are you talking about? Ocean terrain? Fish don't have maps! What are you on about? What are larger fishes?' Fired off Moey.

'Ahh, you know, whales, dolphins, sharks'. Babbled Matt.

'Seriously Matty, I'm beginning to wonder about you. Have you ever heard of satellites and GPS tracking? Data? It's a very big ocean and I doubt if the larger fishes would be bothered by our corrupt little section of coastline'.

'Yeah, I know, but I just wanted to get a local feel on things'. Explained Matt, apologetically.

'Well, why didn't you say that? I'll be in the air in a couple of hours but don't call me because I'm turning off the phone. I will pay attention to any whales, dolphins, sharks or large fishes that I see. I'm going to the kiosk afterwards, so we can talk then. Oakey Dokey', stipulated Mo.

'Yeah, yeah that's great, Thanks Moey. Cheers dude'. Matt was a bit embarrassed. Moey was a very direct and intelligent girl who had the habit of putting him on the back foot. As far as his make-believe stories go, he had to be extra careful when asking for help, otherwise she would see straight through him.

Back at the club, Mel had arrived for work upstairs. 'Good morning, O wise Bean, how are you?' She quipped on her way past the kiosk.

'Normal. How about you?' Replied Bean.

'I need to have a chat with Starch, do you know where he is?'

'Yeah, I think he's in the storeroom. Is everything alright?' Asked Bean.

'Yeah allgood, thanks... Errr has anything else happened?' Quizzed Mel, referring to Bean's pathway love quest.

'Nah, too hard. Hopeless. Given up', moaned Bean.

'Again!' Groaned Mel as she walked off to find Starch in the storeroom. 'Hi Starch, can I talk to you for a minute please, if you're not too busy'.

'Of course. I'm never too busy for you, Mel', replied Starch.

'I need to ask a favour, and if it's not possible I won't mind. My son Benny is doing a skills course and part of the course is retail food. This involves serving, ordering and stock taking in a retail environment. He has to have eighty hours of hands-on experience and training from a qualified chef in all of it'. Explained Mel.

'Benny?' Asked Starch. 'I know Benny and of course it's possible. Let me know when he wants to start and I'll tell Adrian'.

'Oh, okay. Well, next week would be good if that's possible.'

'Very possible', said Starch. 'I'll let Adrian know when I'm finished here and you can fill him in on the details, on your way upstairs. There won't be a problem. Adrian will look after Benny. He's a good bloke.'

'Thanks, Starch. I wasn't sure whether to ask you or not. Benny loves coming to the club and hanging out on the beach with the boys. He's been taking surfing lessons and talks about it non stop', related Mel.

Starch looked at her for a second, then gave her a nice little, "it'll be ok" pat on the shoulder. 'He's a good kid and like I said, no probs. Who knows he might bring some sanity to the kitchen'.

Buoyed by the good news, Mel headed upstairs to start work. As she walked past the kitchen everything seemed unusually quiet so she decided to have a look inside. Adrian was there by himself sorting out some menus for the day, so she seized the opportunity to talk to him.

'Hi Adrian, can we talk for a minute?'

'Sure Mel, what's wrong?' He replied.

'Oh, nothing's wrong. Well, Benny has been doing a skills course and to cut a long story short. He has to spend eighty hours of manual work under the supervision of a qualified chef'. Before she could go any further Adrian interrupted:

'No problem. When's he wanna start?'

'Well... Well, I was thinking, maybe next week'. She replied.

'Too easy. I'll let Starch know'.

'Oh, okay. I've already floated the idea to him and he seemed alright with it'. Explained Mel, being as diplomatic as possible.

'Okay, it's a done deal. It'll give me a break from Brian anyway'. Sighed adrian.

'Oh, I think he's alright, just a bit mixed up, that's all'. Suggested Mel which caused Adrian to raise an eyebrow.

'Whattt!!! Have you heard him? The kid's a walking enigma!' He blurted.

'Well he can be testing at times, that's for sure. Well, I have to go, so I'll catch ya later. Thanks once again, I really appreciate it', and off she went to sort out the office.

Mel's son Benny had Down Syndrome, and like Jackson's mum Susanne, Mel's life was an uphill battle. She had raised Benny on her own from birth when her partner left after hearing Ben's diagnosis. She worked long hours at different casual jobs but like everybody else was taxed heavily on the second job - so her income did not reflect the amount of work she did. The Australian government was no friend of the bottom tier workers and taxation was disgusting. There were no shelf companies or overseas tax havens. No trustees and No tax free financial gifts for the wage earner. Just a herd of overpaid gutless politicians who focused on the little man whilst the big end of town enjoyed their tax nullius unabated. Despite everything stacked against her, Mel would never give up. She loved Benny unconditionally and cherished every moment they spent together.

Matty had let enough time pass for Moey to be in the air, so he climbed back into his secret cave and got into his secret pet fish rig. He adjusted the new bluish camouflage side to up, and double-checked all the safety settings. He was happy with the conditions so he made his way through the cave opening. It was much easier with the small hydro motor fitted. The water was clear and for the first time he appreciated the fun factor of his pet fish. Even cruising around a little under the surface was exhilarating as his body temperature remained normal, thanks to his clever wetsuit alterations. Deciding to test the automatic snorkel/oxygen tank safety switch, he dived down about ten meters and stayed there for five minutes. The automatic changeover was so good it surprised him, so he zoomed about for over an hour watching the motor use half the battery pack charge.

Being more than pleased with his test run, the potential of his design had suddenly dawned on him. This was a low cost, safe, ton of fun, underwater sports craft. There was nothing like it for the money and the possibilities were endless. This was a case of necessity, being the mother of invention. He had set out to save Bean and boost the kiosk economy but had been forced into going beyond his perceived limitation. He was now being more innovative than his wildest dreams would have predicted. The first thought on his mind was, 'WOW'.

His second thought was whether his stealth, camouflaged, disappearing shark design had worked. He stored his rig on the shelf in the cave, then climbed out of the dry entrance and made his way up to the top of the headland. There were at least twenty people sitting around watching the surf and the boardriders. With nothing unusual happening, he headed down to the club.

'Hey Bean, how's it going?' He asked as he popped into the kiosk.

'Good mate. All normal. How are you going?' Replied Bean.

'Allgood, any dramas here today?'

'No. Why did you ask that twice? Queried Bean.

'No problem. Just making sure you're okay. I'm just goin for a quick surf, I'll see ya later'. He answered, grabbing his board and jogging off. On the way down the beach he spotted Starch, so he headed toward him for a yarn. As he got close, Starch's phone rang so he detoured to the surf.

Starch fumbled frustratingly with the phone answer button. 'Hello', he muttered without identifying himself.

'Hi Starch, it's Molly Baxter here. How are you?' Said the spirited female voice.

'How do you know it's Starch?' He asked.

'Put it down to experience', said Molly. 'You owe me a coffee, so when's a good time?'

'Whoa! Well don't be shy about it! I don't know'.

'Great, next Tuesday morning at nine it is then', quipped Molly. 'I just want to run a few things by you'. Then the call went dead.

'Hello, hello'. Said Starch into the phone, but Molly had gone. 'Fair dinkum', he gasped. 'More bloody push than a rugby scrum'.

As he started to walk up to the kiosk Jackson came down to meet him, so they walked back together.

'Aren't you supposed to be working today, what's goin on?' Starch asked.

'Yeah on my way, just called in to see if you're going out in the inflatable today'. Replied Jack.

'Yeah, this afternoon if you wanna come. How's the Dive Centre going?'

'The reef is covered in sand at the moment so we're mostly doing dives along the rock wall, and night dives and stuff'. Answered Jack.

'Hmmm. This sand's a curse. Do you go on the night dives?'

'Yeah. Andrew gets me to go in the swift currents and stuff of a night time. It's pitch dark but he ties a cord between us. He's very strict on emergency procedures and operating under adverse conditions and stuff. He keeps telling me, never ever panic, keep your heart rate down, your mind calm, and go through the processes'. Replied Jack.

Starch nodded in approval and replied: 'Excellent advice. You're doing great, Jack. This sand build-up is a bit of a bloody worry though. Kirra is starting to look like the Gobi Desert, and this place is no better'.

'Andrew said the same. Do you need help with anything at the moment, Starch?' Asked Jack.

'Nah, not at the moment mate, call in after work and we'll give the inflatable a run. You'd better get going'. Replied Starch, appreciating Jackson's never-ending willingness to lend a hand. Then within a flash, Jack was on his pushbike and gone.

Moey had arrived at the kiosk and made herself something to eat then settled down at one of the tables. As usual, she said little and tapped away on her small laptop computer whilst eating, with a predator-like focus. She finished her food, wiped the table and was leaving when Matthew came running up from the beach carrying his board and yelling: 'Moey, Two seconds. I need to talk to you. Hang on a minute. Did you see anything?'

Moey rolled her eyeballs and replied, 'Nooo, no again, and no again'.

'What? Hang on, wait a minute. Did you look? Are you sure?' He asked, doing a poor attempt at sounding normal.

'Matty. I did look and I looked again, and to be sure I looked again, but I did not see any large fishes today'.

'Oh, okay. That's great', replied Matt.

'Why is that great?' Fired Mo, straight back.

'Oh, I mean, it's great that you looked. Thanks, heaps. Catch you later'. He said without elaborating. He then rushed off to contemplate his next move, leaving Moey without an explanation for the odd behaviour.

Shark sightings close to shore were uncommon along that section of coastline and he had been spotted twice. One of those was unintended so he thought it best to rest his pet fish for a while. Bean was cashed up in the kiosk, so his attention turned to improving the recreational viability of the craft and the one thought that kept coming back to him was safety. As he arrived back at the kiosk, he sat at one of the tables and tapped out mathematical equations on a calculator. He needed enough buoyancy to float to the surface if forward propulsion stopped. Just as he reached a conclusion Bean wandered over.

'Hey Matt, are you busy? I have to do a few things that'll take about an hour, can you watch the place? It's alright if you can't. I'll just do it this arvo', enquired Bean.

'No, no it's cool. I'm just hangin'. Do you wanna get going and I'll take over', replied Matt.

'Incredible, you're a lifesaver! Okay, I'll get going. There's nothing going on at the moment, so I should be back shortly. Thanks mate'. Said Bean as he headed off.

Matthew sat in the kiosk trying to think of a solution to his safety idea. His mind kept repeating, buoyancy, buoyancy, buoyancy. Then he had an "I wonder" moment. He hopped up and went into the club junk room and rummaged through the lost and found and washed up bin. He found two old adult style life-saving vests with the straps broken, that had been in there for over a year. He looked at his equations and looked at the weight size for the vests and muttered to himself: 'This can work'.

He took the vests back into the kiosk and laid them out on a table. With his mind ticking over he found a pair of scissors and started cutting the material apart until all he had was the buoyancy blocks. Everything looked good except for the colour. The blocks were fluro yellow. He raced out to his van and grabbed bits and pieces of his new camouflage wetsuit material. Covering the fluro yellow blocks with the material was simple, so he busied himself with the task. The kiosk trade was quiet except for the occasional coffee, so he worked quickly and had nearly finished the job when Fins Walton suddenly appeared at the counter.

'Have you seen the boys? What's that you're doing?' Asked the gravelly voice of Fins.

Matty's heart sank. Any exchange with Fins was testing.

'Errr. Hi Fins. It's just some stuff I'm working on'. Answered Matt.

'Is that still the colour project excuse thing you came up with last time? Or is this a new thing?' Quizzed Fins.

'Ahhhh, no. I'm just mucking around. Just making nothing really'. Matty tried to survive the moment by appearing boring, but Fins wasn't buying it.

'So you're cutting up a flotation vest and covering highly visible fluro green with painted blueish wetsuit type material to make nothing?' Asked Fins, putting the pressure on.

Matt could feel the walls closing in so he tried the baffle with bullcrap approach.

'Awww no, not really. I was wondering if the flotation vest could be made more efficient by making it out of wetsuit material. It's a matter of water displacement'. He replied avoiding eye contact.

'Matty. You're the brightest young bloke I've ever known, but you're the worst bullshit artist I've ever heard. See ya later and stick these reef fillets in the fridge for Jacko and his mum". Said Fins, and walked off with Sharkbait closely behind.

Matty paused for a moment to savour the sense of relief. He had survived another Fins grilling. The buoyancy squares were finished and he attached some strips of industrial velcro as an attachment device. He was happy with the safety addition but was once again planning something bigger. Matty was addicted to innovation and the what if bug, had got to him again. He had an idea on how to make a portable seawater desalination device that could easily fit on his fish thus making fluid replenishment endless. His new idea would lift his pet fish into a whole new level of day tripping recreation - or a serious small, independent, exploratory underwater craft. He sketched out a few drawings and equations for the seawater desalination device, and decided to fit the buoyancy squares after work, on his way home. He decided to test them at a later date when things were quiet and he could float to the surface unnoticed and perform any adjustments.

# Chapter 15

# Feel The Burn

The week passed and the status quo remained with the club grant. Starch would not endorse the dredging and the application for government assistance remained buried somewhere in Flowers' office. Mel's son Benny had arrived to start his work experience training at exactly 8.30 am on Monday morning. Adrian and Brian had started earlier and were busy in the kitchen preparing for the lunchtime trade, when Benny knocked on the door and caught Adrian's attention.

'Hi Benny, good to see you. Are you ready to start?'

'Yes please Adrian, thank you', replied Benny.

'Great. Come on in and I'll introduce you to Brian'.

Adrian called Brian over to meet Benny. He had been told there was a work experience junior starting today but he had not been told it was Mel's son. He also wasn't aware the work experience person had down syndrome.

'Benny', said Adrian. 'This is', but before he could finish, Brian interrupted.

'Hi Benny, my name's Brian, pleased to meet you. You can come over and work with me if you like'.

Adrian was a bit flabbergasted by Brian's interjection, but Benny seemed happy with the suggestion.

'Would that be alright, Adrian?' he asked.

'Yeah, well, I suppose so. Just remember Benny is on work experience and not a paid staff member, please Brian'. Said Adrian, concerned and wary of the invitation but deciding to let them have a go.

'Of course!' Replied Brian, surprised and a bit puzzled by Adrian's cautious response. He very openly embraced Benny in a friendly manner and was keen to help him.

'Let's go, Benny. I'll show you how we do meal prepping. Do you want a drink or anything?'

'No thank you and thank you for letting me help you.' Replied Benny, as the pair walked over to a food prep bench where Brian had a bucket of potatoes.

'Ok Ben, we're gunna do spuds, you can peel or cut. Peel just means peeling the skin, and cut just means cutting them. What do you think you would like to do?' Asked Brian.

'I think I would like to cut them,' Benny replied.

'Okay, I'll peel. Just give me a couple of minutes and I'll have them done, then you can cut them'.

Brian took the bucket of spuds to the sink and very rapidly peeled them. Benny looked on and was greatly impressed by the authority and virtuosity he displayed, quietly thinking to himself: 'If ever a man was born to peel spuds, this was him.'

After the peeling exhibition was finished, Brian put the spuds back on the bench and fetched a cutting board and knife.

'Ok Ben, have you cut spuds before?' He asked.

'Yes', came the quiet reply.

'Okay, when you're finished put them in the bucket and I'll check them, then we'll give them to Adrian. After that we'll do carrots, but just take your time and do the spuds first then we'll do the rest. I've just got to go downstairs but I'll be back in ten or fifteen minutes. If you're unsure of anything just wait til I get back'.

Brian then left to go downstairs and Benny set about cutting the potatoes. After cutting two thirds into a suitable size, he took them over to Adrian.

'Here's some of the spuds, Adrian. Are they done right?'

'Yeah mate, that's great', replied Adrian. 'Just give me the rest when you've finished them'.

Ben went back to the bench and put a slight cut in the rest of the spuds, but left them whole. Just as he finished, Brian came back.

'How did it go, Benny, any problems?' He asked.

'Nope', answered Benny.

'Okay, well you can start cutting them now if you like', said Brian.

'I have', replied Benny.

'What do you mean? Where are they?' Quizzed Brian.

'There', answered Benny, pointing to the spuds with cuts in them.

'But they're not cut up,' Brian stated.

'You didn't say to cut them up, you said to cut the spuds, so I cut the spuds', explained Benny.

Adrian was listening to the conversation and started to smile, very broadly.

'No, it's ok. You misunderstood me', Brian counselled.

'No, I didn't. I did exactly what you told me to do', explained Benny.

'Well, it's not what I meant', replied Adrian.

'But it is what you said'. Benny politely insisted.

'Benny, people don't always have to say exactly what they mean, they say things generally. It's kinda like taking shortcuts or dressing up words. It's ok to do that, everybody does it. So if I say, "cut the spuds", it means to cut them into pieces, not put bits of cuts in them'. Brian patiently explained.

'Did I make a mistake?' Asked Benny.

Brian's heart softened, and he replied: "No Ben, I made the mistake".

Adrian kept silent and smiled in rapturous appreciation of Benny. He had exposed a caring side of Brian that Adrian thought never existed. There were another seventy nine and a half hours of Benny's company left to share, and Adrian was looking forward to every second of it.

Brian organised their next task of carrot prep as Benny finished off the spuds.

'Ok, now we can do carrots. What do you want to do, peel or cut them into pieces?" Asked a wiser Brian.

'I don't care, whatever you want to do', answered Benny.

'Well alright, let's swap this time. I'll cut, you peel. When they're peeled, just put them on the bench and I'll chop 'em up'.

The boys worked quietly away with Brian doing odd jobs and Benny peeling carrots, everything was running smoothly until Benny mentioned a discrepancy with the carrots.

'Brian, we need more carrots'.

'No, that's enough. That's plenty', replied Brian.

'We need more. We don't have enough', Benny insisted.

'Benny, you have peeled them perfectly and that is heaps', insisted Brian.

'We need more', said Benny.

Puzzled by the thinking, Brian asked: 'Why do we need more?'

'Because there are more spuds than carrots', reasoned Benny.

'Yeah, that's right. That's how we do things', declared Brian.

'But it's not fair,' appealed Benny.

'Well, it doesn't have to be fair. Vegetables don't have feelings so they won't get upset', explained Brian.

'But what about the carrot eating people? They won't get as much as the potato eating people, and then they won't feel as important and then they will be unhappy'. Reasoned Benny.

'Ben, the carrot eating people are the same as the potato eating people. They're all the same'. Brian patiently clarified.

'But it's not correct', insisted Benny.

Brian gave a deep sigh and explained: 'Some things don't have to be correct, they're just guidelines. No one worries about it because it would drive us all stupid. We use our common sense to tell us what's going on. If carrot eaters and potato eaters are confused, well maybe it's just them'.

'Okay, but I still think it is incorrect'. Benny was resolute.

Adrian was listening to the interaction between Ben and Brian and found it very interesting. Ben was forcing Brian into a non-pedantic approach to everything.

The kitchen flowed along smoothly for another couple of hours. Brian was being very patient and quite enjoyed looking after Benny. At the end of the shift, it was time to clean up and Adrian was happy to let Brian delegate the work, seeing the pair were getting along so well.

'Benny, do you want to clean the benches or empty the bins?' Asked Brian.

'Can I do bins, please?' Replied Benny.

'Yeah okay, just tie off the bin liners then throw them out and we'll scrub the bins later', said Brian, as he set about cleaning the benches. Ben did just as he was told. He tied off the bin liners then picked up a couple of the bags to throw out - however, he headed for the office instead of downstairs to the bin, which prompted a reaction from Brian.

'Whoa Benny. Where are you going? You've got to take them to the bin downstairs. Not to the office'.

'You said "throw them out", and mum said you threw some stuff out of the office window, so I'm going to throw them out the office window'. Maintained Benny.

'Yeah but, I was just being stupid. Who's your mum?' Asked Brian.

Adrian was listening to the conversation as usual. When he heard Brian's admission about the office window fiasco, he snorted and dropped his jaw in astonishment.

'My mum's name is Mel. She also works here', answered Ben.

'Is Mel your mum?' gasped Brian, with his mouth wide open.

'Yes. Now I'll take the bags downstairs', said Benny.

'Were you going to throw the bin bags out the window because your mum told you that's what I did?' Asked Brian.

'No', replied Benny.

'Well why?' Said Brian, trying to make some sense out of the situation.

'Because I was pulling your leg. Mum said you like upsetting people, so I thought you would like to be upset a little bit', explained Benny.

'Whattt?!!' Blurted Brian.

'Mum said you like arguing with people about silly things, so I thought you would like to talk about silly things'.

'Have you been geeing me up all day?' Asked Brian, who was struggling to believe what he was hearing.

'Yes', stated Ben.

Brian was halfway between gobsmacked and disbelief, struggling to get his head around Ben's honest answers.

'Are you serious?' He drawled. 'Are you serious? You've been setting me up all day'.

'Yes,' replied Benny.

'I can't believe this!' Brian continued.

'Am I a mistake?' Asked Ben.

'No, I just didn't know you could do that because you suffer from Down syndrome', replied Brian.

'I don't suffer from anything. My mum tells me she loves me every morning when I wake up and every night before I go to sleep and I love her, so I don't suffer from anything. I have Down syndrome but mum loves me and always hugs me. Does your mum hug you and tell you she loves you, Brian?' Asked Ben.

'No... But it's not important'. Quietly answered Brian, bowing his head.

There was a period of silence between the two of them as they stood there. Adrian was gobsmacked listening to the conversation. He had learnt more about Brian today then he had ever done. All of a sudden his behaviour started to make sense. Brian never spoke about anything personal, but he opened up to Benny with genuine trust. After an awkward minute of standing in front of each other without speaking, Benny broke the silence.

'Can I be your friend, Brian?' He humbly asked.

'I thought we were friends', answered Brian quietly.

'Oh okay. That's happy', said Benny.

From that day forward Benny and Brian were best friends. Brian never spent time on the grommets pole again, and Adrian never raised his voice to Brian again... Almost...

Simmo had a chat with the girls and floated the idea of entering the Australian Surf Boat Championships that were being held on the coast in a month's time. The girls had decided to grab the opportunity with both hands and voted a resounding 'Yes'. They took charge of the gym and a sign had gone up at the entrance, "No mobile phones or crap like that in here". The club members were unreserved in their support with every single member chipping in some expense money - creating an overwhelming feeling of mateship in the club.

Rooster had caught wind of the news and seeing he was the self-appointed Team Guidance Officer, he decided they needed his help. Because of people trying to smear his character in recent months, he decided to help them secretly. Rooster believed this was humility in its purest form and he believed himself to be a humble human being.

The surf boat was kept in the storage room under lock and key and as usual, Rooster had gotten access to the keys. When the club had closed or quietened down for the night time, he would set about improving the performance of the boat. Every day the girls trained he would polish the hull secretly that night, reasoning this would decrease any drag through the water. He also cleaned the seats to guard against any infection thus decreasing the chance of any type of disruption to training due to illness.

Starch had kept clear of the training, as far as he was concerned it was Simmo's responsibility and he already had enough problems to deal with - but he was always on hand for any help that was needed.

They crossed paths on the beach one day when Simmo was leaning on the surf boat and deep in thought. Starch used the opportunity to have a yarn.

'How's it going, Simmo', he asked.

'Not bad mate, just got a bit of a problem with the boat seats', he replied.

'The seats? What's wrong with them?' Asked Starch.

'The girls have all got what looks like a burn mark on their butts. It's never happened before, so I'm wondering if it's something in the water or maybe in the wood of the seats. I hose the boat off after every training session, so it's got me stuffed. It's getting worse', he related, sounding frustrated by the problem.

They both stood there quietly for a moment looking at the seats. Both of them were puzzled and overcome with an answer drought.

'Well, that's a newie. It has to be the wood or the water unless someone is having a go at us', concluded Starch.

'Yeah, I didn't want to think someone would be interfering with the training. I had a yarn to Soapy at the markets and he gave me a heap of goat's milk soap for the girls and said don't use anything else. It calms them down when they have a shower, but their arses go red raw as soon as they hop in the boat again. They're training through it, but I can't expect them to put up with that. It's got me stuffed!' Lamented Simmo.

'Okay, leave it with me. We can't blame the dredging for this one, so I'll just have a think about it. You can bet your bottom dollar there'll be an answer. Dunno what it is at the moment, but we'll find it'. Said Starch as he gave Simmo a pat on the back.

Simmo gave a relieving smile as Starch continued on his way thinking about the mystery of the burning butts.

With the application for the club grant still sitting in Flowers's office, Robyn had decided to call a meeting of the board members. Andrew Coleman from the dive centre had requested permission to attend and discuss the environmental and financial impact of the bar dredging. The meeting was held mid-week and went late into the night with the board members being unanimous in its decision to bypass Flowers, and directly approach the government minister responsible. They were also unanimous in conducting an independent impact study into the effects of the dredging fiasco, with the costs and labour being shared between the club and Colmie. One of the major hurdles facing them would be the board riders club and surf shop mogul, who had embraced the new superbank and sprouted it's worth daily. Even though there were more fights than ever due to the massive influx of out of towners, that led to overcrowding and a complete disregard for surf etiquette.

After the meeting finished Starch was left to tidy up and turn off the lights. On his way out he noticed someone had left the storage room light on, so he backtracked to turn it off. When he opened the door he was greeted by a sight that left him speechless. Rooster was busy polishing the boat and hadn't heard him come in. He stood there baffled for a minute then walked up slowly behind him wondering, 'why is Rooster polishing the surf boat late at night, in secret?'

'Having trouble sleeping, Rooster?' He asked.

Rooster jumped and straightened up as if he had been hit with a cattle prod. He spun around to see Starch and felt his life flash before his eyes.

'Errr, ah, errr, no mate. Just looking after the team. Been too busy through the day so just doin what I can for 'em'. Blurted Rooster, sounding amazingly confident compared to the way he felt.

'Oh really. And what would that be?' Asked Starch.

Rooster's reply was preceded by a look that suggested it was a silly question.

'Awww mate, just the usual equipment maintenance. Every second counts in this game. Gotta do the right thing. Someone's gotta do the hard yards, mate'.

'Exactly what hard yards are you doing?' Asked Starch.

'Awww, mate. Completely hand buffing the hull, mate. All the time, true grit, spit and polish and dedication, mate. The hardest yards, mate. This is where races are won and legends are born, mate. In the storage shed, mate. I don't want any thanks or accolades. Been doin it for years, mate. The wind in the sails of champions, mate. No one sees the wind, they just feel his effects'. Rooster spoke in a very wise, selfless tone that would boggle the mind of anyone prepared to listen, but not Starch.

'And what else are you doing?' He asked.

'Awww. Just a bit of sterilisation, mate. Athlete infection control… Sort of", replied Rooster.

'Infection control? How's that?' Asked Starch.

'Only the seats, mate. Just making sure everything is sterile and ship shape', replied Rooster.

'And how do you sterilise the seats?' Asked Starch, starting to smell an information bone.

'Caustic, mate. Good old Caustic Soda. Best sterilisation you've got. Kills everything'. Rooster's voice took on a scientific, knowledgeable tone.

'And what is the method?' Said Starch, with the manner of an interested student.

'Just simple, mate. Just brush the caustic on and leave it, let it soak in'. Informed Rooster, enjoying the interest.

'Rooster. I think you should know that the boat crew are walking around with severely burnt arses. If they get wind of your athlete infection control, it'll be RIP Rooster. But however, they will have to line up behind The White Pointers, Donga and who knows how many others. Everything to do with the boat and crew goes through Simmo. Although what you are doing is well intended, and I welcome the change, I'm assuming Simmo knows nothing about this. Would I be right?' Asked Starch, showing incredible patience.

'Yeah well, I've always been one to stand in awe of humility, mate. I'm always doing something privately that changes people's lives', confessed Rooster.

'So I've noticed', drawled Starch. 'Okay, you can knock off and leave me the keys. I'll let Simmo know about your good deeds'.

Rooster sensed now was a good time to bail and declared: 'Yeah, good idea, mate. I've stuffed my back doing all this work - kindness has its drawbacks I suppose'. And he started for the door, but Starch wasn't finished.

'Just a couple of questions before you go. First, why were you really doing this?'

'Oh, just a bit of recognition for a change, mate', Rooster answered.

'But you said you didn't want any recognition', replied Starch.

'Yeahhh, nahhh. Recognition for not ever being recognised, mate', answered Rooster.

Starch looked down and gave his head a mini shake, then continued.

'Next question, why don't you answer your phone? Do you want to be taken off patrol duty?' He asked.

Rooster looked alarmed and exclaimed: 'No, no, no, definitely not, mate. My phone company cut me off! They reckon I didn't pay my phone bill, which is ridiculous. I'll get an apology off 'em and I'll be back online next week'.

'Okay', said Starch. 'Cyclone season is approaching up north and the school holidays are coming. The council is thin on lifeguards so the volleys have got to number up'.

Rooster took a deep breath in and his chest swelled out. He was needed.

'I'm on it, mate. I'm all over this. If someone needs me, I'm there like lightning in a thunderstorm. I'm attracted to hardship, mate. A service to humanity I am, no worries, mate', blurted Rooster.

'Yeah, yeah, yeah, just be available at the start of holidays. I'll talk to you before then if possible. I'll see ya later', said Starch as Rooster walked off, feigning a limp.

Starch went back upstairs to the kitchen to get a bottle of apple cider vinegar, then washed the boat seats three times and followed that up with a hosing off with water for ten minutes. Realising that was all he could do, he decided to head home. It had been a long, challenging day and his mind kept returning to the financial woes of the club, and whether Flowers should be entitled to breathe oxygen. He reasoned there was nothing he could do, other than hang on and hope.

The following day Starch waited until after the girl's boat crew finished training, to have a yarn with Simmo.

'How'd it go, Simmo? Are the burning backsides still an issue?' He asked.

'Actually, that'd be the first session in a while that they haven't said anything. Don't know, maybe it's gone', replied Simmo.

'Just between you and me, I may have solved it', said Starch.

'Whattt? What'd you do? What was it? It had me stuffed. It's sent the girls off the deep end', blurted Simmo.

'Well, I don't want this to go any further, but Rooster has been secretly polishing the boat and sterilising the seats'. Said Starch quietly.

Simmo stood there for a moment with his mouth open.

'Who told him to do that?' Said Simmo aghast. 'What'd he do to the seats? How'd you find that out?'

'He was trying to help. He soaked the seats with caustic. I came across him last night after the meeting when I was locking up', explained Starch.

Simmo was mortified and struggled with what Starch was saying.

'They will kill him! If the girls get wind of this they will kill him.

He is a dead man walking. Donga will seem like a baby compared to this lot. If they get wind of this he will pay big time', he exclaimed.

'How are they gunna find out? Just don't say anything', consoled Starch.

Simmo gave an eyeball roll and replied: "I can't lie to them. I just hope they don't ask me anything".

'Nah, all good. The problem has been fixed. That's it. Can you also remind the girls the school holidays are coming and we're going to need everybody on the beach. Other than that it's back to normal, so I'll see ya later'. Said Starch as he headed off, happy that at least one problem had been solved.

It was one week to the day, when Starch came across Bean handing out free coffee vouchers on the path.

'Hey Bean, how ya goin, have you seen Rooster around here lately?' Asked Starch.

'Yeah, he's just over there', replied Bean.

'Is that him? Strewth, he's got fat! It's gone straight to his arse! How'd he manage that?' He asked, looking at Rooster who was about thirty meters away, talking to a couple of ladies.

'It's a nappy. Apparently, he washed the surf boat seats with caustic soda, which burnt the girls. As soon as they found out they knocked off his undies from the change room, soaked them in caustic, dried them, sprinkled a little bit more inside, then hung them back up with his clothes. Soon as he put them back on things went bad. Roasted his nuts badly. Burnt his anas to the point he can't fart. Everywhere round the nether regions burnt like an active volcano. It's bad, mate. They drove him to the outpatient emergency ward up at the hospital and said he was crying the whole way, and wailing like a banshee. The whole deal is soaked in Aloe Vera and the nappy is soaked with Aloe Vera. The doctor said it'll be a month before he shows any sign of improvement. Even Donga squirmed when he heard the news'. Recounted Bean.

Starch was lost for words and muttered: "Ohhh nooo".

'Who told the girls about the boat seats? When did this happen?' He asked.

'He told them. Apparently, he wanted recognition for not being recognised, so he told them what he'd been doing, humbly and quietly. You don't try it on with those girls, I can tell you. Dunno when it happened, just saw him wander in today with his nappy and a pillow to sit on', explained Bean.

'I think I'll leave this alone. Does Simmo know about nappygate?' Asked Starch.

'Dunno. As I said, I just found out myself', replied Bean.

'Oh well, if you see him it might pay to let him know. I'll see ya later', said Starch and he continued on his way being careful to avoid Rooster.

# Chapter 16

# Business as Usual

Three weeks had passed and Flowers was still sitting on the club grant, while the beach sand continued to build up from the dredging. With the school holidays approaching rapidly, two cyclones started to form off the coast of North Queensland. This meant huge surf. The hinterland was enjoying heavy rainfall and the Tweed River and estuaries were at the high watermark. The coastal weather forecast for the weekend was hot and sunny. Starch knew Saturday was the beginning of the holiday season and judging by the forecast, Sunday would see a massive increase in beachgoers. The tourists arrive, get changed and head for the beach.

Most of the club members had made themselves available for the weekend as a virus had swept through the council lifeguards, making them thin on the ground. The shortfall was easily covered by the clubs so everyone was expecting a bumper holiday season. Starch was busily going over the equipment, double-checking everything when Jack rolled up on his bicycle.

'Hey, big fella, what's going on? What's happening on the diving front?' Asked Starch.

'Not much, the water's pretty dirty at the moment because of the rain in the hinterland. The Tweed river banks are breaking and there's some localised flooding, so the water's just too muddy. Andrew thinks it'll rain for at least the rest of the week, so we can only do learners in the pool. I've been refereeing underwater rugby which is great. The scrums are hilarious', laughed Jack.

'Underwater rugby!!! What the hell! How did you get into that? Underwater rugby? How do you blow the whistle?' Starch bellowed.

Jack gave a hearty laugh, knowing he'd get a reaction when he told Starch what he was up to.

'Well, Colmie asked me to do it because everyone was arguing and fighting with the ref. He said I'm the only person they don't argue and fight with, so he asked me to have a go, and it's been fun. I use flags instead of a whistle', he explained.

'So what happens when you go up for a breath? Is that when they put the biff in?' Starch asked.

'Nah, I have oxygen tanks, they have snorkels. Colmie got the tanks from Bull. They're shaped to fit the body and really cool. He had two pairs. He said he gave Matty the other pair for his environmental research', informed Jack.

'What? Matty the environmentalist. That's a newie', replied Starch.

'Yeah, but there is one problem. Danny asked me if there was a spot on a team for him. I didn't know what to say but he's waiting to find out. Andrew said, whatever I think is fine but I don't know what to say. What do you think?' Asked Jack.

'Actually yeah, that's a good idea because one thing that could shut him up would be a snorkel and six feet of water. Tell him, yeah, I'd reckon'. Advised Starch.

'Ok, I will. There's nothing on this weekend so I'll be able to help all day if you need me', said Jack.

'Yeah, we'll definitely need you. It's gunna be flat out'. Replied Starch, which was exactly what Jack wanted to hear.

Once he was satisfied with the readiness of the equipment, Starch checked the tide times and let out a groan. To add to his concerns there was a king tide on Sunday with the top of the tide at 3pm. He let out another sigh. The conditions for the first weekend of the holidays were, king tide with huge waves propelled by the cyclones up north. There was also localised flooding in the hinterland which meant a huge body of water coming down the Tweed River. To add to all this, all holiday accommodation on the coast was fully booked, which meant big, big crowds on the beach.

The week slipped by relatively quietly as if it was the calm before the storm. Bean and Mattew had discussed the possibility of a quieter start to the holidays but Bean had decided to risk it, and ordered up big for the weekend. Matthew decided if it was quieter, then a shark sighting might be appropriate, especially as he wanted to test his new flotation safety device. He had also made a prototype portable desalination device that adapted easily to the drinking water supply that he wanted to test. There hadn't been a shark alarm for a while so rather than risk food wastage, a shark sighting might be needed.

Despite the large surf on the points, Rainbows End was a sheltered beach which made for an excellent family spot. There was just enough of a wave for the holidaying Boogie Boarders and calm enough for swimmers of all ages. The only shortfall was the one hundred metres of sand between the club and the surf. The sand build-up was a result of the unchecked dredging of the bar and had created a potentially dangerous situation. If there was a serious shark attack or life-threatening injury, suburban ambulances could not traverse the soft sand. There were only a few four-wheel-drive ambulances on the coast, so station to situation time wasn't at emergency standard - meaning the rescue helicopter was usually always needed.

Starch had rostered eight volunteers for Saturday and ten for Sunday. This was around double the normal roster and did not include any council full-time lifeguards. Rooster had declared himself fit and available and urged Starch to use his experience. He called this the "Rooster Factor", and insisted he was a game-changer. Starch reluctantly accepted Rooster's offer and offered him either day in return. Rooster took both days with a vow of total commitment and an alcohol-free weekend, but Starch didn't believe any of it and instead, just hoped for the best.

Saturday morning came around and Jack, Starch, Bean, Matty and Simmo were all at the club before sunrise. Starch and Jack set up the patrol equipment and double-checked all the radio frequencies. Bean and Matty greeted the local baker and set about making one hundred lunch rolls. Simmo hosed off the pathways, lined the garbage bins and filled the ice freezer in the med room. The board riders were already surfing the points in the predawn darkness and more were unpacking their gear in the car park before making their pilgrimage to the waves. It was an eerie, surreal scene that looked like moving shadows in the dark, gravitating to the beach and being drawn into the tribalistic festival of surf.

About mid-morning the beachgoers started to arrive and their numbers built up fairly quickly. There were the familiar faces who spent their summer holidays at Rainbows End every year, with questions about the sand and what happened, being asked repeatedly. There were a lot of new faces and many were unfamiliar with beach conditions such as rips and sweeps, so the lifeguards had their hands full trying to keep people swimming between the flags. Most of the holidayers were completely unaware they could drift so far out, until the lifeguards made them aware of it.

Upstairs in the kitchen, Adrian, Brian and Benny were flat out as lunchtime approached. No one had kept count of Ben's experience hours so he just came and went as he pleased, although Adrian always made sure he went home with a full box of groceries.

At midday the beach was a hectic scene, the patrol had performed nine rescues in two hours - then there were the back and neck injuries from being dumped in the surf. Everyone was busy except Rooster who was sound asleep in his chair. The kiosk had run out of rolls by midday and Bean had lost count of the bacon and egg rolls, but it was a big number. Looking like it was kiosk armageddon, Bean called in Jules and Moey to help out, the four of them barely coped. Just when it seemed things couldn't get any more chaotic, Danny and Grizz turned up for their Saturday morning eat and chat but couldn't get a seat causing Grizz to growl - which was nothing new. Danny, however, asked Bean for a 'please explain', as to why his seat wasn't reserved.

'Bean, mate. I just thought I'd let you know, I don't have a seat'. Announced Danny diplomatically.

Bean was under enormous pressure and didn't have enough time for Danny's feedback on the seat situation.

'Yes, you do mate. It's attached to your hips, it's called your arse', he replied.

'What? That's not right, I've got training. I've got to prepare. You should be aware of the seat situation, you know', retorted Danny.

'I am! Council laws restrict me from putting any more out. If you want anything it's a one hour wait', said Bean.

'Whattt! One Hour? You're joking, aren't you?' Blurted Danny.

'Yes, I'm joking. Whaddaya want?' Asked Bean.

'Aww... Just the usual and Grizz will have a coffee', said a relieved Danny.

'What do you mean, 'usual'? What is that these days? Bean sprouts on chocolate?'

Danny raised an eyebrow and took an aloof tone: 'Errr. No. I'll have a burger, coffee and a high protein muesli bar with dark chocolate. I'll organise the seats, we'll be back in a minute'. The two of them then wandered upstairs to borrow a couple of seats.

Starch had his hands full on the beach with three lost children, men taking uninvited photos of females on their mobile phones and board riders encroaching on the flagged area. The Superbank created by the dredging was producing a big wave, and the club med room was busy with board riders bleeding from fin cuts and abrasions from rocks. Just about everything that could float was being ridden on the Superbank wave. There were constant arguments and fights about surf etiquette and it was much the same on the points. The Out of Towners were present in large numbers, and "Water Town" was stacked.

The barrage of holidayers was constant til around 4pm when they started to thin out. Bean took stock of what they had left and it was nowhere near enough for Sunday, so Matty was dispatched to buy more supplies. Starch and the Lifeys pulled the flags at 5pm and called it a day, everyone was exhausted and went up to the clubhouse for a meeting. They definitely needed more lifeys on the beach, so Starch rounded up extra help for the next day.

Jackson's mother Suzanne, called in to pick him up but because he was still working she decided to go up to the headland and wait. After he had finished, Benny, who had recently learnt how to use the coffee machine, made a Chai tea as a present for Jackson to give her. It was her favourite tea, and the gesture took Jackson by surprise so he let Benny know what a special person he was, to do such a kind thing.

Jack then walked up to the headland to find his mum sitting on the grassy point. She loved all of Jackson's little surprises and was very surprised with the tea - it was one of those little things she would cherish forever. He explained to her that it was Ben who made the tea and he would have been too shy to ask, but "Ben just seemed to know what I wanted without me saying anything". They both sat on the headland for a while watching the boardriders on one side squeezing every last second out of the day, and the angry Tweed River bar on the other. The bar had been shut by the Waterways Authority the night before, after two boats had capsized. It was very dangerous.

While they were watching, a familiar fishing boat came up the Tweed River and approached the bar. Jackson and his mum stared in disbelief.

'You're not serious? No way!' said Jack.

'Oh dear, I'm afraid he is Jacky', said his mum.

The boat approaching belonged to Fins Walton. Sharkbait was standing on the bow, a one-legged seagull stood on the mast and Ben and Sushi were hanging out each side of the back. Fins could be seen inside calmly steering the boat straight for the heart of the bar. As the boat approached the impassable, Fins slowed slightly - approaching cautiously.

'You're not serious? No way! You're joking. Is this a prank?' Said Jack.

'Oh dear, I'm afraid he's going to take the bar on', replied Suzanne.

'This could end very, very badly', gasped Jack.

As the boat moved closer to the huge waves, Sharkbait left the bow and ran down into the cabin. The one-legged seagull took flight and Ben and Sushi put on their life vests. Without warning Fins accelerated, full power into the heart of the bar. The old vessel dug down in the stern as it powered into the first wave, which smashed across the bow. Fins spotted a channel through the middle and kept the throttle on full. The boardriders spotted the boat in the middle of the bar and stared in disbelief. The locals knew who it was and started laying bets on whether he would make it or not. The old rig was smashed from one side then another. There was nowhere to hide but Fins kept going forward.

Suzanne sat there stunned with her hand across her mouth as Jack pondered ringing the Air Sea Rescue. All seemed lost when all of a sudden the boat seemed to slide down the back of a big wave and make it to the ocean side of the bar. The sea was still rough, but Fins had handled much worse in his time. Ben and Sushi breathed a sigh of relief as Sharkbait briefly stuck his head out of the cabin, then went back inside.

The rest of the fishing boat skippers had decided to wait til the bar and the sea calmed down, but Fins knew that would take days and fresh fish stocks in the coast's high-end restaurants would run out. If he could land a catch of quality fish the restaurants would pay a premium, so they decided to stay out for a week and see what happens.

Jack and his mum watched the old boat head out to the eastern horizon as the sun went down in the west. The one-legged seagull returned to the mast while Ben and Sushi started to prep the gear. It would be a very long, hard week. As Jack and his mum started to walk home, the boardriders were still queuing up for waves. It was as if they had no home to go to, or they simply never wasted good surf.

Starch was exhausted and went home as soon as all the gear was packed away, leaving Tom Green, the bar manager, to close the club. Mel stayed back to help and the pair of them cleaned up and finished around 11pm - they both left without noticing the storage room light was on. Rooster was back polishing the surf boat again, although he had given up the thought of Athlete Infection Control, and left the seats alone. He worked into the early hours of the morning with a set of earphones on, belting out music at an enormous volume from a band called Creedence Clearwater Revival. Such is the Rooster.

# Chapter 17

# Why?

Starch pulled up in the club car park just before dawn, Sunday morning. The boardriders were already there, getting changed and running down to the surf. He sat in the car for a minute watching a big man with a torch on his hat measuring out spaces adjacent to the path and numbering them with a powder. The man was Damo, who was one half of the Art and Craft on the Coast management team. The other half was Kay, his wife, who Starch could see walking up and down in the darkness organising other workers.

'Oooh no,' Starch muttered to himself. He had checked the market itinerary and they were scheduled to be further up the coast this weekend. He hoped there was a mistake and went to have a chat with Damo.

'Morning Damo, how ya going? What's going on with you blokes?'.

'Morning Starch, how are ya mate? The council is doing revegetation work up at Broadbeach so they relocated us down here. We would've gone to Burleigh if they wanted, but it's better here', replied Damo.

'Yeah ok. I'll have to get a couple of extra lifeys. The beach is always busier when the markets are on. How big is it?' Asked starch.

'Today there are about 250 permanents and whatever casuals roll up before 6.30 am. We're expecting a big crowd', answered Damo.

Starch knew his day had just got a whole lot more difficult. The local market crowds were huge and some of the younger parents had a tendency to drop their children off around the patrol tent and expect the lifeys to babysit. This was a nightmare unfolding as far as work goes, and expecting everyone to cooperate wasn't an option.

'Yeah, that's big. The beach was packed yesterday and I'd say it'll be bigger today. I'd better start to get things organised. I'll see you later mate, hope you have a great day'. Said Starch as he headed off to the club. Jackson arrived on his pushbike soon after and set to work helping set up, but couldn't help commenting as he looked across the beach to the silhouettes of boardriders in the surf.

'Do those people ever go home?' He muttered.

'I think that is their home', replied Starch. 'I hope everyone turns up for work today, otherwise we're stuffed'.

It wasn't long before everyone arrived and the club was up and running. Matthew had decided to hedge his bets by setting up his pet fish. He was unconvinced the kiosk could be that busy two days in a row, so he made a pre-dawn dash and double checked everything was good to go. The safety modifications and his new portable desalination device for drinking water were connected and operational. All he had to do was climb in and everything would switch on automatically - but he hoped he wouldn't have to and the kiosk would make a squillion dollars.

It was 8 am when Rooster fronted up to the kiosk, looking as striking as ever in his nylon DT's.

'Morning Bean. Matty throw me on three bacon and egg rolls please, mate. I'll have them on my tab, please mate'.

'You don't have a tab and are these for Starch and Jack?' Replied Bean.

'Yes I do mate, I gave you fifty short ones in advance ages ago, and Nah mate, they're all for me'. Reasoned Rooster.

Bean did the usual look down and shake the head routine.

'This is the last time! The kiosk does not say, eat now and pay whenever. Grab a seat and Matty will put them on'. Replied Bean, already running out of patience.

Just as Rooster parked his frame into a chair, Danny arrived at the kiosk window.

'Morning Bean, my good man. Can I have a bacon and egg roll with tomato, cheese, a couple of chips and sauce, please mate? And I'll have another with just bacon and egg for Grizz, please Mate', said Danny.

'Yeah ok, just grab a seat and they'll be a couple of minutes', answered Bean.

'Thank you but I'd better stand. We're on standby assistant patrol today. I'd better keep on my toes so I can keep both eyes on the beach.

I believe Starch is relying heavily on us'. Related Danny, sounding very serious.

'No comment,' replied Bean.

Just as Bean spoke, Bull the plumber came round the corner.

'Gidday Bean, how are ya. Can I have a couple of bacon and egg rolls please, then I can head down to patrol, mate. Starch has got half the bloody country here today. A little bit of surf and everybody starts to panic. I could do it all myself if I had to'. Said Bull, whilst Rooster and Danny nodded their heads in approval.

'Well I'm glad you're here, I thought you'd be in court today, although it is Sunday. The rolls will be a couple of minutes'. Said Bean, with a smirk.

'Yeah, nah. I'm just suing a bloke at the moment for defamation. Can't do that these days, especially when you've got an excellent reputation'. Explained Bull.

'No comment', replied Bean.

Just as he turned to help with the orders another customer fronted the counter. Bean spun back around to serve but froze in his tracks. Right there before him was the unfulfilled love of his life. He opened his mouth to speak but as usual, his voice went missing in action. Thankfully, the lady was busy looking through her handbag for money and was unaware of the frozen Bean at the counter. She looked up and saw Matty at the coffee machine.

'Hi, how are you?' She said.

'Hello! Good to see you again. Are you having a coffee?' Replied Matt.

'Yes please. Same as last time'.

'Ok, I'll do it straight away, it'll be two minutes', said Matt.

'Great, I'll leave the money on the counter', she replied.

Bean was still standing there frozen and dumbstruck and only just managed a nervous smile as the lady looked at him. As promised, Matty had her coffee ready in a matter of minutes and placed it on the counter.

'Sam', Matty called out, sending Bean further into emotional oblivion with the realisation that Matty knew the woman.

'Thanks, Matthew, see you next time,' she said.

'Thanks, Sam', he replied.

Bean was mortified, gutted, hyper shocked and still without a voice. He had one nagging question tearing his head apart: 'HOW?'

It was mid-morning before the crowds had well and truly arrived. The Art and Craft market was packed, while down on the beach the situation was similar with the patrol being super busy. Rooster was quietly sitting in his chair watching the goings-on and handing out advice on proceedings. The patrol was happy to let him have his way and just ignored him most of the time, and all was good, until, without warning, he stood up and announced: 'I'll be back in a minute, I've just gotta go to the airport'. Then he walked off.

The lifeys looked at one another and decided not to ask anything - the less they knew about Rooster the better. Not long after he left, Starch and Jackson came along to check on everything. Although the lifeys were short in numbers they were doing a great job, but Rooster's absence started alarm bells ringing with Starch.

'Where's Rooster?' He asked.

'Don't know, he just got up and said he had to go to the airport and he'll be back in a minute'. Replied Shannon, who was on duty.

'Stuff a duck! I knew yesterday was too good to be true. That bloke is about as reliable as whatever! Never fails to disappoint. Unbelievable', rattled off Starch.

'It might have been important. Airport sounds important and he said he'd be back', reasoned Jack.

Starch looked at Jack with one eyebrow raised. 'Ahh, the voice of reason. Let's see what happens then, Mr Optimistic. I'll wager one of Bean's double milkshakes, he won't make it back'.

Jack gave a smirk and a little fist pump before replying: 'Done! Come on Rooster, you can do it'.

To which Starch dryly replied: 'That'll be the day!'

The Superbank continued spewing out wave after wave of cyclone assisted boardrider bliss. Bean was working in the kiosk when he paused for a moment to watch the circus unfolding. He had seen it all before, the waves building in size and intensity signalling the impending arrival of the monster, leaving only the brave or foolish to tempt fate. Bean smiled and watched as he counted the time between the sets of waves, muttering to himself: "Any minute now". Then, without warning, a seeming jaw shaped, massive, rogue-wave came rolling through perpendicular to the beach. It was big and nasty, smashing everyone in its path. Surfboards were being spat out the top whilst every boardrider succumbed to its power. Bodies were being tossed about as if they were in a giant washing machine. No one was left standing.

Matty stopped to have a look and see what Bean was smiling at.

'Oh nooooo… Did you enjoy that?' He asked, wondering about Bean's dry sense of humour.

'Loved it', replied Bean. 'Loved it'.

Moey and Jules arrived just after the surf armageddon and in time for the lunch hour crush. Even with the four of them, it was another titanic struggle to feed the masses. Matty had abandoned any plans for a run in his pet fish and wondered if he would ever need it for the kiosk again. He was chafing at the bit to try out the new improvements although he had grown so much in confidence of his own ability, he had no doubts about everything working. Upstairs, the bar trade was normal with the kitchen crew performing like superstars. Even Mel was impressed and proud of the dynamic duo, Brian and Benny. Adrian couldn't be happier - for the moment anyway.

By around 2 pm the Art and Craft markets had closed and the stallholders were packing up. The beach was still packed and the king tide was living up to all expectations. The lifeys were exhausted and Starch was at the end of his tether. Jacko was doing his best to help by keeping an eye on everything when he spotted Rooster pushing a young boy in a wheelchair up to the point of the headland. As Rooster made it to the top, he parked the chair in a spot where the lad could get an uninterrupted view.

'There you go young fella, that's the Pacific Ocean', said Rooster.

The young boy just looked and said nothing. After a minute or so Rooster asked.

'Well, what do you think?'

'It's just so big', answered the lad.

The two of them stood there silently for a moment, then Rooster replied.

'Yeah, it is. I never thought of it like that… Let's go get our heads wet'.

The boy was very excited but seemingly overwhelmed by the volume of water. He knew he was seeing just a small part of it, and tried to fathom the enormity of the whole ocean.

Rooster wheeled him down to the club and transferred him into a wheelchair the members had built to go over the soft sand. When the boy saw the chair and sat in it, he exclaimed excitedly: 'Woooo, tractor chair! Unreal'. Rooster pushed him over 100 meters of beach, to the water. The patrol, Starch and Jack looked baffled.

'What flavour was that milkshake, Jack'. Muttered Starch.

There were two elderly people with Rooster and the boy, who found the soft sand tough going - so the little group took their time. Rooster pushed the chair to the edge of the water then lifted the boy up and carried him into the surf.

'You alright', he yelled as he walked backwards through the shallow sets of surf. Once he got between the waves he squatted down for a few seconds in the calmer water.

'Climb on my back and just hang on with your arms around my neck. When I yell, take a deep breath and hang on tight'. Rooster's voice was reassuring.

The lad hung on and excitedly yelled back: 'Ok, it's incredible! It has so much power'.

Rooster swam around body surfing and duck diving under the waves while the elderly couple stood smiling and watching the pair enjoying themselves. The young boy laughed and yelled with excitement as Rooster dived under wave after wave after wave, then swam out the back and body surfed back in. After about 20-30 minutes, Rooster decided to give the young fellow a break, considering he was sure the boy had swallowed half the Pacific Ocean. He carried the lad back up the sand and placed him back into the special wheelchair. He pushed the chair back up to the patrol tent and parked it next to his chair, and announced:

'Everybody, this is Michael Hadfield from Thargomindah out the back of Bourke, and this is the first time in his life he has been to the coast - and these two beautiful people are Micheal's grandparents'.

The lifeys, Starch and Jack just stood there and stared for a moment with their mouths open, then all at once moved towards young Michael to shake his hand and introduce themselves. Jack was first to shake hands and start asking questions. There was a lot of enthusiasm and the patrol positioned themselves on each side of him chatting non-stop. Starch stood there quietly listening and was mystified as to how the notorious and totally unreliable Rooster fitted into all this. He eventually walked over to Michael and introduced himself, had a brief talk and joke then went to talk to his grandparents.

'Gidday, my name's John, I'm the club president. Thanks for coming along to the beach. That certainly made our day a bit special', said Starch.

Both grandparents smiled and Starch could feel the warmth and sincerity in them. They were country people alright.

'Oh, thanks John, we didn't expect this much attention. I think Micheal might be a bit overwhelmed by it all, but in a good way - everybody is so accommodating and friendly. No wonder Rooster speaks so highly of the place'. Said the grandfather whose name was also John.

'Well, that's good to hear. He's been around here a long time and knows just about everybody', smiled Starch.

'Oh, he sure does. He tells everybody this is the greatest place on earth", replied grandfather John while grandmother Hadfield added: "And you're the greatest champion that ever walked planet earth'.

'Oh I'm not sure about that', said Starch, feeling embarrassed.

'Well, I think he's pretty close. I've been a Saints supporter for 50 years and I remember this player called John 'Starch' Lawless. Toughest forward I've ever seen. Break a man in half. The most feared player on the planet. That's you, isn't it?' Asked Grandpa John.

'Well I did play for St George for a while, but I took every bit as much as I gave, and I think I got cut in half every weekend. Did they give you life membership?' Asked Starch.

'Yes, he was given life membership at 40years and they gave us a beautiful dinner at 50 years membership', answered Mrs Hadfield.

'That's really good to hear. Do you mind if I ask how you know Rooster', probed Starch.

Grandpa John gave a smile and replied: "Well we have a family farm just out of Thargomindah that my son and his wife now run. I met Rooster on an online chat group that was set up for drought affected farmers. Rooster is good company for the farmers and loves a yarn so I asked him if there was much water where he was? "Much water!" he said. "I've got a whole bloody ocean, trouble is you can't drink it!" He's one in a million, young Rooster, that's for sure'.

'Yep, I would agree with that one hundred percent', said Starch with a grin. 'Are you just up for a holiday?'

'No, we couldn't afford a holiday, we're only on a pension and the drought has been going on for four years now so the family is just getting through from day to day - it's taken everything we had. When Rooster heard that Michael had never seen the ocean, he used all his savings to buy us plane tickets and paid for a week's accommodation across the road. He gave us a month's notice and said the tickets were non-refundable, so we had to come or he'd lose the money. It was such a kind thing to do, it was overwhelming. We still can't believe it. On the other hand, I've never seen Michael so excited. Rooster never told us he was a lifesaver so that's another surprise', Related Grandpa John.

Starch stood there silent for a minute. He was having one of those moments when you learn about the little things that are a part of a person's character, you never would have thought existed. He had been thrown another Rooster curveball.

'Well, that's a very generous and extraordinarily kind thing to do. It's a busy day so I'd better get going. It's been great to meet you both and great to find out about the footy club. Let's catch up again before you go back', said Starch.

'Oh yeah, for sure. It was a pleasure to meet you. I just wish I would have bought some of my Saints stuff for you to sign,' replied grandpa John.

'No problem, we have plenty of time', said Starch as he walked off. Jackson and Michael were having a huge conversation so Starch didn't interrupt them and continued up to the clubhouse by himself.

Towards the end of the afternoon, the beach crowds began to thin out with mainly people from overseas and the southern states arriving who preferred the much gentler afternoon sun exposure. Young Michael and his grandparents were feeling exhausted so Rooster walked them back to their holiday unit across the road, and organised a dinner for around 7pm. After that he headed back to continue the day's patrol. The lifeys were still pretty busy with people drifting out of the flagged area and sometimes needing to be rescued, but everything was under control.

Rooster settled back into his chair and true to his word he was going to stay with the patrol until the end of the day. Within ten minutes the rumble of his snoring had alerted the other lifeys. They quietly discussed how a human being could switch off so quickly, but they rationalised he was probably partly asleep all the time.

Suddenly, Rooster stopped snoring, his eyes flashed open as he stood bolt upright. The lifeys were puzzled and thought he must have had a daymare, but Rooster had been on the beach a long time and his intuition was second to none. The superbank had gone flat as the boardriders floated listlessly waiting for a wave to build, the outgoing water on the beach had gone a long way out and was still going. The swimmers and people on the beach hadn't noticed it, and children, young toddlers and their parents were just standing on the wet sand expecting another remnant of a wave to wash up.

Rooster screamed at the top of his lungs: 'RUNNNN. RUN, GET OUT'.

Everyone stood there perplexed and didn't move. Jodie looked at the surf thinking he must have seen a shark but then noticed the rapidly receding water. Everything seemed to be very still.

'Oh no!' She said to the patrol, then yelled: 'Quickly! Get them out of the water'.

Rooster ran across the sand yelling at people to get out, to pick up their children and run. Starch was on his way back down the beach when he saw him running and yelling. He studied things more closely then had an awful feeling in his stomach. He started to run and yell:

'Get them out, get them out'.

The water looked to have gone out about a hundred metres more than usual, but it had turned and a block of foaming water or wave about one and a half metres high was on its way back in. Behind the first wave, there were other bigger waves building and rolling toward them. The lifeys scrambled shouting at people, grabbing their children and ordering them to run. Jackson was thinking quickly and grabbed the alarm and kept blasting the siren whilst pointing and motioning people to get up the beach. By this time everyone had seen the wall of water coming toward them and panic had set in. People started to run, but some had multiple children and were moving too slow to escape the approaching wave. Astonishingly, there were still other people who just stood there wondering what all the fuss was about - they were the first to get smashed and were splattered like ten pins.

Although there were swimmers getting washed up the beach the lifeys were able to grab them and drag them up further. Everyone knew the danger would be in the outgoing water and a rip would form quickly. The inflatable and jet ski started to drift up the beach, along with the tent, the beach umbrellas, eskies, towels and everything else that would float. The kiosk staff and people upstairs at the clubhouse saw what was happening and raced down to help. It was a huge amount of water and it kept coming. The lifesavers never panicked but Starch knew they were in trouble so he put out a call for help to Coolangatta, Greenmount and Kirra who responded immediately. He then gave a distress call to the rescue chopper:

'Rainbows End patrol to chopper. Urgent. Come in over', blasted Starch.

'Chopper to Rainbows End. We heard your previous communication, what's happening there? Over', said the familiar voice of Rotors.

'We've had some kind of freak wave that's about one hundred and fifty metres across and a face height of one to two metres that's come out of nowhere. There is a huge body of water behind it that has gone up the beach about eighty metres taking out everything. It's beginning to suck out whilst there are other waves building. We have people stuck in the surf we are trying to reach, we request urgent assistance. Repeat, urgent', beseeched Starch.

'Struth! On our way', replied Rotors.

As the wave reached its peak the water seemed to pause for a few seconds then suck back out again. There were too many people to save all at once so the lifeys grabbed the weaker swimmers first and got them to shallow water. The other clubs started to arrive in inflatable rescue craft and jet skis. They were stunned at what was happening. The boardriders who had seen what was happening were also paddling over to save people who were being dragged out. The undercurrent was too strong for the average person once they lost traction and the situation grew worse as the waves kept coming. Jackson was able to get the jet ski started, but Shannon was unaware Jack could drive it, so he told him to hop on the back with a couple of life jackets and a rescue board. The waves coming in were unusually dirty and this made it difficult to work in, but they did their best to get as many people as they could up to the dry beach. The scene was one of complete anarchy. None of them had seen anything like this before and it had taken them by complete surprise with everyone wondering, 'what happened'.

There were just too many people to save with more getting drawn out the back. The chopper, the inflatables and the boardriders, who were coming across in droves from the point to help, were doing their best to get to them. Up on the dry sand it was like a field hospital with children crying and the odd swimmer throwing up, but most were just exhausted and thankful to be on dry sand.

About half way out through the wash there was an Asian family. The man and his wife had three children, a little girl and twin boys that were all toddlers. The dad had the twin boys in his arms and his wife had hold of their daughter. They were just hanging on in water slightly above waist level. In between the waves the water was a bit shallower and even though they had to battle the outgoing undercurrent, they had made good progress toward the dry beach. It looked like they would make it, but with their backs turned toward the surf a big wave caught them by surprise. They were both knocked off their feet and sent tumbling through the surf. All three toddlers were lost from their arms.

Jackson had spotted what happened and yelled at Shannon to get to them. The father who was now standing in chest-deep water was distraught and yelling for his children as he kept his wife's head above the water. Jackson was standing up on the back of the ski and spotted a patch of black hair. He pointed Shannon in the right direction and with only a few seconds to spare, Jack dived into the surf where he had seen the black hair. The toddler was about a foot under the water trying to come up for air when Jack grabbed an arm and pulled what was one of the boys to the surface. Shannon reached down and dragged him up onto the ski, as Jack spotted another patch of black hair about five metres away. He quickly got to the second child which was the little girl, just in time. She was too exhausted to stay afloat so Shannon reached down and dragged her up on the ski as quickly as he could. The father was still screaming for the second boy while he tried to keep his wife's head above the water. Jack stood up as high as he could on the back of the ski. He spotted the second twin about twenty metres away getting sucked out in the rip. He pointed for Shannon and yelled: 'THERE'.

With the two toddlers on his lap, Shannon maneuvered the jet ski through the surf to where Jack had pointed. The boy had gone under, and the water was too dirty to see him clearly, but Jack spotted a patch of black for a split second and dived in. He couldn't find the boy, so he went under again but still couldn't find him. He came to the surface, took a deep breath then went down again with his hands out in front of him, trying to feel for anything. He touched something like seaweed and grabbed a bunch of it then swam to the surface - if it was seaweed he had, it was heavy. He got to the surface and took a much-needed breath of air, then, as he looked at his hand he felt relief - he had the second twin but he was barely clinging to life. Shannon grabbed hold of the toddler and yanked him out of the water and onto his lap with the other two. As he pulled the boy's arm up he suddenly spewed out a heap of water and coughed, then started to breathe, this was a good sign. Shannon yelled at Jack to get on the ski or the rescue board being towed by the ski, but Jac said "no" and pointed to the parents who were in real danger.

'Get them on the ski, quick. I'll be okay, I'll get a wave in. It's Ok. Just get going before a wave comes', shouted Jack.

'No. Get on the back. It's too dangerous', Shannon shouted back.

'No, just get going. I'm not getting on. Get the parents'. Yelled Jack, and he started to catch a wave into the beach.

Shannon made it to the parents and yelled at them to get on the board at the back of the ski. When they had pulled themselves on he headed to the beach in conditions that were akin to rogue waves on steroids.

The parents were too physically depleted to stand upright, and the father wept with relief. Shannon, Danny and Bean worked on the toddlers to expel any water out of their lungs. They were shaking but breathing. A couple of paramedics took over and the whole family were taken to hospital where the toddlers were kept in for observation overnight.

The treacherous conditions continued for about another twenty minutes, although it felt like an eternity. Then things slowly evened out. The four patrol crews were still kept busy treating swimmers on the beach. There were neck injuries, back injuries, cuts, abrasions, people throwing up. Eventually, everyone recovered and made their way off the beach. The lifeys stood in a bunch and hypothesised on what had happened. Rooster was adamant the tectonic plates had shifted and caused a mini tsunami, but this was met with a chorus of "Nah". Looking at the surf they were at a loss for an explanation. Starch was quietly watching the surf when one of the lifeys asked: 'What are you thinking, Starch?'

'Tell me what you think about the wave on the superbank', Starch replied.

The lifeys and people that were standing close by heard what Starch had said and watched the Superbank for a couple of minutes.

'Well, I'll be stuffed', said Rooster.

Jodie quipped in, "What's going on there? What happened to the wave? You don't suppose?"

'We don't know yet what happened, but I'd like to take a look under the water at the so-called superbank and see just how stable it is'. Replied Starch.

'Do you think the sand bank could have collapsed?' Asked Shannon.

'We don't know without getting an image or having a look but it's too dirty at the moment. What we do know is, there has been a lot of fresh water from the rain in the hinterland going out. There is a king tide and there is very big surf because of the cyclone up north. There was a big swell on the points and superbank when we got here this morning, but there is no break at all on the superbank now - although the points are still raging'. Answered Starch.

'Well I'll be stuffed'. Blurted Rooster, again.

'That sand built up very quickly and that could have been the problem. We're lucky we didn't lose anybody', reasoned Starch.

One of the penguins named Monty, who was in his 80's and had served around the club for most of it, was standing beside Starch and nodded his head in agreement.

'I think you're right. The bank collapsed then the water sucked out. There was no warning about the size of the wave coming in when the bank broke. It was a disaster waiting to happen, and you don't have to be a scientist to work that out. That bank's as flat as a maggot now, look at it!' The lifeys agreed with Monty's assessment of Starch's theory, but it begged the question: What happens now?

The TV news crews had started to arrive and were eager to talk to anyone who witnessed or was part of what happened. Starch avoided talking to them because of the politics surrounding the dredging and related sand build up on the bank. Rooster, however, was first to be interviewed and gave a riveting account of what had happened. He relished the moment of being broadcast across the nation as he stood in his nylon DT's and tradesman suntan, speaking very confidently which was reminiscent of a popular world leader. The News crews lapped it up and the interview made national news that night. Out the back of Bourke at Thargomindah the locals recognised the name of Rooster, and the place of Rainbows End Beach. Rooster was quickly written into folklore and acquired living legend status. "That bloke from the coast ought to be the bloody Prime Minister", was proclaimed far and wide through the pubs and clubs of the bush.

Starch went round and personally shook everyone's hand that had helped with the rescue and treatment of those affected. There were the Greenmount, Cooly and Kirra lifeys that reacted immediately, the boardriders and everyone in the club and kiosk, the penguins, the boat crew (who were lifeys anyway), and the people on the beach who rushed to help. He then phoned Rotors, Stitches and Gills (the chopper rescue swimmer), who were the chopper crew and thanked them. Even Danny received a pat on the back, which had Grizz's eyeballs rolling.

After everything had settled down Starch decided he just wanted to go home to his family so he asked the crew upstairs to lock up when they closed. As he finished packing up, his phone was still being bombarded with messages. Robyn needed to talk to him the next day, Molly Baxter, the journalist needed to see him, Flowers the politician wanted him to call. Hordes of media outlets were trying to contact him, and Colmie wanted to catch up, first thing. Starch was dog-tired, worn out and at a loss as to what to do next. Did the superbank collapse, endangering all those people, some of whom were still in the hospital? Where does he go from here?

Just as he closed the door to the office his phone rang yet again. Even though he knew he'd probably regret answering it, he pressed the answer button.

'Hello', was his cautious response.

'Hi Starch, sorry to bother you but it's Suzanne Gave. Jackson's mum. Is Jacky still there? He isn't home yet and he has never done this, he always calls me', related Suzanne.

'Hi, Suzanne. No, he's not here but give me a minute and I'll check the storage room and see if his bike is still here. Just give me a minute and don't hang up', replied Starch.

Jack's bike was still there.

'Hello Suzanne', said Starch.

'Yes, still here', replied Suzanne.

'Yeah, his bike is here but he might be across the road with a young boy and his family from the country he met today, or he could be up at the Dive Shop. Do you want me to check?' Asked Starch.

'I've already phoned Andrew and he's not there, but I'd appreciate you checking across the road please'. Continued Suzanne.

'Ok, I'll do it straight away, then I'll phone you back'.

Starch went through his phone for Rooster's number and decided to call him to find out the unit number the family were staying in.

'Hello', came the croaky voice of Rooster.

'Rooster, it's Starch here mate. I'm trying to find out where Jackson is. His mother's looking for him', said Starch.

'Dunno mate. Last time I saw him, he was on the beach when all the drama happened. There's nothing wrong, is there?' Asked Rooster.

'No, not yet. I thought he might be with the family from the bush. He struck a chord with them', replied Starch.

'Nah mate, we're all at the club on the verandah, just finishing dinner. Mate, do you want a hand to look for him?' Asked Rooster.

'Well at the moment I don't know where to look. He just doesn't do this. I'll try ringing the patrol to see if they know anything. I'll ring you back', said Starch.

'Ok, thanks mate. I appreciate that'. Replied Rooster.

He went through all the lifeys that were on duty that day and started calling them one by one. He had called eight of them and no one had seen Jack since the afternoon turmoil. His next call on the list was Shannon.

'How ya goin Shannon, it's Starch here. I'm trying to find Jacko, his mother's looking for him. You don't know where he is, do you? Did he say he was going somewhere or something?' Asked Starch.

'Hi Starch. No, he didn't mention anything to me. The last time I saw him, he was on a wave heading for the beach'. Answered Shannon.

'When was that? Did you see him on the beach?' Asked Starch.

'No. He was on the back of the Jet Ski and rescued an Asian family. He did it all by himself. Three kids. Then he insisted on me getting the parents with the ski and he caught a wave in. That was the last time I spotted him. He looked okay. Like, he wasn't struggling or anything and he was on a good wave', recounted Shannon.

'But you never saw him make the beach?' Quizzed Starch.

'No. I had the three kids and their parents who were in all sorts of trouble. Then someone else took over on the ski. You don't think anything happened to him, do you?' Asked Shannon.

'Well I can't find him and you know what he's like with his mother. He'd never, ever, not let her know where he is', replied Starch.

'Okay, okay. I'm getting the message. What can I do? I need to help find him'. Implored Shannon, as he felt the anxiety rise.

'Phone everyone. Try to find anyone that saw him after you did, then call me straight away'. Said Starch, and the call ended.

He sat there quietly for a minute or two trying to decide what to do. He decided the path of honesty was his only route, and so he rang Suzanne.

'Hello Starch, did you find Jacky?' Was the question Starch wasn't looking forward to, but he replied:

'No sorry, I haven't been able to find him yet but I've got help phoning around. The last person to see him was Shannon, which was in the afternoon during the rescues on the beach. He told me that Jack was on the back of the Jet Ski and rescued three children, then insisted Shannon keep going on the ski to pick up the parents, who were rapidly going under. He last saw Jackson on a wave heading into the beach and there was no sign of trouble, but I cannot find anyone who can remember seeing him on the beach afterwards'. Explained Starch, trying to be calm.

'Oh dear, that definitely isn't Jackson. I'm really worried about him, Starch. What can we do?' Asked Suzanne.

'Well, like you I'm beginning to worry. I'm going to call the police straight away and let them know what's happened'. Replied Starch.

'Okay, I'm going to wait here in case he does come home. Can you please, please keep letting me know what is happening'. Said Suzanne.

'Definitely, I'll call the police now. If he comes home, phone me. Talk soon'.

He still had Senior Constable Kelly Follent's phone number on a card, so he decided to ring that number.

'Hello, Coolangatta police, Senior Constable Follent speaking. How can I help you?' Said the voice on the phone.

'Oh gidday. My name is John Lawless, I'm the president of Rainbows End Surf Lifesaving Club. We've met before when a drunk left his clothes on the beach after his girlfriend dumped him', said Starch.

'Oh yes, Starch. What's going on? Everyone's talking about the surf or mini tsunami that happened this afternoon. Is everything alright?' Asked Kelly.

'Well, sort of. We didn't lose anyone in the surf but there's a junior club member who is unaccounted for this evening. His name is Jackson Gave', said Starch.

'Jackson Gave. I remember him. His father was hit and killed by a drunk driver a few years ago. I'll never forget it. They were a beautiful little family and he's a really nice kid. So when was he last seen?' Asked Kelly.

'He was last seen during the freak event this afternoon. He was on a wave heading back into the beach after he had rescued three toddlers. He wasn't injured in any way and didn't look to be in any trouble, but no one can remember seeing him on the beach or anywhere afterwards. His mother contacted me just before because he hasn't come home, which he has never done', related Starch.

'Start looking,' said Kelly.

'Where?' Asked Starch.

'Where he was last seen. I'm putting this in the system now', said Kelly.

'What? Do you think we should look in the surf?' Said Starch.

'Wherever it's possible. He could have washed up. Best case scenario is, he's sitting on a rock somewhere injured or unable to climb or get up. If that's the case, time is critical', warned Kelly.

'Okay, I'm on it. Can you give me a ring if anything happens?' Asked Starch.

'Yes of course. I've notified the police chopper. They have powerful lighting and heat sensors. They'll be there shortly. We'll come down and have a look in a couple of minutes. I'll see you then', said Kelly and hung up.

Starch phoned Suzanne and gave her an update, then phoned Rooster and Shannon and gave them the task of alerting club members. Everyone they phoned, including the Penguins, turned up at the club with a torch of some description. There were also the families and friends of the clubbies. The ladies boat crew were all there. Adrian, Brian and Benny from the kitchen, along with Bean, Moey, Jules, Matthew, Tommy Green, Mel, Danny, Grizz, and Simmo. Some of the boardriders found out what was going on and joined in. Constable Kelly

Follent and some other cops arrived and started to search and organise everyone. The copper chopper swept up and down the coastline looking for anything that could help the search.

By midnight, there were flashlights all over the points and beaches within five kilometres of Rainbows End. Some of the Kirra, Cooly and Greenmount clubbies had got out of bed when they heard what was happening and joined in the search. The Penguins had formed a line across the sand into the high water mark and walked up and down, searching for any clue of what could have happened to Jack.

About 4.30 am people were still searching, nobody had gone home, so the cops called a meeting and announced that the police chopper had not found anything. One of the problems was the very dirty wash from the floods in the hinterland, hampering vision. There was also a lot of debris floating around, which made the search more difficult. The surf rescue chopper was going to start sweeping the coastline at first light. Seeing as there had been no other information presented and Jackson had still not been located - it was more than likely he had met with an accident in the surf around the time he was last seen. It could not be assumed whether he was still alive or deceased. That was a very sobering police announcement.

The police advised everyone to have a break and an organised search would start again in daylight hours. Everyone felt gutted. Simmo and Starch stood there silently. Neither of them had any intention of resting. Andrew Coleman walked up behind Starch and put his hand on his shoulder.

'What are we going to do boys? We know we're not going home until we find him', said Andrew".

'Well, we'd all better get our noses in the air and keep searching', said a voice in the darkness. It was Rooster.

At first light the TV media choppers were in the area above Rainbows End Beach, the story was headline news and Starch's phone was in overload with missed calls. The reason behind the freak incident had experts from all over the country with an expert opinion. But now the disappearance and possible drowning of Jackson had added to the controversy of the Superbank, and the associated Tweed River Bar.

Colmie had decided the most effective way for him to search would be to use the dive boat and start working out in deeper water, while

Simmo used the inflatable to look closer in. Starch continued to search the headland with Rooster, who intermittently checked in with young Michael Hadfield and his grandparents. Jackson's mother had spent the longest night of her life, sitting in a chair beside her front door, waiting for Jackson to come home. She could not wait any longer so she left a large note on the front door and decided to go to where Jackson was last seen. The note on the front door read: "Jacky if you come home please ring me. Love you, Mum." For friends that came around to visit and support Suzanne, the note was heartbreaking.

Suzanne phoned ahead and told Starch she was on her way to the club, so he made his way through the car park to meet her. Jackson's school friends had turned up at the beach and were standing and sitting on the sand, they weren't saying much but their faces told how they felt. Other locals started turning up, some of them knew Jack and some didn't. Water Town was a close-knit community and if someone goes missing in the surf or elsewhere, they all feel it.

Starch met Suzanne in the carpark and explained the search situation, then they went to the temporary police control centre in the club house. The cops explained what they were doing and the reasons behind their decisions - she listened quietly and thanked everybody for their concern. Outside, the hearts were heavy amongst the searchers, Jackson did not have a life jacket, he was an asthmatic, and he had no protection at all against the conditions. If he was in the water, it is unlikely he would have survived the night. The developing cyclone up north meant the sea was still very rough and the search boats were being tossed about like corks, making any search activity extremely difficult.

Suzanne excused herself and asked if it would be okay to sit on the rocks at the base of the headland where it met the beach. She would be in plain sight of everyone and could easily be reached if needed. Starch tried to comfort her and asked if he could get her anything but she was neither hungry nor thirsty, so he sat with her for a while until some of the ladies from the club found her. He made his way back to the clubhouse where there was nothing more he could do other than wait and hope. The overwhelming feeling around the club was one of shock, disbelief and denial. How could this happen? Why? Everyone was falsely optimistic about finding Jack, because thinking about any other outcome was so soul-destroying it was unbearable.

Robyn turned up at the club to let Starch know that she had put everything on hold as far as chasing Flowers was concerned. Molly Baxter had weighed into the fight by asking him some very probing questions, so Flowers was not taking calls about the bar and had reportedly left town on a fact-finding mission overseas. Robyn was in the same frame of mind as everyone else concerning Jackson - shocked and inundated with disbelief. In less than 24 hours, everyone's world had been turned upside down and despite all their effort, it was getting worse every second.

Bean and Matty were in the kiosk supplying food to the cops and volunteer search and rescue people. There was no charge, Bean would not accept any money. The usual playful banter that was common around the kiosk had gone and both he and Matty spoke very little. Danny came and went without uttering a word. Grizz was the same. Bull walked past the kiosk window and nodded his head, then kept going down to the headland to help search. The constant sweeping of helicopters and light planes further out to sea amounted to nothing, but still, the search team remained optimistic. The constant searching in and around the headland amounted to nothing, but still, the search teams remained optimistic. Colmie, Starch and the Penguins studied the tidal flow trying to predict the most probable location Jack could be found, but the Superbank or dredging had changed things a lot. It was pretty well accepted by now, the cause of the freak surf condition was the result of the sand bank collapsing. It was confirmed by the absence of waves on the Superbank, or the Blooperbank, as the locals were calling it.

The volunteers and professionals kept looking until the daylight had gone. Then the cops announced the search would continue at first light the following morning, and urged everybody to stay positive. But, once again it was going to be a very long night. Suzanne remained sitting on the same rock until there was total darkness, then Heidi and Marie from the boat crew convinced her to let them stay with her overnight. Suzanne's family were scattered around the world and had phoned every hour for updates. Starch never went home at the end of his working day. He put his head on the office desk and fell asleep. He had been awake for two days. Downstairs in the storage shed Rooster had gone to sleep in the surf boat, and like Starch, he was running on empty.

The next morning everyone turned up again to search. There was still an air of hope amongst the searchers and as soon as they had reasonable vision, they were at it again. Up and down, up and down, rocks and sand. The surf rescue and police helicopters flew high and low, up and down looking for any sign of Jack. Colmie once again scoured the water about a kilometre offshore, while Simmo used the inflatable and searched beyond the break. Suzanne once again walked up to the club and met with police who shielded her from the media. The ladies from the surf club and parents of Jack's friends once again came down and sat beside her on the same rock. The mood was still hopeful despite the chances of finding Jack alive were diminishing by the hour.

Day two was a repeat of day one - nothing upon nothing. At the end of the daylight, the police called a meeting before addressing the media. The cop in charge spoke very solemnly and respectful. Jackson was known to him and he had been through this once before with the loss of Jack's father. The big cop wasn't a religious man but he had been saying a mountain of silent prayers, pleading for help to find this young fellow alive. He called the group of searchers together for a talk, away from the media.

'I want to thank all of you for what you are doing. We all have a connection to Jackson and we are all feeling the same way. Tonight will be the third night he's spent out there and tomorrow will be the third day. The chances of finding him alive are becoming more remote every day, so we'd better start preparing ourselves for the news we don't want. I'm sorry that I don't have anything better to tell you. The chopper crews and boats have covered every centimetre of the search area, time and time again. They have inspected every bit of floating debris out there, with no luck. At first light tomorrow we'll do it all again. Thanks, everybody. Starch, do you want to say anything?' Said the big cop.

'No thanks mate, you've covered everything, and big thanks to you and your team for what you are doing'. Replied Starch, who was only just holding himself together.

Three of Jackson's school friends' parents stayed with Suzanne that night - she had not eaten since Jack had gone missing. Starch slept with his head on the office desk, Colmie fell asleep in an office chair and Rooster slept in the surf boat.

The sun came up for the third day and the searchers turned up again, although the optimism was giving way to grief. The faces were becoming drawn and the talk was quiet and subdued. But still, they searched up and down, up and down, over rocks and sand hoping upon hope to find Jackson alive. Suzanne arrived at daybreak and went again to her rock and sat quietly looking out to sea. Friends came at once and sat beside her hoping to give her some support, but by now her grief had set in. There wasn't anything anyone could say or do that would ease the dull ache she felt inside. Every hour her family would ring from somewhere around the world, and every hour she would relay the same message. All of her immediate family had booked flights to Australia and were leaving the following day.

Starch, Colmie and Rooster picked up a coffee each from the kiosk. Matty had opened early to give Bean a break. Nobody said much, they just sipped their coffee and looked out to sea. Simmo arrived, ordered a coffee and joined them standing there silently, trying to come to terms with the situation.

'Okay, let's do it again', said Rooster.

And so without saying a word they all went about the search with everybody else. The chopper crews had extended their search radius a further thirty kilometres down the NSW coastline and north to Stradbroke Island, in Queensland. The surf club was virtually empty, all the members were either working or involved in the search. The clubbies from Kirra, Cooly and Greenmount had stayed committed, with many of them taking holiday leave from work.

Suzanne sat silently on her rock, not saying too much and surrounded by people who had by now, run out of things to say. It was a horrible situation, despite all the prayers, positive affirmations, hopeful positive attitudes and everything else offered up - there was no change in the situation. The tragedy was beginning to cast a cloud of dismay over all of them, the tears among the searchers were beginning to show and the feeling of helplessness was now permeating all of them. At the end of the day, it was another brief talk by the cops and then a media update. It was the worst of news and a story the journos were getting emotionally drawn into. There was nothing good about it. If he was alive he would be in agony if he had already passed away, the thought of Jackson's body floating in the sea was simply too much to bear. It was a soul searching moment and coming to grips with what had happened was near impossible. The club and the people would never be the same again.

That night Starch fell asleep on his desk, Colmie fell asleep in the office chair and Rooster slept in the surf boat. Suzanne left her rock late into the night and the ladies boat crew, Jack's school teacher and some friends all spent the night at her place. It was the fourth night Jackson would have spent in the water.

It was first light on the fourth day and although the police and Air Sea Rescue didn't mention it, they were now looking for a body. Starch, Simmo, Rooster, Colmie, all of the Penguins and some club members from neighbouring SLS clubs, mingled on the beach. Brian and Benny were spotted around the base of the headland, they had been there searching all night. Mel was aware of it and slept in her car in the club carpark.

When is the time to accept death? Do we hang on forever hoping, or do we simply accept the death of our loved ones, as it will eventually befall all of us? How do you love someone that is no more? How do you reconcile a tragedy that is so wrong on all levels? How do the realms of divinity explain the death of someone loved by so many people? A death that was so unfair. There were thousands of questions but no answers, just overwhelming heartbreak and grief. The men remained stoic on the surface but underneath they were totally gutted. The women had nothing they could say or do to ease the pain of a mother that was too heartbroken to say more than a few words at a time.

Suzanne came down to the beach and sat on her rock - she was simply dressed and as elegant as ever. Her eyes were blackened from lack of sleep, though her manner never changed. She had not eaten but sipped the occasional water. As she sat on the rock a Samoan lady and two young Samoan girls, who looked very lean and fit, came up and hugged her. Suzanne started to cry. The Samoan lady and children were Starch's wife and daughters. They had been in Samoa visiting family when Starch told them what had happened. They came straight back.

Starch's wife was his inner strength and his life's greatest treasure, her name was 'Talia', which is a Samoan name meaning 'to wait'. The girls' names were Natia, which by itself means "hidden" as in a secret, and Manala which means "nice, good or beautiful". The girls were club nippers and both loved being around the water. Like everybody else, they were close to Jackson. Talia, like many Samoans, had a deep Christian faith and although she was a quiet, humble lady, Suzanne always felt a confident calmness when they were together. Talia sat on one side of Suzanne and held her hand and the girls sat on the other side. There was minimal talk between them, just a resolute kind of silence. The big cop knew where they were sitting on the rock and continued to shield them from the media.

The monotony and disappointment of the unrewarded effort had started to take a negative toll upon everybody. The choppers, boats and land crews were relentless in their quest to find Jack, but their quest was in vain. There was absolutely no trace of Rainbows End's favourite son. It had all happened so quickly, it was only now that reality was beginning to sink in. All of the rescuers on the beach the day Jack was taken, had the thought of "I should have seen it, I should have been there, I should have done more." Everybody pondered the pain and fear he must have felt in the water. It was all so unfair for a kid that had never wronged anybody. A young gentleman who was dealing with life's harshest cards then had his own life taken from him in such a violent and unforgiving way.

Amongst the grief and overwhelming sadness the locals were feeling, there was a quiet anger building. Many people wanted answers, in particular to the bar dredging and subsequent developing Superbank. Was it to blame for the freak surf conditions that day? The unofficial summation was "yes", but the rising levels of anger needed to know who was responsible. Starch, Colmie and the big cop kept the lid on things, and focused everybody's attention on the search, and support for Suzanne.

At the end of the day, the big cop called the search crews together and gave his usual pre-media address.

'Hello everybody and once again thanks for your unconditional support. This is not an easy moment and there is no easy way to say this, but please bear with me. It's now been four days and this will be the fifth night and we have found nothing. Tomorrow the search will be expanded again, there will be police and SES four-wheel drives constantly on the beaches in northern NSW and north to Stradbroke

Island. Police divers have searched the rock wall at the bottom of the headland, but so far have found nothing. It is not easy to say this, but the chances of finding him alive are slim to zero. We will not be officially conducting a land search tomorrow on the headland or local beach, but if you decide you want to keep looking, then that is entirely up to you. As I said the search will now focus mainly on the tidal flow and probably places of landing. I have been told by Jackson's mother that she is overwhelmed by the love shown toward her son, and although she can never repay you, she will always remember you. Well it's going to be another long night, but I'll be here in the morning so if need be, we can talk then. Thank you'.

The volunteers had their heads down. The big cop only stated the obvious. The sense of denial and unacceptance of the situation was slowly being eroded by the brutality of the real situation. The searchers slowly made their way home, the choppers made their final sweep, the search boats headed back in. Up on the headland sat an Asian man, who had been sitting there on and off for a couple of days. Each day he sat there until last light with his face resting in his hands. It was the father of the toddlers Jackson had saved. It was Jackson who insisted on Shannon going to save the man and his wife on the ski, with the toddlers on board. The man saw what happened and knew he and his family would have drowned that day if not for Jackson. His children had been released from the hospital and he had been coming to the headland to watch the search. He was a good man and a very loving father and husband. No one had noticed him sitting on the point by himself. He was extremely distraught and living his own hell, blaming himself for a large part of what happened.

The sun finally set on the fourth day and the stars were dotted across a dark sky. Starch went to sleep with his head on the office desk, Colmie fell asleep in the office chair and Rooster slept in the surf boat.

The following morning Starch, Colmie and Rooster were up and about before dawn, Starch made some coffees in the club kitchen, then the three of them walked down to the beach.

The mood was as sombre as the day before and each of them was battling the sadness they were all feeling. They were all bracing themselves for the acceptance of what they knew was the reality. Jackson had now been missing five nights and four days in rough seas. The thought of finding his lifeless body was horrific. There was a notion among the searchers that finding his body would help bring closure but the three of them knew through experience, the loss of a loved one doesn't have closure - one just learns to live with the loss, if that's possible. For some, it is not.

As they stood on the sand in the dark, the sun started to come up over the ocean. On the rock Suzanne had been sitting appeared a dark silhouette of four people, two adults and two children. It was Suzanne with Starch's wife Talia, and his two daughters Natia and Manala, sitting each side of her, they had been there all night huddled together. The three men didn't say anything but quietly walked toward them without startling them.

'Can I get you coffees and hot chocolates', said Colmie.

'Thank you, Andrew, that would be welcomed, and good morning Rooster. John, are you okay?', Said Talia.

Natia and Manala turned to see their father and immediately jumped up and hugged him.

'Allgood darls. Suzanne, can we get you something from the kitchen?" Asked Starch, as his two daughters hugged him from both sides.

'I'm okay at the moment thanks Starch, but thank you for asking. Talia and the girls have been more than wonderful to me'. Replied Suzanne.

Rooster looked up to the rocks, above where the girls were sitting. There were two figures sitting up on the face of the headland. It was Benny and Brian. They had been there all night watching over them. At the same time, Mel came walking down the beach, she had once again slept in the car park. Together they formed a little group around Suzanne and quietly talked about possibilities of survival they knew were near impossible.

As the sun continued to rise, all of the searchers returned. The big cop wasn't surprised and had expected it. He knew that if the day didn't produce anything, then the afternoon's talk was something he was not looking forward to. A police officer's life sometimes involves delivering the worst of news to families about a loved one. To the big cop, this was one of those times and he did not know whether he could do it without breaking down. The searchers wandered around for most of the day, hoping for a miracle. The four-wheel drives combed the beaches, the helicopters combed the sea, Colmie and the search boats continued to search. Unbeknown to everybody, Moey had used all her savings to hire a plane over the last four days and did loop after loop after loop looking for Jack. She was now broke and had found nothing, but her thoughts were still with Jack. It was the same with everybody.

As the sun went down on the fifth day, the big cop called everybody together for one of the saddest days in Rainbows End's history. He choked out the words he always dreaded he'd have to say.

'Okay everybody, can I please have your attention for a couple of minutes. The decision has been very regretfully made to scale back the search tomorrow. After five days, and tonight will be the sixth night, we have found no trace of Jackson. The search will continue at a scaled-back level mainly through the helicopter and boats. On behalf of everybody involved, I would like to express our deepest sympathies and condolences to Mrs Gave. We are all deeply saddened by what has happened. Our prayers lay with you... On another note, while I have you here. There is a lot of anger being directed at the dredging company and associates. I am asking you to be patient and not to do anything you'll later regret. There has been an investigation started and this will cover every decision concerning every grain of sand that has been dredged by the relevant company. We have to look at the facts first. Thank you'.

The big cop then went off to face the media. Starch, Colmie and Rooster walked down the beach to where the girls were still sitting on their rock. Starch's daughters got up and hugged him, then he sat down next to Suzanne. There was silence for a moment then he softly said:

'I am so sorry'.

Suzanne turned to look at him, as the tears rolled down his cheeks. This was a very tough man that had been broken to pieces. Talia stood up and hugged him. It was clearly evident that Talia was his rock, her strength of character sustained him. Suzanne held his hand and for a minute there was silence. Colmie and Rooster broke the ice and spoke.

'We'll be back in a minute with some cups of tea and stuff', said Colmie.

'Can you young girls give us a hand', added Rooster.

The girls let go of Starch as he took a deep breath in and realised just how damaged a human being can get. Talia sat back down next to Suzanne as Starch asked:

'What's the answer, Tal'.

'Sometimes there is none, not as far as we're concerned anyway', she lamented.

On the way back up to the kiosk, Colmie, Rooster and the girls looked up to the headland to see the Asian man sitting with his family, quietly looking out to sea. They weren't familiar with the full story of the little family's involvement, so they didn't think it was anything unusual.

It was a long, long night as usual with Starch wandering around the beach, Colmie fell to sleep in the office chair, Rooster slept in the surf boat and the girls and Talia sat with Suzanne on the rock. Everybody knew that tomorrow, they would have to let go.

# Chapter 18

# Sometimes
# There is an Answer

The cyclone up north had dissipated, leaving the sea calm after five days of rough weather. About twenty kilometres off the coast, Fins Walton's trawler sat in water that was like glass. Fins knew nothing of what had happened to Jack. There was no radio or communication of any sort on the boat so Fins, Ben, Sushi, Sharkbait and the one-legged seagull were oblivious to anything that happened while they were working. Fins had four days of empty nets in a tumultuous sea, but then his luck changed. The crew worked for fourteen hours straight and his trawler was packed with a quality catch. They had finished in the early hours of the morning and decided to get a couple of hours sleep before heading back into port at first light. The boys were exhausted but in good spirits knowing they had a massive payday coming.

Sharkbait was asleep in the cabin when his eyes slowly opened. His nose gave a twitch and he slowly stood up, trotted up to the deck and gave another sniff while looking around. A flock of seagulls were hovering over a school of fish about twenty metres away, he gave a bark then put his nose down toward the water and had a big sniff. He lifted his head, looked at the seagulls and gave a whine that sounded like dog anxiety, then gave a couple of big barks. The crew were still asleep and Fins was snoring his head off, but Sharkbait kept barking.

'Shut up', groaned Fins, but Sharkbait kept barking loudly. Ben and Sushi opened their eyes and sensed something wasn't right, so they went up to investigate. The seagulls and school of baitfish were drifting closer to the boat. Fins appeared on deck to see what was going on. The sun hadn't broken the horizon, so the light was dim.

'Come on boy. He barking at seagull and baitfish,' said Ben.

'Not baitfish', replied Fins.

'How do you know?' Asked Sushi.

'Because ol' mate's still sitting on the mast'. Replied Fins, referring to the one-legged seagull.

Within minutes the gulls were hovering beside the boat.

'What is that?' Asked Ben, looking at what the seagulls were hovering around.

'Dunno. Get the bait hook', said Fins.

Sushi grabbed the bait hook and cautiously dragged the floating object closer. At first they thought it was a dead shark but then it looked like a pile of pipes and junk. The light was still dim so they were cautious. Sharkbait continued to whine anxiously. Sushi dragged the pile of pipes and junk to right beside the boat. They all leaned over for a closer look. It was just barely on the surface, but Fins could see a full face divers mask and a body floating in the junk.

'JACKSON'!! Screamed Fins and jumped overboard. Ben and Sushi screamed something in Japanese and followed him over the side.

'Get his head up', yelled Fins with his mind going a million miles an hour.

'Is he alive?' Yelled Ben.

'Can't tell', yelled back fins.

Sushi climbed back on the boat and grabbed a couple of ropes.

'Wrap around junk', yelled Sushi.

'No', yelled Fins. 'Get him out of it'

'Listen to me, I know what I'm doing. We don't have time. Just trust me,' shouted Sushi.

Fins recognised a sense of control in Sushi's voice and Ben was acting very methodical so he decided to do things their way. They were all stunned by the situation, but the two young men had reacted very quickly and professionally. They carefully, but quickly wrapped the rope around the junk, criss crossing to form a cradle. Fins carefully held Jackson's head up although there was no water in the mask. Sushi pulled the junk out of the water as Ben climbed back onto the boat and Fins stayed cradling

Jackson's body. They lifted him out of the water and laid him down in the boat. It looked as if he had become entangled in the junk. Fins and the boys were aghast at what was happening, but the control and calmness of the boys was astounding. Fins had never seen them like this. They were like a pair of angels racing to save Jackson. If it wasn't too late.

Ben grabbed two large sharp knives and handed one to Sushi, they said something in Japanese and methodically started cutting the junk away from Jack's head. Fins examined a piece of the material they had cut off. It was a rubbery wetsuit type of material and it looked like it had been painted in patches. The pipes were PVC and looked as though they had formed some type of craft. Fins studied it for a moment then quietly said: 'Matty'.

Sushi turned to Fins and yelled: "Quick! Help clear from Jack. Must work fast".

As the three of them cleared the junk away from his head and neck, Sushi removed the mask. He then did a rapid assessment, feeling for a pulse, lifting eyelids and more. It was very clear to Fins the boys were definitely not just deckies. They were extremely well trained medical personnel. He was stunned and shocked allround.

'HE'S ALIVE! But only just. Quick must work fast', yelled Sushi.

'You stabilise, I'll call it in', yelled Ben as he reached for the radio.

'That doesn't work out here', yelled Fins.

'Does now! I fix', yelled Ben as he selected channel sixteen.

'Pan pan, pan pan, vessel VMQ 2022 to lifesaver 101. Come in. Urgent', instructed Ben in a calm clear voice.

Rotors and the crew just happened to be in the base early, preparing for the days searching when he heard the message come through on the radio and immediately responded.

'Lifesaver 101. Ben is that you on the Walton vessel?'.

'Yes Rotors, this is Ben on Fins boat. We have just found Jackson Gave floating in the sea trapped in some sort of floating junk. I repeat. We have just found Jackson Gave floating in the sea trapped in some sort of floating junk. We have him on board. He is alive but suffering extreme exposure. He is not conscious. Over'. Said Ben, maintaining a very professional manner.

Rotor's mind raced, as the other two chopper crew stood transfixed around the radio.

'Ben, please repeat. Did you say Jackson Gave and he is alive? Over', asked Rotors.

'Yes, repeat. Jackson Gave from Rainbows End. He is not conscious but alive. We are stabilising him at the moment. Over', Said Ben.

'We are on our way, the paramedic will tell you what to do. Over', replied Rotors.

'Jackson in very, very good hands. Sushi is an emergency trauma surgeon and has many, many years of experience with acute life-threatening injuries. I have set off the EPIRB. Hurry, we must work quickly. Over,' ordered Ben.

Rotors and the crew were gobsmacked but the adrenaline kicked in as the emergency channel search teams picked up on the transmission. The hospital was notified, the police and rescue services were notified, the Jackson news had gone through them like a lightning bolt.

Ben went straight back to helping Sushi treat Jack and cut away the junk he appeared to be trapped in.

'He has a right side clavicle fracture and bruising around the right side Glenohumeral joint. Everything else seems okay', reported Sushi.

'What's a Gleno whatever?' Asked Fins.

'Shoulder joint. How long do you think he's been in the water?' Replied Ben.

'Bloody too long by the look of him', replied Fins.

'Three, maybe four days. This material is from a diving suit, it has a breathing apparatus.' Said Sushi, just as Jackson partly opened his eyes.

'Lifesaver 101 to VMQ2021. Are you there Ben. Over', said Rotors.

'Yes, lifesaver 101. Over', replied Ben.

'Can you give an update on the condition of Jackson? Over', asked Rotors.

'He has a right side clavicle fracture, bruising around the right Glenohumeral joint, breathing is stable, pulmonary edema unlikely. He is regaining consciousness. Over,' said Ben.

'Thank you. Our ETA is approximately fifteen minutes. Out,' replied Rotors.

Jackson slowly opened his eyes again and gave a very faint smile, he seemed to know who they were. The boys had cut him loose from the junk and Fins piled it into a bundle. In amongst everything was a shark fin attached to a rod that Fins immediately pulled out and inspected. 'Matty', he muttered. He took the shark fin and hid it in the cabin then continued to pull the junk apart. He found oxygen tanks, an electric motor, a breathing device for the face mask, a water bottle type of container with a tube to the facemask. There was other stuff but he didn't have a clue what it was or what it did. Fins kept one eye on the boys treating Jackson as he knelt beside them. He was baffled at the knowledge and skill of both of them and astounded at the sight of Jackson. Why was he floating in the sea? What had happened? He couldn't stop thinking.

The top speed of the rescue chopper was around 260 kilometres per hour, and it was doing every bit of that and more as it roared over Rainbows End Beach on its way to pick up Jackson. Suzanne was sitting on her rock with her head on Talia's shoulder, the girls on either side of them fast asleep. The noise of the chopper woke them all. The sun still hadn't broken the horizon but it's rays gave a soft light. None of them said anything, they just assumed the chopper was going out to do its sweeps as usual.

Brian and Benny had gone up to the kitchen early, after spending all night on the beach again. Benny turned on the SLSC radio as usual and was startled to hear people talking on the rescue channel. Brian heard it and said: 'Turn it up, Benny'. Their mouths dropped open when they heard the chopper paramedic's voice talking to Sushi.

'Lifesaver 101, to VMQ2022 our ETA is approximately seven minutes. Can you give me an update on Jackson Gave, please? Over', said the medic.

Sushi replied: 'He has almost fully regained consciousness. He has identified who we are and managed a smile but is too exhausted to speak. We have taken precautions with his skin but everything else is as reported. We will have him ready to go when you arrive, over.'

Brian and Benny looked at each other, then at the radio, then at each other again as Brian shouted:

'Ring Starch straight away and tell him they've found Jackson, they've found him and he's alive. I'm on my way to tell Mrs Gave. Quick Benny, we've gotta do this fast'.

Brian raced out of the kitchen onto the verandah, put one hand on the railing and jumped straight over hitting the ground running. Ben rang Starch's mobile and it's ringtone came from the office. Starch was head down on the desk asleep, and Colmie in the chair.

'Yeah, hello,' mumbled Starch into his phone.

'Hello Starch, it's Benny from the kitchen, they have found Jackson and he is alive', said Benny.

'What', said Starch as he launched to his feet. 'How do you know? Where are you?'.

'I'm in the kitchen at the club and Brian and I heard it on the radio', replied Ben.

Starch ran outside to see Benny talking on the phone. 'When did you find this out, Benny?' Gasped Starch, trying to remain calm.

'About one minute ago. Brian has gone to tell Mrs Gave. He jumped over the balcony', said Ben.

Colmie came racing out to see what was going on as the radio crackled again.

'VMQ2022. This is Lifesaver 101. ETA is five minutes, Over'

'VMQ2022. That's Walton's boat. He must have found him. We have to get Suzanne to the hospital', said Starch. 'Turn on the TV Benny and keep an eye on the phone'.

The extremely relieved and excited Starch and Colmie ran out to the verandah, put one hand on the railing and jumped over. There were loud thuds as both hit the grass below and both let out a grunting type of "uhhh" sound. They looked up to see and hear Brian shouting and running toward Suzanne and the girls.

'They found him, they found him, he's alive'. Screamed Brian.

Suzanne looked up to see what was happening but couldn't understand what Brian was yelling about. As he came closer everyone could clearly understand what he was shouting and started to run toward him. Suzanne grabbed Brian by the shoulders and calmly pleaded:

'Slow down and tell me what you know'.

In between breaths Brian blurted out: 'They found him! A boat found him out there. He's alive on the boat. The people on the boat are treating him and the rescue chopper is on its way to pick him up'.

The girls looked at each other and remembered the chopper roar overhead just minutes before.

There was excitement, relief and astonishment allround as they began to run back to the clubhouse. Starch and Colmie met them halfway and exclaimed to Suzanne:

'You've heard the news. Come on, we've got to get you to the hospital'.

Starch's daughters raced off ahead as Talia grabbed Suzanne's hand and started to run.

'Are you sure he's alive?' She was almost too afraid to ask.

'Alive and conscious and managing a faint smile. He's on Fins Walton's boat and the deckies are treating him, apparently, they have some medical experience or something'. Explained Colmie.

'Mr Walton's boat, how on earth did they find him?' Asked Suzanne, trying to talk while she ran.

'Don't know, but we'll find out soon enough,' replied Colmie.

Benny was watching everything from the clubhouse verandah, and listening to the radio conversation when the phone rang.

'Hello, Rainbows End Surf Lifesaving Club, how can I help you?' Said the well-rehearsed Benny.

'Hi, it's senior constable Kelly Follent from Coolangatta police here. I'm trying to locate Suzanne Gave. Her home phone isn't answering, neither is her mobile. Would you know how I can contact her?' Asked Kelly.

'Yes, I do. She is on the beach running up to the clubhouse. I can tell her to ring you', replied Benny.

'No need. There'll be a police car there in a couple of minutes to pick her up. They have found her son Jackson and the police car will take her straight to the hospital. Can you give her that message immediately, please?. Who am I talking to?' Asked Kelly.

'My name is Benny and I will give her that message now. Thank you. Bye', he replied and hung up the phone. With his mind racing, he ran out to the verandah, put one hand on the railing, then paused and looked over the railing to see how far the ground was below. He wisely decided against jumping and ran down the stairs instead. It was only a matter of seconds before he met Suzanne and the others running up to the clubhouse.

'Mrs Gave, the cops are coming to pick you up and take you straight to the hospital. They'll be here in a minute and they know about Jackson and they have been trying to ring you, but said your phone isn't answering'. Exclaimed Benny, pausing between breaths.

Suzanne checked her phone and it had zero charge.

'Thank you, Benny, the news is very much appreciated. I had better get up there'. Replied Suzanne, still showing incredible composure.

Brian gave him a pat on the back to acknowledge his contribution and said: 'Well done Benny'. Starch and Colmie did the same which had the effect of putting a huge smile on his face. Everyone was zinging. The nervous excitement between the group was electric.

Suzanne reached the car park as a police car with two lady cops arrived at speed. Kelly the cop, jumped out from the driver's seat, shook Suzanne's hand and asked:

'Do you have everything you need, Mrs Gave?'

'Yes, yes, thank you', replied Suzanne.

The other lady cop opened the back door for her as she gave Talia a hug, and said:

'See you at the hospital, sister'.

Suzanne sat in the back of the police car by herself and began to tremble. She had spent the previous night accepting Jackson's death and planning how to end her own life. She could not have endured any more pain. She had gone through six days of hell and now was almost too afraid to believe Jack was alive. The never-ending waves of emotion had taken its toll as the tears streamed down her cheeks and her mind raced with questions: "How bad is he? Will he make it? Is he permanently affected? Will he live?" Her hope had become her reality and now it was time to accept. Sometimes we win.

The siren of the police car screamed with urgency as the cops raced toward the hospital. There wasn't any early morning traffic to slow them, so the speed was breathtaking. Kelly the cop and her offsider kept counseling Suzanne and this helped immensely. She was slowly gaining the courage to believe.

The chopper had reached Fin's trawler and as promised Jackson was ready to go. Ben and Sushi had placed him in the appropriate position for his injuries and Sushi had given him a small amount of water with sugar. Jackson did not appear to be suffering from any sort of shock which puzzled the boys and led them to the conclusion that this is a very tough kid.

The stretcher, and Stitches the paramedic, were lowered from the chopper to where Jack lay waiting wrapped carefully in foil. They loaded him very carefully onto the stretcher as the paramedic had a quick look at what the boys had done. In a matter of minutes the signal was given and they were hoisted skyward. Once loaded on the chopper and locked in, the nose of the aircraft dipped and they headed for the hospital at maximum speed.

'How is he?' Asked Rotors.

'Considering how long he's been in the water, he's very good. Unbelievable! The boys on Walton's boat have done this before', replied Stitches.

Just as they were talking, Jackson slowly opened his eyes.

'Jackson. Welcome home mate. Can you understand me?' Yelled Stitches.

Jackson gave a faint smile and Stitches yelled again:

'Stay with me Jac. You're a champion, mate'.

The crew kept treating Jac and confirmed to the hospital everything Sushi had reported.

Back on the trawler, Ben was going over the junk and determined it was some sort of sophisticated underwater recreational craft with electronics and parts he couldn't discern. He did find some type of water tank and tasted its contents which was a mix of glucose and something else. He packed it up in a bundle and stored it on deck.

Back at the clubhouse, a breaking news flash interrupted the TV's morning news Bulletin. The media had heard the emergency radio calls and were in a frenzy. The club phone was ringing non-stop, Starch's phone was in meltdown and Colmie couldn't keep up with the calls. A celebratory Big Cop appeared on TV and confirmed reports Jackson had been found alive. It was a national headline news story. People that had been part of the search started rolling into the club desperate to know what was going on? Jackson's school friends were all on deck begging their parents to drive them to the hospital. All in all, it was total mayhem in a good way.

The police car with Suzanne onboard arrived at the emergency department of the hospital. The lady cops and a couple of nurses escorted her up to the helipad just as the chopper was landing. There was medical staff everywhere, doctors, nurses, specialists, you name it, they were there. Suzanne's trembling turned into shaking as she struggled to contain herself. Senior Constable Kelly drew her in affectionately and calmly said:

'As soon as they get him clear of the chopper they'll give us the all-clear. We're almost there'.

The medics carefully loaded Jackson onto a trolley bed and cleared the chopper. Suzanne raced to the trolley and broke down when she saw him. Although the medics were surprised at his resilience to the conditions and assessed his condition as good, to his mother he was a mess. Suzanne had never seen him like this and was distraught until Jackson heard her voice and opened his eyes wide for a moment then focused on her. He gave her a smile and held onto her finger with his good hand. That touch was all it took for them both to know he was home and he would make it.

The news choppers were starting to hover over the hospital and the media circus was building out the front. Talia and the girls arrived, followed by Starch and Colmie. Rooster had stayed at the club to talk to the media which scared the hell out of Starch, but he had asked Simmo to try and contain the Rooster effect. The mood in the waiting room was jubilant. Jack's smile had settled his mum and grief had given way to relief. Next to arrive was Big Cop, who smiled at Starch and Colmie as he walked in and declared:

'How good is this? They don't always end this good. You blokes must have said a lot of prayers'.

'Didn't we all?' Answered Colmie.

'Fancy, Walton finding him. The last time I dragged him out of the water he was punching me in the face on Greenmount Beach', bellowed Big Cop.

It wasn't long before the waiting room was overflowing with Jack's schoolmates and clubbies, prompting Big Cop to make a speech and thank everybody for coming - but they had to clear the room. He assured them Jack was in the best of hands and it was now just a matter of time before he would be back at the club. He urged everyone to start preparing for what would be the biggest party Rainbows End has ever seen. Starch and Colmie decided to head off with everybody else, leaving Talia and the girls with Suzanne. As he was walking out the door Starch turned to wave goodbye and noticed the only person other than the girls in the waiting room was an Asian looking man, who was sitting quietly with his head bowed. He looked like the man who was sitting on the headland all week, but he concluded it was just a coincidence.

By around 8am there was mayhem at the clubhouse. Media from every news service in the country were crawling all over the place, and the very unusual circumstances of Jack's survival were beginning to attract international attention. Everyone wanted to talk to Fins Walton and crew, but Fins was unavailable until he reached his mooring. Ready to fill in the information gap, Rooster was talking the house down and featured heavily on morning news bulletins across Australia. Out the back of Bourke at Thargomindah, the Rooster phenomenon had become folklore as the locals watched the morning news. The Rooster tales grew larger and larger with the most uttered phrase in the district being:

'That bloke from the coast has done it again. He ought to be Prime Minister. Bloody fair dinkum champion'.

Young Michael Hadfield and his grandparents were constantly at Roosters side in the middle of the media cyclone and loving every minute of it. Michael nor his grandparents had never seen or felt such excitement. They were having the holiday of a lifetime. The phone calls from home were relentless with their faces on national TV news bulletins. Everyone from his schoolmates to the town mayor wanted to know, 'what's goin on?'

Starch had tried to contact Fins but in true Fins fashion, he wasn't or didn't respond to calls whilst working. The news choppers had watched the trawler make its way home, and it wasn't long before the media crews started to set up on the edge of the bar. A crowd of locals had also started congregating on the headland. Coming into view approaching the bar, was the unmistakable boat of Fins Walton. Sharkbait stood proudly on the bow with his nose in the air, the one-legged seagull perched on the mast, Ben and Sushi were working on the deck and Fins behind the helm. In normal Fins Walton style, his speed didn't alter as he approached the still very unpredictable Tweed bar.

Fins noticed the forming media juggernaut and immediately doubled the price of his catch. This was the "Jack Catch" and had to be priced as such. With the locals on the headland clapping, Fins went straight over the bar and up the Tweed River to the co-op, where the buyers were waiting - but they weren't alone. Throngs of journalists, onlookers, sticky beaks, and more clapping locals crowded the wharf. Standing out in front of them all was Big Cop with a couple of water police waiting to interview Fins and crew. As Ben and Sushi tied up the boat, Big Cop stepped onboard.

'Hello, Mr Walton. Before we get blasted with the media questions, can you tell me what happened with young Jack. Who, by the way, is expected to make a full recovery - thanks to you and your onboard medical professionals'.

Fins looked up with a raised eyebrow and replied.

'Well, I've got a few questions for you too. As far as young Jack is concerned, we found him a couple of hours ago at first light, floating in the Pacific Ocean, tangled up in that junk next to you'.

Big Cop looked down to see a conglomeration of PVC pipes, wetsuit material, water tanks, oxygen tanks, and other containers. There was also a bunch of what looked like switches and a divers mask with hoses attached.

'What the hell is all that?' He asked.

'Wouldn't have a clue, but it obviously kept him alive. So what happened to him? How did he end up out there?' Asked Fins, as Ben and Sushi listened in.

'There were a series of very big, freak waves that happened last Sunday afternoon. It caught everyone by surprise, the beach was still busy with people. It was a catastrophe. Everyone, including the neighbouring clubs did what they could to help, it was very lucky no one was killed. Jackson went out into the guts of it all on the back of the jet ski to save three toddlers and their parents. He had to work hard to save the toddlers, then made the jet ski driver get the parents because they were going under and starting to get swept out. The last time the jet ski driver saw him was when Jack caught a wave heading into the beach. The driver had to drag the parents onto the ski board at the same time. Jackson didn't appear to be in any trouble at that time, but that was the last time anyone saw him. He was discovered missing that night when his mother was concerned that he hadn't come home for dinner. We did a massive search for him for six days. No one spotted a thing, land, sea or air'. Recounted Big Cop.

'Freak waves? What, did this hit the whole coast? Was there a storm? What?' Questioned Fins.

'No, it was localised to the Rainbows End part of the beach. It is now widely accepted that the sandbar build-up called the Superbank suddenly collapsed, which allowed a massive volume of water to surge onto the beach. There was no warning whatsoever', answered Big Cop.

'The bloody dredging. They're the scum of the earth that mob. Where's Flowers? So that little germ of a 'polly' and his bullshitting European experts caused all this to fall on young Jack, did they. Well, they'll be getting a bit of a thank you, won't they'. Growled Fins.

Big Cop paused for a minute to let Fins settle down. He had seen what happens when he gets wound up - and it wasn't good.

'Mate, I'd rather you let due process take its course first before any public lynchings. What about all this stuff you found him floating in, whaddya make of that?' Big Cop asked.

'Never seen it before in my life. Wouldn't have a clue what it is'. Replied Fins, avoiding eye contact.

'Who were the medics on board that treated him? Apparently, they did a very professional job?' Asked, Big Cop.

'Still trying to figure that out myself. Apparently, it's Dr Sushi and Dr Ben. The boys have been a bit shy about coming forward with who they really are. What's the latest on Jack?' Asked Fins.

'He's in intensive care where they expect him to make a full recovery. He's a bit smashed up but the boys did an excellent job of getting him out of whatever this junk is without further harming him. The team, up at emergency, said the treatment applied was very intelligent and innovative'. Answered Big Cop.

'That's good! Alright, I've got some fish to sell. I haven't got anything else to tell ya. I haven't got anything to say to the media either. We'll all be up to check on Jacko at the hospital when we finish. The medics can have a yarn to Ben and Sushi then, if they agree', said Fins.

'Yeah ok. We all appreciate what you and the boys have done. He wouldn't have lasted any longer if you didn't find him and the way you responded was excellent. Thank you'. Acknowledged a grateful Big Cop.

Fins was quiet for a moment. Being appreciated by a policeman was something he wasn't used to. In fact, it was the first time in his life he had actually been appreciated by the police.

'Well, to be honest, I think it was more a case of him finding me. We weren't even aware he had gone missing, and the boys were guessing how long he'd been in the water. I didn't do much, it was all those two. I'm still a bit stuffed about the whole matter, to be honest. Even that boofhead dog has stopped growling at me - but that'll be temporary'. Replied Fins, quietly.

191

Big Cop smiled and couldn't believe the humility coming from Fins Walton. Could it be that Fins actually had a heart? He extended his hand and the pair shook hands with each other for the first time in their lives. That moment was almost as big as the Jacko rescue news. Fins Walton and a cop shake hands. Unbelievable!

The Rainbows End clubhouse was packed by early morning with jubilant club members and locals. Everyone who had been involved in the search had or were dropping in to have a yarn and to catch up with 'what's goin on'. The news networks were going berserk with the story, especially with the Fins factor thrown in. The hospital phone lines were going into meltdown and a plea had to be issued not to phone for updates. The emergency wards were unable to function properly because of the overwhelming concern for Jacko jamming the switchboard.

Suzanne sat beside Jack's bed as he lay in intensive care. The girls had gone back to her home and picked up some clean clothes, so she was able to shower and clean up at the hospital. When they returned they talked her into joining them in the cafeteria as Jack rested. It was the first time she had eaten in a week. Although Big Cop had shielded her from the media, her face was still instantly recognisable because of the constant avalanche of photos taken of her sitting on her rock. Just about everyone in the cafeteria recognised her and wanted to chat and give her a hug. After they had finished eating, she hugged the girls and thanked them. She wanted to go and sit beside Jack because that's where she needed to be, so the girls went home to rest. When Suzanne walked back into the intensive care unit, she stood beside her son's bed looking down at him. He immediately sensed her presence, opened his eyes and held one of her fingers, before giving a faint smile and drifting back to sleep. The following day he was taken out of intensive care and placed in a private room. Suzanne was still by his side and looking a lot better. Jack was getting stronger and stayed awake for a few minutes at a time throughout the day, and managed to say 'sore throat', when the doctor asked how he was.

With Jack safe and sound and expected to make a full recovery, Starch's thoughts turned back to the clubhouse grant. Things were looking pretty grim on the financial front and there had been almost no income for the past week with everyone contributing to the search for Jack. He decided not to dwell on it for the moment and instead would concentrate on getting the club running smoothly again. The beach was back to being busy so there was work to be done, and he had confidence in Robyn.

Rooster was relishing his new media portfolio and had become the nation's greatest media star with at least 15 television interviews and 40 print media quotes in one morning. Most of the TV interviews were done with him in his DT's, so they were head and shoulder shots only. Starch decided to take over dealing with the media after seeing some of Rooster's work on live TV, but once the journalists had Starch in their lenses, the questions turned straight to the dredging. He tried to be diplomatic but it was clear, the cat was out of the bag and everything was being put under the microscope.

Around the club, things were in recovery mode. Bean and Matthew were trading the house down. All the regulars were back and most were looking for answers about the dredging fiasco and demanding accountability. Danny was back doing what Danny does, Grizz was unhappy and grizzled about everything. Liz was still on her cruise, Bull was back in court over impersonating a plumber. Rooster was looking after young Michael and his grandparents from Thargomindah. He had also gone back to polishing the surfboat, although the girls were quiet about the Aussie Surf Boat Championships. Brian, Benny and Adrian were serving up some excellent food upstairs and high fiving each other all day long. Tommy Green was pulling beers like a champion at the bar, and the tips were coming thick and fast.

At the end of his shift, Matthew decided to wander up to check on his pet fish and make a couple of adjustments. After doing a quick scan to check he was not being watched he climbed into the cave's secret entrance, only to discover things were not as they should be. His pet fish was gone, complete with oxygen tanks, new portable water desalination system, power motor and everything else. Matty was not happy, he had poured so much time and energy into his project and had so many improvements to make. He was disgusted that someone would steal it.

With his mind racing, he made his way back to the kiosk trying to think of why someone would steal something like that. They wouldn't know how to use it or whatever. Maybe they just wanted the tanks but stole everything.

Bean was happy to see him back at the kiosk as he needed to go to the bank.

'Can you give me half an hour? The account looks pretty ugly so I have to deposit the takings', he asked.

'Yeah, no probs'. Replied Matt, masking his disappointment over the pet fish theft.

Feeling unsociable and peeved off, the young bloke pulled up a chair and opened a newspaper on the servery counter. Flicking through the pages he never noticed a customer approaching. All of a sudden there was a rod with a large shark fin attached, placed across the page he was looking at. He did a very big 'gulp' and with his heart in his mouth slowly looked up. There before him was Fins Walton, looking twice as big as he usually does. Matty had never felt so vulnerable before in his life. There was nothing pretty about Fins. His orange/red hair and beard coupled with his cold stare always made things worse.

'I believe this belongs to you', eloquently growled Fins.

Matty froze and decided silence was his best option.

'The rest of it's on the boat. You'd better come and get it. Bit chopped up but might be salvageable'.

Seeing Matty had nothing to say, Fins started to walk off upstairs to the bar, but stopped, turned around and added:

'By the way, some bloke was around at the boat asking questions about who built your toy. He took some photos and asked if I could find out and get a contact name or number. I don't know how he knew about it, only the cops knew where it was. He was a nice sort of a bloke, bought every fish I had left - paid cash. Was an Asian looking sort of bloke. Will I tell him?' Asked Fins.

Matty was still reeling from the encounter and only just managed to say: 'Okay'.

Fins turned and walked upstairs. Sharkbait growled and showed his teeth as Fins walked in front of him, but to this day, Matty swears, Sharkbait turned and winked at him.

Jack continued to improve hour by hour and Big Cop continued to support his mum with anything he could. He was very interested to know what had happened but would have to wait. Starch's problems continued to mount with the structural faults in the club building worsening. There was also the media interest in the superbank collapse and any possible corruption. The phone calls for comment were constant. He had spoken to Robyn a few times and had stepped around the subject but the elephant in the room needed to be addressed so he decided to call a meeting for the following week to bring everything to a head. Molly Baxter had been hounding him and he expected her to eventually corner him some time soon. He decided to answer next time she phoned to hear what she had to say. He had no doubt she would have a wealth of information. At least Flowers was still overseas which meant there was one less lunatic he didn't have to worry about. Life was edging back to normal.

A couple of days passed and Suzanne was up before dawn for her early morning shower at the hospital special accommodation unit. Afterwards, she made herself a cup of coffee before settling down beside Jack. To her enormous surprise when she walked into his room, Jack was sitting up in bed and greeted her with:

'Good morning Mum. Love you'.

The sound of his voice rang like church bells and the weight of a thousand dreads lifted from her shoulders. With her mouth wide open she did a double blink to make sure she wasn't dreaming, then walked around to the side of his bed.

'I love you too Jacky, and good morning to you, and boy didn't you have us worried'. Said Suzanne, still reeling from the sight of him sitting up.

'Sorry about that mum, but I think I can explain some of it,' replied Jack.

'Well there's plenty of time for that later, are you hungry? How's your throat? Is your shoulder painful?' Suzanne fired off.

'Mum! I'm in a hospital. They're doing everything they can to make sure I'm okay. Did everyone get out of the water okay? Did that family get out alright?' Asked Jack.

'Yes, luvvy. Everyone got out of the water. There were lots of people looking for you, it was Mr Walton who found you'. Replied Suzanne.

'Yes I know, I could see his boat but I just couldn't swim or paddle to it. My arms wouldn't move. Then I remember he was in the water with me, then I remember Ben and Sushi fixing me and taking the strain off my arm. I think I was in a diving suit'. Explained Jack.

'Do you remember how you got into the diving suit? Do you remember what happened? How did you hurt yourself?' Suzanne gently asked.

Jack took a breath and replied: 'I was on a wave when another bigger wave picked me up and dumped me really hard. I felt a lot of pain in my shoulder and neck and couldn't move my right arm to swim. It was like being in a front-load washing machine. I tried not to lose consciousness and remembered the training Andrew gave me. I kept repeating to myself 'don't panic, don't panic'. I felt the bottom and pushed up, but it was only for a breath, then I felt the current drag me under, it was too strong, it sucked me down and out very quickly. It's force was too powerful and my shoulder and arm were killing me. I had no vision. The water was so dirty and my lungs were burning but I came up and took another breath, then another wave smashed me. I hit the bottom and it felt like a giant hose just swept me out further. I thought I was going to die, then, then I felt dad. I didn't hear or see dad but I felt him. It was like sitting on his shoulders again and walking through the shopping centre. It was so high but I was never scared because he was there. I was above all the people and I always felt safe. He always made me feel safe. I sort of relaxed and did what Andrew taught me. I felt around and touched something. It was soft and smooth like a divers suit. I grabbed hold and hung on, then all of a sudden I popped through the surface and managed to stay there for a minute or so. Then another wave broke on top of me but the thing I was hanging on to, just floated me back to the surface. I could only hang on with one arm so I tried to find a better grip. When I tried to figure out what it was, I found it had a divers mask and custom air tanks and a sort of snorkel and other stuff. I put the mask on with my good arm and had clean air straight away then started to figure out how to get into the wetsuit thing. I managed to get in then zipped it up with my good hand. The suit was good but it had broken pipes and stuff so I could only float face up. Even when a wave smashed on top of me the suit would just go down then float back up to the surface. I couldn't do anything so I just floated. The first night was the hardest, but I had long talks with dad and I was never scared. When the sun came up I didn't know where I was, I was just floating. I watched the rescue helicopters fly over but I couldn't wave and they never saw me. I sucked on a tube in the mask and it had some sports drink or something, so I just took tiny sips. That's what every day was like, just floating and hoping. The ocean was still pretty rough so I just bobbed about. Some days, dolphins would come past and have a look at me. The helicopters were still going overhead but they didn't see me.

On the last day at first light, the sea was like glass and there was a flock of seagulls hanging round me that just wouldn't go away. I saw a fishing boat in the distance but I couldn't paddle or wave. Somehow we drifted closer to each other. I was so tired, hungry, thirsty and tired that I could only stay awake for a short time. I remember looking to see the boat and there were people on it looking toward me. We were getting closer to each other. I was too tired to care about anything, the seagulls were everywhere, then I felt something pulling me, then I heard someone yell my name and then there was a huge splash then another splash. Then I saw Mr Walton's face looking at me.

Next thing I remember was being on the boat and Sushi was looking at me and gently touching my shoulder. I remember him and Ben taking me out of the wetsuit and treating me. Everyone was talking but I was too tired to understand. I was just so happy to see them. I remember a little about being on the rescue chopper. I remember everything about seeing you when they unloaded me. That was my happiest day. I knew when I woke up this morning dad had lifted me off his shoulders and put me on the ground. It was time for me to walk on my own again. I must accept the way things are but I know things won't be like this forever. When I was floating out there I asked him if one day he could carry me on his shoulders again. He said: 'Maybe. But one day I would be carrying him on my shoulders'.

Jackson's answer had left his mother stunned and momentarily lost for words. She paused for a moment without saying anything. Both of them just smiled at each other. Sometimes, nothing needs to be said.

As they both sat back a mature and business-like nurse entered the room to check on Jack.

'Good morning Mr Gave, how are we going? And good morning to you Mrs Gave. The police phoned and checked on Jackson's condition. They'll probably want to talk to him when you're ready'. Said the nurse.

'Yes, that's okay anytime is fine', replied Jack.

'Thank you, I'll give them that message. The doctor will be around shortly to check you over. How's the shoulder?' Asked the nurse.

'It's sore, but that's okay', replied Jack.

The nurse gave a slight smile. There was a sense of connection in her conversation and it sounded like she had been a nurse for a very long time.

'We'll have a look at it in a minute, I'll just go and tell the doctor that you're sitting up, first'. Said the nurse, as she left.

Suzanne listened to the conversation and pondered the change in Jack's demeanour. He had changed. He was still Jack but he seemed different, he acted and sounded much more mature. The week had definitely affected him, but not in a traumatic way but more of a toughening way. He leaned back, closed his eyes and rested as Suzanne continued to wonder about the change in him. How frightening must it have been to be out there in the darkness night after night, not knowing if you would live long enough to see the next day? The constant pain of a broken collarbone and shoulder damage. The hopelessness of the rescue choppers passing overhead day after day. She was staggered with how he articulated his experience and the resoluteness he spoke about his father with. What had happened out there? Did he really experience what he thought, or was it just his mind using the memory of his father as a coping mechanism? Did he become so inundated with fear that he became resilient to it?

The police and medical staff had warned her he would suffer from some sort of post-traumatic stress because of what he had been through, but it seemed just the opposite had happened. She decided to wait and see what the doctor had to say.

# Chapter 19

# What a Day

The surf club was in a jubilant mood and preparations were underway for a thank you day, in appreciation of everyone who had helped look for Jack. The biggest problem facing the club was how to thank Fins Walton and crew for finding and saving Jack, when Fins was serving a ban from the club. Although no one had tried to enforce the ban. How do they thank him without getting their heads bitten off? They decided there ought to be some sort of appreciation presentation, and hoped for the best.

Bean had resumed his love quest and was busy handing out free coffee vouchers, hoping to meet the lady he didn't have the courage to talk to. Matthew was in a dilemma trying to decide what to do about his future. Despite all the scholarship offers on the table he just couldn't see himself committing to any of them. His parents decided not to intervene and as usual, left the decision entirely up to him. He spoke to career advisors and his school teachers but no one said anything that helped. One of his biggest problems was, he didn't know himself well enough to know what he wanted to do.

Rooster was still writing drunken, anonymous poetry for married ladies whom he was sure fancied him, but remained sober enough to recognise and step around Donga's wife. He had paid for an extra week's accommodation for young Michael and his grandparents so he could show them more of the coast while he wasn't busy. He didn't have the cash for the extra week so he used his car as surety, if he couldn't pay the rent in thirty days.

Danny had hit a new high of annoying people by talking about his exercise and use of energy boosters to build his iron man type fitness. Grizz was busy and cranky with his painting business, although he was chuffed with the fact Liz had sent him a text and not Danny. He had kept this to himself.

The ladies surf boat team had now completely fizzled out. During the week-long search for Jack, their will to compete had been lost, so they asked Simmo to withdraw them from the national titles. They decided to go back to the way things were and leave the dream of winning to the dreamers.

Benny, Brian and Adrian were breaking all records in the restaurant. Much to the delight of the members the food was first class and bookings were rolling in. Adrian had asked the board members to consider offering Benny a permanent position as a kitchen hand/apprentice chef. The board were waiting on the outcome of the grant before giving their answer, as the outcome of the government grant money could decide the future of the club. Robyn had told Starch there had been a development in the grant submission and requested a meeting with the full board to discuss what had changed. She didn't say what was going on.

Jack's condition continued to improve and Suzanne was able to go back to work and visit every night. Big Cop had also been to visit him and recorded a statement about what had happened in the surf. There was a lot of head shaking as Jack told of the events during his week, which left Big Cop struggling to comprehend how the rescue and police choppers missed him. It was almost as if he was hidden in plain sight. The media was finally allowed an interview and the reaction was pretty much the same as Big Cops. There were clearly lots of questions that needed to be answered, ranging from the dredging to how he managed to survive for so long.

Big Cop went back to have a yarn to Fins Walton and inspect the pile of junk Jack was found floating in. Any meeting with Fins was a bruff affair but fortunately for Big Cop, he was sitting on the back of his boat having a beer and homemade pie - which meant he was in a good mood.

'How are you, Mr Walton,' greeted Big Cop.

'Gidday copper,' replied Fins.

'I need to have another look at that junk that Jackson was found floating in.' Said Big Cop.

'It's gone, mate! Chucked it out, bloody health hazard. Full of sea lice and crap. Don't know how the kid's still alive.' Blurted Fins.

'Where did you chuck it?' Enquired Big Cop.

'In the garbage, mate. Long gone!' Answered Fins.

'When you found him, how did you manage to spot him?' Asked Big Cop.

'Sharkbait must have sniffed him. He started barking his useless head off', replied Fins.

'So was he clearly visible?' Questioned Big Cop.

'Nah, couldn't see him until we got him beside the boat'. Said Fins.

'Can you please explain to me what you saw when the dog started barking?' Big Cop asked, battling with Fin's non-committal attitude.

'Seagulls, mate! Lots of bloody seagulls and no baitfish. It's still got me wondering what the seagulls were doing there! If it wasn't for them he would've floated straight past. No way we could've seen him', recounted Fins.

Big Cop looked down and shook his head.

'Well, you're not the only one! Both the choppers missed him and he was right under them for a bloody week', exclaimed Big Cop.

'Well, it seems to me like someone wasted a hell of a lot of money on some bloody useless search helicopters'. Fired off Fins.

'Yeah well, we need some answers, that's for sure. Thanks, I'll see you later... Oh, just off the record... Have you seen any improvement in the bar since the dredging started?' Queried Big Cop.

'No', was the short answer from Fins.

Big Cop had the experience to know Fins was lying about the pile of junk, but it wasn't a malicious lie, it was more likely he was protecting someone. But why? He decided to let it be, after all, no law had been broken and it was a welcome change to be able to talk to Fins without the boxing match.

Life had pretty much returned to being manageable for Starch. Although he did appear to be a bit lost without his little buddy Jackson following him around checking things, and testing the water craft. Things had at last settled down. As he walked up the beach toward the clubhouse pondering his next move, Molly Baxter came around the corner. Being a straight to the point type of girl, Molly walked right up to him, and blurted out:

'Alright! Whose shout is it?'

Starch gave a grin and replied: 'Well it's probably yours but I'll pay because I'm generous. It'll have to be a takeaway. I'm busy'.

'Done'. Molly agreed, trying not to laugh at the 'generous' quip.

'So, what do you know?' Asked Starch.

'I was going to ask you, actually', replied Molly.

'Well it's too early to see what will happen, because of the superbank collapse'. Said Starch.

'Yeah, lots of questions being asked there. I just wanted to know if you knew anything about the developer putting forward a proposal to the government, about the club?' Asked Molly.

Starch's jaw dropped. He couldn't believe what he had just heard.

'What!!! What proposal? What developer?' Gasped Starch.

'Apparently a foreign-owned company with some serious money has started talking to the government about buying the club site or something'. Replied Molly.

'You're joking', drawled Starch.

'I've been trying to get in contact with you but you didn't answer my calls'. Said Molly.

'You're joking', drawled Starch again. Hoping it was some kind of bad joke.

'No, no joke. I thought it could have been the dredging company, trying to stem the fallout from the superbank disaster. But if you haven't heard anything, I don't know what is going on', replied Molly.

Starch was standing in front of her with his mouth open and feeling like he'd just been hit by a truck.

'Unbelievable! Thanks, Molly. Sorry about the unanswered calls. It's been a trying time, although that's no excuse. We needed this like a hole in the head. Where is it all going to end?' Lamented Starch.

'Don't know Starch. These are interesting times. I'll let you know if I dig up anything else. I have to go. See you next time and it's my shout', said Molly. Then walked off.

Starch was left feeling like the world had gone mad. 'What next?' He thought to himself with his head still spinning. He decided to give Robyn a call and let her know what Molly had said.

'Hello Robyn, it's Starch, how are you?'

'Hi Starch. I'm good thanks. What can I do for you?' Asked Robyn.

'Well I've just had a visit from Molly Baxter and she tells me there's a whisper about some foreign developer wanting to buy the club land or something', related starch.

'Yes, well, that's what our meeting is about. I managed to push the grant through whilst Flowers is overseas, and I've heard the same as Molly. I don't know who the developer is but I've been told they're big. Very big. Global'. Replied Robyn.

'So where's that leave us?' Asked Starch.

'Well, nothing's changed. We're still applying for a Community Assistance Grant, so the government will say, yes or no. What might happen is, they might send out their own building inspector to look at the clubhouse, then if the developer story is true, weigh up the options'. Explained Robyn.

'Then what about the beach patrols, who'll be doing that?' Beseeched Starch.

'I'd say they'd propose a tower onsite, and man it with the neighbouring clubs. But that is just speculation, we don't know anything for sure, yet'. Answered Robyn.

'Well, what a kick in the guts this is. Strike me pink I can't believe this, what next?' Blurted Starch.

'Nothing has been confirmed. At the moment it's all rumour, so carry on as usual. If I get more news, I'll let you know at the meeting', replied Robyn.

Starch gave a sigh and replied: 'Okay, thanks, Robyn. Much appreciated, I'll see you then. Bye'.

It seemed as if the winds of positive change would never come for Starch. He, like many others, had given their time and energy to the club, day in day out for many, many years. The thought of someone just coming along and buying it because they had the money, sickened him.

Matty picked up his pet fish from Fins without any questions being asked. He pulled the mangled pieces apart and packed what was salvageable into boxes and put them in the kiosk storeroom. It was obvious that his secret cave had been flooded when the bar collapsed and his pet fish was swept out.

He knew he had to make some decisions about his future and had started to spend long hours of a night sitting on the headland and looking at the stars, agonising about what to do. The beach was crowded with tourists so there were plenty of kiosk work hours which helped take his mind off things. Around 2pm was usually clean up time and both Bean and Matty were cleaning up when a youngish Asian looking man walked up to the counter, and politely asked:

'Would Matthew be around, please?'

'Yeah mate', said Bean. 'Matty you're wanted at the counter', he yelled.

It was rare for Matty to have callers, so he was puzzled as to what this could be about. As he approached the counter the man gave him a respectful smile.

'Mathew?' The man asked.

'Yeah', replied Matt a bit hesitatingly.

'My name is Larry. Would it be possible to have a chat whenever you're available', said the man.

Matty thought for a moment and wondered how an Asian man received the name of Larry.

'Yeah, what about?' Asked Matty.

'Innovation in recreational submersible watercraft', said Larry.

'Did you speak to Fins?' Asked Matt.

'Yes', answered Larry.

'Okay… we can talk now', said Matt. 'Hey Bean, can I have a couple of minutes please'.

Bean was listening to the conversation and wondering: 'What the hell is this about?'

'Yeah, no probs', he answered.

Matthew and Larry sat down at one of the kiosk tables and a couple of minutes of chat turned into a one-hour discussion. It was over an hour when the pair stood up and shook hands. Bean watched on, mystified as Matty walked back to the counter, and couldn't help asking: "What's goin on?"

'I think he just introduced me to myself. That is the most intelligent person I've ever met. My head's still spinning', said Matt.

'What!!! What's goin on?' Blurted Bean. 'What's it all about?'

'He just wanted to find out how much I know about science and innovation, human physiology, ideas on air and submersible water recreational craft. He said he enjoyed our conversation very much and would like to talk to me again. He may have a career opportunity for me but said it might be better if I spoke to my parents first, to see if it's okay. I explained they think it's better if I decide my own future, so he's going to come back and have another chat'. Explained Matt.

'Who is he?' Quizzed Bean.

'Wouldn't have a clue. All I know is his name's Larry, and he's a very, very smart person', answered Matt.

'Well what career is he talking about?' Asked Bean.

'Wouldn't have a clue', answered Matt.

'This is crazy!' blurted Bean. 'Who is this bloke?'

'I don't know, he has an accent. He said he's Canadian, he's a really nice bloke', replied Matt.

'Canadian!!! He looks Asian', blurted Bean.

'Give me a break, Bean, maybe Canada floated over to Asia somewhere. I'll tell you straight away when I find out what's going on', said Matt.

The conversation was interrupted by Danny who walked up to the servery window and slapped a pile of pamphlets down on the counter.

'Okay to leave them there? Thanks, men.' Said Danny, then walked off without waiting for a reply.

Bean and Matt just looked at each other without saying anything, then picked up a pamphlet each to read.

'Is he fair dinkum? He's gone mad', babbled Bean.

'Maybe you should have a talk with him. He's lost the plot', said Matty.

The pamphlets read: "Danny PT - Globally recognised fitness and superfood consultant. Book your Appointment in advance and receive a 2.5% discount. Escape your limits - Think Danny PT. Non-achievers and slow responders counselling available".

'We can't leave these on the counter, we'll get sued. Better let Starch know', fired off Bean.

'Is he serious? He can't be serious,' questioned Matty.

'Danny is never not serious. Let's get them off the counter and let Starch know'. Said a bewildered Bean, then turned around to see his secret love standing at the counter.

'Hi Matthew', said the lady.

'Hi, how are you? Are you having the same as last time?' asked Matt.

'Yes please, I'll be back in a minute. The money's on the counter', replied the lady.

Bean froze. First, it was Larry, then it was Danny, now it was his secret infatuation. The day was spiraling out of control. Matty made the coffee whilst Bean pretended to clean, positioning himself to talk to the lady when she picked up her order. Just as the talk started about 'who is Larry', the lady swooped in, picked up her coffee, said "thank you", then left without Bean getting a word out. He paused for a moment then thought, "stuff it, I give up". At that moment Mel pulled up in the carpark, which prompted him to go for a walk. He wasn't up to talking about anything else, enough had happened already and his world was spinning.

Matty mulled over the conversation with Larry. He seemed to be able to read people with great accuracy which was a little unnerving, but encouraging. He remembered him casually saying: "He had inspected his project and it was not the work of an enthusiast but a passionate individual committed to solving some very intricate engineering problems. He could see the learning curve and the problems solved along the way. The most impressive thing about the project was the simplicity of effectiveness". Matty took this to heart. It was the first time someone had knowingly recognised and appreciated the scope of his ability. It gave him confidence.

It would take a lot of courage for Matty to step outside his comfort zone and the thought of such a big decision was daunting. Meeting Larry had given him direction and he couldn't wait to talk to him again and learn if there was a career opportunity, and what kind of career. But Larry was very private and played his cards close to his chest. After a lot of deliberation he decided to confide in Moey. After all, she knew everything.

Rooster had gone back to maintaining and polishing the surf boat with obsessive detail, although he was unaware the girls had decided not to compete at the Aussie titles. In true Rooster style, he managed to keep doing his secret maintenance without anyone's knowledge. Jackson was now on his feet in hospital and spent the day chatting to other young people in the ward. Rooster took young Micheal Hadfield up to see him most days, seeing as the pair got on so well together. The week passed quickly and soon it was time for Michael and his grandparents to return home, although it was good to be going back to family, they were a bit sad to leave the coast - what an experience it had been. What an extraordinary gesture from Rooster to organise and pay for everything. He had arranged all their meals through the club kitchen and served them all himself. He had thought of every little detail that would make their stay special, he did all the little things.

Starch had rounded up some old football photos and had his legendary football mates sign them. His wife Talia made a special photo album to preserve the pictures and gift wrapped the lot with a personal message from each of the players. Needless to say there was a tear in the eye of both grandparents when they opened their presents. The kindness, especially in the middle of so much tribulation was overwhelming. When they arrived back in Thargomindah, the talk went on for a week with the local paper printing the story - not surprisingly, the legend of Rooster grew more and more.

It finally came time for Jack to go home from the hospital. The doctors and nurses had become very fond of him in the short time they had known him, whilst the absence of any post-trauma stress was still puzzling them. Going back to the surf club and back to the dive centre felt strange, he realised for the first time he had changed - he no longer felt he had to prove himself to anyone. Everyone noticed the subtle differences in his manner. He was tougher and more direct, he was still 'The Big Fella' and everyone was glad to see him back, but he spoke and acted much more mature.

Everyone associated with the search for Jack had in some way been affected by it, How a seemingly normal day could be turned upside down at any instant. How the gift of life could be extinguished in a heartbeat, without any warning whatsoever. There are no second chances with death, it is absolute and final. The more sudden and unexpected it is, the more paralysing the effect. The closer it is to us the harder it hits. But Jack was a survivor and an inspiration to everyone. His million to one chance of being rescued had lifted everyone - sometimes, we win. Some of the people that were involved, reassessed their lives and made changes. Some relationships ended and others began, some careers ended and others began. There were lives taking new directions. Rainbows End had a wake up call and many of the locals were embracing it, but for others it was business as usual.

Danny had a good heart at times but whenever humility was handed out, he had unfortunately missed out and clearly overdosed on self-belief. Bean and Matty had sheepishly shown Starch the "Danny PT" pamphlets, and hoped it was not contagious. It was decided that any advertising pamphlets left on the club premises would attract an advertising charge of one thousand dollars per spot and pamphlets must be no bigger than a postage stamp. Starch wrote the rule on a club letterhead and gave it to Bean and Matty, hoping to fix the problem. Needless to say, Danny didn't accept the decision and argued discrimination, but his pleas fell on the sometimes deaf ears of Starch. He continued to distribute the pamphlets by hand.

Bull Jackson was buoyed by a recent adjournment of his court case involving himself being sued for falsely representing a plumber and gross overcharging. He had proudly and mistakenly declared himself exonerated and his detractors on the run. He had continued to trade and offered his services free of charge to Jack and his mum, although the Penguins had cautioned her about dealing with a Bull Jackson bearing plumbing gifts.

The kiosk had a quiet afternoon so the boys packed up early. Matt was to have another meeting with Larry, and Bean decided to hand out some coffee vouchers. He had noticed his secret love walking past in the early afternoon so he staked out a spot on the path and waited. Larry and Matt sat down at a table and picked up the conversation where they left off last time. Bean watched on as the pair talked their heads off, drawing diagrams on pieces of paper then squashing them up and throwing them away, then drawing some more. Bean was happy for Matt, he had never seen him so excited just talking to someone - it was just what he needed. Maybe Larry could help him with a career in something after all.

The path was pretty quiet so after about an hour and a bit, Bean decided to give up the love quest for the day. As he turned to leave he looked up to see the lady of his dreams walking toward him on the path. She was holding hands with a large, overweight, heavily tattooed man who looked to be in his late 50's or thereabouts, dressed in a blue singlet and jeans with long untidy grey hair cut in a 'mullet' style. The man was known to Bean. His name was Nohair Nelso n and was a local feral longboarding legend. He had made a name for himself by way of his 12 hour plus surfing benders after consuming buckets of magic mushrooms. Bean had mixed emotions. On one hand, all his dreams had gone up in smoke, on the other hand, he was relieved - his dreams could have ended up a nightmare.

As the lady and her boyfriend walked past she spoke to Bean:

'Working hard?' She asked.

'Always... Always', replied Bean, without hesitation.

He walked back to the kiosk in a philosophical mood - how could he have become so infatuated with someone he had never spoken to? What was he thinking? The lady had nothing in common with him at all. But still, he felt sad about the whole experience. Why couldn't she be single and like kiosk operators? What on earth could she see in that bloke? Maybe he's filthy rich? The more he dwelled on it, the more downhearted he became. Why couldn't it have just worked out? He was so sure. Do dreams ever come true or is love just a rumour? Or, was it him? It was time to face the awful truth. He was boring... He made himself a hot chocolate and dropped a marshmallow in it, then sat out in front of the kiosk by himself, watching the waves roll in.

Matty and Larry continued to chat at a million miles an hour. They had made enough diagrams and stuff to cover a cathedral ceiling. Bean watched on and laughed to himself thinking, 'at least someone's enjoying themselves'. The pair eventually stood up, shook hands then started walking over to Bean.

'Bean, this is Larry, Larry this is my best friend, Bean', said Matt.

'Hi Bean, pleased to meet you', said Larry.

'Thanks, mate, pleased to meet you too'. Replied Bean, thinking, for a person that is very, very intelligent, he sounds surprisingly down to earth. Bean liked him.

'I watched the work you and Matthew did at the time Jackson went missing. It was and is greatly appreciated by myself, my family, and everyone else that was affected', acknowledged Larry.

Bean was a bit embarrassed but appreciated the gesture. Larry was a cool bloke and he warmed to him straight away.

'Thanks, Mate. It was just one of those times when you do what you can. I just hope it never happens again', replied Bean.

Larry and Matt agreed to meet the next day and Larry would have an offer for Matt to consider. There were going to be some big decisions to make so he headed off home. It was Matt's life and his decision alone and any offer could mean leaving home to work/study in the United States. He knew this would cause angst in his family so he needed to carefully consider everything. Larry and Bean continued to talk for a while about things. Bean was a closet 70's music enthusiast so when Larry mentioned he collected vintage guitars, Bean was quick to ask about them. Larry had collected a plethora of instruments that were used by some of the '60s and 70's biggest superbands, Bean was wrapped, so wrapped that the disappointment of his non-eventuating romance temporarily left him.

He couldn't resist asking Larry what he did for a living, to which he simply replied:

'Heaps'.

The following day Simmo had gathered the girls together for some training, plus there were some new members who wanted to have a go at rowing in a surf boat. It was a good training session and the new girls loved it. Some say there is an adrenaline rush that comes with crewing a surf boat, especially in good surf and to some it is instantly addictive whilst to others, it is a good place to avoid. After the boat was hosed off and pushed back into the storage shed everyone sat down at the kiosk for a meeting where the new rowers were welcomed and a training schedule worked out. Just as Simmo was going over things with the girls, Jackson walked past with his mother. The rowers all jumped up and were eager to give him a hug and excited to see him back at the club, even if it was just for a quick visit. When everybody sat back down, Jackson used the opportunity to thank them once again for everything they had done.

'I really appreciate what you have done for mum and I. I'm sorry about getting smashed in the surf and throwing everybody into search mode, but I'm just glad that it happened here and not somewhere else - because even in my darkest days I knew you wouldn't give up. I'm really looking forward to seeing you compete at the Australian titles. I'm very inspired by your toughness and never give up attitude to training, especially the little things like banning mobiles in the gym. That was fair dinkum. I've got to get going but once again a very big thank you from myself, and especially mum'. And then Jack and his mum continued on.

The girls felt the sincerity in Jack's appreciation but it had left them questioning themselves. 'Toughness and never give up attitude? What have we done?' They thought.

'Oh crap', blurted Charlie.

'Oh nooo', added Steph.

'Well we didn't know it'd turn out like this,' said Marie.

'How are we going to tell him?' Groaned Charlie.

The girls had a collective look of failure on their faces. All of them felt like crawling under the nearest rock, when Steph stood up and laid down the law.

'We were too quick to give up!' Declared Steph. 'It was a mistake! It's not what he would have wanted if this turned out differently. We tapped out way too early. We weakened and took the easy way out. We quit! He believed in us and we let him down. It was never about winning, it was about having a go! How many times has that kid gone back for his bronze? 8 at last count? And what about the people that gave us the money to pay for everything? Strewth! Even the Penguins were getting excited and they're nearly dead! We've been having ourselves on. We could build fitness but we had the resolve of a ripe banana. One squeeze and we all squashed. All of us looked for the back door!... We'd better go find him and tell him the truth about our decision before he hears it from someone else. Let's go'.

The girls all stood up with heavy hearts and bowed heads.

'Stuff it', mumbled Charlie.

As they started to walk off to find Jack, Simmo interrupted.

'Hang on, hang on! Just sit down here for a minute'. The girls walked back and sat down, as Simmo explained the situation.

'You're still in the race. I never withdrew you from the competition. It just didn't feel right. If you want to have a go, it's still there waiting for you'.

The girls sat there with their mouths open before Steph asked: "What? Why didn't you tell us that straight away".

'I was enjoying the show. Talk about entertainment. Never heard so much remorse. Beautiful', he replied.

Steph was livid and blurted back: 'You're a piece of work Simpson! Do you want your punch in the head now or later?'

'That wasn't good coaching Simmo', added a simmering Charlie.

'Really?' Replied Simmo. 'I thought it was brilliant. I had eighty five to ninety percent commitment before, and now I've got one hundred and ten percent. I'm a genius!'

'Bullshit!!!' Roared Steph. 'Get that boat out of the shed and down on the beach. Come on girls, let's do this'.

'Hang on, I need someone to help me', reasoned Simmo.

'Do it yourself, we need entertainment and hurry up'. Yelled Charlie.

The new rowers sat through the conversation without having a clue what was going on. 'What do you want us to do?' Asked one of them.

'Come down the beach and we'll explain everything', replied Steph.

The girls walked off and Simmo was left with the task of getting the boat and gear down the beach by himself. He couldn't help but think he may have just created a monster.

Bean was working the kiosk by himself and was still trying to be philosophical about his failed romance when Mel put her head in the back door.

'Any news, Romeo?' she enquired.

'Yeah, we made contact, we spoke, she's got a bloke, I'm busy.' Replied Bean.

'What! Well hell, that was a much ado about nothing', quipped Mel.

'Yeah, you said it. What's going on upstairs?' Asked Bean.

'You heard the rumour?' Asked Mel.

'What rumour', replied Bean.

'The place is being sold for development', said Mel.

'Whattt? That's impossible! The club owns it', replied Bean.

'Not the land. Looks like we may be getting evicted'. Said Mel as she walked upstairs. 'Bad luck about your dream machine', she yelled.

Bean wasted no time in getting straight on the phone to Starch.

'Hey Starch, Bean here. There's a rumour going around that the place is being sold for development and we're getting kicked out. Do you know anything about that?'

'Yeah, it's a rumour. I'll talk to ya later', replied Starch and hung up.

Bean hung up the phone and turned to see Liz cruise past the servery window.

'Hello Bean, are the boys around?' She asked.

'Hello Liz. Haven't seen them much since Danny got married', replied Bean.

'What? Danny got married? What? When did this happen? That couldn't be right, who'd marry Danny? Where's Grizz? He never said anything about that. When did this happen?' Blurted a wide-eyed Liz.

'Dunno. Just heard it on the grapevine. Apparently, she's very young and wants to have more children, so they fell in love and got married.' Gushed Bean.

'Whattt? Are you serious? That is the most ridiculous thing I've ever heard. Why on earth would he want more children, when the ones he has now won't even talk to him. How ridiculous! Young? How young? Ten? Love? How could he love anybody when he's totally devoted to himself? The man is a walking bean-bag! Even his thought processes are enough to make him tired!' Blurted a disgusted Liz.

'Yeah, well not anymore. I believe he's a full-time athletic conditioner these days', informed Bean.

'Oh, this is just too much. I'm going home. Don't tell anyone you saw me', replied Liz.

Bean gave her the nod of approval, and she walked off shaking her head and muttering. As she distanced herself, Bean gave a mischievous smirk, raised an eyebrow and murmured to himself: 'Rumour? I'll give 'em a bloody rumour'.

Jack and his mum Suzanne had baked the penguins a cake in appreciation of their concern during the search. Of course, it had loads of cream and sugar which resulted in the Pennies not leaving a crumb. After chatting for a while and laughing their heads off at some Penguins Logic, they headed home. As they walked past the kiosk on the way to the car park, Larry came walking toward them. Jack immediately broke out with a huge smile.

'Hey Dr Larry, what are you doing here? Checking up on me? I'm feeling heaps better', beamed Jack.

'Hah. Hi Jackson, you always look great. Everybody needs a hero Jackson, and you're mine. Is this someone I should meet? Are you going to introduce me?' Asked Larry, referring to Suzanne.

'Oh yeah, sorry. I thought you knew my mum. Dr Larry this is my mum, Suzanne', replied Jack.

'Hello. Nice to meet you, Mrs. Gave. You're a beautiful family and an honour to know you', said Larry very sincerely.

Suzanne was taken aback by Larry's polite and gracious manner.

'Well thank you, and it's an honour to meet you', she answered.

'What are you doing here, Dr Larry? Wanna join the club?' Asked a cheeky Jack.

'That sounds great, but I have an appointment with someone so it might have to wait'. He answered, appreciating Jack's confident manner.

'Oh okay, we'd better let you go then. It's so cool to see you. Do you think we'll ever see you around the club again?' Asked Jack.

'Yes, I'm sure you will. Next time let's have something to eat and drink and maybe you could show me around. My shout', replied Larry.

Jack had a mini draw drop. 'Are you serious? Yeah, that'd be great. I'll see Starch and we'll go for a run in the inflatable'. Jack relished the idea of taking the Doc for a cruise around the headland.

'Okay deal', said Larry. 'I'll see you both soon'.

Matty and Bean were standing in the kiosk and overheard the conversation. They both turned toward each other with puzzled looks on their faces.

'Doctor? You never told me he was a doctor', blabbed Bean.

'I didn't know he was a doctor, he never mentioned it. I thought he was some kind of scientist, business man or something. He has such a massive breadth of knowledge, I'm not surprised', replied Matt.

'So when's the meeting about the offer?' asked Bean.

'Today. Then he wants me to sleep on it', answered Matt.

'Well that'll be interesting', said Bean, as Larry knocked on the counter.

'Morning Matthew. How are you today Bean? What time do you think you'll be free, Matt?'

'You can go now if you want, Matty. I can handle this for a while', quipped Bean.

'Oh, okay. Is that alright with you, Larry?' Asked Matt.

'Yes of course. Thanks, Bean. I really appreciate your generosity', replied Larry. Then the pair of them sat down and Larry explained what was possible and what Matty needed to bring to the table. Bean watched on and tried to read their body language, as the pair conversed. Whatever they were talking about, sure was interesting because both were busy drawing and writing things again. Bean was in deep surveillance when without warning, Danny and Grizz appeared at the counter.

'Hello, my man Bean. Top of the morning to you', said Danny in true Danny fashion.

'How ya goin, Bean', added Grizz in a typical Grizz manner.

'Can we have the usual please, and can you sprinkle some muesli on mine please. I've really gone up a gear going forward', announced Danny.

'Yeah well, that wouldn't be hard, seeing you've been in freakin reverse most of your life! Can you grab a seat and I'll bring it over', replied Bean.

'Who's that Matt's talking to?' Asked Grizz.

'That's Larry. Why?' Said Bean.

'I've just seen him around a bit, that's all". Replied Grizz, as he gave a nod of knowledge, then made his way to a table with Danny. As Grizz sat down, Danny stood up and announced: 'I'll be back in a second. I just forgot something', then walked over to the counter and quizzed Bean.

'Bean my good man. It isn't important, but I was wondering if you had seen Liz around?'

Bean raised an eyebrow and replied: 'Nah mate, it's been ages since I've seen her. I heard she became a vegan and went off with some bloke to live in a forest and meditate five hours a day. She gave him all her money and they're gunna plant trees all over the world and make us live like fruit bats. I read it in the paper somewhere actually'.

Danny's jaw dropped and he unloaded with a barrage of emotional responses.

'WHAT? When did this happen? You've got to be joking! Five hours of meditation? Stuff a duck, she gets drained ordering a coffee! Vegan?!! She's a bacon terminator! A bloody baconator! Everything she sticks in her gob has bloody bacon on it!'

Bean paused to savour the moment, then delivered his coup d'etat.

'I'd suppose you'd know all about that Danny'.

Danny stood there transfixed for a moment, caught somewhere between flattered and disgusted. He grunted, then walked back to sit with Grizz.

Bean had the look of a champion plastered all over his face, as he quietly muttered to himself: 'They want rumours, I'll give 'em bloody rumours'. It was obvious the news about the possible club sale and closure were playing on his mind, but for the time being he kept an eye on Larry and Matt, and was chafing at the bit to find out what was going on.

A couple of hours passed before they finished their discussion. Bean watched as they both stood up, shook hands and walked over to the counter.

'Thanks for your patience, Bean. I'll see you later on, my family wants to go to the beach', said Larry.

'Thanks, Larry, that's great mate. Does your family like the beach?' Asked Bean.

'Oh yes, they love it', he replied.

Larry made his way to the car park and Matty watched as he cruised off in his VW Kombi. It was a similar car to his but older and perfectly restored, with an electric motor.

'So, what's going on', inquired Bean.

'I'm going to be leaving', answered Matt.

'What, for a holiday?' Asked Bean.

'No. I accepted his offer of a job, but the workplace is in the United States', replied Matt.

Bean had a dumbstruck moment before finding his voice.

'Are you serious? Your parents will go nuts', babbled Bean.

'Probably, but it's my decision. I think it's a very good offer and he's going to personally recommend me for a scholarship over there', explained Matt.

'Oh man, I don't know, this sounds like a very big deal to me. What is the job anyway? What does Larry actually do besides being a doctor?' Asked Bean.

'Well, he said he wears many hats, but one of his companies is a world leader in marine leisure equipment. That's part of what we've been talking about. I will be working with three other people designing and building underwater sports craft', explained Matty.

'What on earth would a doctor want with marine leisure equipment and why is he hiring you? I mean, don't you think that's a bit suspicious?' Said Bean.

'Someone gave him my name and that's what we have been talking about. He was looking for someone my age because part of the incentive to work for his company is the opportunity to sit for a scholarship at an American Uni - that's why I have to be on a plane in three days. A physical assessment is also part of the scholarship'.

Bean was struggling with what he was hearing, he couldn't get his head around the enormity of what Matty had been offered. It was all very sudden and unexpected, but his heart lay with what his young mate wanted, and if he wanted to have a go at something that was legitimate - well he would support him all the way.

'Matty, I'm stuffed if I know but if it's what you want, I'm behind you 110%. Do you have money for the plane fare and expenses? I've got a few bob saved up that you can have', offered Bean.

Matthew was humbled. Bean was as true as they come, and his generosity and support never ceased to amaze him. He could see the panic on his face about him leaving so suddenly, but he was still willing to give everything he had to help him have a go.

'It's okay, Larry is paying for everything and giving me an expenses card, so I'm not out of pocket. I'll be back in three weeks when I'll know if I've won the scholarship or not, plus I have to meet the other people on the team. They're not attempting the scholarship exam, they're my project team', explained Matt.

'This is freakin big, Matt, we've got to have a go. You've got guts young fella, I'm really proud of you. Larry's no mug and he can obviously see your potential, plus he's putting up a whack of money to back you. Bloody scary if you ask me! Strewth, I'm getting goosebumps just thinking about it. What do you think your old man will say?' Asked Bean.

'I don't know', said Matty, 'I really don't know'. And with that, they both went back to work cleaning up, and trying to get their heads around what was going on.

Sitting at one of the kiosk tables, Ben and Sushi were doing their own bit of soul searching and decided it was time to move on and continue their plan to surf around the world. They still wanted to be a part of Australia and the thought of life without Fins, Sharkbait and the one-legged seagull seemed too boring to contemplate, so the boys hatched a plan and decided to offer Fins a business deal. The boys were environmentalists at heart so they decided to surf on it first, then get some costings and make an offer to a couple of third parties, before speaking to Fins.

After the boys left, the kiosk was very quiet and Bean was starting to stress about Matthew leaving. He talked him into finishing early so he could explain his decision to his parents. It was a conversation Matt was dreading, but his mind was made up. He wanted to have a go at the scholarship, and working with Larry is what he wanted to do.

Deciding to take Bean's advice, he knocked off and headed home to front the olds, being fully aware this was a turning point in his life. As he turned into the driveway of the family home he took a deep breath. His parents were both there so it was a good time to tell them. He took another deep breath and walked inside.

'Hi mum, hi dad. Can I talk to you for a minute and let you know what I'm doing?' He requested.

'About the scholarships and stuff?' Replied his dad, George.

'Yeah, it's a little more complicated than that', replied Matt.

'Oh okay, well you'd better let us know what you're doing', said his mum.

'I've decided to work for Larry, the man I told you about. I've also accepted his offer to sit for a NASA scholarship at the University Of Florida in the United States. I have to go through a vetting process starting in five days time so I have to be there in three. If successful there is a further fourteen days of physical, academic and psychological assessment without any breaks. It's ten to twelve hours a day of rigorous evaluation. Larry is organising my ticket and paying all expenses so all I have to do is pack my things. I'll be back in three weeks when I get the results. Love you'. Matty rattled off, as cool as a cucumber.

His parents just sat there with their mouths open, and a look between disbelief and horror etched all over their faces. To say they were stunned, would be an understatement.

'Would you mind just running that by us again son? Especially the parts about NASA and having to be in the United States in three days time', his dad asked cautiously.

Matthew explained what he intended to do again, making sure he was very clear about the message.

His parents suffered the same reaction which could best be described as gobsmacked. There was a long pause of silence as his parents sat staring at him with their mouths open, trying to think of a response. Unfortunately, they were grappling with the situation and unable to come up with a response, so they played the parent card, and let fly.

'Matthew, have you lost the plot?' Asked his dad.

'What is this? Scare the crap out of your parents day?' Blurted his mum.

'Matthew, that is the most ridiculous thing I have ever heard you say. Are you feeling ok?' Asked his dad.

'Who is this Larry? We've never heard of him! Does Bean know him? Does Bean know what you want to do? Matty, I think you should be a bit more realistic with yourself', gasped his mum.

Matthew could sense the anxiety in their voices, so he tried to reassure them.

'Yes, he knows him. Yes, they get along like peas in a pod. Yes, I told Bean what I wanted to do. Yes I'm okay and I am being realistic. I know this is sudden and you're worried but so am I. To be honest, I'm scared stiff, but I still want to try.' Declared Matty.

'Matthew, if you are scared stiff, don't you think it would be a good idea to just sit back and rethink what you're talking about doing? I mean, it's a lot to digest in one lifetime', said his dad.

'I agree, but that doesn't mean I shouldn't try, does it? The pain of regret will last longer than the disappointment of defeat', replied Matt.

'That's ridiculous, how stupid and misleading. Who told you that?' Blasted his mum.

'Dad', answered Matt.

Both parents stood up and started rolling their eyeballs and throwing their arms in the air. Matt's father paused for a moment, then said.

'Matthew! What you have just said is madness, no matter how you look at it, it's pure nonsensical madness. You have so many offers for scholarships here already, it's like a dog surrounded by bones. There is no need whatsoever to go anywhere with someone you've known for such a brief period of time, in an attempt to become an, I don't know what. You cannot expect us to support you with an endeavour that is no better than a bet on a roulette wheel'.

Matty couldn't hide the disappointment that had just washed over him. His resolve was being tested. He wasn't going to argue, he just choked out the words:

'I completely understand'.

He then went to his room, closed the door and started packing his bag. As he pondered the future, his phone signalled an incoming message that read: "Ticket in attachment. Check-in is at 2.30 pm. We will meet you at the airport. Cheers. Larry".

Matty opened the message attachment, it was a first-class ticket to the US. The realisation that this was really happening began to sink in, even deeper. He couldn't ignore the disappointment he felt from his parent's reaction, which had left him with mixed emotions. This was going to be so much tougher without their support, but he loved and respected them too much to try and argue with them. He bunkered down in his room and thought about the best way to prepare for the assessment, but he soon realised the problem with preparing was he didn't know what he was preparing for. It was a blind assessment, which meant no one knew how they were going to be tested. The only strategy was to wing it and back himself in.

He started to wonder about the new job and how it would all fit together if he won, and the confidence Larry had in him when he said: 'It will work out, just do your best'.

Starch was trying to keep up a brave front by talking to the patrol members positively to keep spirits up, and continually taking time to stop and have a yarn to all the club members. The Penguins had heard the rumour of a developer buying the club and had immediately reacted with a stoic, that'll be the day response. The old boys were fired up and already planning a fight back, or possibly overthrowing the government, and tar and feathering every politician from local councillors upwards.

Although he did a convincing job of hiding his disappointment, Starch was running on empty. He had to deal with the club major structural repairs grant, the dredging, the pressure to conform to the requests of Flowers, the burgeoning amount of sand on the beach, the Superbank fiasco, the collapse of the Superbank, the near loss of Jackson, and now the possible sale and closure of the club. He decided to end his time at the club and began writing a letter of resignation and appreciation. It was a very sad thing for him to do, but he sensed the sale rumours were true and he didn't have the energy to fight another greedy developer - that he knew would have corrupt political backing. There was too much easy money on the table.

The club board had decided to have an appreciation ceremony in three weeks, and everyone who had taken part in the search would be invited and thanked for their efforts. The Australian Surf Boat Titles were in two weeks so the week following seemed an ideal time. Robyn had told Starch the government department handling the grant had guaranteed them an answer by then, so he penciled in that date as resignation day.

Back at the kiosk, Bean was starting to feel a bit overwhelmed with the impending changes to his life. His secret love had revealed itself to be nothing more than an over-eager infatuation, so his fake living happily ever after dream had gone up in smoke. The clubhouse was terminal and a greedy developer was circling like a shark, which could mean the end of the club. Matty was leaving, but for all the right reasons, and he knew this day would come. Nevertheless he was unprepared for the stress that came with Matt's announcement. He hadn't served anybody for an hour which made things worse, because he was alone and kept dwelling on different outcomes. He decided to call it a day and started locking up when there was a knock at the back door and a feminine voice enquired:

'Excuse me, the First Aid room is locked. You wouldn't happen to have a band-aid I could buy, would you?'

Bean walked out to the back door to see who it was, and standing there with a bleeding foot was a very beautiful lady.

'I'm sorry to disturb you but I was walking on the beach and I must have cut my foot on a shell or something. It's not hurting too bad but I can't stop it from bleeding. I don't suppose you would have a band-aid I could buy, would you?' She politely asked.

Bean paused for a moment to assess the situation, then replied:

'No, no, no. We'll have to clean that up. Just sit on a chair and I'll get the First Aid kit'.

The lady looked at him and smiled, she appreciated his concern and kindly manner.

'Oh, okay then. I'll just sit down here so I don't scare any customers off', she replied.

Bean went off to get some water and the First Aid kit. He had recognised the lady from a couple of previous visits to the kiosk. She always came with her mother and once bought her husband, who was a tall good looking man with a closely shaved beard. He noticed how caring she was to her mother although she tended to be a bit bossy with her hubby, who seemed to be accustomed to it.

He arrived back with the water and medical kit and knelt down in front of her, gently lifting her foot to inspect the cut.

'Okay, we're going to have to dip your foot in the water. This might sting a little but we need to clean it up'.

The lady trusted him and did what he said as he cleaned the cut and tried to minimise any stinging. After a couple of minutes of super cautious first aid he dried the area and applied a temporary bandage. Then after all was done, he asked her where her car was and if she could walk okay.

'Oh, no it's okay, I can get there', she replied. 'You're amazing! I certainly got the VIP treatment. I don't think I've ever met a more chivalrous man. Can I pay you for that please?'

Bean blushed and felt embarrassed. The lady was super good looking and her appearance intimidated him, but with the shyness of a young schoolboy, he replied:

'Nah, nah, nah, that's fine, it happens all the time. It's a Surf Lifesaving club, that's what we're here for'.

'Well you're a very generous man and I greatly appreciate what you did for me', she replied.

While he watched her limp back to her car, she turned and left him with a gorgeous smile he would never forget. Life was suddenly good but normality was beckoning, so he finished locking up the kiosk. As he clicked the padlock shut on the front door he stopped and stood still, just to watch and listen to the surf roll in for a minute or two. No matter how bad things get, how much change is on its way, life still goes on. Mrs Super Beautiful had reset his happy compass, by simply being there. Every day brings its surprises, both good and bad. The lady was like a ship in the night, passing quietly and briefly interacting, then leaving him with a little bit of joy in a worrying time. Some human beings have that gift and they always seem to appear at the most unexpected moments, then as quickly as they appear they're gone, never to be seen again. For some, they're treasured moments that are kept locked away with the little things.

As Bean started to walk off his phone rang. Matthew's dad was calling. Thinking the proverbial must have hit the fan at the Binge household, Bean tentatively pressed the answer button.

'Hello, Bean speaking', was the best he could manage.

'Gidday Bean, Matt's father, George here', said the caller.

'G'day mate, how ya going', replied Bean.

'Aww, not bad, mate. Bean, I'm just trying to find out a little more about this scholarship or job offer thing in the US, Matthew has been offered', explained George.

Bean could sense the concern in George's voice and explained patiently.

'As far as I know, he's had a few discussions with a bloke called Larry, who comes to the club. He saw some of Matt's work and came into the kiosk to meet him, then they had a couple of meetings which were skyped with someone in America. The meetings were vigorous discussions with diagrams etc. being exchanged. Larry offered him a job with his company but also offered him the chance to sit for some sort of NASA scholarship in the US. The scholarship offers had closed, so the only window of opportunity was in three days time. I've met Larry a few times and he seems alright to me, I also know he's a doctor because Jackson met him in hospital'.

'Oh! So it's all real!' gasped George. 'Well if this bloke's a doctor, what's he doing with authority to grant scholarship offers, and a private company?'

'Mate he's a mixed bag, and personally, I like him. I think he's far more wealthy and successful than he makes out. He's a very intelligent man and in case you're wondering, this isn't about an indigenous thing, Matthew was given the job offer and scholarship opportunity purely on merit. Larry looks Asian but has a sort of American type accent and he's definitely a switched on honcho', related Bean.

'Well, I trust your judgement, but why on earth would NASA offer a kid from Australia, who they know next to nothing about, a chance at a scholarship. It just doesn't make sense. And then there's the job offer! What's that? It's all too hairy fairy. We're all stunned, this just came out of the blue', gasped George.

'Yeah, well join the club. It seems, coming out of the blue is the new norm around here. George, I don't know what to tell ya, only judging by the conversation between him and Larry, Matt is far more intelligent than what we gave him credit for. I mean, what the hell is Ionic Propulsion? And what the hell is an Oxygen Extraction Synthesis Modulator? I mean, fair dinkum! It's a bloody long way from burgers and coffee!' Exclaimed Bean.

'Well, I don't know what to do. Are you sure Larry didn't talk him into this? It just seems too good to be true', said George.

'Definitely not!' Answered Bean. 'They're both on the same wavelength, that's for sure. He hasn't got anything yet, other than the job offer. The scholarship thing is an opportunity, not a promise. Obviously, he must have something they think they can utilise otherwise he wouldn't have been invited'.

'I just don't know what to do. Why doesn't he just take the sensible option and go with one of the scholarships offered here? It just doesn't make sense', reasoned George.

'George, maybe we don't know him as well as we think we know him. There was a lot of soul searching going on during the week Jackson was missing, and maybe he's decided to go for it. If that's the case, and he's a young bloke that's willing to have a go, then we don't have a choice other than to support him. If we don't do that - well we're useless!' Counselled Bean.

'Agreed, but I don't want to support him with the wrong advice. I don't know what to do, his mothers worried sick. Our only hope is he'll wake up in the morning and come to his senses', lamented George.

'George, separate the anxiety for your son's welfare from the belief in your son's ability. You know what? I bet he'll nail this. I'll bet he'll give you the proudest moment of your life. I'll bet everything I've got, he brings this home and shocks the crap out of everybody. Do you want to know how I know? LARRY! How many people do you know, can phone up NASA and say, give this kid a go, and they listen! This bloke is a very big dark horse. What was he doing in the hospital helping with Jackson's recovery? I mean, that just doesn't happen. We'll all get the answers one day, but in the meantime, I am very sure he doesn't invest himself in mediocre people. Figure it out George, we can only understand what we can process about Matthew. It is obvious that Larry can see a whole lot more. His ability to understand Matthew and what Matthew does, is a whole lot more than ours. It must be taking a mountain of courage for Matty to do this, and the worst thing we can do is not support him. He's your son, George! He's earnt this and he deserves his chance. Think about it', emphasized Bean. The depth of his respect for Matty was evident, from the passion in his voice.

There was silence on the other end of the phone before George responded quietly: "Yeah okay. I can see why you two are best mates. Thanks, Bean."

The call ended and Bean made his way home. What a day!

# Chapter 20

# If Your Chance Came, Would You Take It?

The following morning at daybreak, Simmo was putting the surf boat into the water as the girls went for a light jog to warm up. The boardriders were already crowding the points and Danny trudged across the soft sand with a set of headphones blasting early morning news bulletins into his ears. Starch arrived and did his usual rounds of loading and checking the equipment. The creaking sound of the kiosk roller door opening signalled hot coffee and bacon and egg rolls were thirty minutes away, as a weary Bean tried to get interested in what he was doing. The first customers were Ben and Sushi, who were getting their daily surf fix out of the way early. They had several appointments booked in and were feverishly putting together their business proposal for Fins.

The early morning passed uneventfully, other than a possible shark sighting over the border. Around mid morning Matthew came into the club to see if everything was alright, and touched bases with Bean before he left.

'Hey, Beans. What's happening? Are you okay? Everything under control?'

'Hey, Matty, what are you doing in here, shouldn't you be getting ready to go?' Asked Bean.

'Yep, it's allgood, just checking you're okay. I've packed everything and my check-in time is at 2.30 pm', replied Matt.

'Whoa! It's all happening', said Bean, as he handed him an envelope with four thousand dollars in it. 'That should help with the ticket, I'll send more when I get it'.

'No, no, no, it's ok. Larry has already paid for the ticket, he phoned me this morning and said he had an expenses card, so I can buy whatever I need. If I need cash he said to just draw it off the card. My accommodation and everything is arranged and already paid. I've just got to meet the two other people I'll be working with, as soon as I get there. They're not going for the scholarship, they're going to be my teammates', explained Matt.

'Well, it's all happening. Too much information. How are your parents holding up?' Quizzed Bean.

'There was no one at home when I woke up, I couldn't get to sleep last night so I slept through. Mum left me a note telling me to think things over, which I have, that's why I'm going', Matt answered.

'Matty! Make sure your folks know what time the plane is leaving. Have you found out what Larry's company is yet?' Asked Bean.

'Yeah I googled it, it's huge. They specialise in powered air and water sports leisure craft, but that's only one of them, he's got heaps', answered Matt.

'Well, it's really important to tell your parents what's happening. Ok!' said Bean.

'Yes, of course, all cool. I will be back in three weeks and by then I'll know what's happening. Everything's okay. Larry's very thorough with organisation', replied Matt.

'Okay, so you're sure everything is good to go?' Pressed Bean.

'Yes, I'm going to the airport early and just relax, so I've got to get going. I'll see you in three weeks. I'll give you a buzz when I get a chance, although Larry said my feet won't touch the ground and my head won't hit the pillow, so get ready to be busy'. Recounted Matt.

The boys were very close and Matt knew Bean would have his back no matter what happened. This gave him an extra little bit of confidence. They shook hands in their own special way and Matt walked off. The rest of the morning the kiosk trade was quiet, except for a little bit of a surge that saw Mel having to step in to help. Until he found someone to replace Matty, things were going to be difficult for Bean.

The girl's boat crew had regained their mojo and seemed more determined than ever to give a good account of themselves. The bounce was back in Simmo's step and it was all systems go. Rooster, as usual, was giving his support by secret boat polishings and the occasional compliment whenever he saw the girls. Bean had heard snoring coming from the medical room that morning and had deduced, Rooster was back sharing the love.

Matty collected his bags, called a cab and headed to the airport. He left his parents a letter telling them how much he loved them, explaining, all he ever wanted was a chance and asked for their patience and understanding. He had tried to call both their phones several times but both rang out. He arrived at the airport ahead of time, found a seat and sat there by himself waiting for Larry. As he sat there he thought about his life and realised most of the things he had done, he had done alone. From his pet fish to his early school days when he would pull apart and reconstruct TVs, laptops, mobile phones and anything and everything that twigged his interest. Apart from his pet fish he had recently made a drone the size of a matchbox with a HD camera, that he controlled with a program he wrote for his mobile phone. He was in the process of making the drone submersible as well as aerial. He didn't show this to anyone.

He thought about how far he had come and how he realised very early in life, that rapidly understanding things and accumulating knowledge others struggled with, mostly came easy for him. It was like a gift. He enjoyed sports and even though he had achieved an excellent array of titles from different sports, it always just seemed like fun to him. He never had to train, the skill and fitness were just there. He thought about his parents and how different their world view was to his. Strangely enough, his love of science and learning had left him at odds with most of his extended family, seemingly because he didn't want to live within the culture box. He avoided any conversation with his parents about this because he knew it would upset them. In a way this saddened him and often meant he didn't share a lot of the things he discovered.

On the upside his solitude had made him more resilient and independent, and he was quite comfortable solving complicated problems on his own - which was exactly what Larry was looking for.

Sitting there alone watching people coming and going, he wondered about the thousands of stories an airport could tell. The tears of goodbyes and the joys of hellos filled the different faces. So many humans, coming and going around the world. Then like a bagpipes player emerging through a Scottish mist, a familiar face came wandering through the crowd.

'Hey dude, what ya doin? Dad said you might be here, I was just next door, hanging out', sounded the familiar voice of Moey.

Matty grinned from ear to ear. The best antidote for loneliness is a friend, and one of the best just showed up.

'Moeeeyy! What ya doin dudess? Are you doing loops or something?' Asked Matt.

'Nah, I emptied the bank account on air hours looking for Jacko, so I've got to save up some funds again. So what's going on? Dad tried to tell me you're going to the US to sit for a NASA scholarship, yeah right! How about the truth, are you going on a holiday or something?' Quizzed Moey.

'No, Bean's right. This bloke saw some of my work then came into the kiosk to meet me. Next thing I know we're hooked up, Skype wise, to the States with some other dudes firing questions non-stop at me. Next day he offers me a job and as a bonus organises this opportunity for a NASA scholarship'. Explained Matt, as Moey stood there with her mouth open and speechless.

He continued explaining: 'The scholarship offers were closed but Larry, who is the bloke I met, just asked them to put me in, and they did. I have two more days to get there so Larry is meeting me here any time soon, and off we go'. Moey remained standing there with her mouth open. After slowly digesting what he said, she hesitatingly asked:

'Matty, who is this Larry person?'

'I'll introduce you, here he comes now', replied Matt.

Moey looked around. 'Where?' She asked.

Larry walked straight up to her and said: 'Hi, you must be Moey. Bean described you perfectly. I'm Larry', he said, extending his hand.

Moey was a bit surprised and was still processing what Matt had told her, but accepted his handshake.

'Hello Larry. Yep, I'm Moey and pleased to meet you', she replied.

'Hi Matt, how are we? Are you ready to go? Where's your family? Are they here?'

'Ahhm, no Larry, they're busy. But we had a good talk last night and they know I'll be back in three weeks anyway', replied Matt.

Both Larry and Moe sensed Matt was faking it. The disappointment in his voice was obvious.

'Oh ok then. Well, we had better make our way to the departure lounge. Can you hang around please, Moey? I need to talk to you', said Larry.

'Yeah sure'. Moe answered, curious as to what Larry wanted to talk about, considering she had only just met him.

Matt picked up his bags and the three of them headed to Check In.

'Where are your bags, Larry?' Asked Matt.

'I just have, carry on. Everything I need is in the States. I do that everywhere I go, it's easier that way', answered Larry.

As they walked through the terminal, Moey's mind was racing. The situation seemed so surreal and made her wonder, 'How did all this come together?' Larry could see that she was a bit concerned, and recognised this as a good thing.

'Moey, I hope you don't mind but Bean told me all about you and your brother. He mentioned that you have a restricted flying license and you're currently grounded, because the hours you spent searching for Jackson drained your savings. I hope you don't mind but before I came here, I had your flying school reimburse you the money for the aircraft hire. I also added on a wage for the cost of you flying the search plane', he explained.

Moey gave a blank puzzled look but didn't say anything as Larry continued.

'I do a lot of traveling when I'm here and sometimes it's inconvenient and costly to rely on commercial flights. So if you are interested, I'm going to need a pilot that can be available when I'm in the country. Of course it will be a paid position and I know that you are on a restricted licence at the moment, but I'm willing to include your cost of flying time hours in the deal. The only thing is, you'll need a fixed wing day/night and rotor wing licence, but the instructor fees and aircraft hire cost will be covered by me'.

Moey was stunned with what Larry was proposing and took a moment to try and make some sense of the situation. To her, his offer didn't make sense and was totally unnecessary.

'Larry, it's really nice to meet you and it's fantastic that you're helping Matty, but there's no need to pay for my search hours because Jackson is my friend and I did that for him. I can't accept the tuition fee payment but I'm happy to be your pilot anytime, when I get my unrestricted license. No charge. Why don't you just hire a pilot when needed, and if you don't mind me asking. Why me?' She asked.

'My wife and children asked me to ask you because they don't like using different pilots all the time. They've seen you at the surf club and spoken to you sometimes when you've been helping Bean. He pointed you out when you were flying over the beach one day and the girls loved it. They call you the Flying Girl, and like you a lot. We were all hoping you would say, yes. The money for the tuition is irrelevant because it's an investment and we have to pay someone anyway. The money for Jackson's search has already been paid so please accept it, it's my way of saying thank you. Bean tells me you're doing a medical degree so I can help you with that too. Please have a think about it and let me know in three weeks when we're back. You have forty hours credit at the flying school, Please use it or it will go to waste", Larry patiently explained.

Moey was completely unprepared for the conversation and at a loss for a reply. Just like bad things can happen unexpectedly, good things can happen unexpectedly. She looked at Matt to gauge his reaction, he smiled and gave her a yes nod. Yes it was real, yes it was happening. She had more than enough time to think about life when she was looking for Jackson, and guided by the look on Matt's face she decided to trust Larry at his word and do something she thought she would never do. She would cautiously accept his offer.

'Well, okay Larry. I think I know who your family are, and I like them a lot too, they're beautiful children and your wife is a lovely person. Will you accept a tentative yes. Then if you decide to withdraw your offer, it'll be okay?' Proposed Moey, as Matty's smile grew larger.

'Well my future pilot's not impulsive or a risk taker. That's a relief to know', said Larry. 'My family will be over the moon, the kids will be so excited. The offer will stand, so if you can organise your training hours and let the flying school know, I will be back in three weeks to finalise everything. That'll be a great help. My wife will let you know everything else. I'm sorry there's not enough time to go over all the details with your Med degree, right now, but there's a lot I can do to help you with that. There's so much to do, but let's get Matt on the plane and take care of that first'.

Moey was happy with his answer, so the three of them headed off to the departure lounge. Once inside Larry answered all the questions they had about the company Matt would be working for, and revealed the rest of Matt's new teammates had already arrived in Florida. They were waiting for him to join them.

He explained to them about how the technology used in spacecraft and the people who invent the technology sometimes get involved with projects his companies work on. Some of the projects also involve medical science and technology and involve the international space station. Matt and Moey started to feel a bit intimidated but Larry was quick to console them, explaining that the complexity of the work takes years to complete. Their age and willingness to learn was a huge advantage, going into the future.

He was also quick to reiterate that Matt's scholarship offer was an opportunity not a promise. He would be given a chance the same as everyone else. The assessment would be brutal and unforgiving. Out of the one thousand initial applicants there were ten left, and Matt was eleven. Larry was one of the university's largest donors so he had used his influence to get Matt an interview. But he could only get the interview that was Skyped, then it was the examiners from NASA who made the decision to admit him. Everyone else had started the testing process.

After about twenty minutes the first call for boarding their flight came over the airport speakers. As they made their way to the departure gate, Matthew heard someone shouting his name.

'Matthew, Matthew', yelled his dad. He turned to see his mum, dad, brothers and sister running toward him. Matt had two brothers, the oldest was Dallas, a fourteen year old self professed capitalist who spent most of his time learning about financial markets. Joshua, who was six years old and absolutely idolised Matty, and Melissa, his twelve year old sister who spent most of her spare time with her mother doing volunteer work. Melissa loved learning about the law and her goal was to be part of the legal system, in particular the social justice side of things. She often clashed with Dallas over what she described as his corporate greed and lack of empathy for poor people. Dallas, of course, dismissed her accusations and insisted he only wanted to be successful and she was envious. The arguments were a constant headache for their parents.

Matt's mum gave him a big hug, followed by a hug from his dad, then his siblings fired off their questions.

'Where are you going? What's going on? Why are you leaving? You didn't tell us! You're in trouble!'

There was an awkward moment of silence after the barrage of questions before Larry stepped forward and extended his hand to Matt's dad.

'Mr Binge, my name is Larry and I'm very pleased to meet you and Mrs Binge. Matthew speaks very highly of you and is very proud of you both'.

George welcomed the gesture and replied: 'Thanks Larry and we're also pleased to meet you, we've heard a lot about you. Can you tell us a little more about Matthew's job offer and scholarship, he's a bit sketchy about the details'.

Larry explained as much as he could and assured them that this was a genuine offer from NASA, but made it very clear there were no guarantees. 'His job offer however is his, no matter what happens. If he feels he doesn't want any of it, there's no problem'. As he was explaining everything, the second call for boarding came over the terminal loudspeakers.

Larry shook everyone's hand, including Matt's siblings, then reminded Moey to check in with her flight school. He told Matt he had to make a phone call then would meet him onboard the aircraft.

Matt gave his mum and his brothers and sister another hug, then shook his father's hand and gave him a hug, which prompted him to ask:

'Well we're still a bit worried mate, I just don't understand why? Why NASA? Why on earth would you be interested in that?'

'Why?' Replied Matt. 'Because I want to be a Captain Cook. That makes sense doesn't it?'

George gave a stunned look then blurted:

'What? And colonise the universe!'

Matthew laughed, picked up his bag and replied:

'Think about it dad. Think about it'.

As he started to walk off, Dallas interjected: 'Can I have his room?'

'No! Keep out of my room', Matt immediately replied.

Melissa then blurted: 'Dallas is trying to get dad to give him the family savings so he can invest it. He told dad he can get a big return. He doesn't know anything!'

Dallas replied with: 'Shut up Melissa, if I want a dodgy lawyer, I'll let you know!'

Matt's parents were both rolling their eyes when his mother firmly declared: 'That's enough! Matty has to leave'.

And with that he shook Moey's hand and said: 'See ya dude. I'll be in touch'.

To which she replied: 'What a day!'

Then he started to walk off. Turning around for the last time to wave, he saw a tear running down Joshua's cheek. He dropped his bag and walked back, kneeling down in front of his little brother, he wiped away his tears and said:

'I promise you I'll be back in three weeks, you can sleep in my room and use all my gear. I'm going to phone you from America. This is something I need to do. I need you to have patience. It won't be forever. I love you little bro, you're the best little bro, ever'.

Joshua nodded his head up and down, then threw his arms around Matt's neck and squeezed, then let him go. As he walked off his dad redirected him: 'Matty, you're going into the first class check in'.

'Yes, I've got a first class ticket', he replied.

George gave another stunned look and asked: 'How much are you getting paid for this job?'

'I start on US six figures a year plus expenses, car, rent, etc'. Answered Matt.

With the stunned look still hanging on his face, George replied: 'Can I get a job too?'

Bean was going through the motions at the kiosk when the rattling sound of Moey's scooter signalled her arrival. He hadn't seen her since Matt left, so he was wondering what was going on.

'Hey dad, I've got some great news. You're not going to believe this, but I met Larry', she gushed.

Bean looked skyward and replied: 'Here we go, don't tell me you're going to the moon too?'

Moey laughed excitedly.

'Almost! I can't believe this guy! Is he for real? He must be! Wait til I tell you what he did!' She exclaimed.

'Well yeah, he's for real, so what's going on? Let's hear it, I probably won't be surprised', asked Bean.

'Well I can't believe it, but Larry reimbursed me for all the aircraft hours I had to pay searching for Jack. Over four thousand dollars and on top of that he left me some money in an envelope at the flying school, to pay for my time. Four thousand in cash', related Moey.

The news left the usually very composed Bean astonished.

'You're joking,' he slowly drawled.

'No, but there's more. His family wants me to be their pilot, and he insists on paying me for it', she added.

Bean gave another look of disbelief.

'But you don't have the hours up for the licence required. Why is he doing this?' Asked Bean.

'I don't know. He's very direct about things and as far as the licence goes he's paying for everything, including the rotor', replied Moey.

'Well I don't know either. Larry obviously lives in a world completely different to ours. He's very genuine and just seems to want to help people. He had no hesitation in helping Matty and now it's the same with you. Something tells me he's seriously wealthy but very private at the same time. It's a wonder he didn't offer to do something with your studies as well', said Bean.

'He did! He's going to help me with that too', replied Mo.

'Well there you go. You might as well take him up on it and go for it. Good things do happen, I suppose', reasoned Bean.

'I did. Thanks dad. I'm just going to make myself something to eat, then head off and start using up those air hours. Unbelievable!' Concluded Mo.

The next couple of days passed without incident at the club. The news about Matthew and his NASA offer had been met with shock and disbelief. Bean hadn't heard anything and like Matt's family, was hoping for the best. The regulars were back to normal and the club committee were busy preparing for The Jackson Search and Rescue Appreciation Day, although the Fins Walton invitation was still being worked out.

Starch was doing his rounds and stopped in at the kiosk for his bacon and egg roll, and coffee.

'Morning Bean, what's going on? Any news from your offsider? What are you going to do for help?' Asked Starch.

'Nah, no news. I'd say he'd be feeling a bit overwhelmed by now. Have you heard any news or rumours about developers or anything?' Replied Bean.

'Nah, it's still in the pipeline. Bit of strange stuff going on around here though. Someone's knocked off all the mirrors in the gym. Who does that? Not even Rooster does that, and Rooster does everything', reasoned Starch.

'Yeah, you're not wrong! I went upstairs yesterday for two minutes and when I got back I found this note and five bucks someone had left me that read, 'Sunny coffee,$5'. I was gone for a second and someone had made themselves a Sunny coffee, and self paid $5. Just unbelievable! I've never heard of a Sunny coffee. Don't know what's going on there, should've been $20,' blurted Bean.

Starch sat down at a table to have his roll and coffee when a tall well groomed man in a suit approached him.

'Mr John Lawless', enquired the man.

Starch sensed straight away that the man was a high ranking policeman, and politely answered.

'Yep, what can I do for you?'

'My name is Detective Inspector David Whitehead. I'm from the AFP, can I ask you some questions regarding the Tweed River Bar, please'. Said the man whilst showing Starch an identity card.

'The Federal Police? Sure, okay', replied Starch.

'John, could you tell me if you have ever been approached by anyone from an Australian government department, or any state or federal member of parliament in relation to providing false information about the dredging of the Tweed River Bar. John, have you ever been offered or accepted money as an incentive to provide false claims about the dredging of the Tweed River Bar?' Asked the Inspector.

Starch went blank for a moment then thought about the conversations with Flowers, the local M.P. Even though the thought of Flowers made his blood boil, he decided not to throw him under a bus. He had no way of proving Flowers had tried to blackmail him by using the club grant as leverage, so he answered, 'No'.

Inspector Whitehead gave Starch a sober look and said: 'Do you know what Mr Lawless, I don't believe you. I don't believe you're telling me the truth. I think you're hiding something and I will find out what it is. I'll leave you my number John, if you remember anything, you can talk to me. Have a nice day', said the Inspector.

'Okay, I will. Thanks', answered Starch, as the policeman turned and walked away. The conversation had been short and to the point which left Starch bewildered and wondering if Flowers was finally going to come undone. He had no doubts about Inspector Whitehead getting his man, so things had just got a lot more interesting.

Around lunchtime Bean was getting smashed in the kiosk. Mel was unable to help and Moey and Jules were busy at Uni, so he made a sign with "Help wanted" written on it and placed it on the counter. About an hour later he was in meltdown, steadily getting buried under a mountain of orders. Then without knocking, the lady with the cut foot he had helped days before, walked in the back door carrying his "Help wanted" sign.

'Sooo, who needs help this time? Let's get amongst it', she announced, and walked straight up to the counter and started to serve.

Bean's first thought was, 'What the?' But he was in no position to argue. Before he knew it the lady had cleared the counter and was starting to clear the backlog of orders, much to the relief of the customers.

The pair chatted non stop with a great rapport between them, and Bean started to laugh and smile more than he had done in years. After two hours of solid trade things started to slow down. The lady had been cleaning in between everything else and the kiosk looked immaculate.

Strangely enough, the pair had been busy working and conversing beside each other for a couple of hours and neither of them had introduced themselves - so Bean bought it up.

'Is it okay if we know each other's names?'

The lady laughed and replied: 'My name's Sunny. And yours?'

Bean giggled and asked: 'Sunny? Is that your real name?'

The lady gave him a surprised look and politely answered:'Well yes it is, and I'm glad you find it amusing. And your name is?'

'Sorry, I didn't mean to laugh. I've never met anyone called Sunny before. Everyone calls me Bean, and that's been my name as far as I can remember', he explained.

Sunny burst out laughing and blurted: 'Bean? Did you say Bean? What sort of a name's that? What's your real name?'

'Well I'm glad you find it amusing. My original name, given to me by my mother, that I didn't choose, was Bohemian. So, I just shortened it to Bean. Most people think it's a nickname but it's not. My mother thought I was a very romantic baby, so she gave me a romantic name', explained Bean.

Sunny had a huge smile and couldn't believe what she was hearing.

'Sorry, I didn't mean to laugh but I've never met anyone called Bean before. So, your mother thought you were a very romantic baby? Okay. Well I'm very pleased to meet you Mr Very Romantic Bean', said Sunny. Loving every minute of the conversation.

Where did you learn all that stuff you were doing when we were busy?' Asked Bean.

'I had a restaurant in Melbourne for twenty years. I just sold it so I could come up here and look after mum. She loves walking on the beach and dining at the kiosk, especially when it's busy', explained Sunny.

Bean gave a happy laugh and suggested: 'Well she can come in and serve herself now'.

'I already have, hope you don't mind. You weren't around so I made myself a coffee and left you five dollars', said Sunny.

Bean thought back to the note he found, "Sunny coffee $5", and put two and two together.

'Oh no, that's fine. Are you going to work or anything ever again? What's your hubby doing?'

Sunny gave him a puzzled look and quizzed: 'Hubby?'

'Yeah, your husband. The tall good looking bloke that comes in with you and your mum, holding your hand', quipped Bean.

Sunny paused, smiled and savoured the moment, then modestly replied: 'Oh, that's not my husband it's my son. He came up to help me get settled then went back to Melbourne. Please don't mention anything about being my husband to him, he'll never hold my hand again. I don't have a husband or whatever'.

Sunny could sense what Bean was wanting to ask, so she made it easy for him.

'As far as work goes I just don't know. After twenty years of non-stop work I'm exhausted. Right now mum needs me so I'll be full time looking after her, but if you ever need help, I can help. Today was fun and I really enjoyed myself. Mum has been a medical doctor her whole life and her dream was to one day have her own beach kiosk. If I could bring her along that would make her very happy, and give her some purpose. You don't have to pay us, we don't want that', said Sunny.

'Oh no, I'd have to pay you', insisted Bean.

'Okay, if it makes you feel better, donate two hundred dollars a week to Camp Quality Kids with Cancer. If you want to do that, mum and I will make this place fly', said Sunny.

'Deal', declared Bean.

Sunny went on her way and Bean spent the rest of the day with a huge smile plastered all over his face. Never in his wildest dreams did he expect 'Miss Super Beautiful' to come through his backdoor and solve his Matty gone to America problems. He only hoped the council ruled against the rumoured development proposal and the kiosk lived on.

Starch continued to do his rounds checking on the patrol members and staff at the clubhouse. Everything was under control, there was no shouting in the kitchen, only bragging about how good they were. Fins Walton was at the bar with Sharkbait, but because of the role he played in Jackson's rescue, Starch now turned a blind eye. Fins had quietened down a little, which was unusual but Big Cop and Fins had been seen having the occasional beer with one another - so maybe he was becoming more human.

Around the other side of the clubhouse, Simmo was hooking up the surf boat for the afternoon training session, when Bean yelled out to him to collect his complimentary coffee. Just as he collected it off the counter, Starch came round the corner.

'How ya going Simmo?' Said Starch, hiding all his club related woes.

'Good mate. What's news? There's that many rumours floating around this place at the moment', replied Simmo. Just as he spoke Colmie walked up from the carpark and the three of them congregated at the counter with Bean listening in.

'How are you going Colmie, what's going on?' Asked Starch.

'Not much. Have the cops spoken to anyone here about the dredging of the bar? I had a Federal cop quiz me about taking bribes or being harassed for positive comments by anyone in government. I think they're after Flowers', asked Colmie.

'Yeah', said Starch. 'I had an inspector cop quizzing me about the same thing'.

'It's gotta be about the superwank collapsing out the front and due diligence, I'd say', suggested Colmie.

'More like who's been bloody paid off', interjected Bean.

'It's a wait and see,' said Starch. 'It's a wait and see'.

The four of them nodded their heads in wise agreement then Colmie changed the subject.

'How are your boaties going, Simmo?'.

'Good, really good. They're doing it all themselves. I just drag the boat down then clean up after them. They're putting in a mountain of work', replied Simmo.

'How do you pick the five crew you're going to go with?' Asked Colmie.

'The girls do it themselves. They line up against a wall and have someone throw bricks at them. Whoever doesn't duck or move gets a seat. That's their mentality. It's called the brick mentality', replied Simmo.

Starch, Colmie and Bean looked down and slowly shook their heads, then Starch asked:

'Simmo, I don't suppose the girls would know anything about who knocked off the mirrors from the gym?'

'Yeah sorry about that. I'll put 'em back after they've done with this thing. No mirrors, no mobiles allowed when they train. Did Rooster or Danny complain?' Asked Simmo.

'Danny? Don't think he's looked in a mirror in his life, and Rooster only sleeps in there'. Quipped Bean.

And with that, Bean went back to work with a smile thinking about his new kiosk helper. Colmie and Starch helped Simmo take the boat down, and continued to speculate on what the cops were up to.

The days passed and there had been no news from Matthew. He wasn't answering his phone and had only sent one text message to his family that read : 'Arrived safely. Wow. Love you.'

His parents were spending long sleepless nights worrying about him. Joshua had said a mountain of prayers requesting "safetyness" for

Matty, while Dallas and Melissa argued about how they would shape a new planet if he discovered one.

Sunny and her mother Janice were a huge success in the kiosk which was a relief to Bean. Their company had transformed him into a new man. As promised, the ladies made the little eatery fly, and were enjoying every minute of work. Jackson was back to normal, with his health fully recovered and no signs of trauma at all from his experience. Unfortunately his mother Suzanne had not recovered as well. She frequently had nightmares and the two weeks of no income and mounting debt had left them broke. Their financial situation was dire at the best of times, but had now become catastrophic. They were behind in rent and late with every bill due, with sixteen dollars in the bank.

Jackson had never mentioned the family he saved and almost lost his life for, other than when he woke up in hospital and enquired if they were okay. The parents of the children never came back to thank him and nothing was ever heard from them. He seemed to accept this as being part of a volunteer lifesaver, although Suzanne couldn't help but feel disappointed. He had deserved much better than what he was given, but maybe the people were so embarrassed they just thought it better to go away and never go near a beach again - or maybe they had to return home overseas the next day. She would never know.

Robyn had phoned Starch and let him know that, to the best of her knowledge, the developers had been successful in their bid to acquire the clubhouse building. They had worked out a deal with the Department of Land and Environment to secure a ninety nine year lease with an option on the land. The clubhouse had never been heritage listed which meant due to its current state, it would be demolished.

Starch was gutted and asked her not to say anything to anyone until after the Jackson Search Recognition Day. He would then call a general meeting and break the news as gently as possible. Until then, he decided to put on a brave face and live a lie. It was all such a waste, and left no doubt in his mind this would tear a hole in the heart of the community.

It was exactly one week to go to the Australian Surf Lifesaving Championship. The good news was, the girls were ready, the bad news was, a cyclone was building off the north coast of Queensland, again. If the cyclone moved down the coast the event would probably be cancelled. To prepare for the conditions, the girls rowed the surfboat around to the mouth of the Tweed River and rowed back and forth across the bar. To the people watching, this was insanity, but the sanity of the boaties was pretty much in question anyway. The bar was no place for the meek and after a few days of being bashed about, the girls decided to taper off and wait for the weather to make up its mind. With three days to go, the sea was well and truly showing its teeth, as strong offshore winds set the scene for treacherous conditions. The governing body issued a statement saying a decision would be made 48 hours before competition regarding the Women's Surf Boat races. So the wait began.

Brian and Benny had gone from strength to strength in the kitchen and Adrian had encouraged them to further experiment by putting their own spin on some classical dishes. The boys lapped it up and the feedback from customers was very positive. After some discussion between the three of them it was decided the boys would enter a television reality cooking competition called "Masters of Culinary". They applied and were accepted for the preliminary rounds. If successful, they would go through to the knockout rounds on live television. They were all super excited and let Starch know what was going on. Starch congratulated them and tried to appear enthusiastic, but didn't have the heart to tell them about the club's approaching demise, which could upset their plans.

The surf continued battering the coastline and the beach lovers stayed away in droves. Any other time this would have meant a disaster for the kiosk, but Sunny and her mum Janice, had lifted the little eatery's popularity through the roof. Janice was always socialising with the customers and waiting on tables and Sunny was an organisational virtuoso. Even the toasted sandwiches looked good with the bacon and egg rolls going next level. Danny had been subdued by Janice who had talked him under the table. Grizz had managed to smile and appear pleasant when being served by Sunny whilst Bull Jackson, Rooster and every other male club member also frequented the kiosk when Sunny was serving. Bean was very happy, the ladies were full of energy and very easy to work with, plus they let him know who was boss, all day long. Matthew still had not contacted anyone.

As promised, forty eight hours before the race the SLSA announced their decision regarding the womens surf boat race. It had been decided to fully refund all entry fees to boat crews that did not wish to compete. For those that decided to run the gauntlet of the weather, a final decision would be made on the morning of the race. There were sixty womens boat crews entered, and in true Brick Mentality fashion, sixty women's boat crews decided to run the gauntlet of the weather. As a matter of fact, they didn't even discuss it. Quitting wasn't an option for any of them. To even mention the word "quit" would be like swearing in church - one would get kicked out of the boat.

Strange things were happening with Bean. Sunny and Janice had the kiosk so under control, that he found himself wandering into the gym everyday and actually using the equipment. There was also other uncharacteristic behaviour starting to surface. An old acoustic guitar he hadn't touched for years was cleaned up and restrung. To Bean, this was like reuniting with an old dear friend. The cool, funky blues riffs oozed out of the old acoustic as his fingers found their way around the fretboard, prompting him to wonder why he had left it alone for so long. There was also the occasional borrowing of Moey's little motorcycle to go for a ride along the beachfront, for no other reason than to just chill. He also wondered how someone as beautiful as Sunny could be single, and flirted with the idea of getting Larry to organise a blind date with one of his rich mates - but, Sunny was a no-nonsense lady and probably wouldn't appreciate it. So he gave up on that idea. Whatever it was that made him spend more time doing the things he enjoyed was a mystery, but he was thankful.

On the evening before the surf boat race, Starch worked back late finalising all the accounts to be paid before he announced the news regarding the clubs future or non-future. Tommy Green and the bar staff had finished work and gone home, the kitchen staff had also cleaned up and left. Starch was the last one on deck and the place felt eerily quiet, almost as if the majestic old building knew it's days were numbered and sat quietly waiting for the demolition teams to arrive. He turned off the last light and was on his way to the carpark when he noticed the store room light had been left on, so he walked back to turn it off. He opened the storeroom door and there was Rooster, polishing the boat for one last time. The pair looked at each other but said nothing, instead Starch picked up a piece of cloth and started polishing the boat. They worked together for a couple of hours without saying a word. Neither of them felt awkward, they were just happy to be there doing what they were doing, and sometimes nothing needs to be said.

The following morning Simmo was up early and had the surf boat at the venue, ready to go. The weather forecast had lived up to all expectations, and the surf was as big and foreboding as it had been all week. At the request of the boat crews the committee had given the women's race the go ahead - although many thought this was irresponsible or insanity. The girls arrived full of enthusiasm and understandably nervous. The occasion was daunting enough, without even considering the conditions. The first round would consist of ten races of six boats, with the top two in each going through to the next round. The Rainbows End crew were not considered a threat by the big teams and were expected to go out in the first round, although the girls were a formidable looking bunch. The weight training and countless hours of boat work had chiseled and hardened their appearance, so they definitely looked ready. The race draw was done early and the girls were in race eight in an event known as the long course, being four hundred metres out and around a buoy then four hundred back to the beach. It was a standing start in shallow surf and sprint finish to the flag or gate to end the race.

The conditions had drawn a huge crowd and they weren't disappointed with the first few rounds showing wipeout after wipeout. Fortunately, there weren't any serious injuries and the racing continued. The local Rainbows End supporters had turned up in numbers with a sizable contingent on the beach behind the girls' start point. All the penguins had come along with most of the patrol regulars. Bean, Starch, Colmie, Rooster, Bull, Danny, and Grizz all stood in a group, whilst the nippers and their parents and Jodie were close by.

Simmo had decided not to say too much on the day and let the girls talk for themselves - they were never short of words anyway. By the time race 8, heat 1, came around their nerves had well and truly set in. They had very little competition experience and didn't know what to expect. At the last moment they decided to ask Starch if he had any advice. The old footballer just smiled and answered:

'Stay loose, think fast, make it out and back and you'll do alright'.

It wasn't the answer the girls expected but it was the answer they needed. They did loosen up, they did think very fast, and they did make it out and back which was an achievement, considering three of the six boats never made it out but were rolled and smashed at the first break. Another boat was swamped on the way back in, so that left only the girls and one other. Round 1 down and twenty boats left. The second round was four heats of five boats, the girls were in heat 4 and once again the advice of Starch proved invaluable with two of the five boats not making it back. The girls managed to scrape into second place and through to the semi final round.

The word "lucky" was being used quite a bit in conversation about the Rainbows End crew, but the club members and locals weren't having a bar of it. They were familiar with the sight of the girls training on the Tweed River Bar and they were proving to be very resilient in the big surf. They weren't lucky, they had prepared very well. The eight boats that had survived the earlier rounds were split into two lots of four for the semi final. With the top two in each heat going through to the final. The Rainbows End crew were in the second heat and were considered to be the most likely to bow out. But, the girls were keeping it simple and were silently determined to prove their detractors wrong. Although some of the boat crews were stacked with professional athletes, the great leveller was the surf. The waves were extremely unpredictable and if a boat found itself in the wrong place at the wrong time, it was game over.

Defying all expectations the girls made it through to the final, and not only did they make it through, they had stamped their authority on the competition by displaying some very uncanny skills in the surf. They were now being regarded as serious contenders, and the final was wide open. The locals had got wind of the news about the crew's success and the beach crowd was building. Everyone was turning up to support the Rainbows End boaties. The clock ticked down to the final start time as the race committee agonised over insurance issues associated with the dangerous surf. The medics had confirmed a horrible toll of injuries.

Out of the crews in sixty boats that had started, there had been, three dislocated shoulders, four broken collarbones, six girls with broken/sprained fingers, three fractured wrists, one broken tooth, eleven split lips. An unknown quantity had also not been reported, and went to the hospital outpatients themselves. Despite all this the finalists were eager to get a confirmed start time. The Brick Mentality ran deep, and was alive and well.

The start time was given. It was to be in one hour, before the conditions deteriorated even more. The girls snacked on watermelon and bananas as Simmo and Rooster checked the boat over. By start time the crowd had swelled with several of the local clubs joining in to support the girls. Someone had found the Rainbows End flag and hoisted it up a makeshift flagpole and the atmosphere started to feel like a national title should. It was electric. As the four crews lined up beside their boats, the beach started to resemble a battleground. On one side were the combatants, on the other side was their impossible foe, the raging surf. The traffic was still rolling in as more and more locals turned up to watch the race. In amongst all the cars a fire truck pulled up and half a dozen firemen jumped out, viewing the surf and shaking their heads. One of them immediately exclaimed: 'They're joking!!! Aren't they?'

The five minutes to go call was given and sounded like a call to arms, riveting through the air. The girls slid the boat into shallow water and took their positions alongside. Marie was on the bow, Annika was the sweep, Heidi, Taylor and Sonia were in the middle and commonly referred to as 'The Grunt'. Marie was a tiny woman in her fifties and a full time firefighter. Because of her size she had to work harder than most when she first started, but her power to weight strength was like an ant and she soon had her job down to a fine art. This gained the respect of the blokes, who now treated her a bit like a rock star. Marie was a dynamo and often viewed as a maternal figure by the other girls who sought her advice when they had a problem. As a bow position she would finish the race, this was a tactic. She was light and very quick across the sand.

At the back was Swedish born Annika, a beautiful looking blonde haired lady, born and bred for the sea. She was the consummate sweep, her feel of the ocean, it's tides and currents, it's ebb and flow was ingrained in her DNA. As a baby she sat on her fathers lap sailing the fjords of Sweden and as a child would spend her days sailing her way along the Swedish coastline in a small dinghy by herself. Her heart and soul were tied to the oceans. Annika was their secret weapon, their X factor. The team spine was awesome. Heidi the hatmaker, another pretty Scandinavian blonde, with an affinity for the sea who had made Australia her home. She feared no surf and salivated at the thought of monster waves and sudden death undercurrents. The conditions suited her just fine. She was also the boat business woman and organiser. Then there was Taylor, who was sheer power and the strongest female in the club, the boat enforcer. When the going got real tough, Taylor took over. Then there was Sonia, The Little Champion, The Quiet Achiever, who was all action, no talk. The supreme athlete. Quiet, strong, focused, enduring and never ever waived in her commitment. Sonia and Taylor bounced off one another in the gym, with Sonia consistently pushing Taylor to her limits. They were the muscle. It was no surprise to some people that the girls had made it this far. Anyone who trained on an angry, messy Tweed River bar was either seriously stupid or very, very gutsy.

With the seconds ticking by the girls could feel the nervous doubt of their own ability trying to force its way into their mind. Anxiety is a funny thing, it creeps up on you, then before you know it, it has its tentacles wrapped around you. But, one person corrected all that. Down the beach, walking toward them came Jackson.

'Sorry I'm late. So proud of you. I hope I can get this far one day. You can do this, you are so good!' Exclaimed Jack.

'Any tips, Jack?' Asked Annika.

Jack looked them in the eye and understood exactly how they felt.

'No tips, just the truth... Making it out and back won't do it for you this time, they can all do that. You are going to have to win it, if you want it. You are good enough, you are ready. There is nobody on this beach that is better than you. You're bringin it! I believe in you, believe in yourself. No one deserves this more than you. You have earnt this, you deserve to be here. You are good enough!'

The girls felt their eyes well up, nothing else needed to be said. Where there was doubt there was now courage, they were up for this. This was their moment. This was their chance.

Jackson turned and walked back up the sand and stood on the beach with the other clubbies. His mother had decided to stay at home, the pressure of mounting financial problems around them was taking its toll. Being careful not to alarm Jack, she kept the gravity of their personal situation a secret and tried to appear happy.

The four crews stood by their boats until the one minute signal was given, then the atmosphere changed. The girls were focused and committed, the crowd on the beach were silently looking at the monster surf breaking right in front of them. The set after set of mayhem was a daunting sight. There were many sports that claimed to be tough, but none could match the ferocity of a raging surf. There was no room for glamour or stars in this arena. This was pure intestinal fortitude where one could easily lose their life. The Brick Mentality would be tested to the limit. There were twenty women in four surfboats and every one of them had the heart of a lioness, and every time the surf roared it was met with total defiance. If they didn't dodge a brick they definitely wouldn't dodge a wave. In a standoff, female boaties don't blink.

The referee raised his arm in the air and fired off the start pistol. The resounding crack broke the silence and it was, game on. The crews launched into their boats and pulled hard on the oars. Annika immediately spotted a sweet line between the break and headed for it, but it closed as quickly as it opened. There was no easy way out. She gritted her teeth and kept the bow pointed into the face of the surf which was horrendous. The waves crashed on the boat, around the boat and over the boat. One second the bow would be pointed toward the sky and the next it would freefall off the back of a wave and land with the subtlety of a head-on train wreck. Every muscle, bone, joint, nerve in their body felt the violence of the jarring, unforgiving surf.

All four boats reached the turnaround buoy with nothing between them, but the way back to the beach was a different race altogether. This is where Annika would come into her own. One slip or one bad read and it was all over, but this lady was in her element. 'Fight girls, heave', she would scream. At fifty to one hundred meters out, things started to get hairy again. All four boats were within striking distance of one another. It was anybody's race but the surf would make them pay a high price for victory. It was about this distance when Annika screamed:

'Wait! Oars up. Wait and be ready'.

The other three boats kept powering toward the beach and took the lead, but the sweep knew exactly what she was doing. She skillfully maneuvered the boat and surfed down a huge rolling wave, then screamed with all her might:

'NOW GIRLS! NOW. ROW'.

The boat bottomed out but the extra force the girls put in, was enough to get them clear of the wave coming over the top. The boat spat out of the surf like a projectile and Annika again screamed:

'Oars up. Hold on. Marie, get ready'.

The girls shot to the lead with the other boats trapped in the washing machine like surf. Annika screamed for all she was worth: 'Come Onnnn', and for a moment the girls thought she had lost her mind. But, they all did a half turn for a quick look and saw the beach coming up on them at breakneck speed.

'Wait for it, wait for it, Marie'. She screamed again, as the girls felt the first bump of sand.

'Not yet', came the order.

Then a second bump of sand came as the boat pointed perfectly to the beach.

'NOWWW!' was the loudest Annika scream of all.

Marie leapt from the boat and hit the sand running, and true to form the little champion did exactly what everyone knew she would do. She flew across the sand and between the flags and it was over. They had taken their chance and they had won.

*Every endeavour to succeed is born out of the willingness to try.*

The girls screamed and hugged each other, tears were shed, the excitement was palatable. Up on the beach there was mayhem as the supporters rushed toward them, the club had never seen anything like this. The crowd hoisted the crew onto their shoulders and carried them along the beach with the local news networks in a feeding frenzy capturing everything for the evening bulletin. Within minutes a media scrum had formed with a battery of cameras and microphones soaking up the avalanche of emotion. The jubilation was extraordinary. The tsunami of media centred on one figure who was passionately articulating the guts and glory of the Rainbows End boat crew. It was Rooster at his vintage best, playing the media like a fiddle. Starch watched on from a distance and didn't intervene. He thought about the impending closure of the club. The secret he would have to carry for another week. He thought about all the late nights Rooster had quietly and anonymously prepared the boat. All the little things he had done and never mentioned or sought approval for. He had learnt about all the little things that made up Rooster, and smiled to himself.

'Good on ya Rooster! Go for it, son! Talk 'em up', he said quietly.

Rooster was a rogue with a heart of gold. That evening the race and celebrations featured in the evening news, Australia wide. Outback in Thargomindah the locals were treated to the sight of Rooster who was once again front and centre on the news. In the local pubs they raised their glasses and toasted Rooster and the girls boat crew. The next day the buzz around town was, "that bloke from the coast has done it again". And the legend of Rooster grew even larger.

Tommy Green had switched to emergency mode back at the club, putting in a desperate last minute order for more beer. He expected a big night of celebrations so a truck load of Queensland's best brew should cover it. He was right, except he could never have imagined how big a night it would be. Everyone converged on the clubhouse. Anyone who had ever been associated with the club turned up. It was the biggest night in the club's history. The following morning it resembled the aftermath of a major disaster, with bodies everywhere. There were snoring human bodies on the front lawn, on the beach, in the carpark, on bonnets of cars. They were scattered everywhere throughout the club. Tommy Green was asleep leaning on the bar with five figures still at the bar discussing everything from the origins of the universe to the secret intelligence of whales. The five figures were Ben, Sushi, Big Cop, Fins Walton and Sharkbait, who was lying on the bar with a belly full of pies. The patrons had managed to drink the truck load of beer and whatever else that was available. Big Cop and the boys had a secret stash at the back of the fridge, which ensured their longevity.

As the sun started to show it's face above the horizon, more and more bodies slowly woke up and staggered home. The kiosk wasn't open as Bean had sold everything he had upstairs the night before, plus he had been caught up in the celebrations and was nursing a hangover. Starch arrived at the club and walked upstairs to find the 'final five' still sitting at the bar. Although they were a bit wobbly he decided to seize the moment and ask Fins to attend the Jackson Rescue Thank You Day, next weekend. Seeing as Fins had been quiet and was having the occasional beer with Big Cop, Starch decided to try the civil approach.

'Mr Walton, there is a, Thank You Recognition Day next weekend, and we'd like you and the boys to come along and receive an official recognition of what you did for Jackson. It'll be brief but everybody would appreciate your attendance', said Starch cautiously.

Fins gave a big breath out then answered:

'Nah, no need. I didn't do anything, but the boys are geniuses. They need to be thanked. I'll pass'.

Big Cop rolled his eyeballs then blurted out.

'Oh bullshit, Walton!! This isn't about you, this is about Jackson having the chance to publicly thank everybody! He'll be there and he's right, the boys are geniuses but they're bloody secretive about whatever they know. That whole search and rescue episode has bloody secrets all over it. I still can't believe we flew over him for a week. Whatever happened to that trash you found him in, Walton? I'd like to have another bloody look at that'.

Ben, Sushi and Fins sat there quietly and shrugged their shoulders.

Starch was happy with the response and left them sitting at the bar. He still hadn't decided on the best time to deliver the news about the club's future, but thought it could wait until after the Jackson Day ceremony. This was a job he was dreading.

Jackson's mum Suzanne was awake early, after spending another sleepless night worrying about their financial situation. She knew they were now behind in the rent, and with $16.80 left in her account the automatic payment would have bounced spectacularly. Then there were the other bills due that she had no hope of paying which only added to her concern. Jackson was still unaware of their financial situation and was awake early, still pumped up about the girls' win. Suzanne was careful not to give him any reason to think something was wrong, but around 10 am the dreaded phone call from the bank came.

'Hello, may I speak to Suzanne Gave, please?' Said the voice over the phone.

'Yes, that's me', answered Suzanne timidly.

'Good morning Suzanne, my name is Roberto, I'm from the Australia Bank, Coolangatta. I was wondering if you would have time to discuss some options on your account today', said the polite voice.

Suzanne's head bowed as she reconciled with herself that it would be better to face the consequences now and get it over with. She did not want a high interest personal loan that she had no hope of repaying, so she would face the ugly truth and the ruthless bank. She felt like a complete and utter failure.

'Yes of course. I'll be there in an hour', she replied.

'Oh no that's not necessary. I can come to you', said Roberto.

Knowing Jackson would overhear any conversation at home, she had to think quickly.

'It's okay. I'm doing some shopping so it's right on my way. I'll be there in one hour', replied Suzanne.

'Great. I'll see you then. Thank you', said Roberto.

To prepare for the doom and gloom, Suzanne had a cup of tea and pondered their future, then headed off to face the music. As she walked through the front doors of the bank she felt as though she was walking into a school principal's office for a 'please explain'. After all she had gone through, after all she had endured, she now had to deal with bankruptcy. Does it ever end? Or is this just life? What is normal? She had faced bigger challenges so she just said to herself: 'Let's get this over and done with!' and walked straight up to the reception desk and announced.

'Suzanne Gave to see Roberto. Can you tell him I'm here please?'

The young receptionist jumped straight to her feet and replied:

'Yes Mrs Gave. Straight away', and briskly walked off to an office, then returned with Roberto.

'Hi Suzanne, I'm Roberto, thank you for coming down. Can I get you a coffee or anything?' He said very politely.

'No thanks. Can we get this over with straight away please?' Replied Suzanne.

'Yes of course, I have some options for you to look at'. He replied and led Suzanne to his office.

They both sat down in the office and Roberto placed an assortment of folders in front of her, saying:

'I thought these might be of interest to you, but of course there are other plans if you are not interested in those'.

Suzanne gave a steely look and dug her heels in.

'Roberto, I don't want a personal loan. What can I do about the rent, other than borrow more? I need a week'.

Roberto returned her steely look with a puzzled look and replied:

'Not sure about your rent. This isn't about a loan. I'm a High Range Investment Strategist. There is no charge for me'.

Suzanne returned his puzzled look and asked:

'What on earth would I invest in? I think we've got our wires crossed somewhere!'

They both sat looking at each other in silence for an awkward moment before Roberto asked:

'Suzanne, when was the last time you looked at your account?'

'Oh I don't know. Maybe four or five days ago, I suppose. It's just so depressing', she answered.

Roberto looked at her for a couple of seconds, then tapped something out on a keyboard. Slowly turning the computer monitor around to face her, he asked:

'Suzanne, is that your account?'

Looking at the monitor her mouth opened as she gave a bewildered look, then replied:

'That's me, but that's not mine. You have made a mistake. How much is that?'

Roberto smiled and tried to maintain his professional demeanor as he very patiently explained to her.

'Suzanne, there is no mistake. The person who put that into your account is a very, very big bank customer who went to great lengths to get your account number. The amount is twenty five million dollars and there is another one million dollars to be paid annually into your account for the next ten years. The same person also paid off every bill you had and the next month's rent, probably assuming you'll buy your own place'.

Suzanne sank back into her chair and tried to think. She had just gone from the outhouse to the penthouse in a nanosecond. She had been through so much she simply could not believe this was happening.

It was a pivotal moment in her life that had completely blind sided her and processing this much information was beyond her. Things like this just don't happen.

'But who? But why? But, but,' was all she could say.

Roberto was very understanding toward her. Such a mammoth sum of money unannounced and unexplained brought with it a multitude of questions. Suzanne had been on the receiving end of life's ill will for that long she was almost too scared to be too happy. Roberto quietly pointed to the payers reference which read:

'Have fun, talk soon. Larry'.

She didn't know anyone by the name of Larry, except the Dr Larry whom Jackson had introduced her to. But it couldn't possibly be him. So she asked Roberto:

'Who's Larry?'

Roberto started to realise this was a very complicated issue and answered as patiently as he could.

'Well I don't know personally, except I do know that the payer is an extremely wealthy bank client. You can rest assured this is not a mistake, the money is yours. Now, how about that coffee?'

'Thanks', said Suzanne, as she slumped in her chair wondering what to do with twenty five million dollars and wondering how on earth she would explain this to Jackson. Roberto returned with the coffee and placed all the folders in a satchel for her. As they started to discuss the best way to shift the money around and make some of it accessible, her phone rang. It was Jackson calling, she pressed the answer button with her head still spinning.

'Hello Jacky'.

'Hey mum', said Jack as he laughed excitedly. 'Guess what? The bank made a mistake and put a million dollars into my account. I'm going to take a screenshot of it with my phone and send it out to everybody. What do you think? Would I get into trouble? Am I allowed to do that? Do we have to tell them? The bank I mean?' Jack blurted out.

Suzanne gave a very sober look at Roberto then replied to Jack:

'Jacky, just wait a minute please. I'm at the bank now, so I will check this out'.

Suzanne turned to Roberto and asked:

'Could you check my son Jackson's account please? It's linked to mine'.

Roberto smiled and replied:

'I've already been notified. You had better brace yourself and it's not a mistake'.

He turned the monitor around and pointed to the payer, which read:

'Have fun. Talk soon Larry'.

He then added: "And yes, there is another million dollars to be paid annually into this account for the next ten years".

Suzanne was now utterly convinced this had to be a mistake, it was almost as if she was pushing the gifts away. Jack was getting impatient on the phone and asked:

'Mum, what's going on?'

Suzanne took a deep breath and slowly replied:

'Jacky, I want you to listen very carefully. The million dollars is not a mistake. Someone called Larry is depositing incredibly large sums of money into both our accounts. How much do you know about Dr Larry from the hospital?'

Jack went quiet for a few seconds before answering.

'Mum, what do you mean it's not a mistake? Am I a millionaire? Dr Larry is really good, he was checking on me all the time. I don't think he works at the hospital all the time but he's something like a consultant or something. Is this money ours to keep, mum? Like, no one gives away a million dollars. It must be a mistake'.

Suzanne looked at Roberto as if to ask, 'are you sure this is right?' Roberto looked back at her and nodded his head up and down as if to say, 'Yep it's all yours'.

Jacko's voice came over the phone again.

'Mum, are you there? Are you alright? What's going on?'

In amongst all the confusion she answered:

'Yes luvvy, I'm here. I'm leaving the bank now to come home and I'll explain everything to you then. Please don't say anything to anyone. We have to find out who Larry is, then we might find out why all this money has been given to us'.

Roberto stood up and shook Suzannes hand and reassured her everything was legitimate. Larry was real and a very wealthy bank client, but he didn't know why he had given them the money. The drive home for Suzanne was one big blur with one big question: 'Why?'

At home, she sat down with Jack and tried to figure out who Larry could be, and why had he focused on them with such generosity? They decided not to say anything about what had happened to anyone and both of them would try tracking down Larry, if there was such a person. This didn't take long as the first person Jack spoke to was Bean, who filled in the details about Matty's scholarship offer and confirmed Larry, the well connected, super businessman and Dr. Larry was the same person. Suzanne and Jack sat down again with the new information and tried to put the pieces of their puzzle together. They tried talking to the hospital and found out Larry was indeed a very experienced medical doctor and trauma specialist, his involvement with Jackson, however, was voluntary and they were very grateful for his assistance. But, the story behind Matty's scholarship job offer and the NASA connections were mind boggling. The only person who could shine some light on the situation with a possible explanation was Matty, and no one had heard from him. So, they decided not to touch the money until the real Larry introduced himself.

The kiosk had become a trendy place to do coffee and Bean was feeling a bit guilty about his deal with Sunny and her mum, and decided to pay them as well as the donation. This was met with a flat, 'no'.

However, they would not object to him giving extra money to the Kids With Cancer charity, which he did straight away. Sunny carefully explained they wouldn't be there forever. She appreciated what Bean had done for her mum, who had at last found her beach kiosk, which had given her a new lease on life. Sunny had never seen her smile so much. But one day it would come to an end. The thought of this troubled Bean. He had grown so used to them. Mum was such a likeable character she had become a best friend to him. Then there was Sunny. She made him feel so special when she stood beside him, and just being around her was enough to make his day. They laughed and joked and ribbed each other all day long. He couldn't remember anyone who made him so happy. Strangely enough Sunny's good looks kept any feelings of romance at bay and he never contemplated being anything other than a friend to her. The more he thought about it, the stranger the whole thing seemed. He thought about the first time they met at the back door, and how he was gobsmacked and fell over himself to do something for her. But it wasn't long before he realised and appreciated her authentic character which prompted him to be on his best behaviour all the time. He thought about how easy it was to relate to her and how much he smiled when he thought about her, and how lucky he had been to meet her. He wanted the very best for her and hoped one day she would meet a handsome billionaire who would give her everything she wanted, and of course he also couldn't wait to introduce her to Matty.

Ben & Sushi had let Fins know that they would be leaving soon to continue their surfing trek around the world, and organised a meeting to offer him their proposal. Fins was wary of any proposal, but the boys were like family so he decided to see what they had to say. With that in mind he set off at the time they allotted and headed to the pier in a neighbouring marina. At the end of the pier the boys and Big Cop were looking at a large, very modern looking trawler. Fins was now even more curious as to what they were up to, whilst Sharkbait was glad to see them and gave a tail wag and happy bark. He had grown very fond of Big Cop who always shared a pie with him. The relationship between Fins and Sharkbait was still very volatile.

'Alright, what's going on?' Asked Fins as he approached them.

'We have proposal for you', answered Ben.

'Alright, spit it out', said Fins.

'Okay, we cut to chase', said Sushi. 'We have agreements in place in Japan and Australia with several universities to provide ten students at a time a working experience on a commercial deep sea fishing vessel. The aim is to study environmentally sustainable commercial fishing practices in Australian waters. Students stay on boat for five days'.

'Hang on, hang on', interrupted Fins. "How are you going to fit ten students on my boat plus my deckies, and how am I supposed to make a living out of babysitting? This won't work, it's rubbish. They'll just get in the road. See ya later'.

'Let them finish', interjected Big Cop.

'Not on your boat, Fins, on our boat. This is our boat', said Ben, motioning toward the large trawler.

'What? What kind of a deal is that? When did you get that boat?' Blurted Fins.

'Boat sleeps fourteen and has huge kitchen for cook. Deal is, you fish, you keep catch. We get paid by the university for students. Big cop is retiring and is investor. He takes percentage of both and cooks and looks after boat. Students will work on boat', explained Sushi.

Fins thought for a minute, then asked: "Who pays for running costs?"

'Fifty-fifty', replied Ben straight away."

'Give me a look at the boat', snapped Fins.

'Of course! Sharkbait come too', said Sushi.

They all went on the boat so Fins could check it out. It was a very impressive vessel, and far better than any other, in that part of the world. Fins was impressed but didn't show it. The one daunting thing that bothered him was all the electronics. Ben and Sushi knew Fins well and could tell the electronics would be an issue. Fins didn't even feel comfortable on a 2-way radio. Sensing the problem Ben spoke up.

'All the data and systems are run by the students with Big Cop overseeing. You are Skipper and in charge of catch.'

That was the compromise Fins was looking for and he could smell a good deal. A boat that big could be very profitable with half the running costs and ten free deckies. He factored in Big Cop and decided he could be handy to have around. Fins wanted time to think about it, so he asked: 'When do you want an answer?'

'Now', answered Sushi. 'Otherwise boat goes back to Japan tonight'.

Fins was taken aback by the suddenness of the situation. They expected him to make a huge financial decision and major life change with less than a breath of time to decide. He knew he would have to drastically modify his behavior, but Ben and Sushi were like family to him, so if that's what they wanted him to do, then that's what he would do. Besides that, Big Cop had become a good drinking buddy, and was probably the only onboard help he could tolerate. The boys were quietly waiting for his answer. He breathed out then quietly said:

'Okay, it's a deal'.

The boys smiled broadly and Big Cop couldn't resist but ask:

'What was that Fins? Sorry, I couldn't hear you. Did you say that it's a deal?'

Fins fired straight back.

'Get stuffed copper! You give me any grief and you'll be burly over the side'.

Big Cop grinned and retorted: 'I'm sure Sharkbait will be upset about that, you replacing him and all that. I'd say you could have a demarcation dispute on your hands'.

Fins ignored him and asked: 'Okay, when do we start?'

The boys looked at each other then answered: 'Maybe six weeks. Students need to be advised and first lot booked, plus few additions to boat'.

'Additions? What additions?' queried Fins.

'Special kennel for Sharkbait and perch for seagull', said Ben.

'You have got to be joking!' blurted Fins. 'It's a commercial fishing boat, not a freakin zoo!'

They all laughed then Big Cop suggested they go and celebrate with a drink and something to eat at the club. He also reminded Fins and the boys to have their speeches ready for the weekend, which drew blank looks all around.

# Chapter 21

# The People We Meet

Suzanne and Jack sat around home wondering what to do next. They found themselves in a awkward frame of mind where they didn't know whether to feel excited, cautious or anything in between. They were sick of asking themselves 'why', so Suzanne suggested:

'Jacky, I'm going to give Starch's wife Talia a call and invite her and the girls to the club to buy them a late lunch. Will you come too? Heaven knows we can afford it these days'.

Jack perked up and replied:

'Yeah mum, let's go. It's a bit hard to sit here overthinking everything. I never thought being an instant millionaire could be so stressful'.

The pair arrived at the club to find it packed to the rafters. The members were still celebrating the ladies surf boat win and some of the locals had thrown together an acoustic bush band that were happy to play for beer and tucker. Honey, mum and Bean were flat out at the kiosk and the boys were dishing it up in the restaurant. Everyone was there and seats were a rarity, so Bean grabbed some benches from the gym and found a couple of cushions to put on milk crates so the girls and Jack could settle in. The atmosphere was fantastic, except for Starch who was very quiet, walking around doing his thing.

Throughout the club there were television monitors with the sound muted until the band took a break. Early in the afternoon when the band decided it was thirsty and headed for the bar the network of televisions lit up with sound just in time for the afternoon news headlines. As usual there was little or no interest until the news reader broadcast the lead story for the day:

'The US president made a surprise visit to the Johnson Space Centre in Houston today to congratulate the next generation of space explorers. The candidates had undergone two weeks straight of gruelling physiological and psychological assessment, lasting twelve to eighteen hours a day. Standout candidate was Matthew Binge from Australia whom the examiners described as an extremely gifted and intelligent young man. The successful candidates will begin their full time training in one months time at the Houston Space Centre, where they will prepare for their future missions in space'. As the newsreader spoke, the television pictures showed the U.S. President shaking hands with Matthew and sharing a laugh.

The sound in the club had plummeted to hear a pin drop level. Underneath, at the kiosk it was the same story. Every single person in the club watched and listened to the bulletin with their mouths open. No one spoke. No one moved.

As the television focused on the President leaving the scene of the meeting, he was surrounded as usual by a multitude of security and staff - but before leaving he stopped to shake hands with an Asian looking man, who was nearby. The pair seemed to know each other and shared a brief conversation, before the president could be seen saying:

'We'll catch up later'.

Bean stood paralysed in front of the TV. He slowly reached out, picked up the phone and rang Matthews' parents. His dad answered: 'Hello'.

To which Bean replied: 'You had better turn on the news'.

To which George replied: 'I just saw it. To say we're in shock would be an understatement. I might just grab the family and come down to have a yarn. Did you notice Larry?'

'Yep!! Unbelievable. I'll see you shortly', said Bean.

As he hung up the phone he turned to see Suzanne and Jackson waiting at the counter to collect their food and drinks. They had both overheard the phone conversation so Suzanne got straight to the point and asked:

'Which one, or where was Larry?'

Bean paused then answered: 'The bloke the President stopped to shake hands with on the way out'.

Jackson then intervened. 'Mum! I was trying to tell you that it was Dr Larry, but you kept holding up your hand saying, "In a minute"'.

Suzanne was lost for words. Dumbfounded by the news bulletin, and super stunned by the Larry revelation. But at least she wasn't the only one looking for some answers. All she could think of to say was:

'Who is Larry?'

To which Bean replied: 'Wouldn't we all like to know, but something tells me we'll all find out shortly. Matty will be on his way home soon and he'll have all the answers. Much to the relief of his family'.

Many, many local people saw the TV news bulletin that day and they all wore the same vacant expression. How could someone who works in the beach kiosk serving coffee and food suddenly be keeping company with the most powerful man on the planet and preparing to go to work in outer space - getting paid truck loads of money? Some of the locals were convinced it was all a set up. A bit like the moon landing. There was heavy discussion among his surfing mates, who sat for long periods out behind the break trying to fathom why he never spoke about it. The national media had been completely blindsided and the news crews descended on the club like locusts. Rooster, who was now known as a heavy media tart, threw himself at them like a bug on a speeding car windscreen. The locals at Thargomindah weren't surprised to see Rooster on the news again, and wondered what all the fuss about Matthew was about.

The Binges had a long chat with Bean about Matty that afternoon, and wondered what had prompted Larry to take such a huge gamble on him. How was it, that he could see all this potential and yet nobody else could. Was it the little things? Or was it because they all took Matthew for granted and never really knew how special he really was. On one hand they were super excited and enormously proud, but on the other hand they were disappointed in themselves for not supporting him more. Their own views, although well intended, had almost prevented him from being free to explore his full potential. They loved their son and both agreed to listen more and talk less.

The next day the locals were still shaking their heads thinking, 'impossible'. The Binge family woke early after waiting up half the night for a call from Matty that still hadn't come. As they sat around the breakfast table, the familiar ringtone of George's phone blasted around the kitchen. The caller identification name was "Matthew" in big bright letters.

'Put it on speaker phone', screamed the kids.

George grabbed the phone like a bargain on a boxing day sale, and pressed the answer button.

'Matty, hello, is that you?'

'Hi Dad, sorry I didn't ring. They had me in lockdown the whole time. I fell asleep in a chair at Larry's place last night. I was pretty much stuffed. Is everyone okay at home?' Said the sweetest voice his family had ever heard.

'Gee, it's good to hear from you son. Yes, we're all well, just missing you a lot. Do you know you're all over the news, shaking hands with the US President and stuff?' Said George, as the rest of the family were shouting greetings and questions all at once on the phone.

'No, I didn't know that, that was yesterday. I'm sitting on a plane at the moment with Larry and my roommates, heading home. We'll be there tomorrow morning. Larry said he has some loose ends to tie up and brought my roomies along for the ride. They're also on their way home. I've got so much to tell you. You won't believe some of the stuff I did, and wait until you see the pictures. It's like another world', relayed Matty.

"When do you find out if you won the scholarship?' asked George, as the family yelled more questions over his shoulder.

'I was keeping it as a surprise, there's a lot to talk about. I still feel like my feet haven't touched the ground, I can't believe how advanced the technology is. It's incredible', related Matty.

'What's the President of the United States like?' shouted little Josh into the phone.

'Matty laughed happily at the sound of his little brother's voice and replied: 'Oh he's cool', which sent his family into rapturous laughter. 'I'll ring again, before we land. Can someone pick me up?'

'Yes, yes of course. We'll all be there', said his mum.

'Okay, say hello to Bean and everyone for me. I hope Bean's coping alright in the kiosk', said Matt.

'Oh yes, he has a very pretty lady and her mother helping him. He's very cheerful', replied his mum.

'Really!! That's interesting. Okay, I've gotta go, I'll phone again when we're closer. Love you. Bye'. And everyone yelled in reply: 'Bye, love you', into the phone.

Suddenly all the worry and anxiety dissipated from the Binge household and a world of possibilities and excitement had descended on them. The siblings launched into social media with the news of their brother whilst little Josh started organising the granddaddy of all preschool Show & Tell visits - featuring his astronaut brother, Matthew.

George gave Bean a quick phone call and let him know Matty would be back tomorrow, and said to say 'Hi'.

At the Gave household, Suzanne and Jac's heads were still spinning with their recent, Larry inspired financial avalanche. Suzanne decided to take the day off and sit down on the headland for a while to contemplate their future, which prompted Jack to ask:

'Mum, do you know what time you will be home?'

'Oh, probably in an hour or two. Why?' Replied Suzanne.

'I was just wondering because I have someone I'd like you to meet', answered Jack.

'Oh, who's that?' Asked Suzanne.

'One of my friends I met in the hospital. Will 10 o'clock be okay?' Replied Jack.

'Yes, that's fine'. Answered Suzanne, puzzled by the secrecy.

So, at around 10am she returned home and was in the middle of making herself a cup of tea, when she heard Jack's voice come through the front door.

'Mum, are you home?' He called.

'Yes Jacky', she replied, and walked into the lounge room to see Jack with a pretty young girl.

Jack was expecting his mother to be surprised as he had never bought a girl home before, and he wasn't wrong. Suzanne had the biggest, "well what's going on here" look on her face he had ever seen in his life, so he wasted no time introducing his friend.

'Mum, this is Faith. We met in hospital and have been keeping in touch. Faith, this is my mum, Suzanne', said a serious sounding Jack.

'Oh, I'm very pleased to meet you, Faith, and what a beautiful name. Are you two hungry or anything', said Suzanne, struggling to think of something to say. Life had just thrown her yet another curved ball when she was in the middle of dealing with everything else, but, this was just as much a surprise as anything.

'Thank you Mrs Gave, it's an honour to meet you. We had a milkshake at the kiosk when Jackson gave me a tour and introduced me to everyone', replied a very eloquent Faith.

Suzanne sensed what was going on and noticed the stars in Jack's eyes when Faith spoke. The boy had been hit by a lightning bolt with the name "Faith" written all over it. She took the everything's normal approach and asked:

'Are you okay now Faith? Jack said you met in hospital'.

'Oh, yes, thanks. I must have picked up some kind of bug on my parents farm. We live out at Canungra and I spend most of my time with the horses and animals. It's an avocado farm but my parents have room for mistreated animals to recuperate. So they just run around in the paddocks. My job is to feed them', replied Faith.

'That sounds amazing. Do you have any brothers or sisters?' Quizzed Suzanne, who was very impressed with the young lady's demeanor.

'Two brothers and a sister. Jackson met them and my parents in hospital. Dad and mum really like Jack and said you're both very welcome on the farm any time', answered Faith.

'Did you happen to meet Dr Larry while you were in hospital?' Asked Suzanne.

'No, he was only looking after Jack. Nice doctor though', replied Faith.

Jackson intervened, explaining: 'Mum, I'm just going to quickly show Faith my scuba gear, then her dad's going to pick her up from the surf club. Is that okay?'

'Yes of course. It was wonderful to meet you Faith and you're more than welcome to come back anytime', said Suzanne.

'Thanks, Mrs Gave, I appreciate that very much', replied Faith.

The pair inspected the scuba gear then headed off back to the club as Suzanne was left to wonder, what next? She was still struggling with the millions in their bank account and had come to the conclusion, that it was ridiculous to believe there wasn't a catch. It has to be money laundering or something like that. Roberto had made a mistake. But only time would tell. Strangely enough she was almost as shocked by Jack's newest best friend, but in a funny sort of way she was relieved to see him so excited. Maybe, just maybe their life had turned a corner and better times were coming. After struggling for so long, it was a nice thought.

Like everybody else, Starch was stunned by the news bulletin concerning Matthew. He had been so preoccupied with worrying about the demise of the club, everything else had gone over his head. He called into the kiosk to have a yarn to Bean and find out the full story.

'Gidday Bean, can I have a coffee please mate. You can tell me all about the adventures of Matty while you're making it, if you like'.

Bean let him know how Larry had popped up out of nowhere and took Matty under his wing. How he paid for everything and opened some very big doors of opportunity. How the young fellow had been given three days to get on a plane and get to the U.S. to take the assessment that was on the news. Bean described Matt's effort as, 'freakin incredible'.

Starch listened to the story and like a lot of other people, he thought it sounded too good to be true. But, he had seen the news bulletins and could only shake his head as Bean told him what had happened. In the end Starch had only two questions.

'So who's Larry? And why Matthew?'. He asked.

Bean thought about how to answer his questions and replied:

'I don't know exactly who Larry is, but, after a couple of conversations, I believe he is a very wealthy, powerful but humble, private man. He apparently saw something Matty made, and found out he worked here so that's when we met him. He told me without any reservation that Matthew was extremely intelligent and given the right opportunity he could be anything. The pieces of paper he gave Matthew when they were talking were problems his engineers had been struggling with. Matthew was able to offer solutions in a matter of minutes, hence the rapid investment and scholarship offers. Not to mention the on the spot job offer. Oh, and by the way, the man the U.S. President stopped to shake hands with on the news bulletin was Larry. I'd say they know each other.'

Starch stood there blank faced for a minute before the penny dropped. Although it was a long shot, maybe just maybe Larry might help him with the demise of the club problem. If he can put Matty into outer space and he's a mate of the U.S. President, then saving a Surf Club would be a walk in the park. But, how does he talk to Larry? Starch was desperate for answers. This could be the club's ticket to survival. He made up his mind to talk to Larry before sounding the death knell to the members.

He quizzed Bean further.

'So, do you know when Larry's coming back?'

'Tomorrow', Bean replied. 'Matty phoned his family, and he's on a plane coming home at the moment. Larry and a couple of mates are with him. I'm assuming Larry would want to talk to Matt's family, which means he'll more than likely drop in here. Besides that, he told me he loves the place, and wants his children to be Nippers here one day'.

Starch was buoyed by this information. Before he had learnt about Larry, the club was a shot duck. Now there was a chance. It might be just a glimmer of hope but when you're hanging by the fingernails, a glimmer can be a very bright light.

Bean handed Starch his coffee and added: 'Can you tell the patrol, Honey and mum will bring their stuff down when they get here. They're going for a walk on the beach'.

'Yeah okay. If Larry turns up can you let me know, please?' Replied Starch.

'Yep! No problem', said Bean.

# Chapter 22

# Plans and Problems

Early the next morning, Matt's family waited impatiently at the Coolangatta Airport. They had so many questions, which was making their excitement even harder to control. It had seemed like forever since he had suddenly left, leaving all of them clutching at thin air for answers. His plane finally landed and taxied up to the terminal, then a short wait later, Matthew, Larry and the house mates came striding through the arrival gates. The whole Binge family jumped on Matty at once with a monster group hug. His mother started to cry with happiness while his dad was so excited he grabbed Larry and hugged him. The hug caught Larry by surprise and he stood there like a telegraph pole as George blurted: 'Thank you, thank you, thank you, for looking after him'. The two housemates didn't know what to make of it all, so George hugged them as well. The Binge household were winning and they were loving it.

Larry and the house mates hired a car and arranged to meet Matty and his family at the club later that day. Matt was bundled into the family wagon and talked non stop for the next two hours, answering questions from everybody about everything he had been through. His family were astounded at his experience and what he had to do to win his scholarship. They would never look at him the same way again.

Bean, Sunny and mum were in the kiosk feeding the masses as usual, when Mattty burst through the backdoor totally unannounced and thoroughly energised.

'Does anybody know where I can get a decent feed around here?' He blurted out.

Bean roared with laughter and the pair grabbed each other in a bear hug.

'Holy smoke!' yelled Bean. 'Astro physics just arrived! Where'd ya park ya spaceship? In the car park?'

'Bean old mate, I need to make some coffee! I'm having some serious coffee making withdrawal symptoms! What's going on?' Yelled back, Matty.

Sunny and mum looked on and were surprised at the raucous comradery between the boys. They had never seen Bean in such a celebratory mood and never realised how close Bean and Matty were. Bean had never spoken too much about him.

'Matt, this is Sunny and mum. Sunny and mum this is Matthew who used to work here before he became an astronaut and friend of Presidents'. Said Bean with a large grin.

'I've been relegated to table wiper and empty cup collector these days, Matt'. He added.

'What!!! The place must have gone up a gear or two. Very pleased to meet you both, Sunny and mum'. Matty replied.

The ladies had also seen the news bulletin and were well aware of what an exceptional young man Matthew was, but they were surprised and delighted at his humility.

'And pleased to meet you Matthew. Bean is being a bit modest, he was considerate enough to let us share the beach kiosk experience and kind enough to generously support our favourite charity. We've thoroughly enjoyed ourselves, although it seems your time has been a bit more exciting', replied Sunny.

'Exciting and demanding', said Matt. 'I've got a short break before I start my new life. I've only been away for a few weeks, but it feels really good to be back for a while'.

Matthew could feel the warmth in Sunny's personality and could understand why Bean was so happy. They were very relaxed together which prompted him to think if there was more to their friendship than what they were showing.

'Well little buddy there's the coffee machine, if you're serious, there are the orders. Let's see what you've got'. Bean suggested with a huge smirk on his face.

'I'm up for this, let's do it', replied Matt, which sent Bean into jaw drop mode. He thought Matty was joking but the girls cheered approvingly and the kiosk swung into action.

As Sunny and mum walked outside, Matty cautiously whispered to Bean.

'Strewth mate, where'd you find them? Sunny's a stunner!'

Bean smiled approvingly and replied:

'She knocked on the door with a sore foot and the rest is history. They're beautiful people. Totally fair dinkum'.

It didn't take long for news to travel about Matt being in the kiosk and the locals started flooding in. His surfing mates, his club mates, his footy mates, his old school mates and the kiosk customers who always liked to have a yarn with him. Everyone was rockin up to say g'day and grab a selfie. Matty was big news.

Upstairs was buzzing with people and the committee members were busy organising the 'Thank you' day in two days' time. Starch was cruising round and soon got word of Matty in the kiosk, so he headed in to have a chat and see if Larry was coming to the club. His visit paid off, not only did he thoroughly enjoy catching up with Matty, but he confirmed Larry would be in the building that afternoon talking with Matt's parents. The load of anguish on Starch's shoulders was getting lighter, maybe there was a lifeline for the club - only time and Larry would tell. But, he was daring to hope.

After a couple of hours of simultaneously making coffee and answering questions from his mates and locals, Matt decided to take a break and go upstairs to his family. He was convinced he had detected something other than just a friendly relationship between Sunny and Bean and it was bothering him like an itch he had to scratch. On his way out, he seized a quiet moment to talk to Bean and maybe give him a nudge in the right direction.

'She likes you, you know,' he said quietly.

'Who? Sunny? Aw, no way. We get on incredibly well, but no way. She's nice to everyone. She's definitely dream material but I'd never put our friendship at risk by entertaining any thought of pushing my luck with her. Nah, no way, she's too nice a person', exclaimed Bean.

'Bean!! Listen to me! You don't see how she looks at you when you're not aware of it. She's confused about her own feelings and you're trying so hard to be her friend, you've completely confused the whole situation. Trust me. Her heart has already made its decision, and you need to give her head a reason to follow her heart. Trust me I know, and her mother knows it too', implored Matty.

'No, no, no, no!' Replied Bean. 'You have never been so far off the mark. You've been in outer space too long and you've lost the plot!'

'You're scared of her aren't you?' Said Matt. 'You're scared to let go and find out. What are you going to do? Just let her walk out of your life? She's going to leave, she told you that, and she will unless you give her a reason to stay'.

'Nah, you don't understand. We're best mates, that's all. I'd never do anything to compromise that. Maybe if I had a billion dollars, yeah, I'd think about it', reasoned Bean.

'She won't be bought for a billion dollars or any other amount of money. Ladies like that don't have a price. You can tell by the way she relates to her mother. She has a clean, caring heart and so do you. Just be honest with her and see what happens. But, you will have to give up your comfort zone and bare your soul, if you try and fake it she will know straight away', counselled Matty.

'I don't know mate. What makes you so sure? I don't know if I could ever do that. How do you know all this?' Asked Bean.

'Bean, I've never seen you happier. Hell! I even saw you smile at Danny, that's a miracle in itself. Think about it. Since you met Sunny, look at all the little things you've started doing that you haven't done for years. You and Sunny thrive off one another. It's very apparent. Her mother can see it, I could see it straight away, but if you don't act on it, it will die'. Matt patiently explained.

'Ohhh, this is sounding way too hard. I don't have a clue what to do or what to say, and what if you're wrong and she thinks I'm some kind of creep? And if she laughs at me, I'd feel totally devastated. Total humiliation! What if, Einstein? What if?' Stammered Bean, starting to panic.

'Bean! If someone else laughs at you, it's water on a duck's back. If she laughs at you you're destroyed. See what I mean! You owe it to yourself and her, to lay your cards on the table. She is worth it,' reasoned Matty.

Bean sat down and put his head in his hands. 'This is starting to terrify me. What am I going to do? How do you bare your soul when you don't know what you're bearing? Tell me what I'm supposed to do'.

'Dude, it's gotta come from the heart. Life will allow you to cross paths with your soulmate but the rest is up to you'. Replied Matty, sensing the despair in Bean's voice.

'Well, give me an idea! Travelling around outer space is one thing, but this is harder'. Been reasoned, struggling with the gravity of what Matt was telling him.

'Don't dwell, just do. It doesn't matter how or what you do, so long as it's honest. You are about to approach the most beautiful person you have ever met and lay down your feelings to her. You are going to be, and have to be totally vulnerable. This is one of life's moments that shape us and shape our lives. You have to go for it. Don't die wondering what might have been', said Matt, emphatically.

Bean sat there staring at the floor with Matt's words reverberating through him.

'Ok, suppose you're right. If I haven't been totally honest with myself then I'll do it'. Came Bean's sobering response.

'Do you promise?' Asked Matt.

'Yeah, no. I'll do it. You're right, I just don't want to offend her or put her in an awkward position', relented Bean.

By giving his promise to Matthew, Bean had backed himself into a corner. There was no more pretending. He tossed and turned all that night with his mind flip-flopping about what to do. By the time the sun rose the next day, he had a plan, and as soon as he arrived at the kiosk he would utilise his options, and put his plan into action.

Jay Jermyn, was the man the ladies boat crew had hired to sing for Charlie on her birthday. He had since used Bean as a supplier for a couple of fundraisers around the coast and Bean had been generous in granting him favours - they had become good friends. As part of his plan, Bean had decided to call in a couple of those favours. What he wanted wouldn't be easy, so he gave him a call to test the waters.

'Hello, Jay speaking', came the voice over the phone.

'Gidday Jay, it's Bean from the kiosk down the club, how ya goin', said Bean.

'Excellent, my good friend. Yes, you are the only Bean I know. What can I do for you?' Enquired the Big Fella.

'I need your help', replied Bean. 'I need a white grand piano on the beach, with you playing it for a couple of hours tomorrow arvo'.

'Wooooooo,' came the big guy's reply. 'Can you just run that by me again?'.

Bean repeated slowly. 'I need a white grand piano on the beach, with you playing it for a couple of hours, tomorrow arvo'.

'Ohhh, that's better. For a moment I thought you said you needed a white grand piano on the beach, with me playing it for a couple of hours tomorrow arvo'. Replied Jay, struggling to get his head around what was being said.

'You got it,' said Bean, 'That's exactly what I need'.

'My good friend, I can do miracles straight away but grand pianos on beaches take a little longer'. Jay patiently explained.

The conversation went quiet for a second or two then Bean quietly asked:

'Does that mean you can't do it?'

Jay could feel the disappointment in his friend's voice, and wondered what this was all about. It was very out of character for him to phone up with such an unusual request. There could be only one reason.

'Is this for a woman?' Asked Jay.

Bean paused, then answered: "Yes. How did you know that?"

'A man wouldn't go to this much trouble for anything else other than a woman. Are you in love with her?' Asked Jay.

Bean paused again, then quietly answered: 'Yes'.

Jay took a deep breath then exhaled slowly and replied: 'Oh well, a bloke's got to do what a bloke's got to do'.

'Does that mean you'll do it?' Asked a slightly more excited Bean.

'Whereabouts on the beach, is this grand piano needed? Asked Jay.

Getting a little more excited, Bean replied: 'Against the headland near the high water mark'.

'Well it won't be too near the high water mark!' Blurted Jay. 'And what time is all this going down?'

'Well I was thinking about three o'clock. The speeches and stuff for the Jackson Search Appreciation Day should be all finished by then and everyone will be upstairs groggin on'. Said Bean.

'Bean my good friend, are you planning to propose to this woman?' Asked Jay.

'No. Actually we've never been on a date or anything, we only talk a lot. I'm arranging a table with a white tablecloth and chairs, and afternoon tea for her near the piano, then I'm just gunna wing it'. Bean declared.

'Well that's a very romantic thing to do, but why does it have to be tomorrow?' Quizzed Jay, wondering if Bean had lost his marbles.

'Well, she told me she would be leaving sometime soon, so Matty and I had a sort of a chat about things I need to do. I've decided tomorrow is the day, regardless'. Answered Bean.

'Matty! So, Matty's mixed up in this too! Well I saw the news bulletin and if Matty says go, we'd better go!' Proclaimed Big Jay.

'Does that mean you'll do it?' Asked a now excited Bean.

There was a big breath out on the phone as Jay replied: 'Well, I'll probably have to organise a forklift and a truck by tomorrow morning. Then we'll have to cover it all up until zero hour. I'm not not promising anything but it might be possible... Ok, I'm in, let's do this! This is very, very big, Bean. Who else knows about it?'

'Just you and me. I promised Matt I'd do something but I didn't say what I'd do. I've got some police tape that we can use to put around everything, til I'm good to go. I haven't got a clue what to expect. I'm flying head first into the unknown, my head is mush,' gushed Bean.

'Well she must be a very special lady and I'm very impressed with your thinking, and more than impressed that you're actually doing it. I think it's a good idea to wing it. Just let your heart do the talking when the time comes. I have a friend with a vehicle that can get the piano across the soft sand and unload it on the beach. He owes me a few favours so I'll call them in. If there's any probs I'll call you, otherwise it's all go for a tomorrow morning set up'. Jay confirmed.

'Mate, I wanna thank ya. I know it all sounds like a pile of crap, but I really appreciate your help', replied Bean.

'No problem. I'm really interested in meeting your lady and seeing how this goes down. There is none so free as he who has nothing to lose, Bean. You're a champion. Who knows, this could end up to be anything. I'll catch you later'. Said the big fella and ended the phone call.

Starch was going through the motions around the club. He had been doing it for so long it was almost impossible for him to contemplate life without it. Like a lot of other people, he was anxious to meet Larry and see for himself who this person was. As he walked up from the beach to the clubhouse, Inspector David Whitehead, the policeman investigating the dredging contract fiasco, came walking toward him.

'Good morning Mr Lawless. How are you today?' Said the Inspector.

Starch was surprised to see the policeman. Like Colmie, he had been wondering what, if anything, would happen to Flowers the politician, and what was the real deal with the dredging.

'Gidday, how are you'. Starch greeted the astute cop.

'Oh I'm okay', said the Inspector. 'I was wondering if you had managed to remember anything more than what you told me when we last spoke'.

'Nah, no, nothing. Did anything happen?' Asked Starch.

'In what way?' Quizzed the cop.

'You were asking questions about people trying to pressure me into endorsing the dredging', answered Starch.

'Oh, I can't comment about that at this stage, Mr Lawless', said the Inspector.

The shrewd policeman made Starch feel nervous, so he pretended to be busy and attempted to avoid the conversation.

'Oh well, I wish I could help you more but no one connected to any government department has spoken to me about the dredging since the so-called Superbank collapsed. But if they do I'll let you know straight away'. Said an unconvincing and shallow sounding Starch.

The experienced cop looked straight at Starch and coldly replied.

'So they spoke to you before the Superbank collapsed, did they? And what did they want? Yours or the club's support? And what did they offer in return? Security? Or maybe rapid approval of your much needed grant? So far your honesty rating is sitting at zero, Mr Lawless. And what about the club's new owner? What now? Rainbows End is going to be the only privately owned SLSC in Australia. That is until the new owner decides what to do with it. What then? Another beachfront tower? That shouldn't be too hard to get past the height limit restrictions with the local council. Think about it Mr Lawless. The more units the more money per square metre for the developer, and all that garbage collection and utilities in the one spot for council. Unlike those nasty houses and backyard suburbs we grew up in. Don't you know? They're stacking people on top of one another to save the world'.

Starch suddenly felt hopelessly inadequate and struggled to reply. He looked down at the ground then muttered.

'I was told the club sale was still pending'.

The steely eyed old cop kept his gaze firmly on Starch and replied.

'Well the information you get is about as credible as the information you give. You're not protecting anybody that's worth protecting Mr Lawless, and you'll end up digging yourself into a very deep hole. Think about this… a large percentage of influential politicians usually get paid for their dirty work when they lose or leave office. That's when they get their new jobs working for people they've always worked for. It's all a sham Mr Lawless! They simply move on and we pay for their stupidity and lack of honesty. I could count the number of honest politicians I know on one hand, so don't waste your time protecting anybody. Have a nice day. Mr Lawless'.

Starch felt like he'd just gone 10 rounds with a good prize fighter, and had been well and truly knocked on his backside. He hated the whole ordeal with the dredging. From the bogus community meetings to the threats from that wimp Flowers, to the collapsing sandbank debacle that almost cost Jackson and others their lives. He would never forget the week from hell when Jackson floated about in the open sea, minutes from death. He had no reason to doubt what Inspector Whitehead had said, so any fancy ideas about saving the club were now dead in the water. He had had enough and did not have the motivation to continue. He made his way up to his office and drafted a quick speech about the club's change of ownership and his immediate resignation as the Club President. He felt sad and relieved at the same time. Life would go on. His time at Rainbows End had come to an end, but life would go on. He gathered up his personal things from the office and asked Tommy Green, the Bar Manager, to lock up that night, when trading had finished. He then did something he had never done before… He went home early.

While the focus of the club members had been on the girls boat crew, Brian and Benny from the club restaurant had been quietly progressing through the qualifying rounds of the television cooking show. Adrian had been meticulously coaching the pair and working to a stopwatch was now standard procedure in the kitchen. The boys were happy that attention had been diverted away from them, and they hadn't spoken to any of the club members or patrons about the TV show. This was all about to change however, with the boys making the cut to go on the live TV rounds. The only other person to know about their success was Mel, Benny's mum. Although she was bursting with pride, she had decided not to say anything, but just go along with the boys and let them fly under the radar. Having no expectations to live up to, allowed the young cooks to behave candidly in front of the cameras while filming the promos. The interaction and constant banter between them was a revelation, and the producers loved it. Brian and Benny were stars and set to take reality television by storm.

The boys' approach on traditional dishes they were tasked with making for the qualifying rounds, was described as Wild Culinary. Nothing was sacred in the kitchen and their take no prisoners approach to cooking, was riveting and very aggressive. Mix this swashbuckling cooking style with the volatile, anything's up for discussion banter between them, and the result was first class entertainment.

The television advertising for the show was scheduled to go to air in two weeks, so Adrian thought it best to let Starch know, seeing as the club was sure to be mentioned multiple times during the series. This would hopefully draw more people to the club. But, Adrian wasn't the only person looking for Starch. The club committee needed to talk to him to confirm Fins Waltons attendance at the appreciation ceremony. Robyn had also phoned several times looking for him, but Starch had turned his phone off and wasn't taking calls.

Jackson and his mum had gone to the club looking for Larry, but he still hadn't arrived. After hearing the news about the disappearing Starch, they decided to see if he was at home and if he was okay. Starch wasn't in a talkative mood when they found him, but he gradually opened up about what was bothering him, although he never mentioned the club's imminent closure. Jackson and Suzanne, also decided not to mention the money they had been given. After an hour of chatting they realised they all had one big question. Who's Larry? They were all looking for answers so Jack and Suzanne persuaded Starch to go back to the club, where they could all wait and see if Larry showed up.

Starch felt relieved to have some support and have someone he could comfortably talk to. Jack and his mum had been to hell and back, so he knew they were incredibly resilient and could weather any storm about club closures. When they arrived at the club they headed to the kiosk to quiz Bean for more information about Larry. But, Bean had some bad news, and it wasn't what they wanted to hear.

'Larry's been and gone, mate. He was here for about an hour talking to Rooster and the mob from Thargomindah. They all came up for the Appreciation Day after Rooster invited them. Actually, Larry did ask if Suzanne and Jack were about and he did ask if Starch was here. He did ask me to tell you, if I saw you, that he would talk to you tomorrow if you were available. He also had a chat with Ben and Sushi, and they seemed pretty chuffed', recounted Bean.

Suzanne and Jack knew what their chat would be about and they knew Larry and Dr Larry were the same person, so tomorrow's meeting would explain everything. Starch on the other hand was mystified as to what Larry wanted to chat to him about.

'Did he say what he wanted to talk to me about?' Asked Starch.

'Nah, I'd say it's something to do with his kids and nippers. You know he's hired Moey as his pilot, don't you?' Replied Bean.

'No. I didn't even know he had a plane, but there you go'. Said Starch as he rolled his eyeballs.

'Adrian is looking for you too. Apparently, there's a rumour Brian and Benny are going to be on some cooking show on TV, and the club's going to get some good exposure. You'd better see what he wants', pressed Bean.

'Anyone else?' Drawled Starch.

'Yeah, Robyn has been ringing upstairs all morning, looking for you', replied Bean.

Starch gave a breath out and replied: 'Thanks'. Then he decided to go upstairs and see what was going on. Jackson went off to the Dive Centre and Suzanne went off to work.

Sunny and Mum gave Bean a list of stock needed for the following day, then sent him off to get it. No one knew exactly what would happen on Jackson's Search Appreciation Day, and for Jack and Suzanne, tomorrow couldn't come quick enough. On the other hand, for Starch, it was a nightmare waiting to happen, but Bean was too nervous to think about anything other than his moment of truth.

# Chapter 23

# The Big Day

Bean woke the next morning before daybreak, and straight away reasoned, 'This is ridiculous. I'm going to make a fool out of myself. Sunny will think I'm an idiot'. Nevertheless, he thought back to his younger days at the school dances where he had worked out a girl strategy, at a very early age. None of the boys wanted to go home from the dance without dancing, as that would make them feel or appear a little odd and undateable. Of course, the girls knew this and were often ruthless in the number of knockbacks they delivered - they were well in control and loved it. Their only problem was if they weren't asked for a dance by any of the boys it was a disaster for them, and they appeared odd and undateable.

For his first school dance in his first year in high school, Bean worked out a tactic that would leave his self-esteem intact. At the beginning of the night, he would walk up to the most beautiful girl in school, regardless of her age, height or anything else, and politely ask: 'May I have this dance?' If the answer was 'no thanks, I'm busy' or 'get lost', it would be okay. There was no shame in getting knocked back by the top rung. He would receive nods of approval from the boys for having a go and all was fine. He was just a dance casualty. So, at his first dance in high school, he walked up to Pamela Brown who was the prettiest girl in school, and politely asked for a dance. To his astonishment, Pamela answered: 'Yes okay'. The "yes" reply sent his plans up in smoke. The problem now was, he couldn't dance. He had never danced in his life and he didn't have a clue how to dance. But Pamela, who towered over him, grabbed his hand and walked him out to the middle of the empty dance floor where he blurted: 'I don't know how to dance'. Pamela laughed and replied: 'Does anybody? Just wing it and let's enjoy ourselves'. And so he did, and they did enjoy themselves and to this day they remain the very best of friends. They danced together at every school dance until their schooling ended. Pamela confessed to him some years later that she accepted his first dance proposal because she was dreading having to say "no thanks" all night, then getting sledged for it. It turned out to be one of the best decisions she had ever made because she had found a 'bestie' (Best friend).

Bean crawled out of bed, had a shower, got dressed and headed off to work with Pamela's advice still ringing in his ears, all these years later. 'Does anybody really know what they're doing? Just wing it and enjoy'. 'Was Sunny worth it?' He thought. 'Yep, all day long, a zillion times over'.

Starch, on the other hand, awoke to a day he wished would never come. Despite all his hopes and dreams, reality had now forecast an end to a treasured part of his life. He thought about the friendships he had formed, the lives that had been saved by the clubbies, the staff that ran the club and their families. He thought about the nippers and their parents and the penguins and their comradery, and the regular tourist families that spent their time at the club. He thought about all the characters in the club, all the different personalities that bounced off one another. They were all so different as people yet they all shared an appreciation of each other, a common love of the beach and the enjoyment of life it brings with it. There was so much to lose and it seemed it was all for a high rise building, that would make some developer richer. The more he thought about it the more he recognised the problem. Friendships cannot be sold, appreciation cannot be sold, volunteers cannot be sold, memories or belongings cannot be sold, community or commonality cannot be sold, none of it has any monetary value. The only value lives in those that share the common appreciation of each other and the environment around them - and that is worthless to a greedy developer.

He crawled out of bed, had a shower, got dressed and headed for the club early. Along the way, he tried to get himself into the right frame of mind for the day ahead. He hadn't bothered to find out who was coming, he had left everything for the committee to do. He assumed the local pollies would stick their noses in at the invite of the committee. He rationalised that once the club had closed, everyone would just drift to other clubs and life would go on. So, maybe he was being too dramatic about the whole closure thing. This frame of mind didn't last long, as he remembered what had happened when he tried to sit on the fence for the sand bar dredging fiasco. Thinking about that just made him angry.

When he arrived at the club, it was already a hive of activity. Bean was there loading stock. The kitchen staff were there working their tails off. Mel and Tommy Green were there organising the refreshments and entertainment area. Simmo and the girl's boat crew were cleaning around the clubhouse and the Penguins were sorting and organising chairs. Rooster was asleep in the med room and the other club members were chipping in where they could. Starch gave a deep sigh then hopped out of his car and tried to find one of the committee members, so he could see how the day's program would run. He also headed for the med room where he woke Rooster and gave him a lecture on, 'How many ways there are to be stupid'. Rooster responded by promising, 'med room emergency sleepovers' would never happen again.

The crowd continued to build all morning for the light lunch scheduled for midday, followed by speeches and presentations starting at 1 pm. Starch was feeling ill with the weight of the world on his shoulders. Although he felt like walking away he owed it to the club to stay and deliver the news. As he walked upstairs, Tommy Green, Adrian, Benny, Brian and Mel all asked him to ring Robyn as she had been calling repeatedly. Starch let it go over his head as he reasoned Robyn would be at the presentation, so he would talk to her then. By mid-morning the club was packed with people. The Thargomindah crew were walking around the place being chaperoned by Rooster. Most of the board riders had turned up at the invitation of the committee, so they could be officially recognised for their help in the search and rescue. Downstairs at the kiosk, Bean, Sunny and Mum were being smashed with orders. Bean was starting to get anxious as it was past 11 am and there was no grand piano and no piano player. He quietly reassured himself things would be okay, and reasoned that it was too early to place the piano on the beach.

Big Cop, Ben and Sushi were at the side of the clubhouse and started to tell Starch about their new trawler business venture when Fins Walton and Shakbait came walking around the corner. At the opposite end of the building, Flowers the politician came around that corner, walking straight toward Fins. As they were about to pass each other, Flowers pretended to talk on his mobile phone. Then, without warning, Fins grabbed Flowers by the throat and pinned him up against the club wall, lifting his feet off the ground. Big Cop and Starch raced over and tried to get Fins to let go, but Fins wasn't having a bar of it.

'You little grub! You almost killed Jackson with your dirty little foreign dredging racket'. Snarled Fins, tightening his grip even more.

'Let him go, Walton. We all know what's going on but choking this piece of crap in broad daylight won't solve anything. Let him go'. Yelled Big Cop, as Starch tried to drag Fins off Flowers.

'You little piece of dog's vomit. How's it feel to be about to die?' Snarled Fins as Sharkbait tried to sink his teeth into Flowers' leg.

'Walton!! Listen to me. He's gunna die if you don't let him go! You're choking him. Let him go!' Yelled Big Cop, as Ben and Sushi joined in and helped Starch trying to get Fin's hand released from Flowers' throat.

'How much did they give ya, ya dirty little maggot. You blood-sucking little bullshit artist. I want you to die slowly so I can enjoy the moment even more'. Growled Fins as Sharkbait sunk his teeth into Flowers calf muscle.

Ben and Sushi jumped on Fins' back trying to wrestle him into letting go. Big Cop and Starch managed to get his hand from Flowers' neck, which resulted in Flowers dropping to the ground gasping for air. Sharkbait was still ripping into his calf muscle so Ben dragged him off. Flowers lay on the ground trying to breathe with a look of terror on his face.

'He tried, he tried to kill me. I need an ambulance. Help me. Help me. He tried to kill me', gasped Flowers as he tried to get up. His face was still red and his leg was bleeding badly.

'Shut up, Flowers!! You threw the first punch, I saw it. Walton was only protecting himself, especially after you kicked his dog', said Big Cop.

'That's not true, that's a lie. They attacked me! Please call an ambulance and the police. He tried to kill me', gasped Flowers.

'Nah. No way. Three witnesses saw it. You jobbed him then you sunk the boot into his little dog. That's not a good look for a pollie, Mr Flowers'. Said Big Cop with an official tone.

'I need an ambulance. Help me. I need an ambulance, he tried to kill me. I can't move, help me', begged Flowers.

'Well, it's obvious this conversation is getting us nowhere, and I'm busy, so I'll let you and Walton figure it out'. Offered Big Cop.

'No, no. Please, I'm badly injured, help me to my car. I'll look after you'. Begged Flowers.

Big Cop felt a little empathy for him and was about to help him, when Fins broke loose again.

'I'll put ya outta your misery. I'll look after you like you looked after Jack. You little blood-sucking parasite'. Growled Fins, as he lunged toward him.

A look of horror came over Flowers' face and he tried to get to his feet. Ben, Sushi and Starch tried to hold Fins back. Flowers managed to stand up with his leg bleeding badly from the mauling he received from Sharkbait. The horror of Fins Walton coming down on him again motivated him to hobble as quickly as he could to his car. Coughing and shaking like a leaf, he started the car and sped out of the car park, fearing for his life and fully traumatised by Fins exposure.

'Alright fellas, if the skipper has finished his morning meet and greet, let's head upstairs and see what's happening'. Said Big Cop as nonchalantly as can be.

The control in Big Cops voice diffused the whole situation and brought some welcome relief for Ben and Sushi. Starch had things to do downstairs so he told the crew he'd meet them upstairs later. He then headed off with a huge smirk on his face. It was so good to finally see Flowers on the receiving end of some good old bush justice. He laughed to himself as he thought about Big Cop and Fins working together on the same boat, with a bunch of Uni students. Who knows what else the day would bring. Although the club was going down, at least the club was going down swinging. 'Bring it on', he thought to himself.

The time for the presentation grew closer and closer and Bean's anxiety worsened. There was no piano and no Jay to play the piano. He started to get that helpless, empty feeling in his stomach, so he started thinking about a plan 'B'. Matthew kept constantly checking on the kiosk to see if they needed a hand, but as always, Sunny and Mum had everything well under control. The media crews had started to turn up and were desperate to talk to Matthew and Jackson, but instead, they were escorted around by Rooster who told them he was running the show.

Matthew had linked up with Moey and the pair of them had organised a game of beach cricket with their mates, the nippers, penguins, the boat crews and anybody else who wanted to join in. Jackson hooked up with Starch and helped with the chores before deciding to cruise upstairs and see what the Fishos were doing. As usual, they were at the end of the bar with Sharkbait on the servery munching down a pie and making himself at home amongst the glasses of beer.

It wasn't long before the committee members found Starch and let him know the presentation would begin in thirty minutes and as president of the club, he would be opening and closing the proceedings. There was also a late adjustment to the program to include the introduction of Larry, with the committee members eager to know who Larry was. Starch was bewildered as to why Larry had to be introduced, but there was a connection with Matthew that was big news and the locals wanted to know more about 'what's going on'. Because of the larger than expected crowd and massive media interest, the presentations and speeches were moved onto the clubhouse verandah, for a bit more room. With fifteen minutes to go, Robyn finally found Starch, but before she could say anything, Starch just moaned and held up his hand to cut her off from speaking, then announced:

'Before you say anything, I know what's happening and there's no point in going over it. I'm going to let everyone know when I finish the proceedings and thank everybody who has been involved in the club. There's nothing we can do about it, it's over and done, let's all move on. I haven't slept for a week and I just don't want to talk about it. We've all done our bit for the club. A lot of members have risked their lives by saving other people, and I'm just too gutted, saddened and angry to talk about it. To you personally, we all owe you so much more than we could ever afford to pay, so from me personally, a very big thank you and best wishes for the future. It's been rewarding and informative working with you - you did your best'.

Robyn started to frown as she listened to Starch pour out his heart. After a couple of seconds silence, she gave him a puzzled, irritated look and replied:

'What the hell are you talking about? So! You're gutted, saddened and angry are you? Oh! And you find me informative, do you? Well, why don't you answer my bloody phone calls and text messages! I've called

283

thirty times and sent seventeen text messages for you to call me and you bloody ignored it. I have rung every committee member, every staff member and heaven knows how many bloody club members with a message for you to phone me, and you bloody ignored it. I hope you have a bloody good reason John because I'm seriously about to lose it'.

Starch was horrified by the aggression in Robyn's voice and tried to calm her by explaining:

'I've accepted the grief that goes with the passing of the club, and like me, you're obviously upset. We don't have the money or connections to fight off developers, so rather than upset everybody let's just make it as painless as possible for everyone, and leave it to the end of the presentation ceremony before I say anything'.

Robyn gave him another extremely strained look before letting fly with a lethal berating:

'What the hell planet have you been living on? You seriously haven't got a clue, have you? Not only are you ignorant and rude and overburdened with self-pity, but you are also absolutely clueless and misinformed and more than likely the victim of self assumption plus idiotic freedom of thought. What developers??? We found out what was going on a week ago when you decided to go into your "man bubble". Freakin 'men!!! You've all got to carry the weight of the world on your shoulders, haven't you! Won't discuss problems with anybody will you?'

Starch felt like a deer, caught in the headlights of a very big truck, and got the awful feeling he might have taken a wrong turn somewhere. He cautiously replied, trying to sound like a man in charge.

'Well, I haven't been informed of any developments'.

Robyn had heard enough and screamed: 'Because you don't answer your bloody phone!!! There is no developer! Larry bought the club building and has already bought the land off the government'.

Starch couldn't process what he was hearing, and with his jaw-dropping to record levels he managed to ask:

'What? How can he? We own the building'.

Robyn came straight back at him with zero patience:

'No! The building inspector has condemned the building as being far too expensive to fix and it's never been heritage listed despite being the oldest SLSC club in Australia. It was going to be a massive loss for everybody. So, Larry agreed to buy it, pay for its restoration and renovation and give it straight back to us. We've basically been waiting for your signature to complete the proceedings, but you won't answer your bloody phone. He's giving the club back to us with a blank cheque for the work and improvement we need, including new equipment'.

Starch's knees buckled and he sunk back into a chair. All he could do was stare at Robyn with his mouth open. 'Whattt' was all he could manage to say. Then after an awkward moment of silence between them, he murmured:

'Who is Larry? How did all this happen? Why on earth would he do all that? What does he want?'

Robyn's patience was running out, but she understood the nightmare Starch had created for himself by retreating into his bubble, and not staying in contact with everybody. Instead of talking about the club problem he internalised it and let it fester into something that made him grossly out of whack with reality. So she let him off the hook and suggested:

'I think it would be better if Larry explained his motive to you himself. He's a very nice man. I've met him a few times and he's a very interesting person. I've actually got some work off him, which is great. He's outside on the verandah sitting with Matthew and his family. But, first I need your signature, so it's all done'.

Starch was astounded and feeling quite stupid and immature. How the hell did he talk himself into such a state. He glanced over the papers Robyn had for him to sign and it was just as she had said. But why? He had mixed feelings about going from the outhouse to the penthouse in the conversation with Robyn, but he still didn't know what the deal was. At least the club was alive and he wouldn't be giving any goodbye speeches. Robyn raced off to finalise the contracts and left him to recover from the tsunami berating he received. But, he deserved it so he accepted it, then took a moment to digest what was happening. He decided to head out to the verandah to meet Larry when he was met by Kelly Follent, the lady police officer, who greeted him with a smile.

Hi Starch', said Kelly. 'Good to see you again. You might be able to help us. We're looking for Mr Fins Walton about an alleged assault here earlier'.

'Oh okay', replied Starch with his head still spinning. 'Actually, he's over at the end of the bar with his drinking mates. The big bloke's a copper, you might know him'.

'Oh yes, I can see them. Yes I know the big bloke, he's a very ordinary cop sometimes. I'll just have a chat with them, then I'll need to have a chat with you also', she replied.

Kelly and an accompanying lady police constable, walked over to the end of the bar. Starch tagged along behind them to see what was going on. At the end of the bar, Big Cop, Ben. Sushi and Fins were deep in conversation. Sharkbait was lying on the bar sound asleep with a belly full of pies and snoring loudly. The rest of the bar area was packed with patrons and the noise was loud and joyous. The club was rocking.

Kelly was about to speak to the crew when young Micheal Hadfield's grandfather from Thargomindah, walked up to Big Cop and asked him a question.

'Excuse me, I don't mean to be rude but I was just wondering if you're Gary Follent', Granddad Hadfield asked.

Big cop looked at him for a moment and replied: 'What do you know about Gary Follent?'

All those within earshot went silent and waited for the answer. The only exception was Starch who murmured: 'Gary Follent'.

Granddad gave a smirk and replied: 'I thought so. Gary Follent was the most feared man in Rugby League right through the '70s and '80s. He was a prop, enforcer, hitman, for the South Sydney Rabbitohs. He was the boss of the appropriately named 'Forward Pack From Hell', which was infamous right across the Rugby League world. I thought I recognised you. Bloody good footballer. Referee's nightmare.

'Nah, grossly negatively exaggerated. I'm strictly a play by the rules man. Fairness, respect, sportsmanship. Time tends to cloud things over and magnify hearsay', replied Big Cop diplomatically.

Granddad's smirk grew into a grin, as Starch murmured, 'Gary Follent', once more. Fins overheard him again and commented: "There's an echo in here".

Starch looked at Big Cop in disbelief and said:

'Gary Follent punched me in the face as soon as I ran on as a reserve in my very first game in top grade. Just walked up and punched me in the head and said, "welcome to A grade"'.

Big Cop looked at him and frowned.

'You probably did something wrong mate or a case of mistaken identity. Don't worry about it mate', he replied.

Starch, whose head was now a swirling mess, dropped his jaw even lower.

"Don't worry about it?" he gasped. "I was on the same bloody team! Mistaken identity? We had the same bloody jersey on! We were both props on the same team! How did you end up in the police force? I owe you one", blurted Starch.

Everybody looked down and held their breath when Big Cop calmly replied:

'Nah, it's okay mate. You don't owe me anything, I can't recall anything like that ever happening. Probably got me confused with someone else. No harm done'.

Ben and Sushi were beginning to notice the similarities between Big Cop and Fins. They put it down to a generational thing whereas, they do anything then deny everything. Meanwhile, Starch stood there overloaded with information and stunned that Big Cop dismissed giving him a punch in the face welcome to his first A Grade game. Rather than spoil the day by starting a punch up in the bar, he asked Big Cop if he knew Kelly Follent, the police lady. To which Big Cop replied.

'Yeah, I know her. Did she book you? She booked me. Got treated very unfairly that day, but she's a good kid with a lot to learn'.

Constable Kelly Follent had heard enough, and let fly with a serious tone.

'Dad, you were doing a ridiculous speed through a radar trap in an unmarked car heading to a fast food joint because you were too lazy to prepare meals for the people in the cells. The reason you were speeding was that it was half-time for the footy on TV. That sets a terrible and embarrassing example for everyone else. Mr Fins Walton, we need to talk to you about an alleged assault on Mr Flowers, the local MP, that occurred here today. These are very serious allegations, sir, and I'd like to hear your side of the story, please'.

Before Fins could say anything, Big Cop fired straight back.

'I saw that incident and had to stop Mr Flowers beating up Mr Walton. There are three other witnesses to this and we all saw it, and I'll give you a statement right now'.

Kelly rolled her eyeballs and replied:

'Yeah well, I thought we'd get the facts. Flowers has abused the hospital staff for making him wait when they declared his injuries weren't life-threatening. I suppose that dog that is illegally sleeping on the bar knows nothing about the bite on Flowers's leg'.

Just as the tension reached boiling point, Jackson's mother Suzanne walked up to Constable Kelly and the whole situation was diffused as the couple hugged each other. It was an emotional meeting between the women that hadn't seen each other since Fins and the boys found Jackson floating in the sea. Suzanne had left a letter at the police station for Kelly and the other police lady, but this was the first time they had met since that awful time.

Starch took advantage of the lull in official business and slipped away quietly before Kelly could ask him any questions. Ben and Sushi stayed with Big cop and Fins and were prepared to play their "I don't speak english" card if needed for Fins defence. The boys had invested too much money in their new venture to see Fins sent to jail, so it was all in.

Starch notified the committee members that he wanted to start proceedings, and he made his way out to the presentation area on the verandah. Just as he was about to start, Larry walked up, extended his hand and said:

'Hi Starch, good to see you again. Robyn told me that you went over the contracts and were happy with everything. There are a couple more things I'd like to talk to you about, but we can do that in the next couple of days before I leave. How's your family and everything else going?'

Once again Starch stood there dumbfounded. He wasn't sure what to say or do. He never had time to properly read the contracts, although Robyn would have agonised over them, so he was winging it and hoping everything worked out. Out of ideas on what to say, he replied:

'Gidday Larry, really good to see you. I've heard a lot about you but we've never had a really good chat. I'm a bit gobsmacked with what's going on and don't fully understand the reasoning behind what you're doing for the club. I'd really like to know why, if you've got the time to tell me'.

Larry gave Starch an understanding look and answered:

'Of course, and thank you for asking. In a nutshell what happened was, Robyn, phoned me and introduced herself, then told me about the predicament the club was in with a private development overshadowing its future. She also told me about the condition of the building and the lack of funds for repair. I was told about a government grant you applied for, then did my own investigation and found the local MP never lodged it until the allotted time had expired. I also found out the same MP's family were involved in the development proposal with financial backing from the company responsible for financing the Tweed Bar dredging. Robyn and I had another meeting and tried to contact you several times but you were unavailable. So, she had one day to save the club. We went to the relevant government body and put forward an offer, at the same time discussing the connection between the developers, the dredging company and the MP. In essence, the guarantee of the continuation of the Surf Lifesaving Club won the day. The conditions are, we need to start the renovations of the building ASAP, shaping it in a way that is of benefit to the community and retaining its Old Queenslander character'.

Larry's answer left Starch with extreme dumbfoundedness. It was as if the world was on performance enhancers, and he couldn't keep up. He couldn't mentally digest how blase Larry was about rescuing the club, and shelving out what must be millions of dollars to purchase and renovate it. Trying to understand Larry's logic and without appearing to doubt his intentions, Starch tried to appear understanding and politely asked:

'That is incredible and I'm sorry that I didn't reply to your calls. The club is overwhelmed with gratitude for what you've done and it's bloody fantastic to have you around. But, I must be missing something because I still don't understand, "why?"'.

Without hesitation Larry replied.

'Maybe it's because I can. Let's talk later this afternoon. Can you do me a favour please? Can we skip the introduction and new club arrangement until next week. I feel that it's Jackson's friends and rescuers day, and we should focus on that'.

Starch raised his eyebrows and replied:

'Well, yeah. Is everything alright?'

If there was one trait Larry had, that tended to catch people by surprise, it was his directness. He never padded sentences and got straight to the point.

'Yes, of course', he answered. 'Jackson is a great kid and we owe him and his mother a great debt'.

And with that, Larry walked off and left Starch just as confused as ever. As he made his way out onto the verandah he tested the microphone, and looked around at the familiar faces in the crowd. One person that stood out immediately was Danny. He had a cocky stance and wore a T-shirt with the statement 'Your day just got better, I'm Danny' written across the front. As he turned around the message on the back read 'Enjoy the view, train with Danny'. Starch thought about that for a moment and wondered if Danny had gone completely mad, swallowed up by his own self-delusion. How can a human being be so ridiculous? But, at least it momentarily took his mind off his rapidly changing world and allowed him to centre himself. To rationalise the Danny phenomenon Starch had the thought: 'Maybe the world needs people like Danny to let the rest of us have a good eyeball roll, and realise we're doing ok'.

The rest of the committee joined Starch and the proceedings got underway, with the notable absence of Flowers the pollie. Everybody who was involved in the search was officially thanked. Everything was going very well, everyone was happy and the media were feasting on the Jackson rescue story and the bolt from the blue Matthew story. The big question the media wanted Matthew to answer, but were becoming increasingly frustrated with him dodging it was, Who is Larry? Matty knew by now how much Larry treasured his anonymity, so he never gave anything away as far as Larry's identity was concerned. This approach gave Larry and his family some of the freedoms of normality.

Getting toward the end of proceedings it was time for some of the final and most involved people of the rescue, such as Fins, Ben and Sushi to be officially recognised. As one of the committee members by the name of Mick Jones gave a detailed account of the way Jackson was found and the very professional manner of treatment he received from the boys on the boat, Starch went for a quick look into the bar area. Fins, Ben, Sushi and Big Cop were still there talking with Grandad from Thargomindah, so he asked Fins to come and accept the official 'Thank You'. Much to his surprise Fins replied straight away:

'Yeah alright'.

Not knowing what to expect, the crowd went quiet when Fins fronted up to the microphone. Everybody was well aware of who he was and most had seen him in action, so there was an air of apprehensiveness. His crusty voice broke the air and jaws dropped immediately as he said:

'Well for a start, my name is not Fins Walton. My name is Alex Dyball. My stepfather's name was Walton so everyone assumed that was my name, but it's not. Secondly! I didn't save Jackson. It was Sharkbait who spotted him and woke us up, then it was Ben and Sushi who were the difference between Jack living or dying. The boys were freaking legends from top to bottom and the Ambos and chopper crew will tell you exactly the same thing! So, the only reason I'm up here is to see these blokes get the recognition they deserve. Whatever their qualifications, they've done a bloody good job of hiding it. The most humble pair of bloody legends I've met in my life. While I'm up here I'll just remind everybody how Jack got in the bloody mess in the first place. We almost lost him because of the bloody stupidity of experts! Think about that! The boys have asked me to thank everybody involved for not giving up, and even when things looked lost, you kept going. Thank you and well done'.

With a wry smile on his face, Alex Dyball finished by saying:

'In the unlikely situation that I'm ever lost at sea I'll expect you to do the same thing for me. I'll expect you all to be bawling your eyes out and never give up looking for me'.

And with that, Alex Dyball walked back to the bar to a mildly shocked Big Cop who was wondering how the cops had not known about the real name. Ben and Sushi were scratching their heads and wondering why this never came up when they made up the contracts for the new boat and business. Everybody else was suffering open mouth syndrome, and collectively looked like fish starving for oxygen. It was from that point in time that Big Cop and Alex Dyball were commonly referred to as BC and AD. The crowd was quiet and wondering what was next? Brian, Benny and Adrian from the kitchen were in the crowd on the verandah listening and watching proceedings and sensed the uncomfortable, gobsmacked silence brought on by the Alex Dyball revelation.

Adrian muttered: 'Hmmm. Alex Dyball? Sounds like an engineer'.

Brian wasn't sure what he said and muttered back: 'Sounds like an engine near?'

Adrian impatiently muttered again: 'An engineer!'

Brian opened his mouth in an, "Oh I get it", type of gesture, then replied: 'Of course. An injured ear'.

Benny was standing in between the two of them and turned his head to whoever was speaking. His only thoughts were: 'What's goin on?'

Before Adrian could unleash on Brian and shatter the silence, Mel, who was standing in front of them, turned around and gave them the mother of all death stares. The three of them stood there in line, expressionless and looking straight ahead. Silence returned as they waited for the proceedings to continue.

Starch stepped back up to the microphone with his head now spinning in another direction on information overload. He took a deep breath then announced the final official award of the day.

'Ok everyone can I have your attention, please. We have the final club presentation for the day and it's very important. This award goes to someone who thoroughly deserves it. Someone who does all the little things, all the non-important things, all the fix-ups, all the someone else will do it things, all the things that don't come with Thank-Yous'. All the little things that don't get seen, but give the club its spirit. Rooster, could you come up here please?'

A perplexed Rooster made his way up to the microphone. It was a strange feeling for him to be asked by Starch to front up somewhere when he wasn't in any trouble for breaching club standards. Nevertheless, he did as he was told and stood quietly beside Starch on the podium.

'Ladies boat crew, have you ever wondered how the surfboat slides through the water so well? How do the oars feel so free yet firm? Have you ever wondered why the boat always shines? How does the gym end up so neat and tidy the next day, after you've left it in a complete mess? Someone does all that and more every night, someone who is still working after everyone's gone home. Yeah, I know Caustic Soda doesn't go well on seats, but it doesn't go well in underpants either'. Related Starch, as the ladies boat crew cast their eyes down feeling a bit guilty about the Great Balls of Fire incident.

'Does anybody notice the absence of empty plastic bottles around the club? Have you ever noticed Rooster's ute full of plastic down at the recyclers, getting cashed in and how the exact same amount of money gets anonymously donated to the nippers? Mysteriously enough the same thing happens to the tractor, no one has ever put fuel in it but it's been going for years. I could go on all day about the jobs that get done, that no one was asked to do, and no one needs to be thanked for, because no one knows or cares who's doing it. So, this year's Clubman Of the Year Award goes to Rooster, also known as the invisible man, doer of all things anonymous. Well done Rooster and from all of us - thank you!' Announced Starch.

There was a loud and spirited response from the crowd as the Rooster phenomenon climbed to new heights. The Thargomindah crew were the loudest, although the ladies boat crew didn't hold back with their flattering remarks which were voiced at maximum volume.

'About bloody time! Go Rooster. Legend.' The cries grew louder. After all the years of waiting to hear someone say, 'Thank you, we appreciate it'. His time had come and it caught him completely by surprise. As he stood in front of the microphone his mouth went dry, his throat went dry and his eyes started to well up. He had never experienced this type of appreciation in his life. He tried to speak but the words weren't there. He relished the chance to get in front of television cameras and talk his head off, but this was different, this was about him.

Starch handed him a bottle of water and quietly said: 'Bit dry mate? You're okay, you've earned this'. Having a Starch endorsement gave him enough confidence to speak.

'Thanks so much. I'm not the only one who does things around here and personally, I'd like to thank all of you for letting me be a part of your club. I can't think of anything to say, other than thank you. If you're wondering why I do stuff, it's because you're worth it. You're all worth it. You're a great bunch of people. Thank you'.

And with that, Rooster stood back to walk away from the microphone, but the crowd started to applaud and Starch motioned for him to just stand still and wait. The applause was like a stampede of wild horses, getting closer and closer, growing louder and louder. There was no yelling or whistling, just thunderous applause. This was the sound of heartfelt appreciation. Rooster stood still and his welling eyes started to overflow. Starch put his arm around his shoulder and said: 'Well done, mate'.

The applause rolled on for a couple of minutes then as it started to die down Starch addressed the crowd.

'Ok, well now you can all buy him a beer, but keep him away from the Med Room, and someone drive him home. Just one more thing, there'll be a special general meeting next week and we'd like all members to attend. There is some very good news for the club, and some big positive changes coming. Thank you'.

Starch needed a settler so he motioned to the bar staff to get him a beer. It was a big day, and his head was still trying to catch up, so when the beer was ready Tommy Green waved his arm and placed it on the bar. Just as Starch was halfway across the lounge to get it, the microphone crackled into action and a voice rang out of the speakers. It was Jackson. Starch turned and headed back to the verandah to see what was happening. Jack had walked up, turned on the mike and decided to say a few words unannounced, this wasn't planned. The chatter around the crowd died down as everyone tuned in to Jack's voice.

'Oh, hi everyone. I know I wasn't supposed to be saying anything today, but I just didn't feel right being quiet. I know I've already talked to everybody about the rescue and how close I came to missing out on my next birthday. I know I've already thanked everybody over and over, and I know I'll never be able to thank everybody enough. But there's one person that hasn't been mentioned today, and it's probably because no one knows about the hours we spent together in the hospital. Day and night he was always there. He is an incredible person. His name is Dr Larry. The whole time I was in hospital he was always there, constantly checking and adjusting everything to do with my treatment. He never stopped caring 24/7, and it never stopped when I left the hospital. He has been mind-bogglingly generous to mum and me to this day. So, I'd just like to say to Dr Larry and his family, thank you so much from mum and I and we are looking forward to having a talk later today'.

Jackson's little impromptu speech took everybody by surprise and after the applause died down, the number one question was, Who is Dr Larry? Starch was once again mystified and couldn't help wondering what did "mind-boggling generous" mean? But, Jack had provided the perfect way to close proceedings, which Starch did. After that, a mammoth smorgasbord of free food, including mountains of seafood was laid out, and the bar was open for free drinks. It was a great and raucous scene reminiscent of a medieval feast. Big Cop, Alex Dyball (Fins), Ben and Sushi were still at the end of the bar chatting away. Sharkbait was awake and listening to the conversation, scoring the occasional ear scratch from other drinkers. Danny and Grizz were mingling with the ladies as Starch, Colmie. Simmo, Rooster and the Thargomindah mob were talking their heads off. Jackson, Moey, young Michael Hadfield from Thargomindah and a bunch of boardriders were having a friendly go at one another. Everyone was involved in the social talk fest. The lady boat crews had roped Jules into a lively conversation with a lot of arms drooping around his shoulders, and touching going on. Jules wasn't sure what all the attention was about, but just like Sharkbait, he was lapping up the ear scratches and appreciating the attention. Jack's mum Suzanne, Starch's wife Talia, Matty's parents and Larry's family were amongst a bunch of non-drinkers and heavy eaters enjoying some serious taste testing. Times were good and the piles of fresh local seafood were very much appreciated by the bunch.

There was one corner that held the most interest and the most frustration for the media crews, because Starch had ruled out disturbing the three people in the corner. Larry, Matthew and a famous billionaire technology/space scientist friend of Larry's called Noel Sumk. The billionaire scientist was famous for his range of innovative electric cars and advances in space technology, even to the point of sending one of his cars into space with a human dummy behind the wheel. Sumk had heard about Matt and was eager to meet him, so the three of them were engaged in deep conversation, whilst Matthew's siblings Dallas, Melissa and Josh quietly listened in. Matt's parents had the occasional look over at the trio and were immensely proud of Matty as he held court in front of the two men.

Larry eventually went off to find his family whilst Matt and Noel continued an intriguing conversation about autonomous electric passenger drones and ionic propulsion. Starch was wandering around the club talking to people when he came across Jackson and Suzanne who were doing much the same thing. As they stood there swapping notes about the 'Larry Effect', they were joined by Matt's dad, George. All four of them were eager to get some answers from Larry. In particular, there was one question they all needed to be answered, and that was, why? Why all the generosity? Why the generosity toward Matty? While Suzanne and Jackson couldn't relax until they found out the 'why' behind the enormous amounts of money they had suddenly found in their bank accounts. They decided to approach Larry together and see if he would speak to them privately, and put their minds at rest. As they started to walk off and look for him, Larry and his family came walking toward them in the opposite direction.

After greeting each other, Starch seized the moment and asked:

'Larry, do you think it would be possible for us to talk to you for a moment so we can better understand your motivation behind all the caring and generosity?'

Larry and his wife gave Starch a puzzled look before Larry answered:

'Well I thought that would have been obvious, but yes, of course, we'd love to talk to you and answer any questions. Can we all grab a table at the kiosk and I'll try and clarify my actions and intentions? Can we please keep our personal conversations private? That's very important to my family'.

Everyone nodded in agreement and answered emphatically: 'Absolutely'.

Once they were settled at the kiosk with a makeshift table and milk crates and cushions to sit on, Larry asked:

'So what would you like to know?'

To which Starch replied:

'Well first of all, why? And second, could we please know, who is Larry? Who are you?'

Once again Larry and his wife looked at each other, somewhat mystified and thinking, maybe this is an Australian thing where they have to go over and over something before they feel comfortable. So Larry asked:

'I don't understand your question. What do you mean, why?'

Larry's reply was met with four blank faces, so Starch tried to broaden the question.

'Well why would you go to so much trouble and expense for Matty? Why would you take Suzanne and Jack under your wing and be 'extremely generous'? Whatever that means. Why on earth would you go to the lengths of buying the clubhouse and land only to give control straight back with an open cheque book for renovations? I mean, I can't even count as high as that would cost. Larry, we are mere mortals, low altitude fliers. We just need you to explain things so we can understand and fully appreciate your involvement in everything'.

Larry was quick to reply.

'Well firstly, Matthew was a 'find' for me. I'm always looking for people with exceptional abilities and with Matthew, I hit the jackpot. I'm not the only one that's staggered by his ability. The education system somehow never identified his potential or capability. To be precise he has an extraordinary ability to solve extremely complex problems across multiple cognitive disciplines. His motor skills are some of the finest we've ever seen. For instance, he threaded a needle whilst spinning in zero gravity with boxing gloves on, and that was just his party trick. Who wouldn't invest in him? Who wouldn't want him on their team? He's the find of the decade! As far as everything else is concerned, I have a question for you'.

'What's that?' Asked Starch, still digesting what was said about Matthew.

Larry paused for a second or two then looked at Jack, and asked:

'Jackson, don't you remember us? Don't you recognise us? Doesn't anyone here recognise us? Starch, is this an 'all Asians look the same, type of thing'? Jackson, you saved my children's lives, they were gone, under the water and lost, but you managed to save them. Then you gave up your own life so we could be put on the Jet Ski. We can never ever repay you enough. I watched Suzanne go through the agony I caused. I was careless and didn't listen to Rooster when he yelled out to run. I was apathetic and too slow to react, but you saved us, Jack. You saved all of us! Starch, you spoke to us on the beach, don't you remember? Although it was very chaotic. You tried to help when I was treating the kids, but I told you I was a doctor and I was okay and other people needed your help'.

Larry stopped explaining for a moment. The four shocked faces were plastered with an incredulous expression. Jackson was the first to speak and asked.

'Dr Larry, was that you?'

Suzanne followed with, 'Oh my Grandmother!!! Why didn't you say something?'

For Starch, the penny had dropped. It was Larry and his family whom he had seen sitting on the headland every day of Jackson's search. It was Larry who was sitting in the waiting room when Jackson was taken to hospital, and he was allowed to stay because he was a doctor. It was Larry who was always there, in the background, hoping, praying and then caring for Jack during his recovery. Starch broke the silence by saying:

'Mate, I'm so sorry. I didn't put two and two together and I apologise for that. I just didn't realise. Mate, I don't know what to say. I've had a head-spinning day but I think I've just found all the answers, a matter of fact I'm sure of it. I'm really embarrassed, to be honest, I've completely missed the mark. I've dropped the ball with the line wide open.'

Larry gave Starch a puzzled look and consoled him by saying: 'That's okay Starch, I'm sure we can move on'.

For Suzanne and Jack the conversation had been a revelation. They now had all their answers. The solution was always there, right in front of them. But Suzanne was a gracious lady and Jack always went with his mum's word. So in true Suzanne spirit, she reasoned with Larry.

'Larry, like Starch, Jackson and I are stunned. We respect your gratitude but it was my decision to let Jackson be involved in surf rescue and it was Jackson's decision to be involved in the rescue that day. We have learnt to deal with life's downturns and we are both very grateful for every second we spend together, and with friends and family. We are thrilled and appreciative enough just to know you and your beautiful family. You have been wonderful enough, but we cannot accept your extremely generous gift of appreciation'.

Larry and his wife looked very disappointed, so Larry replied:

'Suzanne, if you do that you will break the chains of gratitude and kindness. It isn't extremely generous, when you consider Jack saved five lives. We are in a position to show our gratitude and you're not allowing us to do that - all we are asking is to be a part of your family and you be a part of ours. I also hope you don't mind but, Jack told me about your music so I asked him to record it and send me the audio file. Out of the twelve songs he recorded you playing, a movie company wants three as soundtracks, a recording company wants to buy four for their own artists. If you don't want to perform an advertising company wants to talk to you about the rest as jingles for commercials. They are all waiting to talk to you about how much you want for your songs. We would be extremely, extremely disappointed, if you rejected our chance to thank you and Jack for what happened. Please don't do that to us'.

Suzanne looked at Jack and was about to ask him about the recordings, but he got in first and said:

'Sorry mum, but you're really good and you never show anybody'.

He gave her a hug and added: 'Love you mum'.

They both sat there and had to accept they were now very wealthy and life would never be the same, plus, what would she do with her music? For the first time in their lives, they were overwhelmed with good problems. Starch was still wondering about how much was 'extremely generous'? Matthew's father George was bewildered by the conversation, and like Starch was wondering what 'extremely generous' amounted to. Their collective minds boggled.

Larry then addressed George.

'George, while we're here talking, I'd like to run something by you.

I've just got word Flowers quit politics citing an assassination attempt as his reason. There's going to be a bye-election and I think you would make an excellent candidate, and a very honest politician if elected. Would you consider doing that? I'm sure you'll get a lot of support from the club and it won't cost you anything to run'.

It was another 'straight to the point' Larry moment and once again it had caught everybody, including George off guard. Still processing the 'why is Larry generous' reply, George stood there shocked and reeling with Larry's suggestion and briefly thought about the life change that would happen if he did change careers. Larry's generous impact on George's family had been huge and he didn't want to disappoint him, so he took the diplomatic way out and answered cautiously.

'Well I'm sorry about the assassination attempt, sounds a bit extreme for this part of the world, but I don't think I'm cut out to be a politician. It's very good of you to think of me though, and I appreciate that. There'd be other people around this place that could do that job and do it well. I'm happy to help whoever wants to have a go'.

Larry listened to George and wasn't convinced by his answer.

'Well the only other person interested is a man called Rooster who has aspirations of being Prime Minister', replied Larry.

The news about Rooster entering politics had an unnerving effect on everybody, and Starch was first to comment.

'Not a good idea, you have to think about this George, we're all behind you. Mate, why don't you run it by your missus and I bet Matty would like to know what's going on'.

All of a sudden George felt uncomfortable, he was being dragged out of his comfort zone. He was being asked to put a secure job at risk and take the chance on a job that he had to re-apply for every four years. George was a very conservative man and what Larry was suggesting was way out of his self perceived abilities. But because Larry was asking, he agreed to confer with the missus.

'Okay, I'll talk to the boss and include Matt', replied George.

'Well, I'll leave it with you til tomorrow morning". Said Larry and as always, there was a deadline for answers. 'Okay, we've cleared all that up and now we're all on the same page, let's start things happening. Tomorrow morning we'll begin with the club renovation planning. By the way, Starch, there's a new 4WD coming as your runaround. We also have to figure out a remuneration package for work done outside volunteer hours', he added.

Starch once again sat there with a head spin, wondering what the hell was a remuneration package supposed to be. He wondered if this was the new norm, where anything can happen at any time. He thought about it for a minute and came to the conclusion that this was indeed the new norm, and the buck doesn't necessarily stop with him anymore. Larry was a very good man and was in their corner. Life at Rainbow's End Surf Lifesaving Club was now a whole new ballgame.

Starch couldn't help wondering how a man accumulates so much wealth when others struggle. How do people like Larry live day to day in such a high powered decision-making environment? Where did he come from? How did he manage to become a doctor and do all the other stuff? How does he manage to stay so humble and unassuming? There was so much to learn about Larry. He thought to himself, 'this bloke mixes with the most powerful people in the world and yet, here he is having a yarn with us like it's completely normal'. His inquisitive mind got the better of him so he decided to politely ask the burning question, 'who are you?'

'Larry', said Starch. 'I'd completely understand if you didn't want to answer this, but the question gets asked quite a bit around here, "who is Larry?" I know you treasure your privacy and it's fair enough if you'd rather not talk about it, but were you born into some kind of dynasty or something?'

Larry gave a slight smile and looked at his wife, who in return gave him an, 'it's okay' look. He looked at Starch and answered:

'No Starch, there are no dynasties. My mother died when I was in my early teens. I had no brothers or sisters, it was just me and dad. My dad didn't cope very well with mum's death and became an alcoholic. He drank himself to death and passed away during my first year at University. I didn't have any money to pay for the funeral so I sold everything we had. I struggled through my degree, paying my way by doing all the jobs no one else wanted to do. I managed to get 'Honours' and after my graduation headed straight to Africa, on a mission to save the world. I spent a year in a refugee camp in the war-torn Congo and quickly realised that you need more than medicine and knowledge to save lives - you need money and lots of it. At the end of my camp stay, I headed back to Canada to reassess what I was doing. I decided to do more study and try to find a high paying job. I also had to go through dad's things and tie up any loose ends. I was too heartbroken to do it any earlier. I was sifting through the paperwork when I found an envelope with my name on it. Inside were some receipts, a USB, some passwords and a letter. In a nutshell, the letter was very personal. He said he was sorry for everything and had used all the money we had, which was a lot, on an all-in gamble on a new emerging form of cryptocurrency called 'Bitcoin', which he thought would take off. My dad was a neurosurgeon, but the pressure of life dragged him down. He never saw his investment take off and had given up hope, which only added to his problems. He was very drunk when he made the decision to speculate on the new digital currency, and it was to apparently give me some sort of future. I loved my dad and would have given anything to help him, but I didn't have what it takes.

I eventually found the Bitcoin account and realised my father's intuition had been right. Bitcoin had taken off, which at the time I was thrilled about, so I decided to leave it alone.

I then uncovered a treasure trove of different Tech stocks that dad had bought in my name. They were all cent share startups and were all Tech stocks. Dad had been buying and adding to them for years, it must have been a release for him to go collecting shares. He always bought the same very large holdings of emerging companies at a trough in the market. I then found the trading account name and the passwords linked to a bank account I knew nothing about. Dad could not have imagined the seeds he planted would have grown to give this much yield. He was meticulous in keeping notes but probably wasn't aware of the intuitive gift he had. It took me months of reading his notes to understand his logic. There was also another envelope full of cards from the funeral but I wasn't ready to open it. When I did, I found bereavement cards from some of the most powerful people on the planet, I phoned them all and thanked them.

Dad was very clear with instructions, all I had to do was follow in his footsteps, and that's what I have done. Many of those companies are now world leaders in their field. The technology is astounding. And Bitcoin? I never touched it. It's still there worth a ridiculous amount of money.

But, it wasn't all plain sailing. Money can be seductive and seduce me, it did. I became so obsessed with the skyrocketing profits and advancements I became a different person to the young doctor working in war-torn Africa. We were not a happy family so I thought a nice holiday in a place called 'Rainbow's End' would make things better - but I could never have imagined the journey we were about to embark on.

Jackson, you didn't just save my life that day. You saved me, you saved our family. You saved so much more than you could ever be aware of. You put your own life at serious risk because realistically, you weren't physically capable, because of your asthma. You have so much courage. I saw what all of you did that day, and I and everyone else that you saved, owe you all a great debt. I understand what motivates you, it's the 'giving', and we'll work together to make sure Rainbow's End SLSC never runs out of its capacity to give, to save, to help. Does that answer your question, Starch? Is there anything else?'

Starch was a little lost for words and felt embarrassed that he had asked the question. Suzanne, Jackson and George looked at him waiting for a reply. He privately reconciled to himself that when he conversed with Larry, he was way out of his depth, so he sheepishly asked.

'Err, well if you don't mind, I was wondering how much is 'very generous', what is a 'ridiculous amount' of money and what's the American President like as a bloke?'

Larry smiled and answered, "never enough, enough, and, he's pretty cool".

Starch, Suzanne, Jack and George burst into laughter, which was well appreciated by Larry and his wife.

'Oh, Starch,' said Larry. 'There's a young lady called Molly Baxter who's been hounding me to talk about the club and the dredging, etc. Can you find out who she is and answer her questions please'.

'Yes boss', said Starch with a big smile. 'I know who she is and I'll even buy her a coffee'.

Larry raised his eyes skywards. No one ever called him boss, or at least not publicly.

'Thanks. Does anyone know where I can find Moey?' He asked.

'Try the kiosk', replied Jack.

'Okay, will do. I'll catch up later. Oh, Starch I almost forgot. The University in Florida where Matthew is doing his studies is running a clinical trial on a natural form of pain relief that is very promising. It's a very big advancement and a spin-off from the space station experiments. I put you down as a subject with severe sports-related injuries. You don't have to go but everything's been paid for and you can go back with Matty. You leave in ten days.'

Starch found himself in another head spin and all he could think of to say was:

'Wow, ten days! Strewth, I thought I would've been off tomorrow morning. Thanks, I'll let the missus know'.

And with that everyone dispersed. Suzanne and Jack were feeling very settled and marvelled at how fate had let them cross paths with Larry. How their lives had been turned upside down from their darkest days to the brightest of futures. Suzanne wondered what to do about her music, does she sell or perform, or both? Jackson wondered about how he would tell his mother that he and Faith had agreed to be married, even though he was only fourteen. But, after all he was a millionaire and could pretty much do whatever he liked, as long as mum said it was okay.

George pondered his future and suddenly realised the shoe was now on the other foot. He was the one explaining to the family about a 'Larry offer'. He thought about the pressure Matthew must have felt and the courage it must have taken for him to go for it. He thought about how wrong he was, and the fear he felt when Matthew announced he was going to accept Larry's offer. Maybe he was too afraid to even consider it. He felt a bit ashamed of himself for being so complacent and made a heartfelt decision to discuss things openly with the whole family, and go with whatever they wanted. Although, the thought of giving a speech terrified him, and the prospect of debating things in parliament was horrifying.

# Chapter 24

# The Day Continues

Starch had a bounce in his step for the first time in years, and felt incredibly good. He no longer felt the pressure to keep the club afloat and there wasn't any more worrying about money to pay bills and buy equipment. Talking to Larry had bought everything into perspective and gave him back his enthusiasm and energy for life. Just about anything could happen and just about everything was possible. It was like being in a football team with the world's biggest gorilla in the forward pack. Life was exciting and he felt alive. He circled the club looking for Talia, his wife, and found her on the grass area at the front of the clubhouse with a large group of clubbies, board riders, penguins and boat crew, all having a great chat. He walked straight up and gave her a hug and a kiss, which he had never done before. Talia was somewhat shocked although everyone else smiled approvingly. Natia and Manala looked at each other and started to giggle happily. Danny and Grizz were standing nearby which prompted Danny to ask: 'Starch had a few?'

To which Grizz dryly replied: 'Nah, he's in love'.

Which saw them both nod wisely.

Larry made his way to the kiosk where he found Bean looking a bit flat and tired which he thought might be the 2 o'clock fades. Moey wasn't there but he found out she was down on the beach looking after his children, so he decided to join them. On his way out he handed Bean a brown paper bag with something inside, and said:

'Thought you might like this'.

Bean opened the bag and took out a door handle and asked:

'What's this?'

'It's the studio 2 door handle from Abbey road. I got it recently when they were doing a repair. I thought you might like it. A lot of famous people have used that door handle. Life has a lot of doors, Bean. We just need the willingness and heart to open the right ones'. Larry replied, as he left in search of Moey and the kids.

Bean was lost for words and stood there for a couple of minutes looking at the impromptu gift like it was a religious relic, and digesting what Larry had said. He never thought a door handle could mean so much to him, and he started to look at things in a more philosophical manner. His piano mate Jay had not turned up as promised, and he had given up trying to contact him. He looked at the door handle and thought, maybe when a door doesn't open it isn't necessarily a bad thing - maybe in the bigger picture it's a good thing.

He had done a very good job of hiding his disappointment from Mum and Sunny throughout the day, and they were none the wiser. He started to think about life after Sunny, and reconciled to himself that love was a myth, romance was a notion and happy endings were a fairy tale. Bean had learnt one of life's hardest lessons. True love is the most evasive of all life experiences. He could always tell her straight up how he felt about her, but that idea seemed so bland he decided to wallow in his disappointment instead, and let the sun go down alone.

Later in the afternoon when he had reached rock bottom and was living in a semi-conscious state of woe when Sunny raced excitedly into the kiosk and half shouted:

'Bean, they're making a commercial or movie or something on the beach. Quick! Let's clean up and go down and watch. I've always wanted to see how they do this. We might see someone famous!'

Bean looked puzzled and replied:'What?'

'They're building a movie set on the beach. Quick, come and have a look', urged Sunny.

Bean walked outside to have a look, and there on the beach near the headland was a beautiful, white Steinway grand piano. The piano was sitting on a platform with a piano stool. Close to that was a table for two with a creaseless white table cloth and two gorgeous white antique dining chairs facing each other. Around the whole lot were four brass poles and a piece of blue and white checkered tape with the writing. "Police Line Do Not Cross" emblazoned all over it.

'Oh', said Bean quietly.

Sunny looked at him with one eyebrow raised and replied:

'Is that all you've got? Oh? Oh? Come on Mr Boring, let's get this place cleaned up and get down there and watch what happens. Grab some water on the way out'.

As requested, Bean who was by now wide eyed and bushy tailed, cleaned up in record time. As they were locking up, Bean grabbed a cooler box from the fridge, which prompted Sunny to ask: 'What's that for?'

Sounding innocent, he replied: 'Water. You said, "bring water"'.

Sunny gave Bean a condescending look, then checked with her mother.

'Are you ready to come now mum?'

Mum looked at Bean suspiciously but gave nothing away. As every boy knows, it is very, very hard to fool a mother, and Janice was one of the best.

'Might sit this one out and watch from upstairs', replied mum tactfully.

Bean realised he had been partly sprung, but things were still in motion and Sunny was too excited about seeing someone famous rather than suspect anything. So as mum made her way upstairs, they walked across the beach to the piano.

Sunny was very excited, she virtually dragged Bean across the sand, chatting away and firing off questions she answered herself.

'I wonder where the cameras are? Oh, it must be a night time thing'.

'I wonder where the lights are?'

As they walked closer her excitement level soared.

'Oh my goodness Bean, that is a Steinway Grand piano. Do you know how much that's worth? It's absolutely beautiful. Oh I hope we hear someone play it. Oh, it's gorgeous. Oh my gosh Bean, this is unbelievable. Oh no, we forgot to bring some chairs. Never mind, we'll sit on the rocks. Oh, doesn't this look so romantic. I bet it's a love story'.

Bean was feeling very comfortable with the reaction his idea was getting. As they reached the table and chairs, he put the esky on the ground and started to pull down the police tape. Sunny panicked and blasted.

'Bean! What are you doing? We can't touch this! This is a police line. We'll be in all sorts of trouble. Put it back'.

Bean smiled at her, then in gentlemanly fashion, pulled out one of the chairs for her to sit on. This was met with a puzzled look from Sunny, and prompted her to question.

'Bean, what are you doing? Did you have something to do with all this?'

Bean smiled at her again and replied:

'Yes. I did arrange this, although I did have some help. It's all for you, because you deserve it and I wanted to do it for you. There are special people in the world and you are very special. This time you are, the famous person'.

Sunny had a gobsmacked, mouth open moment, then slowly sat down. Bean started to unpack the cooler box, as Jay, the very large piano player came walking down the headland stairs. He wore an immaculate three piece white suit with an aqua coloured shirt and no tie. He didn't say anything but just sat down at the piano and started softly playing a very beautiful, intricate piece of classical music.

Bean unpacked the cooler box and placed a single, long stem red rose on the table in front of Sunny. He set the table with a fresh salad, some light seafood on ice, a plate of strawberries and cream with pieces of dark chocolate, and a glass ice bucket with a very expensive bottle of champagne. He then set some sterling silver cutlery for both of them. Honey was still trapped in her gobsmacked moment, but had the largest smile in the known universe across her face. After Bean had set the table he sat down and they both started to have a slightly awkward conversation. Sunny couldn't believe someone would go to all this trouble for her. She worked in the service industry for twenty years and to suddenly have someone wait on her, and go to such incredible lengths to make her happy was unbelievable. It was all like a fairy tale.

The other people on the beach were watching with great interest, wondering what it was all about. The people up at the clubhouse were lined up across the verandah and front lawn watching the proceedings, also wondering what was going on. The longer Sunny and Bean sat there the more relaxed they became, going back to their natural banter and laughing their heads off at one another. Jay was enjoying listening to the conversation and the piano playing was very romantic. All sorts of stories had begun to circulate among the observing clubbies:

'She's leaving and this is her thank you farewell'.

'Bean won some money and he's blowing it on a fancy dinner'.

'Sunny's rich and she's giving Bean a taste of the good life'.

But, there were two people who knew exactly what was happening. Sunny's mum, who had waited twenty years for this, and Matty who had set the wheels in motion. Both of them were watching with great interest.

An hour or so of joyous interaction passed between them, when Bean started to have doubts again. He had come to the realisation that he would never have the courage to tell Sunny the truth about how he felt about her. Somehow, to him it just didn't feel right.

Nevertheless, he was glad he went to this much trouble and had no regrets. He had never seen Sunny so excited. She was totally overwhelmed by the lengths he had gone to, to make her feel happy. They had enjoyed many conversations with each other, but this time it was different, this was intimacy and he felt so privileged to be in her company. As he listened to her he tried not to stare at all the little things that made her so beautiful. The way she threw back her hair from around her shoulders, without a care in the world. Her expression when she spoke and the way her face shone when she smiled. But he realised Sunny had a different kind of beauty that wasn't on the surface, something that was far more valuable. It was the unfolding beauty of her gentle and quiet spirit. Bean realised some of the most beautiful things are hidden and they can only be seen with the heart. Sunny had worked all those hours just to make her mum happy. She kept nothing and gave it all away to a childrens charity without so much as a blink of self consideration. He pondered how much more she had given away.

During a quiet moment in the conversation, when he looked down at the sand she softly asked:

'What are you thinking about?'

He never looked up. He felt as if he had nothing left to give, so he answered truthfully.

'I was thinking about the sand and how much of it is covering the beaches of the earth and how old each grain is. Then I thought about all the beaches in the world and how each beach has its own kind of sand, kind of like the people who live around it. I was thinking about the ocean that washes up on it and how big it is, and all the creatures that live and have lived in it. Then I thought about the moon and how it affects this enormous body of water and how that affects the earth. It all seemed so large until I thought about our sun and how small a space the earth and moon occupy in it's light. Then I thought about all the other billions of stars in our milky way galaxy, more than all the grains of sand on the earth. Then I thought about all of the galaxies in the known universe, so many that we could never stop counting. It all seems so overwhelming. Then I realised it is all nothing compared to the beauty of someone you love. Someone who is patient, kind, considerate and humble. Someone that lets you feel complete when she stands close to you. Someone that is always on your mind. Someone that has your heart held softly and safely in her keeping. The sand, the ocean, the earth, sun, moon and stars, all of it will end, but not the love of that person. That love is life'.

He paused for a moment, then looked up to make eye contact and said:

'For me, that person is you'.

He stood up with his legs shaking and stepped around the table as Sunny slowly but confidently eased herself out of the chair. With the occasional soft crash from the waves rolling in and the beautiful sound of the piano, Bean held her hand. As they stood there facing each other eye to eye, he almost apologetically asked:

'Did I say too much? Would you like to say anything?'

Sunny immediately replied:

'Prove it!'

Bean was caught off guard. It was not the kind of answer he had been expecting, so he asked:

'How?'

Sunny smiled faintly giving nothing away. Her poker face was unnerving as she replied:

'I want to be treated like this every day, for the rest of my life'.

Bean was again caught off guard. Jay the piano player was still listening and smiled. Sunny had put a deal on the table, and it wasn't a rejection. Sunny had once again, poignantly reminded Bean who was boss.

In a very committed but quiet way, Bean replied:

'Done'.

Sunny maintained her subtle smile and replied:

'A gram of truth is worth more than a tonne of promises'.

Bean felt as if he was in no man's land and was unsure where the conversation was going. With his legs still shaking he asked:

'Is there anything else?'

Sunny stood there as composed as ever with an expression that gave nothing away. But then her smile grew larger and an expression of happiness lit up her face, as she answered:

'Yes! Your mother named you appropriately'.

And with that, she threw her arms around Bean and gave him a kiss that told him his journey was over. He had found his soul mate.

Jay the piano man was caught up in the moment. What an emotional revelation. The beautiful piano melody turned into a joyous upbeat tune as the pair embraced each other as lovers do, then they waded into the surf holding hands, laughing like children.

Up at the clubhouse where the crowd was watching, there was mass jaw dropping. Mel, the love coach could not believe her eyes and muttered:

'You're joking!! Well I'll be stuffed!'

The boys from the kitchen started clapping, as someone else let out a cheer, then the whole crowd broke out in jubilant celebration. Sunny's mum shed a tear. At long last her daughter had found her man.

Larry came along and stood on the verandah next to Matthew and asked:

'What's that all about?'

Matty gave his usual smile and replied:

'Those pair just admitted how much they really mean to each other'.

Larry fidgeted with his phone and muttered, 'Really? I wonder if that piano has Wi-Fi?'

Matty watched as he fidgeted around pressing buttons, then all of a sudden the sound of Jay's piano came over the club's speaker system. Much to the delight of the patrons.

When Bean and Sunny finally settled down, Bean introduced Sunny to Jay. Then, much to both men's surprise, Sunny sat at the piano and asked: 'May I?'

Sunny knew far more about Bean than he realised, and started to play the opening piano piece to one of his favourite songs. The band picked up on the melody coming over the club sound system and started to join in. Then Sunny started to sing, and sing with a voice that prompted Jay to lift his hands in appreciation and yell, 'Oh yeah'.

Bean's mind was reeling with questions. How did she know about his favourite songs? Why hadn't she ever mentioned her musical abilty? Was this a secret female thing? Are they like happy icebergs where you only see the bit at the top, while the huge part is hidden? To say he was the happiest, most surprised man in the universe, wouldn't have been an understatement. A plastic surgeon could not have removed the smile from his face.

Up in the clubhouse the music was loud and clear, which sent Danny gyrating across the dance floor in a very confident display of his self perceived dancing prowess. The rest of the crowd upstairs and down, followed Danny's lead. Rainbows End was rocking. BIG TIME.

Bean reached into the chillbox and pulled out another bottle of champagne which he gave to Jay, who pulled the cork and drank straight from the bottle. The big guy had earned it. The pair sat at the table rocking away, as Sunny sang and played the piano, enjoying herself immensely.

Sunny and Bean lived and loved deliriously happily forever after. But life was not finished with them yet and their lives suddenly took a left hand turn when Sunny discovered she was carrying not one but two brand new human beings. Bean's jaw drop moment was epic when she told him, and mum was over the moon. Both sets of siblings were very excited but unanimously declined any responsibility for nappy changing. The beautiful and very loud twins eventually made their way into the world (mum delivered them on the way to hospital) and every day was a new adventure. Matty was gobsmacked when he heard the news and gave himself a pat on the back for the motivational talk he gave to Bean on that special day. He also insisted on being called Uncle Matty. Larry and Matt immediately discussed the possibility of putting the twins on the space station making them the first babies in outer space. However, the thought of nappy changes and the possibility of "floaters" made them revise their plans to something less ambitious. But that's another story.

Sunny always had those special feelings for Bean but it was mum who insisted she go back to the kiosk and talk to him again after their first meeting. Sunny had kept talking about how nice and how different he was, so mum gave her a big push in the right direction. Mums are so special.

Jackson and Faith were true to their word and married on the day Faith was eighteen. Suzanne never found a partner again but was never lonely, at last count she had thirteen grandchildren to look after. Including two sets of triplets. Jackson and Faith wanted a big family so Suzanne was the most kissed and hugged person on the coast. The grandchildren adored her and everyday was an adventure. She did a deal on her music and continued to write more songs. Jackson and herself set up a charity with some of the money Larry had given them, but kept their names anonymous.

Danny continued to 'exercise' but struggled to make a living as a trainer. Grizz was forever Grizz and never changed. Liz was never seen again.

Starch and his family lived on and were very happy. Starch's pain treatment in the US was a success and his days were spent living a healthy life. Talia spent most of her time helping Suzanne whilst Natia and Manala, their daughters, both became marine scientists. Starch became good friends with Molly Baxter, and the pair would usually meet once a week for coffee at the kiosk and discuss local issues.

Ben and Sushi continued on their way surfing around the world eventually returning to Japan. During their travels they both married Brazilian girls so they spent a lot of time travelling between Australia, Japan and Brazil.

Big Cop and Fins (Alex Dyball), now known as BC and AD, were very successful in their business venture and worked brilliantly together. Sharkbait eventually passed away and received a nice funeral service at the crematorium. His ashes are kept on the pie warmer at the surf club and once a year on the anniversary of his passing BC and AD would shout the bar, then everyone would lift their drinks for a toast loudly proclaiming: "To Sharkbait! Best bloody dog that ever lived". The one legged seagull left one day and was never seen again, but a few days after his disappearance another young seagull with two legs came along and moved into the perch box.

Brian and Benny were wildly successful and won the live television cooking show, which triggered another massive surf club bender. People could not get enough of them as they went on and toured the world as part of an international cuisine grand prix, taking cultural specific food and turning it upside down in their own style. As usual the banter between them was priceless. They remained in constant contact with Adrian and the three cooks always remained as close as ever.

Mel remained in the job she loved (with a pay rise), and became good friends with Sunny and Mum. The girls were the backbone of the club and helped everybody they could. At last report they had agreed to help Danny find a wife, but Danny proved to be mission impossible, so they suggested his life as the apex male may have to be a single one. The suggestion worked and the girls were happy to fade back into club business only.

George Binge (Matt's dad) accepted Larry's offer and was elected in a landslide as the local member of parliament. He went on to have a very successful and popular political career. Dallas, Matt's little brother, finished school and became a full time investment strategist, amassing a small fortune by the time he was 21. His sister Melissa became an environmental lawyer, and the two of them always clashed over profit versus people issues. Joshua had no other dream except to follow in Matt's footsteps. Which he did.

Colmie prospered as more dive sites were added to the coast and business boomed. Jackson was always there to help when needed but wouldn't accept any money. Michael Hadfield from Thargomindah had run the shop one day when he was in town and Colmie was so impressed with his attitude, he offered him work whenever he was available - which Michael accepted. Matthew and Larry built a prototype submersible that would take a custom built chair that gave him full 360 degree movement, while Rooster made a trailer for the submersible from donations. The young bloke was a very, very happy Thargomindian. He always stayed with Jacko and Faith when in town and was a popular babysitter. Rooster made some running boards for the side of his wheelchair, so it was a sight to see when fully loaded with kids.

Flowers was never seen again, but the word was he had accepted a job with the development arm of the dredging company. The investigation into his dealings is still ongoing.

Matthew went back to the US where he excelled in everything he did. He finally achieved his dream of space travel and was always considered an integral part of any space mission. He enjoyed a generous amount of time on a space station conducting experiments and forging new and innovative ideas. His name became synonymous with space exploration. Bean remained his best friend forever and Larry was always there with guidance and support.

Rooster grew into a social celebrity. He started travelling more to the country which gave rise to an idea called "Kids From Everywhere ", where he would recruit sponsors to acquire funds to sponsor a country kids trip to the coast. Larry supplied the aircraft and Moey was the pilot. The kids loved it. It was so successful he started another trip called 'Pensioners From Everywhere", where he duplicated the idea. He was enormously popular at Thargomindah and district, and became an honorary local.

Bull the plumber is still a regular at the courthouse resolving issues.

The Penguins eventually had ladies join them and although the language was tapered the females were just as feisty in the opinion arena. They eventually had their first penguin wedding, which was very special. They continued with their charity work and continued to be a protected species.

The ladies boat crew met every year on the anniversary of their national title win and had a bar-b-q on the club's front lawn with their families and friends.

Charlie from the boat crew cleaned windows on hi-rise buildings for a while then took a job using explosives at a mine site. After she became bored with that she returned to the coast and pursued a career in medicine achieving a Doctor of Medicine Masters Level degree. She continues to study and still remains part of the girls boat crew. The brick mentality rubbed off on her and she never dodged a challenge in her life. Danny asked her to marry him but she declined.

Larry would come and go and had a knack for turning a normal day upside down. For Starch he was the world's greatest human being, and he relished the chance to socialize when he was in town. Larry's children became nippers and his wife would help wherever possible around the club. There were still many people who wanted to know "who is Larry?" But the clubbies and locals were happy to let things be and would always reply, "dunno". At the end of the day Larry was just Larry because that's all he wanted to be.

Moey went on to legendary status eventually flying aircraft all over the world, working for Larry's companies and collecting University degrees at the same time. Larry's family adored her. She remained best friends with Matty for the rest of their lives, and whenever there was a situation which couldn't be resolved Matt would always say: 'Ask Mo, she knows everything'.

Jules continued to study and carved out a career as a respected medical professional, funding his studies from part-time modelling. The girls rowing teams were always claiming to be short of a rower and were constantly asking him to fill in. Sunny, Mum and Mel thought this was hilarious and gave Jules the nickname, 'Lonely Boy'. He eventually became besties with Jay the piano player and the pair of them started a band with Jay on synthesisers and Jules on guitar. They were overwhelmed with work for music and art festivals and enjoyed exposure on the FM radio stations, so they hired Micheal Hadfield as their booking agent.

The Rainbows End Surf Lifesaving Clubhouse was restored to its former glory and its traditions remained intact. 'No pokies, No bull. All are welcome'. The old red tractor can still be heard on the beach at daybreak. Jessica is still a local and can be found most days getting her surf in at daybreak, she is still making clothes on her old sewing machine and selling them at the artisan markets on the coast. The sound of slapping thongs can still be heard at first light around the club and Rooster is still sleeping in the Med room. The more things change the more they stay the same.

Of course, there were the good and the not so good days, but that's another story. Thank you for reading this one.

----------------------------------

Buzz buzz, buzz buzz.

'Hello, Matthew Binge, speaking'.

'Matty?'

'Little Bro? Whose phone is that? What are you doing up? It must be midnight down there. Where's Mum and Dad?'

'Well, Mum and Dad are asleep. Larry gave me my phone and he said it's got international roaming and I'm allowed to call you anytime. I can ring the Pope if I want, Larry gave me his number'.

'Whaaaaaat?'

'Matty, I was wondering. I'm just looking out the window at all the stars and there are so many that when you go over our house in the Space Staion, I won't know which one is you. So, when you go over our house, could you turn the lights on and off in the Space Station, so I know it's you?'

'Yes, Little Bro. When I go over our house in the Space Station, I promise to turn the lights on and off so you know it's me. Now, Little Bro it's very late and it's time for sleep, and please don't ring the Pope. He's very busy'.

'Yes, Matty'

'Night, Little Bro'.

'Night, Matty. Love you.'

'Love you too, Little Bro'.

Click, buzzzzz.

# Authentic Australian Terminology

**B**
Big-note - Exaggerate one's own importance or value. To boast.
Bo peep - Look. Have a look
Bolt / take the bolt - Exit very quickly.
Bullshit artist - Someone who lies convincingly.
Bull - Nonsense or not true.

**C**
Clubby - Member of a club.

**D**
Dacks - Pants.
Dacked - To forcefully remove someone's pants. Usually from behind as a prank.
D.T's - Abbreviation for Dick Togs or men's bathers.
Dunno - Don't know.

**E**
Em/em - Shortened for 'them'.

**F**
Fair Dinkum - Truly, honestly, real.
Fancy - can be interpreted as a word for surprise.
Fella - Fellow
Full sick - A surfing term for outstanding

**G**

G'day. Gidday - Good day, greeting.
Gone - Finished, heavily intoxicated.
Grog - Beer
Gunna - Going to

**L**

Lifey - lifesaver

**N**

Not having a bar of it - Strongly opposed to something.

**O**

Open slather - Without restriction.
Ol' mate (Old mate) - Someone who's name you don't know, or have forgotten, or can't be bothered saying.

**P**

Pigs arse - Not true.
Pulling your leg - playing a trick on someone. Joking.

**S**

Shout - Spontaneously pay for something as an act of goodwill.
Sticky beak - A meddler, busybody, having a close look.
Strike me pink - If that is true. Surprise.

**V**

Volleys - Volunteers.

**W**

What's going on - What's happening.
Whaddaya - What do you.

**Y**

Ya - You.
Yarn - A chat or story.

www.ingramcontent.com/pod-product-compliance
Lightning Source LLC
Chambersburg PA
CBHW010258100726
47904CB00011B/2647